Praise for Nora McFar
A Bad Day's Worl

"Welcome to Nora McFarland and her unforgettable heroine, Lilly, who's as lovably dysfunctional as any character you'll ever read! She's funny, smart, and honest, albeit occasionally tactless—in short, fully human. Packed full of adrenaline and attitude, *A Bad Day's Work* is a roller-coaster ride of a mystery. Don't miss it!"

—Lisa Scottoline, *New York Times* bestselling author of *Look Again*

"A wonderful debut novel! Action packed, with a heroine who's sure to win your heart."

—Marcia Muller, *New York Times* bestselling author

"McFarland, herself a former 'shooter' for a Bakersfield TV station, nails the newsroom as well as her feisty, funny accidental sleuth . . ." —*Publishers Weekly*

"McFarland's debut, the first in a planned series, is often both amusing and touching as Lilly discovers both the truth about the murder and enough about herself to change her life." —*Kirkus*

"Former Bakersfield camerawoman McFarland clearly knows her technical stuff. . . . McFarland has an appealingly flawed protagonist here, and fans of Julie Kramer's Minneapolis TV reporter, Riley Spatz, will likely take to Lilly, too." —*Booklist*

"More than a compelling mystery—it's a unique glimpse into the life of a small-town television news photographer. The story of Lilly Hawkins of Bakersfield, California, may be fiction, but the author's fresh voice and careful attention to detail make the intrigue real. . . . The next installment of this excellent new series can't come soon enough." —*BookPage*

Also by Nora McFarland

A Bad Day's Work

HOT, SHOT, AND BOTHERED

Nora McFarland

A TOUCHSTONE BOOK
Published by Simon & Schuster
New York   *London*   *Toronto*   *Sydney*   *New Delhi*

Touchstone
A Division of Simon & Schuster, Inc.
1230 Avenue of the Americas
New York, NY 10020

First Touchstone trade paperback edition August 2011

TOUCHSTONE and colophon are registered trademarks of Simon & Schuster, Inc.

For information about special discounts for bulk purchases, please contact Simon & Schuster Special Sales at 1-866-506-1949 or business@simonandschuster.com.

The Simon & Schuster Speakers Bureau can bring authors to your live event. For more information or to book an event contact the Simon & Schuster Speakers Bureau at 1-866-248-3049 or visit our website at www.simonspeakers.com.

Designed by Renata Di Biase

Manufactured in the United States of America

10 9 8 7 6 5 4 3 2 1

Library of Congress Cataloging-in-Publication Data

McFarland, Nora.
    Hot, shot, and bothered / Nora McFarland.
       p.   cm.
    "A Touchstone book."
    1. Photojournalists—Fiction.   2. Women photographers—Fiction.
    3. Murder—Investigation—Fiction.   4. Wildfires—Fiction.
    5. California—Fiction.   I. Title.
    PS3613.C4395H68 2011
    813'.6—dc22   2011006865

ISBN 978-1-4391-5556-1
ISBN 978-1-4391-7234-6 (ebook)

For Molly and Lucy

Although Lilly Hawkins's hometown of Bakersfield, California, is a real place, the setting of Lake Elizabeth is completely fictional. Some residents of Southern California may recognize similarities to Lake Isabella near the Sequoia National Forest, but except for a shared proximity to Bakersfield, there is no connection. Mt. Terrill, Lake Elizabeth, their residents, and their way of life have been completely made up by me. The University of California's White Mountain Research Station is a real facility, but it and its satellite stations are almost 150 miles northeast of Bakersfield. Please forgive my artistic license.

ONE

I saw the coroner's van and stopped talking midsentence.

We were parked on the side of the road just before the flatness of California's Central Valley met the wall of mountains known as the Sierra Nevada. I was putting away equipment following my reporter's live broadcast at the top of the six-o'clock news. I'd already worked a full day shooting video on the wildfire burning in the mountains and wanted to go home. Of course seeing the coroner's van changed my priorities.

I'm a TV news photographer—nicknamed a shooter in the industry—at KJAY in Bakersfield. I'm the only female shooter in town and one of only a handful of female chief photogs in the country. Aside from light administrative duties relating to the shooters, my title means I'm salaried and always on call. Nights, weekends, holidays—I've always got a camera just in case we need backup for the backup. That works for me because I'm a bit of a breaking-news junkie.

At the time I saw the coroner's van, my reporter was inside the live truck editing video. Leanore didn't see what was coming down the road and consequently misjudged the reason for my abrupt silence.

"I know you don't like talking about your personal life," she called through the open side doors of the truck. "But you and Rod are a great couple. I think it's entirely possible he'd stay in Bakersfield to be with you."

A Sheriff's Department cruiser followed the coroner's van. Blasts of hot, dry air hit my face as each sped past.

"I know he has to move on to a bigger TV market if he's serious about his career," she continued. "And I know he's never lived in a small town before, but I think he really loves you, Lilly."

I watched the vehicles disappear into the canyon. Above the mountains, a mushroom cloud of smoke rose from the wildfire. I turned and looked in the opposite direction.

We were fifteen miles from town. The dark green rows of an irrigated orchard popped against the pale brown earth. In the distance, the scorching summer heat created translucent waves in the air, but there were no people or cars. I was the only one there to see the coroner's van.

I dropped the cable I'd carefully been coiling. A surge of adrenaline carried me into the live truck in one jump. My hand shook as I rushed to hit the buttons and switches necessary to shut down the truck.

Leanore glanced up. She was editing video at a small built-in desk. Her auburn hair swayed in the blast from a portable fan. "Lilly, did you hear what I said?"

I killed the generator. The fan and everything else died. "No."

"Are you okay?"

Leanore Drucker is one of the few people I look forward to working with. Already a grandmother of three, she'd fashioned a second career for herself as our TV station's historical reporter. Despite an almost thirty-year age difference between us, she was probably the closest thing I had to a friend. I didn't say my next words lightly. "Get out."

She jerked in surprise. "What?"

"Get out of the truck, now."

I jumped back out and ran to my camera and other equipment. I scooped up what I could and rushed it to the truck.

Leanore retreated into the rear as twenty feet of coaxial cable flew at her. "Lilly, what's going on?"

"The coroner's van just drove into the mountains headed for Lake Elizabeth." My cell phone started ringing in the overstuffed pockets of my cargo pants. I ignored it. "I think someone's dead up at the fire."

I hurried to retrieve the last of our equipment. Before running back, I glanced at the slowly sinking pole on top of our live truck. At the top of this mast was the microwave dish that sent a live signal back to KJAY. For safety reasons I couldn't drive until it had completely collapsed.

Leanore stepped out of my way as I leapt into the truck. She had her cell phone out. "Should I call Callum?"

"He's already calling us." I stored my camera and then answered the still-ringing phone in my own pocket. "What?"

"We lost your signal." Callum was our station's assignment manager and in charge of newsgathering. He'd been working in Bakersfield for more than twenty years and was famous for his depth of knowledge, unrelenting crankiness, and one long, hairy eyebrow that stretched across his forehead. "Was I somehow not clear? The producer wants a shot of the smoke over the mountains for the closing credits. You got two minutes to get your signal back up."

"Tell him to use something else. I have breaking news." I took Leanore's blazer off the back of her chair and forced it into her hands. "And then send someone for Leanore."

"What?" Callum and Leanore said at the same time, although Leanore with a great deal more alarm.

"Someone needs to pick her up." I strapped the chair to the wall and pushed the rest of the cable under the desk. "She's at the base of the canyon."

"Lilly," Leanore began. "I don't—"

"Get out." I jumped into the driver's seat up front.

"But, Lilly—"

"You have five seconds or you're going to be stuck riding all the way up to Lake Elizabeth with me." Leanore and her weekly feature stories on local history were great, but she was not a hard-news reporter. She'd only worked the wildfire that day because we were so shorthanded. "You really want to get stuck on breaking news with me for the rest of the night?"

"But you can't go all the way back up there. You'll—"

I pointed into the back. "And take the tape you were editing for the eleven. I might not be back by then." The light turned green on the rack of equipment indicating the mast was down. I started the truck's ignition and put it in drive.

"Wait, wait. I'm getting out." Leanore hit eject on the editor and then grabbed the tape.

"Shut the door," I yelled.

She got out as quickly as her arthritis would allow and then slammed the side doors shut. I hit the gas.

"Callum," I yelled into the phone. "I only have a few seconds before I lose cell reception. Send someone for Leanore. She's—"

I slammed on the brakes. I wasn't on the road yet and a giant cloud of dirt erupted around the truck. "Just a minute." I dropped the phone and put the truck in park. I climbed into the rear, found what I was looking for, then opened the side door.

Leanore ran up. "Lilly, what on earth—"

"Here." I threw her purse at her.

"But you—"

I slammed the door shut and then jumped back into the front seat.

"I only have a few seconds." I put the phone on speaker and then buckled my seat belt. "A Sheriff's Department cruiser just went up the canyon going seventy."

"So?" Callum's voice cut in and out, but his impatience came through loud and clear. "Every government agency in Southern California is up there working the fire."

I floored it across the road and drove straight for the canyon. "They were following the coroner's van."

He gasped. "Are you sure?"

"I'm sure. What about the scanners? Have you heard anything? Is there trouble at the fire line?"

"No, but—"

His voice cut off, followed by a noise from my cell phone telling me I'd lost the signal. "Crud."

I tried to catch up with the cruiser and the van, but the boxy live truck was too unwieldy for any sustained speed on the twisty canyon road. Even a regular KJAY news van, which was really just an old minivan covered in the station's logo, would have been more nimble. Things weren't helped by the increase in traffic coming down the mountain. Earlier in the day there had only been a trickle of cars heeding the voluntary evacuation, but now a steady stream of vehicles were packed to the roof with their owners' belongings.

I had the entire drive to question the swell in traffic, but it barely crossed my mind. My only real thought was catching the coroner's van and being the first to break the story.

Dominating coverage of the wildfire hadn't been a problem when we'd been competing with other Bakersfield news outlets. Then earlier in the week, the winds had violently shifted and two firefighters with the US Forest Service were killed. Larger TV stations had begun making the almost three-hour drive from L.A. Their superior technology allowed them to go live and feed recorded video from almost anywhere in the mountains—something our less advanced equipment couldn't do.

But if there'd been another death, and I could break the story first, my little Bakersfield station would earn some much needed bragging rights and a huge morale boost.

The air in the van became increasingly bitter the higher I drove. Soon I was forced to flip on my headlights. We were still at least forty-five minutes from sunset, but the dome of smoke over the mountains turned daylight into a continuous and dreary twilight.

I caught up with the Sheriff's Department cruiser just as the road crested and the view opened on Elizabeth Valley. This should have been a stunning vision of clear blue water, dazzling mountains, and sunny skies.

Instead, Mt. Terrill rose into a black sky congested with the flashing lights of helicopters and planes. Below the mountain, the body of water known as Lake Elizabeth had been polluted with gray sludge from all the ash and soot.

I reminded myself the view could have been worse. So far the fire had remained on the other side of the mountain. Most of the air traffic was either coming or going from dropping water and fire retardant there. Hopefully the hundreds of fire-suppression personnel working day and night would be able to contain it soon.

My cell phone made the familiar sound letting me know I was back in range, then immediately started ringing. I hit the speaker button and set the phone in a cup holder. "I just cleared the canyon and I'm following the Sheriff's Department cruiser. The coroner's van must have gotten ahead."

"The death's not fire-related." Callum sounded as if his dog had died.

I sounded only slightly less disappointed. "Oh, man. Are you sure?"

"It's an accidental drowning."

"Damn!" Viewers care more about some deaths than others. It may not be polite to say it out loud, but in the middle of a deadly wildfire, an accidental drowning was a big, giant nothing.

"But all I've got are rumors at this point," Callum said. "Everyone's working on the fire. Things are confused and no one is returning my calls."

"Then maybe you're wrong."

"Not likely, but check it out. If it's a drowning, pick up a VO/SOT for the eleven."

VO refers to video that plays underneath an anchor or reporter talking. It's also called B-roll and is really just background images. SOT is a sound bite or interview. Together, a VO/SOT makes a quick story, read live by the anchor and not edited into a package the way a longer, more important piece would be.

"I already made the drive," I said. "I might as well get something."

I hung up. The cruiser took the next exit for the Lake Road. This older boulevard made a full circle around the sixty miles of shoreline, but was a slower and more difficult way to travel than the highway.

I tried to follow, but sawhorses blocked my way. An officer

got out of a California Highway Patrol cruiser and came to the driver's-side window. The CHP had jurisdiction over roads and interstates in California, as well as being the official state police. Despite that, they were probably best known from the 1970s television show *CHiPs*. This officer didn't look like Erik Estrada, but he did have a mustache.

"Are you keeping drivers off the Lake Road?" I asked.

"I can't comment on that, but the detective who just came through okayed you to follow him." He gestured ahead. "They're going to Search and Rescue headquarters at the southern end of the lake."

I wasn't surprised I'd been cleared to go in. Blocking media access for a story like this would have been unusual. Drownings are typically held up by law enforcement as cautionary tales to prevent future tragedies.

What did surprise me was the roadblock itself. "Do you have roadblocks at every entrance to the Lake Road?"

"Yes, ma'am."

"But that's a huge effort. Normally the Elizabeth PD only cordons off near where the victim drowned." I had an idea and eagerly leaned out the window trying to look toward the lake. "Is it a hazmat situation? Has something toxic gotten in the water?"

I must have sounded hopeful because he frowned. "No, ma'am."

He stepped back, effectively ending the conversation, so I drove through the barricade and headed south. The western shore, where I now drove, was home to the town of Elizabeth and had retained its low cost of living and working-class roots. Most of the residents lived in mobile homes or prefab houses. The eastern shore, also called Tilly Heights, had gentrified in recent years. The new, more affluent population had built expensive vacation homes along the lake and up Mt. Terrill.

I passed the two large warning signs promoting water safety. The signs, one in English and one in Spanish, never failed to upset me.

LAKE ELIZABETH
63
LIVES LOST SINCE 1955
THINK SAFETY

The running tally of drownings was creepy enough, but I also had personal reasons to be uneasy. Thirteen years ago I'd spent five months living at Lake Elizabeth. I was almost nineteen and beginning a downward spiral that wouldn't end for several years. One of my many escapades involved vandalizing the THINK SAFETY sign. Seeing it always made me cringe.

Truthfully, Lake Elizabeth stirred up a lot of unpleasant memories—most involving my own bad behavior—and I didn't like spending so much time here covering the fire. My boyfriend, Rod, had noticed I was on edge, but I'd avoided telling him the reason. He knew that in polite terms I'd "lost my way" after my father's death, but I'd never shared the trashy details.

I drove for another fifteen minutes past mobile-home parks and unmarked private driveways. The Search and Rescue headquarters had been placed at the bottom end of the lake where the eastern and western shores met. This remote location was a compromise to appease residents of both shores. I reached the turnoff and followed a dirt road as it meandered down toward the lake. My headlights lit the tracks other vehicles had left in the ash.

I saw bright lights and slowed. The facility was little more than a small dock and several garages for equipment. I parked outside a chain-link fence next to an Elizabeth Police Department cruiser, two pickup trucks, and the Sheriff's Department cruiser I'd been following earlier.

I reached for the door handle and instinctively braced for the smell. The bitter, charred stink filled the mountain air. It had already seeped into my clothing and hair earlier in the day when I'd been shooting video up here with Leanore.

I stepped down from the truck and into the ash and soot. The cypress trees surrounding the facility were also covered in the stuff. The light gray flakes and fine, black grit combined to look like a dusting of dirty snow.

"Hello?" I called. An air tanker flying in the distance rumbled, but no human voice responded.

I paused and chugged half my water bottle to fight dehydration. Normally the temperature would be lower in the mountains than in Bakersfield, but the smoke was acting as a greenhouse and trapping the heat. I took a moment to straighten the ponytail keeping my long, dark, curly hair out of my face. I dusted off my cargo pants and straightened the red KJAY polo shirt worn by all the shooters.

"Hello?" I called again.

I thought I heard something inside the Sheriff's Department cruiser, but I couldn't see past the tinted windows.

I collected my camera, sticks, and gear bag, then walked through the open gate. The main building was dark, but a floodlight lit the compound. Its powerful beam backlit the haze in the air.

After calling out again and getting no answer, I continued toward the lake. At the bottom of a short slope, another floodlight lit the coroner's van, parked with its back end open toward a dock. The doors looked like eager arms waiting for the corpse.

Two deputy coroners standing toward the end of the dock were pulling on rubber gloves. Nearby, two men in wet suits and a male police officer stood inside a motorboat. The lake water and horizon both looked black, save for the flashing lights of a helicopter in the distance.

"Hello. I'm Lilly Hawkins from KJAY."

The police officer and the youngest of the divers jumped at the sound of my voice. Their reactions startled the other three. It was a chain reaction of nerves.

"Sorry. I didn't mean to surprise you." I took a step onto the dock. Water had sloshed onto the wood planks and turned the ash into a dark sludge. "And I don't want to get in the way. I just need a little information and a quick sound bite. The sooner I get it, the sooner I'll be out of your hair."

Everyone looked at the police officer. He wore the brown uniform of the Elizabeth PD underneath his life vest.

He looked around, as if waiting for someone else to answer, realized we were all looking at him, then jumped again in surprise. "I really don't know." He climbed onto the dock, walked around the deputy coroners, then continued toward me. "Media stuff's not my line and the sergeant didn't say a word about it."

As he approached the light, I saw he was Caucasian, but with darkly tanned skin that was cracked and scarred from age and too much sun. "You should talk to the detective from the Sheriff's Department. He's calling in on his radio, but you're welcome to wait."

He removed a pair of rubber gloves. His right hand immediately moved to his back pocket, hovered there for a moment, then pulled away.

Even if I was able to lure him on camera, this nervous, uncertain officer would be a nightmare to interview. I could also rule out the deputy coroners—they were never allowed to talk—and since all I wanted was to get out of there, waiting for the detective wasn't a great option either.

That left the divers, and as luck would have it, one of them was openly gawking at me and my camera. The young man stared, even as he lifted his end of a long, gray body bag from the bottom of the boat. His gaze only shifted for a moment, as he and the other diver awkwardly passed the bag toward the deputy coroners on the dock.

I wasn't surprised by the young man's naked ambition. The chance to get on television can make even the most sober and dignified person act like a goofy jackass.

"I'm sorry I can't give you a statement." The local officer reached for his back pocket again, but stopped himself from retrieving whatever was there. "Elizabeth PD has jurisdiction, but the Sheriff's Department is taking custody of the body, and their guy is the senior officer on the scene."

Behind him, the coroners began carrying their unpleasant cargo down the dock. The officer and I retreated onto the shore and watched as they walked to where a black tarp had been laid out near the van.

A special mesh body bag for retrieving submerged corpses had been used. The fabric clung to its contents like a wet sheet.

I didn't know who was inside. I didn't know what his or her life story might be. I didn't even know if the person would be missed—not everybody is.

But I did know, absolutely, and without even a tiny bit of doubt, that I did not want to see what was inside that bag.

TWO

The deputy coroners gently lowered the body bag onto the black tarp.

I glanced at my watch. "Where's the Sheriff's Department detective?"

The local officer gestured up the slope. Even the back of his balding head was a leathery reminder to wear sunscreen. "He's in his cruiser calling in on the radio. You're welcome to wait, if you want."

Wanting didn't enter into it. I wanted to go home to the house I'd been sharing with Rod for the last seven months. I wanted to take a long shower and scrub away the smell of the fire. I wanted dinner. I wanted to fast-forward to Rod coming home after the eleven-o'clock news and the two of us falling into bed.

The two coroners checked their rubber gloves. "How's the smell?" one called to the officer. "Has she been in the water long?"

"I think my sergeant said about a day." The local officer shook his head. "I'm not sure about the smell. She was bagged underwater by the diver and I sure as heck didn't unzip her in the boat."

"You did the right thing. That's proper procedure." The second coroner knelt down. He was careful to avoid the trail of water leaking from the bottom of the mesh bag. It pooled on the black tarp and then ran in a thin trail down the slope to the lake. "Let's see what we've got here." He reached for the zipper.

The officer and I both turned away and ended up staring at each other.

"You must be short manpower because of the fire," I said.

"You know it." He reached for his rear pocket, but stopped himself. "I'm not even full-time active duty. I retired up here from the Kings County Sheriff's Department. I pick up weekend support-officer shifts, but that's about it." He again reached for the pocket, and again stopped.

I suddenly realized what was back there. The charred odor of the wildfire had been masking his chain-smoker smell.

"You like being a reporter?" he said.

I doubted he really cared, but we each needed something to divert our attention from what the coroners were doing. "I'm a shooter, not a reporter, and I love it."

He removed his life vest. Dark sweat stains covered the shirt underneath. "What's the difference?"

"I shoot video, reporters don't. Sometimes I do interviews when a reporter isn't available—like now—but I'm never on camera and I don't write stories."

"Hey, she's got a lot of lacerations." One of the coroners wrote something on his clipboard. "What can you tell us about where you found her? Were there a lot of rocks or sharp debris?"

The officer avoided looking at them by focusing on one of the life vest's clasps. "You need to talk with Arnaldo. He did the dive and bagged her."

As if on cue, the two divers came down the dock carrying their scuba equipment. The younger of the two, the one who'd been gawking at me earlier, had blond hair and blue eyes. His partner was older with deeply tanned skin and black hair. He didn't look handsome in the conventional way the kid was, but he had a natural masculinity that was probably more powerful.

"Are you both volunteers with Search and Rescue?" I said.

The kid grinned. "You know it."

Elizabeth Search and Rescue was trained and supervised by the local police, but populated and supported by volunteers. Big cities probably had money to keep divers on the payroll, but not here. In fact, most of the equipment in the garages up the slope had probably been paid for through donations and bake sales.

"I'd like to interview you both," I said. "If you have time."

"Cool." The kid's grin deepened. "You mean for TV and stuff?"

The local officer gestured to the coroners and the body. "First, they've got a couple questions about where you found her."

The kid started to turn. He was about to take a good, long, full look at the corpse.

At the last moment, the other diver touched his arm and stopped him. "There's no good in seeing that."

He pulled the younger man a few steps away, then they each set down their scuba gear.

The coroner with the clipboard yelled over. "Have either of you had any experience with body retrieval before?"

The lead diver nodded. "I wish I didn't." He knelt and began sorting his gear. "But at least once a year something like this happens. I guess you never get used to it."

Just as before, the kid started to look at the body.

"Hold on." I grabbed his arm and stopped him just in time.

"I know it's tempting to look." The local officer kept his eyes on the small hole he was digging with the toe of his shoe. "But try and focus on something else."

The coroner wrote something on his clipboard. "What can you tell us about where you found her?"

We all looked at the lead diver. He kept his back to everyone and focused on the equipment. "She was facedown in the rocks at the very bottom. It looked like the current and those rocks had been roughing the body up." He went still. I could see from the way his back rose and fell that he was taking deep breaths. "And I had to break rigor mortis to get her in the bag."

Now it was my turn to take a deep breath. I told myself not to think about it.

The kid clutched his stomach.

"Anybody mind if I have a smoke?" The local officer was already walking up the slope. "I'll just be up here if you need me."

The kid took quick, shallow breaths—not smart—and his cheeks had a waxy gray tint. That didn't prevent him from trying to get on TV. "I promise to give you a great interview. I actually have some media experience." He paused to take several more breaths. "I took Intro to Communications at Cal State Bakersfield last semester. I'm a biology major, but I may switch."

The coroner kneeling next to the body straightened. "Hey, which limb did you break rigor in?"

The lead diver still didn't turn around. "Right arm."

The kid started to look.

"Still a bad idea," I said.

The kid stopped himself just in time. A bead of sweat ran down his cheek. "So anyway, I'd love to give you an interview." He swayed a little. "I'm a great public speaker."

In my peripheral vision I saw the same coroner lift the corpse's arm. "Her right or your right?"

"Her right," the diver called back.

The coroner moved the arm back and forth.

The kid finally turned all the way and stared. He must have seen everything. "Oh, man." He leaned over and threw up.

I jumped back in time to save my hiking boots, which wasn't easy. Despite my five-four height, I wear size ten shoes. They made an easy target.

Pukey the Kid pulled himself up. "I'm okay." He wiped the corner of his mouth. "Really, I'm fine. I'll be great in the interview, I promise."

The other diver rushed over and put a hand on the kid's shoulder. "Are you okay?"

"I'm really sorry, Arnaldo." The kid was still pale and clutching his stomach. "You won't tell my dad, will you?"

"It wouldn't matter if I did." His voice was gentle, but certain. "You dove on a full stomach is all. I can't tell you the number of times I've gotten sick doing that."

The kid looked at me. "You won't mention this in the interview, will you?"

Before I could answer, Arnaldo shook his head. "I don't know if that's such a good idea right now. There's work to do." Arnaldo reached down and picked up his gear. "We need to return the equipment and get changed before we do anything else."

It was a sign of how much I wanted to go home that I actually considered asking the kid to stay and be interviewed. But he needed to get away from the body and I couldn't risk him puking again, this time on camera—or even on my camera, which has happened before. You don't know aggravation until you're cleaning someone else's puke out of a mic jack.

They picked up the diving gear, then retreated up the slope. The local officer passed them coming back down.

He kicked some dirt and ash at several small lizards that had descended on the pool of sick. "Awful things. Get away." The tiny, green bodies with distinctive red stripes bolted into the darkness.

"They used to be worried about those things dying out around here," I said.

"I know. Crazy animal-rights people. Now we're overrun with them." He continued kicking dirt and ash to cover up what was left of the kid's lunch. "You can't light up a cigarette without blowing smoke on one, there are so many."

I joined him and kicked some dirt from the other side.

"Thanks," he said. "Stupid kid."

"Why'd he get sick now? He must have seen much worse under the water."

"Nah. The kid shot up to the surface right after they found the body. We're probably lucky he didn't throw up in his scuba mask." The officer frowned. "Arnaldo only brought him along because regulations say nobody dives alone."

A bright flash momentarily bleached the immediate area. We both glanced over at the coroners, who'd begun taking photos.

"What's someone that young doing out here anyway?" I said. "Is he really with Search and Rescue?"

"His dad is, but they live on the other side of the mountain. He's trying to evacuate their cattle and horses ahead of the fire and couldn't come."

Another flash exploded. I waited a second, then said, "At least somebody's obeying the voluntary evacuation. I thought all the year-round residents were digging in."

He straightened a little. "Yeah . . . I guess." He started back to the boat.

I should probably have noted his evasive answer, but I was so focused on my next question that I missed it. "Are you sure you can't give me a quick sound bite?" I followed him. "The sooner I get something on tape, the sooner I can get out of your way."

"I'm no good for that." He passed the coroners, carefully avoided looking at the body, then walked down the dock. I noticed for the first time that a second boat was attached to the first, as though it had been towed.

"You'll be great," I called. "Please."

He looked back at me, saw something, then pointed. "Ask him."

Another flash exploded as I turned.

"Lilly Hawkins. I figured that was you following us." The rotund figure of Detective Lucero walked down the slope, then around the side of the van. He wore slacks and a blue dress shirt with the sleeves rolled up. His Sheriff's Department ID hung on a chain around his neck and a gun rested in a holster on his belt. He was normally assigned to the Rural Crimes Investigation Unit covering thefts and vandalism on the many farms and oil fields in the county. I'd met him seven months earlier when I'd been involved with a murder investigation.

"You're the only shooter in town crazy enough to chase the coroner's van up a mountain." He stopped at the pool of sick. "Let me guess, the kid?"

I nodded.

"I wish the sight of a body could still make me vomit." He laughed. "Now I'm lucky if I even get nauseous."

"It still makes me sick." I returned to my equipment. "But now I know not to look."

He laughed and stepped over the mess. "How you been, Lilly? You look even prettier than the last time I saw you."

Some jerks won't take any woman seriously as a shooter. It's a physically demanding job traditionally done by men. Being small, with long, dark hair and big, green eyes, makes it that much harder for me. Lucero wasn't one of those jerks, but he delighted in pushing people's buttons.

"Thanks," I said. "You look pretty too. Menopause must be agreeing with you."

"Hey." His arms spread in mock outrage. "Did you just take shots at my masculinity and age?"

"It was a twofer."

"Speaking of pretty men, how's that boyfriend of yours?" Lucero made the sounds of a rimshot and mimed the drumming motions.

I didn't say anything.

Lucero dropped the teasing tone. "Seriously, where is he? I don't see him on TV anymore."

"Rod never liked reporting. He's producing our eleven p.m. show now."

Lucero looked at me and nodded to himself. "You know, being chief photog agrees with you. You look more grounded, more in control." His eyes narrowed. "And you're a little harder to read too."

I made a rude hand gesture. "Guess what I'm thinking, right now."

He laughed. "You have a hangnail?"

I opened the tripod and adjusted it for the slope. "If the comedy portion of the evening is over, maybe we can do some work?"

He shook his head. "Sorry. No statements tonight."

At first I thought he was still teasing. "Very funny. Can we get this over with? I've got a long drive back."

"Talk to the Sheriff's Department's information officer." He looked at the deputy coroners who were in the middle of measuring the temperature of the corpse. "Hurry it up, guys. We don't have a lot of time."

The one with the clipboard answered, "It takes as long as it takes."

"Hold on." I quickly closed the distance between us. "You're not giving me anything?"

"No comment."

The local officer returned from the dock with a cooler and another life vest. He set them down, but didn't say anything.

"But I drove all the way up here," I continued. "You have to give me something."

"I don't like being here any more than you do. You think the RCIU handles drownings? I'm only here because everyone is busy tonight. I mean, so, so incredibly busy."

Sometimes I have a problem understanding other people. Uncle Bud says it's because I'm not naturally curious about them. I disagree. I'm very curious about people when they're doing big breaking-news-type things, such as killing each other, covering up political malfeasance, or releasing toxic gas near orphanages. It's the smaller things I have trouble with.

But to my credit I saw the local officer frown at Lucero. I was about to ask about it, but the divers returned. They wore matching dark green pants and orange Search and Rescue T-shirts.

I walked forward and met the kid. "How about that interview? I know you're in a hurry, but I'll try and keep it short."

Pukey the Kid's face lit up, but Arnaldo shook his head. "Sorry. I promised your mom and dad you'd be back first thing. You know they need help with the horses." Arnaldo started down the dock. "Come on. We're almost done."

The kid gave me a sad look, but followed.

I looked from Lucero to the local officer. "At least give me something off the record."

Lucero grinned. "Ah, the magic words."

"Will you just tell me already?"

"It's a straight-up accident." He took out a notepad and consulted the pages. "A woman drowned in the lake, probably yesterday between seven and midnight. Apparently she was a dippy type who always refused to wear a life jacket. Liked to party and commune with nature."

I grasped for some way to make the story more interesting. "Did she have kids or someone dependent on her?"

Lucero shrugged. "The Elizabeth police got the missing person's call and found the body. It's more their case. I'm only here to escort the body back to the morgue in Bakersfield."

We both turned to the local officer.

He reached for his back pocket, but stopped himself at the last second. "I don't know much either. Just what I heard around the station."

"Lilly's good people," Lucero said. "I vouch for her. If she says it's off-the-record, then it's off-the-record."

"Please, just tell me a little about the dead woman and how she died." I paused. "You can smoke while we talk."

He lit up in the time it took me to take a breath. "No one's mentioned her having kids or a husband or anything. They're talking at the station like the dead lady was a real wild child herself." He exhaled a cloud of smoke. "She was staying with friends who live on the lake, got drunk, and took their boat out."

He gestured back to the one they'd towed in. The simple utility boat had a small engine at the rear. "It's a sad story, but hardly new. Add another number to the THINK SAFETY sign."

I glanced at the coroners. They were placing blue bags on the corpse's hands. "How'd you find the body so fast? Last time you had a drowner up here it took weeks for the remains to turn up."

"We can thank the Forest Service for that." The hand with the cigarette pointed to where the silhouette of a Chinook helicopter lowered over the black lake. Probably for the last time that night, it dipped its water bucket below the surface and then rose into the darkening sky. "One of them spotted the missing boat tied up at Road's End earlier today when they were filling up."

Road's End was a rocky hill in the center of the lake. Vacationers who didn't know any better, or stupid locals, sometimes took boats there to party. Over the years, several people had died in the deep water surrounding it.

"So basically," I began, "she was drunk, no life vest, and fell in the water trying to climb from the boat onto the rocks in the dark."

The local officer nodded. "That's about it."

The divers had returned with the rest of the equipment from the dock. They set it all down next to the cooler and life vest.

"Of course, it's hard to know for sure without any witnesses," the officer continued. "But as soon as the fire eases, they'll send someone out to Road's End to have a look around."

Lucero frowned. "Didn't you go over the scene?"

"Couldn't get out of the boat." The officer gestured to the divers. "Protocols don't allow it while men are underwater."

Lucero didn't say anything, but I could see he was troubled.

The local officer took a final long drag on the cigarette and burned it down to the filter. "Truth is, Elizabeth PD is stretched about as thin as can be. Some of the boys haven't been home in days."

Arnaldo removed bottles of water from a cooler and then handed them around. "It's a difficult time. Even Search and Rescue volunteers are working double shifts helping out. The strain is enormous."

The kid paused from chugging his bottle of water. "You think this lady would have been trying to help, instead of going out to party."

The officer tossed the remains of his cigarette away. It landed in the sludge of ash and soot washing up along the shoreline. "At the station they're saying she grew up here and got a real bad reputation. Trashy stuff with older boys, drinking, drugs—criminal record even. Bad news."

One of the deputy coroners stood up. "We're just about done here." His partner zipped up the heavier, leakproof body bag they'd placed the mesh one inside, then secured it with a tamper-proof seal.

I shot B-roll of the body being loaded into the coroner's van, then a few shots of the dead woman's boat. By the time I was done, the technicians had driven the van outside the gate. It idled by Lucero's cruiser, waiting for him. Arnaldo and Pukey shut off the lights, then secured the gate with a padlock. They each got in their pickups and left, followed by the local officer.

Darkness had fallen. The headlights from the coroner's van now provided the only light.

I decided to give Lucero one more try. "If you call and ask, I'm sure you can get permission to make a statement."

"Not tonight."

"Of course they'll say yes for something like this. All you have to do is ask."

"Normally, you'd be right, but tonight's different."

One of the deputy coroners rolled down his window. "You want to follow us or the other way around?"

"Why don't you follow me? I can put my siren on, if we need it."

"Come on," I said to him. "You can do this one tiny, minuscule favor for me. I drove all the way up here. At least give me a statement."

"Try listening to the very important thing I'm saying to you." He paused and then emphasized each word. "I can't call, *tonight*."

"Can't or won't?"

"Do you know how much I'd like to strangle you right now?" He glanced over his shoulder at the coroner's van, then leaned into me. "Once again, try listening. It's good for picking up hints."

I stared at him. What was he talking about?

"I can't call tonight." He repeated.

"Why not?"

"For the same reason the Elizabeth police force couldn't send their own detective out here. Because everyone is too busy."

"Why is everyone too busy?"

The same coroner leaned out the window. "It's getting late. Shouldn't we be on the road?"

Lucero raised his hand. "You're right. I'm on my way." Lucero walked to his own cruiser.

I followed. "Why is everyone too busy?"

Lucero smiled. "No comment." He got in his cruiser and started the car. Before driving away, he lowered the window. "Like I said, Lilly, good to see you. I'd stay and chat, but we need to get back down the canyon before traffic gets too backed up. I got a feeling a lot more people are going to be evacuating, and you know it's *mandatory* . . . that I get back to Bakersfield."

He drove away, followed by the coroner's van.

I ran to the live truck and opened the side doors so I'd have light. I hit the speed dial on the cell phone.

"KJAY, we're on your side." The voice wasn't Callum's.

I tossed my sticks into the rear. "Rod?"

"Lilly, are you on your way back?"

"No." I stored the camera and shut the doors. "I think the evacuation may have been upgraded from voluntary to mandatory."

His voice rose. "We haven't heard anything. Are you sure?"

"I got a tip." I climbed into the front seat and started the engine. "Plus something major is tying up all the local law enforcement. They sent an old guy who fills in on the weekends to retrieve the body."

"I'll call Callum at home. And probably Trent too."

Rod was the 11:00 p.m. producer and had control over the shape and content of his show, but as assignment manager Callum was in charge of newsgathering. Walter Trent was our station's news director, and although I didn't think much of his news judgment, he was the head of the entire department.

"Great job getting the tip. It'll be a huge if we can break this first." Rod started to hang up, but suddenly came back on the line. "Lilly?"

"I'm still here. What?"

"How about the drowning? Is there a story there?"

"No. It's nothing."

"Okay. . . . Be careful. You must be exhausted."

When Rod and I had become a couple, I'd instigated a strict no-public-displays-of-affection-while-on-the-job rule. Sometimes, such as now, I sensed him chafing at my restrictions.

I replied with a neutral tone. "I'm fine, but thanks."

I returned the way I'd come, but took a detour when I saw a dirt road leading up a hill. I reached the top and got out of the truck. The elevation gave me a good view of the entire Elizabeth Valley. Trails of headlights slithered through the dark landscape. They came from all directions, snaking their way down the mountains and around the lake. They all moved unmistakably toward the only exit. The canyon road was about to get crowded.

THREE

Thursday, 7:50 p.m.

I took the Lake Road back the way I'd come, but got off at the city of Elizabeth. The CHP had blocked off this exit too, but an officer moved the sawhorse for me. By the time he realized I wasn't going to drive through, I'd gotten my camera prepped and exited the truck.

I held the camera on my shoulder with my right hand and pointed the stick mic toward the officer with my left. "Hi, I'm from KJAY, can you comment about the mandatory evacuation?"

"No, and that thing better not be recording."

I lowered the mic and camera. "Why are you blocking access to the Lake Road?"

"I can't comment."

A fire truck approached and stopped. Even though the sawhorse had been removed, my truck was blocking its path.

"Move your vehicle," the officer ordered.

"Are you reserving the Lake Road for emergency personnel? Is that how you're avoiding traffic from a mandatory evacuation?"

"I said move your vehicle."

I drove to the highway and shot B-roll of overpacked cars heading toward the canyon. My presence created a mini-traffic-jam as vehicles slowed to look at the live truck. Fortunately I was able to get what I needed quickly, then continued to Elizabeth.

This was the side of the lake that hadn't gentrified. Sidewalks are rare and parking lots are made of dirt. The one-story shopping district is filled with service-oriented businesses such as the post office, an Elks Lodge, and several gas stations. Five years earlier, Fitzgerald's Groceries—or Fitz's as the locals called it—had departed for trendy Tilly Heights on the other shore.

I passed the mobile-home park where my uncle Bud owned a unit. The electric sign was on for the night, but the *m* had burned out so it read MOBILE HO ES OF ELIZABETH.

Bud is a dodgy character who owns modest properties around the county where he can avoid people looking for him. He's actually old enough to be my grandfather and has spent most of his long life passing from one shady scheme to another. I'd heard from his girlfriend that he was currently in Elizabeth pursuing a business opportunity. The details were typically sketchy, but seemed to involve doughnuts.

I remembered a bar a few blocks ahead where locals hung out and drove in that direction. Bars are great sources of information, especially in small towns. I was familiar with this one because I'd actually stayed in Bud's mobile home thirteen years earlier during my time at the lake. I'd been partying and raising hell until one day Bud made a surprise visit to check on how I was taking care of his place. He kicked me out on the spot. This was like Charles Manson declaring you were dangerous, but it had still taken me another five years to straighten myself out.

I saw the plain white building that housed the bar and slowed. A light outside illuminated the words POOL, SHUFFLEBOARD, COCKTAILS, BAIT. OPEN AT 5 A.M.

Several pickup trucks were in the dirt parking lot. As I entered, two old men turned from the bar where they were drinking beer.

Ten minutes later, I was back in the truck. I hit speed dial for the station. A desk assistant answered, then immediately transferred me to the control room. Rod was in the middle of a meeting with the director and 11:00 p.m. anchors, as well as Callum and Trent, who'd just arrived from home. They put me on speakerphone.

"Lilly, it's Rod. Can you hear me?"

"I confirmed the mandatory evacuation." I cradled the phone between my shoulder and ear while storing my camera. "Residents started getting automated calls around six this evening. The calls have been staggered by area, but now word's getting out. I think there's going to be a huge mess, with everyone trying to evacuate all at once."

I heard muffled exclamations in the background and then Rod's clear voice. "There may be a perfect-storm-type situation in the works. It's possible the wind, humidity, temperature, and terrain are all coming together to feed the fire."

I finished storing my gear, then got in the driver's seat. "How soon? Do I need to evacuate?"

"A blowup is only a possibility." I recognized Callum's voice. "But you don't want to be anywhere near Mt. Terrill tomorrow evening."

I looked out the window. A grimy layer of soot covered the glass, but I could still see the lights from houses on the opposite shore. "Are you seriously talking about the fire burning up from the Terrill Valley, over the ridge, and down into Tilly Heights?"

"Yes, but that's not all," Callum said. "The ridge is a hub. There are all kinds of radio and broadcast towers at the top of the mountain. Bakersfield police and emergency lines go through it, cell phones. If those towers get knocked out, it's going to be a giant crudtastic disaster."

I took a deep breath. A part of me wanted to indulge in a comfy bit of denial. *They must be exaggerating. That couldn't really happen.*

The news junkie in me immediately accepted the truth and got excited. *This is a once-in-a-lifetime story. Cool!*

After a brief debate, we decided to send the evening shooters to the base of the canyon to set up a live remote using Granny Pants, our second and much older live truck. After the eleven-o'clock show, they could travel up to Lake Elizabeth with the reporter who was scheduled to start her shift at midnight. Meanwhile, I'd shoot everything I could, then drive my video back to Bakersfield in time for the eleven.

The only reason there was even a discussion was that the Wonder Twins were the evening shooters that night.

"Teddy and Freddy can handle it," I promised. "They won't let us down on a story this big."

Teddy and Freddy had sarcastically been nicknamed the Wonder Twins because they dressed in the same surfer-dude attire and wore their hair in the same bleached-blond curls. Fortunately, they'd managed to shed most of their sloppy work habits since I'd allowed them to pick up extra work in the sports department. Whenever a spare set of hands were needed to shoot local games, I sent Teddy and Freddy, and in return they had to maintain a certain level of competency at all times.

"It's a risk," Trent said. "If they screw up on a night like this, the entire news department will look bad." He paused. "What do you think, Callum?"

"I won't vouch for those idiots." Callum's voice held his usual contempt, so I was unprepared for what he said next. "But I will vouch for Lilly. If she's backing them, it's good enough for me. Now can I get back to the scanners? I've got a fetus watching the assignment desk."

We said good-bye and I started the truck. Rod and Callum had told me to get an official on camera commenting about the evacuation, so I drove the short distance to the foothills outside Elizabeth. This was where the Elizabeth Union School district had its primary campus. During the school year it served roughly three thousand K–12 students from all over the lake area. Two weeks ago it had been transformed into Incident Command Headquarters.

The war against wildland fires is run by special emergency-response teams. Each team has a command structure comprising firefighters and specialists from different agencies. When a wildfire erupts, officially called an incident, a team is mobilized and its members leave their families and jobs until it's defeated.

Incident Management Team 18 was running the fight against this wildfire. In addition to the incident commander and his staff, Team 18 had other departments, such as Operations, Communications, Logistics, and even Finance. Add to that the firefighters and equipment pouring in from all over Southern California to do the frontline work, and you had yourself a small army.

I slowed where a California Conservation Corps member manned a checkpoint. His flashlight hit the station logo on the side of my truck, then he immediately waved me through. Down the road, the campus glowed like an NFL field at night. Every one of the school's lights was in use. To fill the remaining dark spots, portable work lights had been brought in and ran off generators.

I drove past the overflowing parking lot in front of the school's main buildings. A mishmash of official vehicles had taken over the spaces usually reserved for school buses. Fire trucks and SUVs from Kern County Fire, the US Forest Service, and Cal Fire were mixed with random vehicles from agencies all over the state. I had to stop and wait while something labeled VENTURA COUNTY SHER-IFF'S DEPARTMENT TACTICAL RESPONSE TEAM'S MOBILE COMMAND CENTER crossed the road in front of me.

After VCSDTRTMCC had passed, I continued and followed the road as it cut around the school gymnasium. This was the newest building on campus and where the incident commander had set up his war room. Press weren't allowed inside, which just made me want to go in even more.

I slowed again to accommodate the increase in pedestrian traffic on the back side of campus. I had to stop completely when two uniformed Forest Service rangers hurried across the road in front of me. They barely glanced up from the papers in their hands. No sooner had I started again than a forklift carrying pallets of Gatorade cut across the road. It climbed onto the track field and headed for the trailers where personnel were dropping off and picking up their laundry.

I finally reached the information officer's media trailer. The IO's job was to liaison with the media and disseminate information to the public. The trailer housing him and his staff had been placed on the school's baseball field near third base. The field lights were all on as though a night game were under way. Behind the trailer, a giant tent had been set up in the outfield for the daily briefings.

I turned into my usual parking place behind the first-base grand-stands. My breath caught when I saw the news vehicle already there. KBLA's fancy satellite truck was much larger, newer, and cleaner than my microwave truck. I kissed my scoop good-bye.

I parked and got out. The L.A. shooter was sitting out the open side doors of his truck eating a fast-food hamburger. Behind him racks of shiny new equipment taunted me.

"Hey," he said while chewing. His demeanor was relaxed and disinterested.

"Hello." I casually glanced inside the truck. He was sending video back to his station via a live signal, something I couldn't do in the mountains. On the main monitor, I glimpsed a man gesturing wildly with his hands as he spoke. His gray hair stood up in places and he had a goofy European accent that reminded me of a Bond villain.

The L.A. shooter saw me looking at the monitor and smiled. "He's something, huh? Mad-scientist type." He took a larger bite of the burger, but still managed to speak while chewing. "Nightmare interview. The guy's ego is bigger than the fire. He flipped out when I asked about his stupid lizard research. Kept shouting about salamanders."

I looked back at the L.A. shooter. I had a vague recollection of his name being Jim or Tim or . . . whatever. I didn't care what his name was. He was a slug. No motivation or gumption. I'd been calling him Slim in my head as an ode to his laziness.

He raised the burger, but paused. "I guess you'd have to be crazy to still be living on the other side of the mountain." He put the remainder into his mouth in one bite.

I straightened. "What do you mean, the other side?"

Slim had too much food in his mouth to answer, but by then I'd spotted a bright neon-yellow firefighter's jacket lying on the floor behind him.

On the monitor, the camera panned from the mad scientist to a two shot of a young man and woman. "I figure, why leave?" the girl said. Her voice sounded ditzy and her tank top had a picture of a cannabis plant. "They keep trying to scare us, but if it gets dangerous, the firefighters will come save us. I mean, they can't let us die. It's their job to save us no matter how dangerous it gets."

Normally I would have been struck by what a particularly stupid and insensitive thing that was for the bimbo to say—especially considering two firefighters had died just four days ago.

But I was too full of professional jealousy to notice anything else. "They took you past the roadblock to the other side of Mt. Terrill?"

He jerked in surprise at my tone. "Yeah, but we just visited a couple of the people still in their houses. I hardly got any flames."

"You got flames?" My raised voice attracted the attention of emergency workers passing by, but I didn't care. "They won't even let me go to the ridge and shoot down. You got to go into the Terrill Valley and shoot flames?"

"It wasn't my idea." He actually sounded unhappy about it. "The IO called my assignment manager and requested me. Can you believe that?"

"No, I can't."

Either he didn't realize I'd just insulted him or he didn't care. "My reporter and I were supposed to be in Burbank covering a pastry contest today. Can you believe it? My turn to shoot the food package, and I get pulled to come up here."

"Who's your reporter? At least tell me it's somebody famous."

He shook his head. "They said there was only room for me on the ride-along. First time I've been solo in years."

I entered the field behind home plate and marched straight toward the media trailer. The dead, brown grass was covered in ash and soot, but it still crunched under the weight of my boots. The bright game lights were all on and I probably resembled a coach on his way to scream at an umpire.

My cell phone rang. I ripped it out of my back pocket without stopping. "What?"

"Lilly," Callum yelled through the phone. "Where are you?"

"I'm about to rip the IO a new one, that's where I am."

"Normally I wouldn't like the sound of that, but right now I'm so happy you're in the mountains that almost anything is okay."

I stopped near the pitcher's mound. "They gave a sluggy shooter from L.A. a ride-along. Can you believe that? Do you know how many requests we've put in? I've been here every day. And they—"

"Let me guess. His station is the only one that routinely has a truck there in the evening, and the IO specifically requested the slug, but said he couldn't bring a reporter, right?"

I glanced around the field. Two men in uniforms walked along the third-base line, but they weren't within earshot. "What's going on?" I said quietly.

"The IO wanted to make sure a journalist was there to get the story out, but he also worked it so the journalist wouldn't be aggressive or demanding."

"But as soon as the story breaks, every reporter in Southern California will drive up here."

"No, they won't." Callum paused for effect. "I called in a huge favor and got some interesting information. All lanes on the highways and canyon road are being turned out of the mountains. That way twice as many cars can get out."

"But if both lanes are going west, how will people drive up here?"

"They won't, not until the bulk of the evacuation is finished. Eastbound lanes might reopen tomorrow, at the earliest."

"But then, I'm . . ."

"Not going anywhere. If you come back to Bakersfield, you won't be able to drive back up. Sorry, but we're one of only two news organizations in the world with a camera there, and by the way, the other guy's a slug. You're a pit bull. You can't come home."

I smiled. "Like I'd want to."

"That's the spirit." He quickly shifted gears. "See if you can get the IO on tape commenting."

"But how do I send my video back?" I glanced back at the

grandstands. Slim's satellite dish peaked over the top. "I'm lucky to even get cell reception."

"Stop a car just before they go into the canyon. Tell them if they deliver your tape to Teddy and Freddy at the bottom, they'll get on TV."

It was simple and would almost certainly work. "Okay. Are you sending a reporter up here before the road closes?"

"We won't have anyone until midnight, and by then it'll be too late." He hesitated. "I can always ask Rod. Before he switched to producing he was our ace. Probably the best reporter I've ever worked with."

"I know, but he hates being on camera."

"He might enjoy getting back out in the field."

"I know him better than you, and he'd hate it" Acknowledging our romance in a work context made me uncomfortable, so I quickly moved on. "And it's not like I can go live and need a reporter in front of the camera."

We said good-bye, then I returned to the truck for my gear. I checked the settings and then carried everything to the media trailer. The large mobile office looked fairly generic from the outside. A paper sign had been attached to the clean white metal body with blue painter's tape. The words FIRE INFORMATION were printed in red block letters. Nearby a portable generator rumbled.

The door was propped open by a rubber trash can. I stepped up and through the strand of hanging clear plastic designed to preserve the air-conditioned interior. Despite noise from various radios and scanners, the IO heard me enter and looked up from the desk where he was working. I could almost hear the swear word inside his head.

The information officer was Caucasian, with dark brown hair, and in excellent physical shape for a man entering late middle age. He wore the uniform of the Santa Theresa Fire Department, where he worked when Team 18 wasn't activated. Strapped over his chest was a small pack with radios and other necessities.

He looked at an African-American woman working at a desk on the opposite end of the trailer. "Don't worry. I got this. You keep working on the press release." She nodded, then he glanced at me. "You must be on overtime. Why'd you come back?"

"There was a drowning in the lake." I set down my gear. "It's not much of a story, but I guess it's a good thing I checked it out."

"Really?"

"Cut the BS. I know about the mandatory evacuation and I'm not leaving." I stepped toward his desk. "But more importantly, I know about the ride-along you gave that slug from L.A."

Laughter cracked his professional facade. "That's what you're upset about?"

My hands shot to my hips. "Do you know how hard I've tried to get to the actual fire?"

He stood. "Yes. I do. I'm the one you've been harassing for the last two weeks, remember?"

"Well, I'm sorry, but it's my job to harass you and it's your job to get harassed. The breakdown seems to have been in the harassment not working."

He laughed again and walked around his desk. "How many hours have you worked today? You must be exhausted. Go home and let KJAY send someone else up here."

"It'll be hard for them to do that after all the lanes have turned west."

He froze.

"That's right," I continued. "I know all about it and I'm not going anywhere."

He looked at the woman. "Tracy, would you mind stepping out for a moment?"

"No problem, sir." The woman stood and picked up a walkie-talkie from the desk. She reminded me of a ballerina—tall, graceful, and strong as an ox. I spotted the logo of the L.A. Fire Department on the sleeve of her black uniform. "I should update the board, anyway." She picked up several papers from her desk and didn't let a slight limp slow her exit.

The IO waited until we were alone, then said, "Okay, we need to talk."

I raised the camera on my shoulder and looked through the viewfinder. "Fantastic. Let me set a white balance real fast."

"No." He covered the lens with his hand. "Not on camera."

"What other kind of talking is there?"

"The serious kind." He turned down several radios on which he'd been monitoring audio traffic, then lowered the fan on the air conditioner.

"Listen, Lilly." He sat back down behind his desk. "The evacuation is a serious public-safety issue. We have to get twenty thousand people out of these mountains and we don't have very long to do it. If we fail, people could die."

"Why are you talking like I'm in your way? I'm here to record what happens, not get involved."

"But you could get in the way without meaning to. Even a brief slowdown in traffic can snowball into a traffic jam. Then cars start running out of gas in the canyon. There's no shoulder there." He shook his head. "You have to see what we're up against."

I thought about how I'd already stopped traffic just shooting B-roll.

"All I'm asking," he continued, "is that you try and be aware of how your actions might affect the bigger picture."

I wasn't good at seeing how my actions affected me, let alone the bigger picture, but I meant it when I said, "Of course. The last thing I want is to become a part of the story."

This appeared to satisfy him. "Good. As a gesture of goodwill I'll make calls and get you access to the Lake Road. That way you can get around easily."

"Thank you." I reached for my camera. "Now how about a sound bite?"

He got up to turn the radios back up. "No one is commenting until the midnight briefing."

"I need material before then. We have a newscast at eleven." I pointed at him. "And you owe me for giving away my ride-along."

He laughed and shook his head. "How about you take the briefing live at midnight? I was going to let KBLA carry it, but if you promise to make it available to other news outlets, I'll give you the bragging rights."

"I can't go live." I gestured toward the door. "But I'm sure Mr. Ride-Along will do just fine. It's the perfect excuse to hang out here for the next four hours and do nothing. He'll probably win an Emmy for sitting on his butt."

The IO had a sudden thought. "How about the drowning?"

"What about it?"

"I may be able to get you an interview with the victim's brother?"

Normally, I'd jump at something like that—viewers love grieving family members—but this was hardly a normal night. "If it's not fire-related, nobody is going to care." I started for the door. "And I need to get something on tape about the evacuation in time for the eleven."

"Hold on," he said. "What if the dead woman's brother is a firefighter?"

I stopped. "You mean he's working this wildfire, right now?"

"He's on a Hotshot Crew with the Forest Service out of Tulare. We ordered him brought in so we could break the news."

A grieving firefighter? An emotionally devastated hero? A man risking his life in a desperate fight against the forces of nature, only to lose a beloved sister?

"I'm in," I said.

"Maybe wipe that grin off your face when you see him." He headed for the door and gestured for me to follow. "His sister just died."

FOUR

Thursday, 8:40 p.m.

I followed the IO outside. The woman who'd left the trailer was now speaking with someone at an easel displaying the latest fire information. The white briefing tent sat directly behind her, in the outfield. Although it had so much ash and soot on the roof, it probably couldn't be called white anymore.

"Tracy," the IO called to her.

She quickly joined us. "Sir?"

"This is Lilly Hawkins from KJAY in Bakersfield." He looked at me and gestured to the woman. "This is Firefighter Tracy Bell. She's just been loaned to us from LAFD."

The woman offered me her hand. She had dark brown skin and hair cut close to her head. Like me, she wore no makeup. "Pleased to meet you."

The IO waited for us to shake hands and then spoke to Bell. "Take Lilly and find a Hotshot named Brad Egan. He's the one whose sister drowned in the lake. If he agrees, Lilly is going to interview him. But only if he agrees." The IO stressed this last part. "Tell Egan he'd be doing us a favor, but be respectful."

She nodded. "I understand."

Before we left, I ran back to the truck. I retrieved the tape I'd used to shoot the body and loaded it in the camera.

I passed Slim reading a graphic novel at his satellite truck. He looked up as I passed. "They giving you a sound bite?"

"Yeah." I kept walking.

Behind me I heard him say, "That's good. Hey, if I don't see you again, good luck."

I stopped and turned around. "You're not leaving, are you?"

"I need to be on the road by nine so I can get back to L.A. before my shift ends."

I didn't know what to do. He was a rival, and technically I should try to maintain my exclusivity on this story. After all, the midnight briefing didn't have to go out live. I could record it and send my tape down the mountain.

"But I'm glad you got your sound bite." He looked back down at the graphic novel, then turned a page. "They shouldn't be playing favorites. That sort of thing is no good." He sounded as if he meant it. When I didn't say anything, he glanced up. "Hey, are you okay?"

"Don't go back to L.A."

"Why not?"

"Just don't."

"But why?"

I hesitated one final time. "There's going to be a briefing at midnight and I can't go live. It's important that someone is here to get the story out, even if it's not me."

"That's weird. They don't usually do briefings at midnight."

"It's special." I was close to losing all patience with him. "That's what I'm trying to tell you. Tonight isn't like other nights and you're going to want to be here for it. Don't go back to L.A." I turned and left before he asked me another question.

I found Bell waiting for me back at the media trailer. "Egan was in first aid earlier." She replaced her walkie-talkie in the pouch on her chest. "So now he's probably getting something to eat." She started for the main set of buildings where the classrooms were.

I followed. "First aid? Is he injured?" This story just got better and better.

"Don't worry. Nothing serious."

It's possible I was a little disappointed. I mean, I didn't want him to die or have serious problems, but a nice superficial injury—maybe his arm in a sling or a bandage on his head—would be the cherry on top of my heroic, grief-stricken sundae. He's brave, he's heartbroken, and he's got a heroic injury. Viewers would send us fan mail for a guy like that.

On our way to Egan, we passed a dirt lot where rows of blue Porta Potties had been set up. Bright lights ran off generators here, but farther out individual camping tents dotted the dark landscape. There were probably men inside trying to sleep in the few hours they had free.

Bell walked quickly, despite her limp, and soon we'd reached the elementary-school classrooms. The rooms were laid out in a simple U-shape with an outdoor courtyard. We stayed outside the U and approached the cafeteria from the rear, where the Dumpsters were. A single halogen lamp above the back door lit a group of young Conservation Corps members unloading pallets of food and water from a semitruck.

We entered the kitchen and passed men in aprons opening crates of apples. The school's multipurpose room buzzed with conversation and radio traffic. Long cafeteria tables had built-in benches on each side where clusters of different personnel ate and relaxed with their comrades.

"Wait here. I'll be right back." Bell crossed the room and spoke with a man standing by a table full of coffee urns. Above them, HOME OF THE BRONCOS was painted over a horse logo.

I took a closer look around the room. Most everyone wore casual clothing marked with the logos of their various fire departments or government agencies. But at a nearby table, a small group of firefighters appeared to have come straight from the fire fight. They'd lowered the top portion of their yellow coveralls, revealing navy-blue shirts. Even from a distance, they reeked of the fire. The smell was sharper and more pungent than what was already in the air, probably because it was mixed with the kind of sweat marathon runners experience.

Bell returned. "Egan was here, but left. He's expected back soon. We can wait for him." She gestured to a table stacked with box lunches. "Would you like something to eat?"

I pulled out my cell phone and looked at the time. It was already 8:50. "I can't wait. I have to send video back for the eleven."

She considered for a moment. "We can ask the minister who volunteers with Team Eighteen." She started to walk. "Father Tom might know where he is."

I followed her to where an older man with gray hair drank coffee with a group of younger men.

She introduced herself and explained we were looking for Egan.

"I tried talking to him about his sister." Father Tom looked down into his coffee. "There's history there, I think. The bad kind. He wants to lose himself in work."

"Do you know where he is now?" Bell asked. "I heard something about replacing a piece of equipment?"

"That's exactly what I mean. He's over now having a chain saw fixed. Several of us offered to go for him, but he insisted on doing it himself." Father Tom shook his head. "Right now all he wants is to catch the first ride back to his crew."

Bell began to step away. "Thanks for your help."

We exited through the front door and emerged in the courtyard. People crossed back and forth between classrooms carrying papers or talking into walkie-talkies. It was odd to see uniformed emergency personnel among the bike racks and STUDENT OF THE MONTH signs.

We walked back toward the gym, but this time on the front side of the campus. We passed the camp's makeshift commissary, where anyone could purchase necessities and even custom-made T-shirts commemorating the fire. On the far end of the parked vehicles was a small truck with a GORDON AND SONS logo. Outside, two sets of pallets were covered in chain saws. One set had the sign READY FOR PICK UP.

Bell popped her head inside the open side door of the truck. "Senior Firefighter Egan?"

I heard a voice answer from inside, then Bell climbed the small steps and entered the truck. I followed, still carrying my equipment, but stopped on the top step.

Inside, work counters ran down each wall with cabinets above and below. Several large reels contained different sizes of chain spun up like thread on a spool. A man in a thick apron sat on a stool working at one of the counters. Sitting on another stool was a US Forest Service Hotshot.

Members of these hand crews are the frontline men in the war against a wildfire. They frequently work in remote areas, eating and sleeping in the field when they can. They perform the back-breaking physical labor of cutting down trees and digging lines that create firebreaks. My worst day as a shooter is probably a normal day for them—and I'd had some bad days.

This one wore the usual dark green pants and yellow shirt that was their uniform. His hair was dark with sweat and dirt, as were his shirt and pants.

Bell introduced herself and explained who I was and what I wanted. "You'd be doing us a favor by talking to Miss Hawkins," she told him. "But if you're at all uncomfortable, please say no. We're not trying to pressure you."

He crossed his arms. He had a large, powerful build, and his muscles strained his shirtsleeves. His face looked older than his body, but either way he had to be the dead woman's older brother. "What I want is to get back to my crew, but they say I'll have to wait until tomorrow at the earliest. If I do the interview, will you find me a ride back tonight?"

Bell shook her head. "I don't have control over that."

"But you can make calls and ask around for me," he said. "If you wanted to, you could probably make something happen."

She glanced at me.

He dropped his arms. "You don't realize how bad it is out there. Every time we lay down a line, the fire spots embers right over it, and we're running out of time. I can't afford to sit around here twiddling my thumbs."

I fell hard into shooter love. This guy was an old-school hero and was going to be phenomenal on camera. "You can make some calls," I insisted to Bell.

She looked from me to Egan. "I can try."

He stood. "Then I'll do it."

We went outside. I told him the light would be best if he sat on a masonry fence bordering the parking lot. Truthfully, the bright lights flooding the parking lot were the same everywhere, but by putting him at the fence, I was able to frame an American flag into the background of my shot.

I set up my sticks and attached the camera. "Are you sure you're up to this? I heard you were in first aid earlier. I don't want to bother you if you're injured." Actually, his being injured would only make me want to bother him more.

"Blisters," he replied. "Occupational hazard."

Blisters, though extremely painful and potentially serious, would probably sound mundane on the air. "Oh."

Bell mistook my disappointment for concern. "Blisters are a real problem for the men. If they're not treated, they can go septic."

"Poison oak is the worst," Egan said. "I had that real bad, last year." He paused. "I mean, it's the worst except for stuff that'll kill you."

I set a white balance on the camera. "Have you had some close calls?"

"Everybody has close calls." Egan gestured to the east where the fire was. "Right now we got a couple cougars displaced by the fire and stalking the crews."

Bell rushed to jump in. "But Fish and Game went over this afternoon. They'll take care of it. Nobody is taking any chances."

I made one last check of my camera settings. "So in addition to fighting the fire, you have to worry about getting mauled to death by a cougar?"

He shrugged in a manly, bearing-his-burden-stoically kind of way. "It's all part of the job."

My hand shook with excitement as I attached the clip mic to his shirt. This was going to be award-winning stuff. This was going to be legend. When a guy this heroic opened up about his grief and pain, the hearts of viewers all over Bakersfield were going to break.

"While we're doing the interview, don't look directly into the camera." I couldn't wait to hit record. "You can just talk to me, like we're having a conversation."

He nodded.

I hit the button. "Please say and spell your name for me."

He did, and I was about to ask my first question, but a large truck started nearby. I patiently waited for it to leave so we'd have a clean audio track. By patiently, I mean I wanted to kill someone. Finally, it rumbled away.

"Okay," I said. "Thanks for waiting."

He nodded.

I felt like a gambler who knows, absolutely, that the slot machine is about to show her three sevens. All I had to do was reach up and pull the handle. "Can you tell me a little about your sister?"

I leaned forward slightly in anticipation. If he started crying, I might win an Emmy.

"She was kind of a whore. You know, trashy and flaky and nobody you'd want to know. Happened after our mother died. She was okay before that."

For a moment I couldn't speak. Then, when I could speak, I had no idea what to say.

"Got in with a bad crowd in high school," he continued. "Started drinking and doing who knows what else. Never would settle down with one man."

"Okay," I said, stalling for time. "Why don't you talk a little bit about how her death makes you feel?"

"On one level it's a relief to know she's not going to be a problem for Dad anymore, but mostly I'm angry."

"Angry at who? Is there someone you blame for her death?"

"I blame her." His voice rose and his previously handsome face distorted with anger. "I got pulled away from my crew. Those men are more family to me than she ever was. Now I'm not there to watch their backs and carry my share of the load. Jess couldn't even die without hurting other people." He paused. "What's wrong with you?"

"Nothing."

"It sounded like you were groaning or something."

"Why don't you talk a little bit about your family background?" I said. "Where did you both grow up?"

"Over in Tilly Heights, but my dad sold his land over there when the Starbucks crowd started moving in. Bought a mobile home on this side of the lake."

"Does he know about the tragedy?"

Egan nodded. "I called him in Bakersfield. He evacuated the day before yesterday and went to stay with my aunt."

"Why didn't your sister go with him?"

"She lived down in L.A." Egan shrugged. "I figure she came up here yesterday to check on Dad, not realizing he was already gone."

I cheered for a moment, hoping I might be able to use a sound bite about the dead woman's concern for her father. But then Egan added, "She probably thought she could get some money out of him."

I was standing on the deck of the *Titanic*. There were no lifeboats and I was going down.

Egan jumped in to fill the silence. "I guess Dad should have called and told her he was leaving, but they didn't talk a lot. And with the way things are headed with this fire, it was more important he got out fast."

I straightened. "Where are things headed with the fire?"

Bell jumped in. "We'd prefer you stick to questions about Senior Firefighter Egan's sister. This interview is not about the fire."

"Can't blame me for trying."

She smiled. "I don't."

I turned back to Egan.

He'd taken a small packet from his pocket and was shaking the contents to the bottom. "Truth is, I haven't seen Jess in over ten years. She took off after high school and I was glad to see her go." He ripped the top off the packet. "She came home for the first time last spring. Stayed one night with Dad, and then took off in the morning."

"So that's good, right?" I brightened. "Your family reconciled. Everyone got to make peace before the tragedy."

He pulled a water bottle off his belt and then opened the top. "Not really. I wondered why she visited until someone told me she had a man up here—and he's married to boot. Thankfully, Dad never heard about that."

So much for reconciliation and closure.

Egan poured some of the packet into his mouth and followed it with water. He swished everything around, then swallowed.

Bell actually shuddered. "Wouldn't you rather have that warm and fresh-brewed?"

I looked at the packet in his hand and recognized a popular brand of instant coffee.

A small smile appeared at the corner of Egan's mouth. "I won't make it out on the line if I get used to that kind of luxury."

He finished the packet and swished more water around his mouth. "Are we done here?" He started to get up.

"No, please," I said. "Just a couple more questions."

He reluctantly sat back down on the masonry fence.

At this point, I had nothing usable. I decided to abandon nostalgia and ask about the tragedy. "Did your sister go out on the lake a lot? Was it a special place for her?"

"When she was a kid, you couldn't keep her out of it, but then like an idiot she blew her shoulder out. Never swam after that."

"Could that have contributed to her death?"

"No." His anger flared. "She died because she was stupid enough to get drunk or high or whatever and take a boat out on the lake by herself. Her shoulder had nothing to do with it."

"Okay, I'm sorry. I didn't mean to offend you."

But I don't think he even heard me. "I don't know how she got so stupid. Jess was a smart kid. Mom wanted her to be a lawyer or something, but after she died, Jess got all weird about the environment. I grieved for Mom and moved on, but Jess just got weirder and weirder."

I started to try to steer him into remembering the good times, but he continued, "You know she actually chained herself to a tree, protesting development with some fruity environmental group. The cops had to haul her off. Sixteen and my dad had to get her out of jail."

"It sounds like a very difficult time. Maybe we should talk about the good—"

"She spent her entire senior year of high school grounded. And it worked. For a while things were okay, but after graduation she went out every night partying."

"She must have been a passionate free spirit. You could even say, an innocent who loved nature. Maybe you could talk about that, in your own words." I was basically asking him to paraphrase my statement, which was skirting pretty close to an ethical line, if not over.

It didn't matter, though, because he refused to grab the life preserver. "Innocent girls don't do the kinds of things she did. I'm too ashamed to tell you about her final big stunt, but let's just say it proved she had no decency."

We all turned to look as a Cal Fire truck passed on the road above us. It towed a long flatbed trailer with huge bulldozers.

Once the noise had died away, I tried to take advantage of the pause. "How about when your sister was older? Maybe you have some good memories from when she outgrew that phase."

"She never did. At the end of that summer she turned eighteen and blew town. Joined back up with that environmental group where they were headquartered down in Venice. That was thirteen years ago." He looked down at the ground. His giant boots were caked with black mud. "I have a friend who went down there and says you can't walk barefoot on that beach. There are drug needles and stuff in the sand."

"But you must have some good memories," I stressed. "Maybe

from when she was a child? Try to think of her when she was a little girl. What kind of little sister was she?"

He kept his face down as he kicked at a pebble. "She used to follow me around everywhere. She always wanted me to show her stuff. Fishing, camping, swimming, you name it. If I could do it, she wanted me to show her how." He looked up and smiled for the first time. "I must have tried to teach her how to put a worm on a hook a million times before she got it to stick. She loved the outdoors. She loved these mountains, and the lake." His smile faded. "Maybe it's right she died there. Like she's at peace or something." He squeezed his eyes shut.

My pulse charged. That was my sound bite. No hearts were going to break, but at least it gave the viewer a taste of who the victim was and a window into the loss her brother felt. I waited, just in case he started crying, but after a few moments he shook his head and looked at me with dry eyes.

"I think that's everything we need." I pressed stop on the camera and removed the clip mic. "Thank you for speaking with me." I removed a reporter's notebook from my gear bag. "One more thing, can you give me your sister's name? The coroner probably won't release it for several days."

"Jessica. When she was a kid we all called her Jess or Jessie."

I was writing the E in her last name when it hit me. "Jessica Egan?"

He was too absorbed in his own thoughts to notice the change in me. "That's right."

The chain-saw repairman leaned out of the truck. "All done."

"Thanks," Egan called, then looked at Bell. "Get me back to my crew. I don't care how, but I expect you to make it happen." He returned to the truck without looking back.

Sometimes I wonder what would have happened if Egan had stayed a few moments longer. Would I have said something to him? I was still pretty shocked and unsure, so maybe not.

Bell left. I think I must have mumbled a thank-you, but I was on autopilot.

Jessica Egan?

I hadn't heard that name in thirteen years. I'd only known her for the one summer I'd lived at Lake Elizabeth.

Was it really possible that the thing in the body bag I'd been so careful not to look at had been Jessica Egan?

FIVE

I packed up my equipment and returned to the baseball field. I don't remember the walk. One minute I was on the front side of campus, then the next I was behind the grandstand. Slim's truck was gone.

I took out my cell phone.

Callum answered. "KJAY, we're on your side."

"It's Lilly. When are they doing the autopsy on the drowning victim?"

"I have no idea, but I doubt it'll be anytime soon." His voice receded. "Hey, Bev. How about you try and put the right tape numbers in your scripts? . . . Don't give me that look. I'm the one around here who gives looks." He came back to the phone. "What about the IO? Did you get a statement?"

"No. He wants their midnight briefing to be the first time anyone comments." I paused. "But I did get an exclusive interview with the brother of the drowning victim."

"Oh." He couldn't have sounded less interested.

"He's a Forest Service Hotshot. They called him off the fire line to break the news."

"Oh," Callum said again, but this time his voice was higher and a lot more emphatic. "That's great. We'll slip in a nice VO/SOT about the drowning in the A block."

"The last sound bite is the one to use." Through the grandstand I saw several people crossing under the bright lights toward the briefing tent. I recognized Slim's satellite truck parked out there too. "Have you heard anything more about how she drowned?"

"Is there more than one way?"

"You know what I mean." I wasn't in the mood for sarcasm,

even from Callum. "The story up here seems to be that she was drunk in a dangerous place without a life jacket."

"That's the story I heard too."

"There has to be more to it than that."

"Why?"

An image of Jessica flashed before my eyes. Short, brown hair, jeans, and tennis shoes. A dour, disapproving frown as I offered her a can of beer I knew she wouldn't take. The offer itself a joke meant to provoke someone I thought was an uptight buzz-kill.

"Lilly?" Callum called. "Are you there?"

"Yes, I can hear you." I paused again. "I've been talking to some people who used to know her. Back when the victim lived here, she didn't approve of drinking or partying out on the lake."

"Just a minute." He set the phone down. I heard him yelling at someone in the newsroom, then he returned. "Sorry, Lilly. What were you saying?"

"I think the drowning story is suspicious."

"I'll call about the autopsy, but drownings are nightmares for MEs. It's almost impossible to tell if water in the lungs got there before or after they died."

My voice rose. "But they must be able to find something out."

"Sure. They'll do a toxicology report and check for evidence she struggled with an attacker, but if the body got roughed up underwater, it'll make it that much harder."

I remembered the diver saying the body had been thrown against the rocks. How badly damaged was Jessica's body? Pukey the Kid had taken one look and hurled.

"Call anyway," I said.

"Sure. I'll put it in the planner for follow-up next week." I heard him moving papers around his desk. "Why don't you go ahead and find someone to take your video down the canyon? Make sure they know to deliver it to Teddy and Freddy."

I left Command Headquarters and returned to Elizabeth. My plan was to stop at a gas station and find someone preparing to evacuate. As I drove, I kept thinking about the way the police and Jessica's brother had talked about her—like she was a silly, self-destructive bimbo who stupidly got herself killed. It made me angry. I didn't know why I felt so strongly since Jessica and I hadn't even been real friends.

I thought of calling Rod to talk about it, but he was working. Besides, telling him about Jessica would require telling him the gory details of my misspent youth.

When I saw the doughnut shop I slammed on the brakes.

The lights were all on inside Double Down Donuts, but the door was locked. I pounded on the window until an older Asian woman entered from a door behind the cash register. She wore a hairnet and an apron. She saw me and immediately began shaking her head. "Closed." She had a strong accent and I doubted English was her first language.

"Wait," I called. "I'm looking for someone." But she'd already returned to the interior of the building.

I followed the dirt lot around to the back. The only light came from above the closed rear door. Parked nearby was a delivery van with DOUBLE DOWN DONUTS painted on the side.

I knocked on the back door. After a few moments, a teenage girl opened it. The sweet and creamy aroma of baking poured out and drove away the stink of the fire.

The girl looked liked the older woman's granddaughter. Her long black hair was piled into a hairnet and she wore an apron smeared with batter and flour. "We're closed." Her voice was pure American. She had an iPod attached to her arm with the earbuds draped over her shoulder.

Behind her the older woman saw me. "I said we're closed."

"I don't want doughnuts." I paused and rethought that. "I mean, of course I want doughnuts, but that's not why I'm here."

"Little Sister!" I heard metal crash and then Bud appeared behind the girl. "What're you doin' here?" His hands, covered in oven mitts, took me into a giant bear hug.

I pulled back and looked at him.

Bud wore his usual cutoff jean shorts and five-o'clock shadow.

His wrinkled and tattooed torso was bare underneath the apron. "You should be back home in Bako. It's not safe up here."

"I'm covering the mandatory evacuation."

"Move." The woman pushed past Bud and reached for the door. "You're going to ruin this entire batch."

I stepped farther into the kitchen so she could shut the door. An air conditioner was running, but the heat from the ovens was still brutal. All three of their faces were glossy from sweat. "If I were you, I'd leave it open."

"It's because of the ash," the teenager explained. "If the door's open, the ash gets into the batter, the glaze—everything really."

Despite the threat of ash, the room was remarkably clean. The beige walls gleamed from a fresh coat of paint and matched the new stainless-steel counters. The only thing that looked old and worn, besides Bud of course, was the blue-checkered linoleum floor.

The woman didn't stay for introductions, which was a relief because I didn't have the energy to engage in polite chitchat. She and the teenage girl resumed pouring flour into a large mixer at the other end of the room.

"I'm up here workin' too." Bud walked to a rack of stainless-steel trays holding freshly glazed doughnuts. "I'm bakin' for all those brave men fightin' the fire, and no government organization ever did nothin' without doughnuts." He rolled the rack to a counter piled with pink cardboard bakery boxes.

I followed. "Should I translate that to mean you're gouging the government and the money is too good to stop?"

"This here rodeo's on the up-and-up." He put his left hand, still covered in the oven mitt, over the right side of his chest. "On my honor."

I ripped my eyes away from all that creamy, sugary goodness on the trays. "It's supposed to be your right hand, and it goes over your heart."

"Never do remember that right." He grinned. "But I'm not shootin' a line this time." He gestured to the woman. "Mrs. Paik here has this first-class shop, but when they started signin' up local contractors, she didn't have the people-type skills to put herself forward proper."

He gave Mrs. Paik his trademark grin—the one that had charmed women and separated fools from their money for longer than I'd been alive.

Mrs. Paik frowned at him. "You're wasting time talking," she yelled over the mixer. Her immunity to Bud's charms was impressive.

He nodded as though he agreed, but then went right on talking. "She was set to miss this here gravy train so I stepped in on her behalf. I got a real good way of talkin' with the boys runnin' this here show, on account of my bein' a smoke jumper up in Alaska all those years ago."

"Translation—you charmed them with tales of the good old days and made them think you were part of their club."

He nodded while swapping out the oven mitts for disposable gloves. "I'm gettin' fifty percent of the take, and as you said before, there may be some gougin' involved, so the take is considerable."

Mrs. Paik yelled across the room again, but this time in another language. Bud listened and then glanced at a clock on the wall with a KOREAN FOOTBALL ASSOCIATION logo on the clockface.

"It's awful late." Bud looked back at me. "Head on over to my place, if you need a place to sleep." He began filling the boxes with doughnuts. "It's close by. I'll give you directions."

"I know where it is. You let me live there after Mom kicked me out, remember?"

"That takes me back a piece." Bud grinned. "Sure put a crick in her neck, my lettin' you do that. She said how you was goin' to the devil and I was helpin' you along."

"No good deed goes unpunished."

He looked confused for a moment, but then smiled. "That's right. I forgot about my missin' TV."

"I seem to remember selling a lot more than your TV. You were right to kick me out. I wasn't a very good person, back then."

"You'd just lost your way, Little Sister. It was a bad time, but you came back 'round right." He grinned. "I've never quite gotten there myself."

I didn't return his smile. "That time is what I came to talk to you about." I glanced at the woman and the teenage girl. They were each focused on the mixer as its massive paddles churned. "A woman drowned on the lake last night."

Bud continued putting doughnuts into the pink boxes. "I heard about that. What kind of idiot goes out partyin' at a time like this?"

"No, that's just it." I put a hand on his arm and forced him to stop. "I knew the dead woman back when I lived up here, and she wasn't like that. She's the last person who would have gotten drunk and gone out on the lake."

"I'm sorry, Lilly." His face looked genuinely pained. "I never would've talked bad about her like that if I'd known she was a friend of yours. You must be right upset."

"No, it's not that." I hesitated. "We weren't friends exactly, but I know she wasn't reckless or wild. She was into protecting the environment and animal rights. She was smart and strong, not stupid and frivolous like people are saying."

He resumed filling the box. "She wasn't mixed in with that hippie-type group who came in protesting development a ways back?"

I nodded. "Yes, but that's exactly what I mean about her not being wild. She gave up all her free time volunteering for that group while everyone else her age was only interested in having fun."

"Well, I can understand how she got herself a bad reputation. Those environmental folks rubbed most of the locals the wrong way, and there were all kinds of stories about drugs and such."

"No. She never would have approved of that kind of thing. She didn't even approve of me." My voice rose. "It's all wrong. The things people are saying about her, the way she died—it's all just wrong."

"Is there some other reason you got for thinking that, other than you not believin' the lady was the type?" I didn't answer.

" 'Cause a person can be on the straight and narrow for years and fall right off."

That hit a little too close to home, but before I could think of what to say, Mrs. Paik approached. She spoke to Bud again in the other language, and to my surprise he responded. Soon they were having an argument.

I tried to get Bud's attention. "What language is that?"

He didn't answer, but the teenage girl took one earbud out. "It's Korean. My grandmother says you're slowing us down and you need to leave. Your uncle is saying . . . she's colder than . . . the flip side of a pillow . . . on the dark side of a hill." The girl paused. "I may have lost some of it in translation."

I shook my head. "No, that sounds like Bud."

After a few more moments of arguing they both broke off.

"I'm sorry," Bud said to me. "We're pressed for time and I need to get back to work. How about, if everythin's not on fire by mornin', you and me can rustle up some breakfast?"

Mrs. Paik forced a bag of doughnuts on me and pushed me outside. "Good-bye," she said, then slammed the door.

I'd already finished one of the doughnuts by the time I returned to the van. I quickly ate a second and then started to get the tapes ready to send down the canyon. I stopped when I saw the one labeled ELIZABETH, DROWNING.

Something was nagging at the back of my brain, but I had no idea what it was. Why did Jessica Egan's death bother me so much? Bud was right. People can change a lot in thirteen years. For all I knew Jessica had become a Playboy Bunny.

I switched on the suitcase editor Leanore had been using earlier. It sat on a small counter in the rear of the truck. I unhooked the chair from the wall and sat down to look at my video.

I saw it the third time through.

Elizabeth police headquarters is grouped with city hall and some other county offices in a newer complex of buildings. Previously most of these services had been located in Elizabeth, but as the population had shifted to the other shore, a change had been demanded. Just like Search and Rescue, as a compromise it had also been placed where the eastern and western shores met. I passed the dirt road I'd taken down to the body retrieval a couple hours earlier, then made the right up to the city government buildings. Despite the late hour, the lights were all on.

I left my gear in the truck and entered the police station. About half a dozen empty desks filled the room. Several similarly empty offices lined the back wall. The only person there appeared to be a support officer watching a cable news channel's coverage of the wildfire.

I recognized the video Slim had fed back to L.A. The girl in the cannabis tank top was talking as a boy with glasses and a ponytail looked on. My work had never been picked up nationally, and it was galling to see a slug get that kind of honor.

I put aside my momentary professional jealousy and spoke to the officer. "Pardon me?"

The support officer was a plump woman in her fifties. Her dyed hair had been carefully arranged in a way that contrasted with the drabness of her brown uniform.

She jumped at the sound of my voice. "Sorry. Didn't hear you come in." She pointed to the monitor. "Can you believe this girl? Says she doesn't have to evacuate because the firefighters will save her. That's how good men get killed—airheads like that."

Now that the clip had gone national, I suspected most of America would have a similar opinion of the girl.

"I'm a shooter from KJAY," I said.

She glanced at the logo on my polo shirt and straightened. "I'm sorry. None of us are authorized to talk."

"I know all about the evacuation, but that's not why I'm here. I need to speak with someone about the drowning today."

She looked surprised, but shook her head again. "I can't comment about that either."

"I have important information." I leaned around her and tried to see into the offices. "Is the sergeant here? It's urgent."

"He's getting his first sleep in twenty-four hours. I can't wake him unless it's an emergency."

"I don't think the drowning was an accident."

She glanced over her shoulder toward the hallway. "Wait here." She walked down the hallway and returned a minute later. "It'll just be a minute. He's pulling himself together."

"Thanks." I shifted my weight to the other foot. Scanners played in the background. The cable news channel moved on to the latest political fight in Washington. I shifted my weight back to the other foot. After another minute I sat down on one of the hard plastic chairs in the waiting area.

The feel of the chairs reminded me of the waiting room at the old police station in Elizabeth. I remembered sitting there thirteen years ago while they questioned Jessica in the back. An officer stood nearby in case I decided to bolt. I was sure Jessica would tell them everything. She had nothing to lose and everything to gain by telling the truth.

But I'd underestimated her. Jessica was strong. She'd withstood everything they threw at her and kept her mouth shut. Not many teenagers, let alone adults, would have been able to do that.

Jessica and I had never been friends—if anything we'd been using each other—but thinking about her thirteen years later, I wished it had been different. I wished that I'd been the kind of person who could have been friends with Jessica, instead of the shallow, immature jerk I was back then.

I'd only seen her once more after the police station. She'd turned eighteen the next day and left town. What had her brother said during the interview? She'd gone to be with the environmentalists where they were headquartered down in Venice?

I had a sudden idea and stood up. "Have you lived here for very long?"

"Twenty years." The support officer smiled. "I came on vacation and never left."

"Do you remember back in the late nineties when that group came into the area protesting development?"

She walked back to a small table with a coffeemaker and poured a cup. "Sure. They raised a fuss because Mr. McClellan wanted to subdivide his land and build it up. Those environmental folks said how the lizards would go extinct or something." She paused from adding creamer. "And wouldn't you know, now we're overrun with those ugly little things with the red stripes. Can't shake your hair out without hitting one of them."

"Is there anyone who might still be mad about it?" I eagerly leaned against the counter. "I remember tempers running pretty high at the time. Could someone have held a grudge all these years?"

She returned and set the coffee on the end of the counter, but didn't drink it. "I don't know. All that land on the other side of the mountain belonged to the McClellans and they fought hard to build on it, but the whole mess dragged on with environmental studies and all kinds of bureaucratic stuff. Finally, they ended up selling everything for a nature preserve."

"What happened to the preserve?"

"It's still there. If you go up Mt. Terrill and over to the other side, you'll see the fence soon enough." She frowned. "Of course the preserve runs all the way down into the valley and a lot of it's been burned up in the fire."

"Do any of the McClellans still live around here?"

She shrugged. "Old Mr. McClellan built his dream house over there and called it Bonny Hazel after the hazelnut trees, but it had to be sold with the rest of the land. Now there are students living there studying the nature preserve, or something."

The sergeant walked in. He wore a wrinkled Elizabeth Police Department uniform. His shirt had come untucked on the side. He looked tired. "I can't comment about the evacuation, even if you already know about it." The support officer handed him the coffee as he walked around the counter. "So if that's why you're really here, do me a favor and don't waste my time."

He stopped a few feet from me and took a long drink of the coffee.

I waited for him to lower the cup, then said, "Jessica Egan couldn't have died the way you're saying."

"Why?" He raised the cup and inhaled the smell before taking another drink.

"I was there when they towed her boat in—the one she supposedly drove all by herself out to Road's End." I held up my tape. "I looked at the video and the motor is an old two-stroke. You need some serious strength to pull a cord on one of those."

"Sure you do," he said. "But I've seen plenty of women do it."

The support officer, leaning on the counter, raised her hand. "You're looking at one right here. It's a pain, but I used to get it done."

"You don't have a bad right shoulder." I looked at the sergeant. "Jessica Egan blew hers out when she was a teenager."

No one spoke for a moment. The scanners and the TV filled the silence.

Finally the sergeant nodded. "I'll make sure that gets added to the report." He raised the cup and swallowed the last of the coffee. "Do you have a business card I can take in case someone needs to follow up?"

"You don't understand." My voice rose. "You have a woman dead under mysterious circumstances."

My tone didn't ruffle him. "When the autopsy results come in, we'll get together with the Sheriff's Department and take another look at the case. Your information will be carefully considered."

"But the autopsy could take weeks and might not even show anything conclusive. In the meantime, evidence could be lost or the killer could simply pick up and leave town."

"Killer?" He glanced at the support officer. "Isn't that a little melodramatic?"

"Jessica Egan was one of the protesters thirteen years ago when the McClellans tried to develop their land. Maybe someone is still angry about what happened and decided to hurt her."

His mouth contorted as he tried to suppress a laugh. At least he managed to keep his tone neutral. "I promise, we'll carefully consider all the possibilities when we get the autopsy results back." He stepped back in preparation to leave. "Thank you for bringing us your information. I'll definitely add it to the report." He turned to go.

"Look, I get it." I stepped toward him. "You're exhausted. You're short manpower and resources. Believe me, I have been there, but you aren't even doing basic police work."

He stopped. "Excuse me?" His professional tone broke. "We diverted resources from a deadly natural disaster to look for the body. Do you know the pressure we're under right now? And we stopped everything to look for her."

The support officer bristled. "You have no business saying something like that. We even got a helicopter to fly over the lake looking for her. That was time it could have been making water drops on the fire."

The sergeant stepped toward me. "Most people wouldn't even have gone after the body. Do you know how hard we had to hustle to get her to the coroner before the evacuation tied up the roads?"

"You had good intentions," I said. "But maybe if you hadn't gone so fast, you'd have realized you were making a mistake. Have you even done a single piece of forensic work? The geezer you had out with the divers didn't even check Road's End."

"This conversation is over." He turned and started to walk away.

I followed him. "At least tell me who she was staying with?"

He stopped again. "What?"

"Who's this friend who conveniently provided Jessica Egan with alcohol and a boat—which she couldn't start on her own, by the way—and then reported her missing?"

A look of recognition flashed across the support officer's face and she pulled back from the counter. "So that's what you're after. You're doing some kind of smear story."

"What do you mean, what I'm after? I'm after this person's name because they might be involved in a woman's death."

The sergeant walked back to me. "We will follow up on the information you provided at the first opportunity, but if I find out you've been harassing witnesses, I will arrest you." He stepped forward until we were almost toe-to-toe. "Now get out."

SIX

I returned to the van. I took deep breaths to try to slow my racing heart. A soreness had begun to creep into my chest from the smoke. I tried drinking some water, but it didn't help. Had I really just been thrown out of the police station? Even I knew that was bad.

I took out my phone, but instead of calling the assignment desk, I dialed Rod's personal cell. He answered almost immediately.

"It's Lilly," I said.

"Is your video on the way?"

I managed not to say the swear words in my head. I'd completely forgotten. "Yes," I lied while starting the truck.

"Why don't you give me a description of the car bringing it down? I'll text Teddy and Freddy so they can be on the lookout."

"I'll call them directly, eliminate the middleman." I put the phone on speaker and started back to Elizabeth.

There was silence for a moment, then Rod said, "Just a minute." I heard him get up from a chair and walk a short distance. After a brief pause, a sliding glass door swooshed closed. "Okay, I'm alone in an edit bay. Nobody can hear us. Why are you lying?"

"Is it that obvious?"

"Yes. What's wrong, sweetheart?" His voice was warm, even over the phone.

"I've been thinking things over." I hesitated. "I need your help up here."

"Okay."

"I know the roads are going to close any second, but can you try and make it?"

"Sure."

"You're already at the station and have a better chance of succeeding than a reporter Callum calls at home." I paused. "Wait, did you just agree?"

"Of course. I'll throw a few things together and be on my way."

"Oh."

"Isn't that what you want?"

"I'm just surprised. I know how much you hate reporting."

"A change will be nice. Sometimes I miss reporting." He paused. "And you said you need me. I don't think that's ever happened before."

"Of course I need you."

"You've never said it out loud. Is the fire that bad?"

"No. It's something else. I'll explain when you get here."

We hung up quickly so he could get going. I didn't waste time worrying about Rod's new enthusiasm for reporting or my being blindsided by it. I had to find someone to drive my video down the canyon. It proved remarkably easy. At the gas station a line of cars stretched into the street. I promised a family of four inside a Subaru Outback that they'd be interviewed upon delivery of the tape, and they eagerly agreed.

I got back in the van and dialed Freddy's cell phone.

"Dude," he said for a greeting. "So how bad is it up there? Has it turned all *Lord of the Flies* yet?"

"When did you read that?"

"High school, dude. So has anybody, like, eaten anybody yet?"

"There's no cannibalism in *Lord of the Flies*."

"For real?" I heard a soda can pop open. "I totally must be thinking of *Lord of the Rings*."

"There's no cannibalism in *Lord of the Rings* and none up here. People are evacuating. It's not a zombie movie."

"Wait till the fire gets there." In the background a plastic bag crinkled open and I guessed Freddy was putting Fritos in his Coke. He'd stopped doing it in the newsroom because it grossed so many people out. "I bet society, like, crumbles and you have to go all solitary loner."

I laughed, despite myself. "Are you and Teddy set up at the canyon entrance to go live for the eleven?"

I heard him take a drink and then chew. "We're good to go. Don't sweat it, chief."

I gave him a description of the Subaru bringing my tape down the canyon and said good-bye.

I bought a Mountain Dew from a vending machine at the gas station. It was the only thing that didn't have a massive line. I drank it in the truck while thinking about how to make the police launch an immediate investigation. Rod's combination of charm and intelligence might work where my forward assault had failed, but there was no guarantee he'd make it before the road closed.

I reached over and flipped the windshield wipers on. The cleaning fluid cleared away the latest layer of soot and ash. Of course, the glass outside the wiper's path was almost opaque, making the clear part look like a pair of eyes. I wasn't alone. Almost every other vehicle now had these same windshield-wiper eyes.

I could call Callum and ask for his help, but the minute I told him I knew the dead woman, I'd be yanked from the story. I could always try lying by omission, but Callum was good at reading me. Whom else might the police listen to? That's when I remembered Jessica's brother, Brad. Not only was he the next of kin, but he could confirm Jessica's bad shoulder.

I drove back to Incident Command Headquarters and parked in the same place as before. Slim's truck was still over at the tent. He and the truck would need to be there to carry the briefing live at midnight.

I returned to the multipurpose room where Bell had taken me earlier. A new group of men and women were eating and relaxing. I didn't see Brad Egan among them, but after a moment I spotted Father Tom. He was sitting with three recently showered men drinking coffee. Their conversation stopped when I approached.

"I'm sorry to disturb you," I said. "Have you seen Brad Egan?"

Father Tom shook his head. "He's not here."

"Do you know where I can find him? It's urgent."

"I'm afraid that won't be possible. He's already gone back to the fire line."

"What?" My voice carried across the room and I saw several faces turn to look. I tried to calm down. "How did he manage that?"

"Firefighter Bell got him a vehicle. He left ten minutes ago." Father Tom sighed. "He said getting back to work was the best thing, but I'm not so sure."

I wasted several more minutes trying to convince them I needed to contact Egan on the fire line. They all insisted there was no way for a civilian to do it. I tried explaining that it was an emergency, but they remained unmoved. Finally I asked when Egan would return to headquarters.

"Not that long," one of them said. "His crew has three days left on a fourteen-day rotation."

I mumbled thank you and left. I stepped out into the courtyard and stopped. In the background of my thoughts, I heard trucks coming and going. Men and women went by. Several weak, yellow-tinted bulbs hung outside the cafeteria. This area seemed dark compared to the blinding lights in the nearby fields and parking lots. I wondered what the students would think if they could have seen what had happened to their campus.

I thought about finding Jessica's father's house and searching it. I don't know if the insanity of the fire created a false sense of reality, but the idea of breaking and entering didn't bother me. What did give me pause was how unlikely I was to find anything. Jessica's father had already left by the time she got here. She probably hadn't even been inside. Also, it wasn't the house she grew up in, and from what her brother had said she'd only been to visit once before.

Then it hit me. It wasn't so much an idea as a realization. I was standing in a place where Jessica had come every day for most of her young life.

I stopped a man walking by. "Pardon me. Have you seen a library around here?"

"The school library is locked up. Only room on campus." He wore a blue vest with National Weather Service patches. "You want to read? I've got some paperbacks. I really should get an e-reader for these assignments, but I can't quite pull the trigger."

"I'm looking for old school yearbooks."

He looked puzzled, but gestured down the courtyard. "Why don't you go to the yearbook office?"

"Because I didn't even know such a thing existed."

He pointed again. "It's down a little bit. Display Processing took it over."

I thanked him and walked until I reached a room with a DIS-PLAY PROCESSING sign taped to the door. Unlike the signs on other doors, which had been scribbled in marker, this one had been done on a computer and included a faded image of an old world map behind the words.

I walked in. This room wasn't a classroom. It was full of long, flat tables covered in giant maps. They were similar to the ones on the media trailer's walls and appeared to be drying after coming off a giant, industrial printer.

A woman looked up from an extremely large computer monitor. She had four different pencils stuck behind her ears, and a pen on a cord around her neck.

"I'm looking for yearbooks," I said.

She pointed to a bookcase in the rear of the room. A bulletin board with proof pages from a yearbook had been taken down from the wall and leaned against it.

I quickly passed her and stopped at the bookcase.

"Wait a minute," she said. "Are you with the media?"

The yearbooks were a hodgepodge of different years. They were probably kept as examples for the new student editors each year and not as an archive. "I'm with KJAY in Bakersfield."

A man walked in wearing a Mojave Fire Department uniform. "We're getting intel from one of the hand crews that the crown is shifting south."

"I've got that from the latest infrared." She frowned as she used her mouse to pull something up on the computer. "I told you I'm on top of it."

"I'm sorry to keep bugging you, but the governor's staff has called twice. They're freaking out about—"

She jerked up from the computer and pointed at me. "This lady is from a TV station."

Whatever he'd been about to say, I doubted they would tell me. "Don't worry, I'm leaving." I grabbed three of the oldest yearbooks and left.

I returned to the multipurpose room and sat down at an empty table. I'd looked through one yearbook, without learning anything, when an orange shirt caught my attention. I whipped around to look at the retreating figure. The back of her shirt said SEARCH AND RESCUE. I slid off the bench and followed as she picked up a white box lunch.

I caught up with her at the coffee urn. "I'm sorry to interrupt." I waited for her to turn and look at me. "I'm from KJAY. My name is Lilly Hawkins. Can I ask you some questions about the body pulled from the lake today?"

She set down a bottle of nondairy creamer and turned excited eyes to the logo on my shirt. "I don't know very much about the drowning, but I could talk about how Search and Rescue is helping with the evacuation."

I opened my mouth to say no, but she continued, "We're helping people evacuate large animals on the other side of the mountain, and we're doing first aid down at the spike camps and—"

"That's great," I said as though I could not care less. "But I need to know about the drowning. The dead woman's name was Jessica Egan. Do you know who reported her missing?"

She shook her head. "No, I'm sorry."

"When the police requested a diver, did they say anything at all about who owned the boat out at Road's End?"

"I wasn't involved. You could try asking Arnaldo Bedolla. He's the one who did the actual dive." She paused. "Or Pete Barton, but he's just a teenager. His dad is usually the one who dives with

Arnaldo, but he was too busy trying to evacuate their cattle and horses. The family's place is on the other side of the mountain and the fire is real close now."

I doubted Pukey the Kid and his father knew much. "How do I find Arnaldo Bedolla?"

She returned to fixing her coffee. Her enthusiasm was waning the more she realized I wasn't going to interview her. "After the dive he went home to make sure his wife and kids evacuated. Once they're safely out, he's taking an overnight shift for Search and Rescue."

"Can I leave a message for him at Search and Rescue headquarters?"

She shook her head. "Nobody's there. We're all using this as our base." The woman pulled out her cell phone. "But I can give you his personal number. He's selling real estate now so he checks his voice mail a lot."

I thanked her and dialed the number. I left a message explaining that we'd met at the body retrieval and asked him to call me.

I decided to take the yearbooks back to the truck. On my way, the cell phone rang. I saw KJAY on the caller ID and answered immediately. "Hi, Callum."

"Freddy just called in. He says CHP officially closed the road to eastbound traffic. You're cut off."

I stopped. I was standing in front of the field of Porta Potties. The rough grumble of generators powering the portable lights ran in the background. "Does he know if Rod made it in time?"

"He passed them five minutes ago."

I exhaled. My relief frightened me. Yes, it was good Rod was coming—he'd be a big help—but what if he hadn't made it in time or had even said no? I needed to be able to take care of myself.

"My guess, he'll reach you in half an hour or so." After a pause Callum continued, "We may have worked out a way to go live. Rod's bringing a laptop and the digital camera with him. The engineers are working on streaming the feed directly into the control room."

Trent, our news director, had bought the digital camera as an experiment. Eventually, he hoped to make the switch to digital shooting and editing. It would be portable, easier to use, and substantially cheaper than the ancient system we now had.

What Trent hadn't said, but Rod had warned me about, is that small digital cameras are more convenient for one-man bands—reporters who shoot and edit their own material. If Trent put that kind of system in place, he could save a fortune on payroll by eliminating most of the shooter and editor positions.

Needless to say, I hated Trent's puny little camera.

"Wireless service is spotty up here," I cautioned. "Even if we can get a wi-fi signal or a cellular network, it's going to cut in and out."

"That's why you need to find a hard connection to a high-speed modem."

"Oh, is that all?"

A man emerged from one of the Porta Potties. The perfumed chemical smell escaped out the open door and mixed with the fire stink.

I started walking again.

"No, that's not all. Try to rustle up someone for Rod to interview live."

I pulled the phone away from my ear to glance at the screen. It said 10:37. "Why don't I put out the wildfire instead? That would probably be easier."

"Do your best," Callum said. "Give it a try."

"And by try, I'm assuming you mean, do it right and on time or risk being fired."

"Yes, the usual."

A propane tanker rumbled up behind me. I got off the narrow road and stepped into a tanbark playground.

"Lilly, are you there?" Callum said.

"Yes, I'm here." The tanker passed and I continued walking.

"There's something else we need to talk about. The Elizabeth police chief called Trent to complain about you."

I stopped again. "What?"

"He said you were verbally abusive to an officer and harassing witnesses."

"I can't harass the witness because they won't tell me who it is." I told him about Jessica's shoulder and my visit to the police station. I left out that I knew Jessica.

"I don't know why," I said at the end, "but they both freaked out when I started asking questions about the friend. Maybe they're covering for this person. Maybe it'll turn out to be a bribery or corruption story. I know how much you love those."

"I do love a good corruption story." Callum paused to savor the thought, then got back to business. "And I agree, the death sounds fishy." I heard his chair move. "We'll put a reporter on it in a couple days. As soon as the evacuation is over and the fire is better contained."

"But by then it may be too late."

"Too late for what? If Elizabeth PD is guilty of incompetence or even covering for someone, we'll nail them."

"I don't care about nailing them. I care about catching whoever's responsible for Jessica Egan's death. And you know as well as I do that homicides that aren't solved in the first forty-eight hours are almost never solved."

"You're right." I heard a high-pitched buzz in the background alerting Callum to a story coming over the video feeds. "But it's not our place to catch murderers. That's the job of the police. It's our job to inform the community if the police are screwing up, which you can do in a couple days."

I didn't say anything.

"Listen, Lilly. This is serious. You've got a front-row seat for the biggest natural disaster we've seen around here in fifty years. I need you focused and in the game. We're all counting on you. This is big for the entire station."

"I know."

"Lilly, I want to hear you promise me you'll drop the drowning."

Truthfully, I wanted to drop it. The evacuation and approaching wildfire were once-in-a-lifetime stories. Would I ever have a chance like this again? But wasn't I just sitting in the police station wishing Jessica and I had been friends? Would a friend abandon her now when she couldn't even speak up for herself? Plus, I owed her. She covered for me with the police.

When I didn't say anything, Callum continued, "I vouched for you with Trent. He doesn't take complaints from police chiefs lightly. And I had your back earlier about Teddy and Freddy. I put my reputation on the line to protect yours. Don't make me sorry."

I took a deep breath. "Okay."

"Okay, what?"

"Okay, I promise."

"Good." He paused. "Now go find an Internet connection and someone to interview."

I returned to the media trailer. The door was locked and no one answered my knock. I started toward the briefing tent, but paused at the sandwich board. New maps of the wildfire were posted, and it was clear we were losing ground.

The science of stopping a fire is simple. You remove all vegetation and trees in a wide line. The fire burns to the line, runs out of fuel, and stops. These firebreaks can be roads, rivers or streams, or just a stretch of land cleared by bulldozers and chain saws. All that matters is that there's nothing there to burn.

The only hitch is if a fire is spotting—spewing embers in the air—it could jump over and continue on the other side. That's why ideally you wanted the line to be as wide as possible. Sometimes fire retardant was even dropped in advance to try to prevent the embers from igniting.

Judging from the new maps, a firebreak was being created on the other side of Mt. Terrill, just below the antennas on the ridge. In case this didn't stop the fire, a second line was also being constructed on this side, just above Tilly Heights.

Callum and Rod had been right. The worst-case scenario, that the fire burned up from the Terrill Valley, over the mountain, then down this side, now appeared to be the likely scenario.

I continued to the large briefing tent. Inside, a group of ten to fifteen men and women stood on or near the raised platform up front. Several maintenance men were going through the tent with Shop-Vacs sucking up ash and soot from the brown grass floor. Above us, the baseball field lights shone through the white tent fabric, highlighting the dark patches where ash had accumulated on the roof.

Slim had set his camera up in the main aisle facing the podium. He was reading a graphic novel and eating a burrito, so I didn't stop to say hi.

The IO stood with several men in Cal Fire uniforms up at the podium. The man I'd seen in Display Processing was also there. He was taping maps to the canvas wall behind the podium. They were similar to the ones I'd seen outside, but much larger.

As I approached the platform, everyone turned and saw me.

"Just a moment," the IO told them, then stepped to the edge. "If you want to set up a camera in the back, that's fine, but we need to keep the side aisles free."

"I've got a reporter on his way up the canyon. We want to go live for the eleven-o'clock show. I need access to a cable modem and someone to interview."

He shook his head. "No one is commenting on the evacuation until after the midnight briefing. Not me, not anyone."

"Then we'll use the interview to get an update on the fire." I began backing up as though it were decided. My only real talent, other than shooting great video, was being a human steamroller. "And I'm sure you've got Internet access in your trailer. We'll make it work."

He stepped off the platform. "I said no."

"I might have an idea." The voice came from a woman in an elegant updo and dark purple suit. Her face was heavily made up and her skirt was just short enough to show off her well-toned legs. But the most noticeable thing about her was at the end of those legs. She had on the only pair of high heels within twenty miles.

"How about the Forest Service airstrip?" She took several careful steps to join us. She appeared to be favoring the balls of her feet. When she stopped, I saw why. Her pointy heels punctured the grass and the back end of her shoes sank to the ground. She must have lost at least two inches in height. "I'm sure the Forest Service has an Internet connection out there."

The IO started what looked like a rejection, but stopped himself. He paused and appeared to be considering it.

"But that's fifteen miles up the lake." I looked from one to the other. "And no one will be landing or taking off at night. I need a live picture of something actually happening."

The woman's smile deepened. Her voice sounded upbeat. "This is a good compromise for you because someone important is landing there." She looked at the IO. "And it's good for you because it keeps her out of the way while you're trying to get organized."

"Who's landing?" I said. "And how important are they?"

They glanced at each other, but neither answered me.

"Just a minute." The IO jumped onto the platform. It swayed in a way that should have made everyone nervous.

The woman in the heels was the only one who appeared to care. "Excuse me," she said before yanking her heels out of the ground and marching over to a maintenance worker on the balls of her feet. I watched as she spoke to him and pointed at the platform. She was smiling and had that same upbeat energy, even though she was reaming him out.

The IO returned from speaking with several men on the platform. "Do you know how to get to the Forest Service airstrip?"

"Yes, but I'm not driving all the way up there unless I know who's landing."

"How about the governor of California? Is he important enough?"

SEVEN

Human steamroller or not, that gave me pause. "Seriously?"

"He's coming for the briefing." The IO began walking me out of the tent. "Firefighter Bell, who escorted you earlier, is already at the airstrip. I'll call over and tell her to expect you, but you need to get going."

"Why? What time is the governor landing?"

"Eleven."

I looked at my cell phone's screen. "You mean ten minutes from now?"

"Don't worry. Politicians are late for everything."

I bolted for the van. On the way I made a quick call to Callum telling him to redirect Rod to the airstrip.

I drove quickly across the back side of campus. A man with a clipboard started to cross the road headed for the gym. He held up his hand for me to stop. I hit the horn. He jumped back and I cruised through without slowing. On the streets of Elizabeth I zigzagged from one lane to another dodging traffic.

It was seven minutes past eleven when I pulled up to the airstrip's main gate. It opened and a Sheriff's Department officer checked my credentials before allowing me in.

The facility wasn't fancy. The only structures, besides a large hangar for storing aircraft, were simple one-story buildings. Several huge trailers containing helicopter equipment and spare parts had been trucked in and were parked near the hangar. The runway itself, which was being used as a giant helipad, was lit with large floodlights that backlit the haze in the air.

I drove past a group of six or seven officers waiting next to four

SUVs with the CHP and Elizabeth Police logos. They screamed official entourage so I relaxed. If they were waiting to drive the governor to headquarters, then I hadn't missed the arrival. I parked at the largest of the buildings and grabbed my camera.

Firefighter Bell walked out the main entrance to meet me. She wore the same black L.A. Fire Department uniform as when she'd taken me to interview Brad Egan earlier. "Hi. This is quite a scoop for you. Congratulations."

"How long before he arrives?"

"We don't know. The governor's plane landed in Bakersfield, but apparently the chopper bringing him here hasn't taken off yet."

"You mean he hasn't even left Bakersfield?"

Bell shook her head. "Nope. Politicians always run late. The bigger they are, the later they run." She hooked her thumb behind her. "His aide is inside, but I doubt he'll tell you anything."

At my request, Bell enlisted the help of one of the Forest Service rangers to tackle the Internet situation. Meanwhile, I cranked up the generator in the live truck, opened my sticks, and set up the TV monitor and a light for Rod.

A male Forest Service ranger brought out a cord through the front door. "This is the longest one we've got. Let's hope it reaches."

I'd set up directly in front of the building, so the cord did reach, but without the laptop or camera I couldn't do anything more.

Bell and the ranger both decided to go inside and escape the smoke. As soon as they were gone, I called Arnaldo Bedolla again. He still didn't answer so I left a second message.

I rationalized breaking my promise to Callum with the old I'm-not-really-hurting-anyone excuse. I was covering the fire, after all. What did it hurt if I used some downtime to follow a few leads for Jessica?

I retreated to the live truck and looked through the two remaining yearbooks. They were only slightly more helpful than the first. I found headshots of a much younger Jessica in the alphabetical listings of middle-school students. Her hair was long and she was smiling and happy. She was very different from the young woman I'd met several years later. Those middle-school headshots were the only mentions of Jessica. The pages with clubs and extracurricular activities were reserved for the high school students.

High school students such as her older brother. A young, handsome Brad Egan stared out from page after page. He was captain of the football team, a varsity shot-putter, captain of the archery team, prom king, and a member of the division-winning basketball team. The caption under his photo read *Future Olympian*. He'd chosen it himself.

"Come on." The voice belonged to a woman. I looked up and saw an attractive female ranger following a man in blue coveralls. She tried to keep up with him as he walked from the hangar toward the runway. "Everybody knows you pilots always have obscenely good coffee and in massive quantities."

He kept walking. "I don't know what you're talking about."

"Give me a break." The ranger had short brown hair and a graceful body. "The medevac practically smells like a Seattle coffeehouse."

He stopped and turned around. "You don't even have a grinder. I'd have to loan you mine."

"Please. We won't make it through the night."

He considered for a moment, then reluctantly nodded. "Maybe I saw a bag of French roast somewhere."

She gushed with thanks, then ran into the office.

The pilot continued toward the runway, but I jumped out of the truck and intercepted him. "Were you here today when they found that boat out at Road's End?"

"No. I'm on standby at night in case there's a medical emergency." He gestured behind him to the hangar. "The fellas you're looking for fly the Chinooks. They'll be back a little before sunrise." He started to leave.

I stepped in front of him. "I won't be here then. Did you hear anything about what happened? I'm trying to find out who owned the boat."

"Can't help you with that." Despite the refusal, he glanced over each shoulder.

"No one can hear us and this is off-the-record."

"I don't know, but before I left this morning, the deck coordinator denied the police's request to search the lake. We couldn't spare the time or manpower."

"Why'd they change their minds?"

"I wasn't here." He stepped around me and started down the runway. "But somebody must have called in a huge favor."

I went back to the truck. Someone had wanted Jessica found. Judging from the tone of her brother's interview, I doubted it had been her family. Did she have a boyfriend? Brad Egan had mentioned a married man. Could her lover, if he even existed, have quietly pulled strings? What about friends? Did she still have any in Elizabeth?

I opened the first yearbook—the one I'd looked through in the cafeteria. This was from Jessica's senior year of high school, when her brother had already left for college. She wasn't on any of the sports or club pages. She wasn't in any of the candid shots of the high school students.

Brad had said she'd been arrested at the beginning of her senior year for chaining herself to a tree during a protest. If her father had indeed grounded her for the rest of that school year, it might explain her lack of extracurricular activities.

I took a deep breath. I forced more and more air into my already sore chest. I pushed it to capacity, cringing as the ache spiked and then receded with my exhale.

A memory surfaced. Floating in an inner tube, just a little buzzed, despite being underage. The smell of barbecue cooking somewhere I couldn't see. My cutoff jeans and tank top wet with lake water. My peroxide-bleached hair up in a ponytail.

The start of summer.

Jessica Egan was standing on the shore of the lake looking at me. "Is your name Lilly?" Her was hair cut short in an uneven way she'd probably done herself. She wore jeans and a PETA

T-shirt. She'd just graduated high school, but was still only seventeen.

One glance at her and I was bored. "Nope."

She looked around confused. "I heard that was your name."

I didn't say anything. The current moved my inner tube farther down the shore.

She hurried along the water's edge, trying to keep up. "I also heard you're from Bakersfield and nobody around here really knows you."

"That's nice." The inner tube spun and I was no longer facing her.

"I have a business proposition," she called.

"I'm not in the business of business."

"Could you be in the business of lying to my father?"

I paddled around until I faced her. She suddenly seemed a lot less boring.

"My dad doesn't approve of how I want to spend my time," she said. "If you tell him we're friends and hanging out, I'll pay you."

"What makes you think he'll approve of me?" I took a drink of beer. "Why don't you get some nice local girl to lie for you?"

"Nice girls don't lie."

I heard metal hit metal and then a long squeak. I leaned out of the truck in time to see the front gate admitting a KJAY news van. Rod parked the old minivan next to my much larger live truck. He raised a hand in greeting before getting out. He wore a charcoal-colored three-piece suit with a maroon handkerchief peeking from the pocket. His wavy, blond hair was perfectly groomed, and his expensive Italian-leather shoes were shiny and polished.

Unlike other people, I've never been impressed with Rod's packaging. When he'd first arrived at KJAY, the ladies around the station all swooned over him. I wrongly assumed it meant he was a shallow jerk who just wanted to look good on TV. It had turned out that he was a shy geek, albeit an incredibly well-dressed one.

He approached carrying a laptop and some other equipment. He made eye contact and smiled. I may be immune to his packaging, but the smile gets me every time. I felt like Superman getting hit with kryptonite.

"Thanks for coming," I said.

"Are you kidding? What an opportunity." His face was lit up and I realized I hadn't seen him this happy at work in a long time. "Why didn't you tell me the governor was coming?" When I didn't say anything he continued, "That's why you asked me to drive up here, right?"

"It's a long story." I heard a noise and saw Bell coming out of the office. "We can talk about it later."

After polite introductions, Rod set the laptop down on a milk crate and waited for it to boot up.

"You don't appreciate how bad the smoke is until you're actually here." Rod looked at the ground. "And the ash everywhere, it's surreal." He raised his arm and examined the fabric of his suit coat. "Will it get on my clothing?" He brushed the sleeve. "Should I be taking precautions?"

I attached the small camera to my sticks. It wasn't even as big as the head plate and looked goofy sitting there. "It will get on your clothing. And there are no precautions you can take."

Despite my issues with the camera, Rod and I got it prepped and connected to the laptop. After several minutes of tweaking, one reboot, and multiple calls to Callum and the control room, we had a live signal. KJAY used the live image of the airstrip to tease the governor's impending arrival and ordered a report from Rod for the next segment. They were in breaking-news coverage now and probably wouldn't go back to regular programming until after the briefing.

KJAY went to commercial break and I called out the three-minute warning.

A tremor ran through Rod's hand as he straightened his tie for the eighth or ninth time. "Lilly, can I have a quick word about the feed." He pulled me into the live truck. "I can do this, right?"

"You're going to be great." I held his arm. "Piece of cake."

"I was so excited to be out in the field with you again, and it's the governor and everything, but I forgot how scary being on camera is."

"You don't have to worry, Rod. You can do this. I have no doubt at all, and you always know when I'm lying."

He relaxed. "Thanks for believing in me." He swooped down and kissed me. I decided to relax my no-public-displays-of-affection-while-on-the-job rule.

We were interrupted by Callum calling over my cell phone. "Thirty seconds. Where's Rod? Why don't I see Rod?"

"We're here," I yelled back into the phone. We hurried to our places behind and in front of the camera. The live shot was almost flawless. Rod was perfect. I'm ashamed to say my camerawork was the weakest part. Did I mention that I hate that puny camera?

A few of the officers from the waiting entourage had walked over to watch the live shot. They quickly dispersed when it was over. Only Bell came forward to congratulate Rod. "I'm a public service officer with the L.A. Fire Department, so I'm used to working with some of the best reporters in the country. You're very, very good. What're you doing in a backwater market like Bakersfield?"

I didn't say anything, but Bell recognized my irritation. "I'm sorry," she rushed to say. "Nothing against Bakersfield. I'm sure it's very nice, for a small town."

"You're right," Rod told her. "It's both nice and small, and that's why I like it. I grew up in L.A. and that was the first market I ever worked in. I had my fill of traffic and celebrity car chases."

While they chatted about the L.A. media market, I used Rod's laptop to google Jessica Egan. I found a listing for her on the Green Seed Foundation's website. This large, national nonprofit promoted environmental and animal-rights causes. Jessica was listed as the executive director of the Southwestern region. Her office address was in Venice, California. The website looked elegant and professional. It did not look as if it represented a bunch of fringe environmentalists living on the beach and doing drugs—as her brother seemed to think.

Under a tab marked CONSERVATION, I found a page devoted to the Terrill Nature Preserve. The map showed a wide strip of green starting at the top of Mt. Terrill and then running all the way down and into the valley. Unless I was mistaken, the most eastern part of the preserve was currently on fire and the rest of it in danger.

I clicked through a few more links and found a picture of Jessica at a fund-raiser. Her hair was still cut short, but instead of jeans and a frumpy T-shirt, Jessica wore a strapless, black evening gown. An elegant, older gentleman in a tuxedo had his arm around her back while a second woman stood to the side.

Despite his posing with Jessica, the man and the second woman were identified as Dr. Sebastian Polignac and Ceasonne Polignac. Ceasonne Polignac wore a striking sarong and had long, gray hair. She was described in the caption as Green Seed's executive director—the title Jessica now had. I wrote down the woman's name. Even if she no longer worked for Green Seed, it might be worth trying to contact her.

Bell and Rod were still trading gossip about the L.A. television market, so I checked the Bakersfield newspaper's website. Skimming an old article, it appeared that Green Seed had been responsible for the protests in Elizabeth thirteen years ago.

Green Seed claimed that the McClellans' land was the only known habitat for the Terrill Mountain slender salamander. Their attempts to stop the McClellans from building housing and retail developments had dragged on for over a year. How Green Seed ended up owning the family's land and turning it into a nature preserve wasn't explained.

There was a particularly unattractive photo of the salamander. Its beady eyes and slimy body were made more sinister by its trademark red stripe.

Bell took a business card out of her pocket and handed it to Rod. "If you ever do come back to L.A., I'd like to keep in contact."

Rod took the business card and slipped it in his pocket. "Any chance you might give us a quick interview now?"

Bell shook her head. "The IO has decided no one is making any statements until after the briefing."

"What about the governor?" Rod asked. "He can do whatever he pleases. Any chance he might talk to us after he lands? Even just make a short statement on his way to the car?"

I laughed. "I think it's more likely the governor will put the fire out by peeing on it."

I'd shot the governor twice before—with my camera, not an assassination attempt. The first, when he made a campaign stop in Bakersfield, and the second, when he toured one of the oil fields in Taft. Each time I was kept at least twenty yards back.

Bell chuckled and pointed to the building behind us. "One of his aides is working in a back office, but I doubt he'll help you get an interview. All he seems to care about is keeping the governor on schedule."

"I might as well introduce myself." Rod stood. "As gets go, the governor has to be tops."

The *get* is the one interview that everyone wants for a certain story. For instance, if a UFO landed in someone's backyard, you'd want to interview the homeowner who met the aliens, not someone who lived two blocks away and had seen some strange lights. At KJAY, someone had turned the idea of the get into a game, and the shooters had been playing with one another for years.

I perked up. "Are we playing Who's the Get?"

Bell looked from me to Rod. "What's Who's the Get?"

"Nothing," Rod said. "Something Lilly does with the other shooters. Very boring stuff."

In my enthusiasm for the game, I missed Rod's attempt to change the subject. "It's a great way to kill time. You make up breaking news and then argue over who's the most important interview to land."

"In that case, I agree with Rod." Bell momentarily paused as the pilot entered the building carrying a package of coffee beans and a grinder. "The governor will always be the get, even if he doesn't have the most useful or up-to-date information."

"Not true," I said. "Right off the top of my head, I can think of a scenario where the governor is a distant second place."

Bell raised an eyebrow. "Okay, I'll bite. Who trumps the governor?"

"I have a better idea." Rod took a step toward the building. "Why don't we go talk to the aide?"

"Come on. I want to hear this." Bell looked at me. "Who's better than the governor?"

"If someone tried to kill the governor," I started—Rod probably tried to give me a warning look, but I didn't see—"and a little girl bravely jumped in front of the bullet and saved his life . . . and the little girl was an orphan because her mother had just died fighting in Afghanistan." I nodded in satisfaction. "In that situation, the little girl is the get, and the governor becomes the guy standing behind the brave orphan."

"But Lilly isn't hoping for any of that to happen." Rod looked at me in a panic. "Are you, Lilly?"

"Of course I'm not hoping for that to happen." I tried to think of the right words to explain. "But if it did happen, I'd want to be the one to cover it."

Rod opened his mouth to try to do more damage control, but Bell cut him off, "It's okay. I get it."

The pilot exited the building, now without the coffee and the grinder. Bell nodded to him and then turned back to us. "I haven't always worked public relations. Back when I was on an engine crew, I developed a pretty thick skin too. In these kinds of jobs you have to, or else you go crazy. Cops are the same. When you see terrible things every day, you have to depersonalize it." She rubbed the knee on her bad leg. "The aide is inside if you want to speak with him. I'm going to see if the coffee's ready."

After she was gone, I stood from the milk crate I was sitting on. "I don't know if I explained that right."

"It probably would be best, going forward, not to tell people about Who's the Get." Rod smiled. "Sometimes you get a little too enthusiastic when you play. Not everyone would understand."

I nodded.

We covered some of the equipment so ash wouldn't get on it, then followed Bell inside. A small counter sat on the right with pamphlets and brochures. A large topographic map of the Sequoia National Forest covered the back wall. The two rangers were running a small grinder next to a coffeemaker in the rear. Bell had commandeered one of the four desks and was working at a laptop.

"Don't let us interrupt you," Rod told her. "We're going to give the aide a try.

"You're not interrupting." She used the laptop's mouse to click something. "While we wait for coffee, I was going to watch this clip again that's going viral. I escorted the shooter on the ride-along and feel responsible."

I rolled my eyes. "The blond girl in the tank top who said the firefighters had to save her?"

Bell nodded.

"I saw it on the feeds." Rod looked from me to her. "You could tell it was going to upset people, and even more so because those two firefighters died on Monday."

Bell's expression hovered between sadness and anger. "The Twitter response is vile—really inappropriate things being said about the poor girl."

I remembered watching as Slim had fed his video back to L.A. "I saw some of the raw material. I'm surprised the ranting mad scientist hasn't gone viral too."

Bell nodded. "He's getting some play on television, but crazy, middle-aged men will never be as popular as a blond girl in a tank top."

The female ranger had been eyeing us from the back of the room. She came forward now. "Are you Rod Strong?"

Rod hesitated. "Yes."

The woman reached us and stopped. Her short haircut accentuated pretty, brown eyes and perfect skin. "I used to watch you on TV all the time."

"Thank you." Rod's embarrassed smile made him look even dreamier—in a completely involuntary kind of way. "That's very kind of you to say."

Her face melted into a love-struck gaze. "You were wonderful. Why don't you do it anymore?"

"I'm a producer now."

"But your fans miss you."

Bell made eye contact with me, and we each smiled at Rod's obvious discomfort. A lot of men would love this kind of attention, but not Rod. Even when he'd been single, he hated it. The women who were attracted to his good looks and investigative-journalist persona would always dump him once they discovered his secret life writing *Star Trek* fan fiction, or that he was a level six mage in Dungeons & Dragons.

"My wife's a huge fan too." The other ranger joined us. He'd brought me the Internet connection earlier, but I hadn't noticed that his brown mustache had gray roots. He probably hadn't had time to dye it since the fire started. "She's not going to believe it when I tell her Rod Strong was here."

The door opened and one of the waiting officers poked his head in. "Please tell me it's ready."

The male ranger returned to the coffeemaker. "We're just about to start a pot. We'll let you know."

"Thanks." The officer turned his tired eyes to the female ranger. "Would you mind calling on your landline and letting headquarters know we're still waiting on the governor? Orders are to stay off the radio and cell lines as much as possible."

"No problem." The ranger pulled herself away from Rod and walked to her desk. "We're on speed dial with you guys at this point."

The officer thanked her and left.

Bell gestured down a short hallway. "The aide is in the back office if you want to give him a try."

On our way to find the aide, I heard the female ranger speaking into her phone. "That's right. It's me again." She laughed. "I guess the police would have caller ID. Just to let you know the governor still hasn't landed."

I had an idea. It was impetuous, dangerous, reckless. So much for personal growth.

EIGHT

I glanced inside a second door off the hallway. I was hoping to see an empty office with a phone, but saw a toilet and sink instead.

We reached the only other door. It was ajar so we entered. A desk was pushed up against one of two windows. A man sat at a small, round conference table working at a laptop. His shirtsleeves were rolled up and his suit jacket hung from the back of the chair. He faced the wall, giving us an excellent view down on his bald spot.

"Pardon me," Rod said loudly, trying to be heard over the blasting air conditioner.

The aide didn't respond, so Rod tapped him on the shoulder.

The aide jumped, then turned. He removed one of two earbuds connected to the laptop. "No interviews."

Rod laughed. "Let us introduce ourselves. We're—"

The aide turned back to the monitor and started typing again. "No interviews. Now or later. We're already behind schedule."

I looked around the room and spotted a phone on the empty desk by the window.

Rod refused to let the aide's rudeness dim his enthusiasm. "Let me give you my card. You can call me on my cell if things change."

The aide exhaled loudly, then turned away from his computer. "My job is to keep the schedule. I'm a schedule Nazi. I don't write speeches. I don't schmooze for legislation. I don't even care about reelection. I'm a schedule Nazi. My only ambition is to keep the governor on schedule. There will be no interviews." The aide turned back to the computer and put the earbuds back in.

After an uncomfortable silence we left and returned to the main office.

The female ranger rushed over to Rod. "You must be an expert at reading people. Can you look at something for us?"

"That's a great idea." The male ranger pointed to Bell's laptop. "Tell us what you think about the boy who's standing with the blond girl. I think he's a creep."

"No way." Bell glanced at the monitor and shook her head. "I was there when the video was shot. I met him. He's a nice guy. He has a ponytail and glasses, for goodness' sake."

"Maybe it's because I've got three daughters of my own, but there's a moment where he's looking at her . . ." The male ranger mimicked fangs with his two index fingers. "It's like he's a wolf and she's Bambi."

We all laughed, then Rod said, "I don't know if he's a wolf, but I agree that the girl is an innocent who didn't realize what she was saying."

The male ranger leaned around Bell and started the video playing. On the laptop screen, the girl spoke while the boy watched her. "They keep trying to scare us, but if it gets dangerous, the firefighters will come save us."

"Now." The male ranger pointed. "Watch him now."

"I mean, they can't let us die," the girl continued. "It's their job to save us no matter how dangerous it gets."

We all saw it at the same time. A kind of sly, predatory smile from the boy in the glasses as he watched the girl making an ass of herself.

"I don't believe it." Bell stopped the video. "I think his name was Farris. He was so nice and polite."

The male ranger smiled at Rod. "I bet you've met all kinds of nasty characters in your line of work."

I saw my chance and went for it. "You know, it's too bad neither of you have a camera. You could take a picture with Rod Strong to show everyone he was here."

The woman's eyes popped. "My cell phone's got a camera in it." She ran to her desk.

The man went to a filing cabinet and began opening drawers. "And we've got that old Polaroid too."

"I'll be outside with the equipment." I got all the way to the door before Rod took gentle hold of my arm.

"Hold on. I need to ask you about that Heimlich cable for the live shot." He glanced over his shoulder, then still smiling quietly added, "What are you doing?"

I raised an eyebrow. "Heimlich cable?"

"What are you doing?" He repeated with more urgency.

"Nothing. I'm checking on the equipment."

The male ranger rushed to Bell's desk. She pulled back as he began opening drawers. "I know it's here somewhere."

"Take your time," Rod said to him. "I'm sure you'll find it." He turned back to me and whispered, "You're lying. Why?"

"I don't know what you're talking about."

"Why did you throw me into this photo op? Usually when pretty girls say they're fans, you start growling."

"Maybe I didn't realize she was pretty."

For a moment he panicked, but then smiled. "Oh, no. This does not get turned around on me."

I smiled back. "Just stall. Keep them occupied."

The female ranger joined the search for the Polaroid. "After we take a couple regular pictures, maybe we can think up some fun poses. Do we still have that Davy Crockett hat?"

Rod frowned, then whispered, "I'm not doing this."

"I'll watch *Doctor Who* with you. Any of them you want. Even the one with the crazy hair."

"They all have crazy hair." His eyes widened and he took a quick breath. "Wait, you mean Tom Baker?"

"You pick. I don't care."

He thought for a moment, then countered, "How about instead you go with me to Jareth's Ball?"

I shook my head. "I don't know who Jareth is or why he's having a party, but that does not sound like a fair trade."

"It's whatever the market will bear, and right now that's the price for my cooperation." He paused. "And you have to wear a costume."

"Hey, everybody." The female ranger hit buttons on her phone. "I think I can upload pictures straight to the Internet."

Rod grimaced.

I rushed to agree before he could take back the offer. "I'll go to the party, but you have to keep all three of them occupied for at least ten minutes."

I left before Rod could say anything else. Outside, I passed the truck and camera, then I casually walked around to the back of the building. The first window had the blasting air conditioner in it. I crouched below the second, then cautiously peeked into the office. The aide still sat facing the wall. I found the Swiss army knife inside my cargo pants. I opened the nail file and inserted it into the space between the lower and upper panes. I soon had the window unlocked.

I quietly pushed the frame up. I reached for the phone, but the cord stuck on the side of the desk. I pulled and maneuvered, but it wouldn't budge. I hoisted myself up over the ledge so my stomach rested on the sill and my legs hung out behind me.

I heard Rod's voice just as the door opened. "I think I saw it in here." He appeared in the doorway, saw me, and abruptly stopped. He wore a Santa hat.

I froze, still balanced on the sill and with my outstretched arms holding the cord.

"Or not." Rod grabbed the doorknob, then jerked it toward his body.

The aide took one of the earbuds out and turned his head toward the door. "What now?"

Behind Rod I saw movement. "No, I think you're right." The female ranger tried to look around Rod. "I saw it in there last week."

Rod stepped backward. "This isn't a good time." He pulled the door tight to his body. "The room's being used." He looked at the aide. "Sorry to bother you. Go back to work."

"What did you want?"

"Nothing." Rod gestured to his ear. "Put your headphone back in. We didn't mean to disturb you."

"Too bad, you have disturbed me. At least tell me why."

Rod stammered, unsure what to say. He was actually a pretty good liar, but he was terrible at thinking up the lie.

I curled my hand into a C-shape and tilted it up and down toward my mouth to mean coffee.

"We're drinking," Rod said.

"What?" The aide ripped the other earbud out.

I violently shook my head.

"No," Rod rushed to say. "We're not drinking."

I shook my head again and repeated the cup motion.

"I mean, yes. I think."

"We're looking for the Polaroid," the female ranger called from behind Rod.

The aide paused. He looked at Rod in the Santa hat. "Are you drunk?"

Rod glanced at me. I shook my head and cupped my hand again. This time I tried to mimic steam rising off the top of the cup.

"I think we're dancing, maybe."

The aide shook his head in disgust. "Go away and don't come back." He put the earbuds in and turned back to his laptop.

Rod gave me a nasty look before shutting the door.

I waited a few moments, then freed the cord from the side of the desk. I pulled the whole thing outside. I crouched down under the window and dialed information. I scribbled the Elizabeth Police Department's nonemergency number on my hand with a Sharpie from my cargo pants.

While I waited for someone to pick up, I took deep breaths. Without realizing it, I tend to telegraph what I'm thinking and feeling. Lately, I'd gotten a lot better at holding more of myself back, but would that be enough to pull off this kind of lie? At least it wasn't in person.

After a few more rings, a woman answered. I couldn't hear well over the air conditioner, but it sounded like the support officer I'd met earlier.

"Hi," she said. "Is the governor there yet?"

Caller ID is a beautiful thing—to subvert. "No, he's late. But they sent someone from the IO's staff to babysit us. She says politicians are always late."

"What a waste of manpower." She paused. "So what can I do for you?"

I took a breath. "I'm doing some advance work for tomorrow's crew and we're wondering about that boat parked out at Road's End."

"What about it?"

"The deck coordinator left a note that it might be a hazard for the choppers filling up on the lake tomorrow."

I froze as a mechanic walked past the side of the building toward the hangar.

"Don't worry," the officer said through the phone. "Search and Rescue brought it in this evening. There's another waste of manpower."

I waited a moment to make sure the mechanic wasn't returning. "How'd we even know where it was? When I left work this morning, the deck coordinator said we didn't have the time to search for it."

"Yeah, but then the mayor's office pulled some weight."

The Elizabeth government wasn't big or glamorous. Most elected officials had day jobs, if they weren't already retired. My best recollection was that the title of mayor passed to a new city council member each year.

I tried to sound disinterested. "Why was the mayor involved?"

"It's Lee Fitzgerald's boat, so you understand." I didn't know who Lee Fitzgerald was, but his last name was on the biggest store in the area. "A friend of the family took it out last night and fell overboard or something."

"You don't say."

"Sort of poetic justice. The dead woman is that Egan girl who spray-painted the THINK SAFETY sign back in '98."

My jaw literally fell open.

"Hello?" The support officer waited and after a moment said, "Are you still there?"

"Yes, I'm here. It's just . . . You know they never caught the person who did that."

"Everybody knew it was her. Even her dad always said it was her. And she left town right after it happened."

My grip on the receiver tightened. "That's because she turned eighteen. She was a minor before that and couldn't leave. She didn't paint the sign."

"How do you know?"

Suddenly the air conditioner cut out. That's when I heard it—the soft rumble of a helicopter. I paused and the sound got louder as it approached the airstrip. "I have to go. The governor's here. Thanks."

I slammed the phone back into its cradle and jumped up. I found myself face-to-face with the aide. He leaned over the desk and stared at me through the open window.

"I can explain," I offered.

He followed the sound of the helicopter and looked toward the sky. "Is getting involved going to drag me into a local drama and wreck the governor's schedule?"

"Yes."

"Then I don't want to know." He ripped the phone out of my hands, then slammed the window shut.

I ran back around the building.

Rod was standing at the camera. "What's going on?"

"Later." I handed him the stick mic and pushed him back to his mark.

Since KJAY was in breaking-news coverage, they were able

to cut right to us. Rod did another fantastic job going live. He'd actually gotten better at it during his time producing. Despite the hated camcorder, I managed a nice pan as the entourage walked from the chopper to the SUVs. I spotted the aide glowering as the governor made a point of shaking hands with each of the officers. Finally they all boarded the vehicles and the entire convoy rolled out for Incident Command Headquarters.

And that's how I met the governor of the great state of California for the third time—from twenty yards back, and with absolutely no personal contact.

Before she left, Bell called the IO on her radio and confirmed that the briefing had been moved back to one thirty. Rod and I called Callum to make plans for the rest of the night. He confirmed KJAY would take the L.A. station's live feed of the briefing, but said Rod was expected to be there in case the officials took questions. Then KJAY would return to normal programming until four thirty, when Rod and I would need to be ready to go live again.

"But hopefully you won't be using the Internet for this live shot," Callum said through my cell phone's speaker. "We're working on something. I'll let you know in an hour or so for sure."

We all said good-bye and I ended the call. I raised my hand before Rod could speak. "Let me make one call and then we'll talk about what happened in the back office."

I walked away and dialed information. Soon I was calling Fitzgerald's in Tilly Heights. The harried saleswoman who answered said they were still open, but couldn't guarantee for how long. I managed to keep her on the phone long enough to confirm that Lee Fitzgerald was at the store.

I returned to the live truck.

Rod had finished packing the equipment and was waiting for me. "So you want to tell me why you were hanging out the back window of that office?"

"I needed information. Making a call using their phone was the only way I could get it."

"Really? Lying, breaking and entering, making the governor's aide think I'm a drunk—those were the only possible ways to get information?"

I cupped my hand and tipped it back and forth. "This is drinking coffee. You were supposed to ask him if he wanted some coffee."

Rod's voice rose. "That's the international symbol for alcohol."

"Then what's coffee?"

"There's no way to silently communicate drinking coffee because nobody would ever need to keep that secret." He pulled the silk handkerchief from his suit pocket and ran it along his forehead.

"I know you're upset, and I would be too, but I think the woman who drowned in the lake may have been murdered."

I gave him a quick rundown and explained about Jessica's shoulder, the mayor's involvement, and the police seemingly protecting Fitzgerald. When the time came to tell Rod that I'd known Jessica, I hesitated, then chickened out. I rationalized my silence by telling myself it wasn't the time or place to tell that complicated story.

Fortunately, Rod had calmed down by the time I'd finished. "I understand your interest in the drowning, but Callum was right. The fire has to be everyone's top priority, and that includes you and me."

Except I owed Jessica. Not only had she covered for me, but now it sounded as if she'd been blamed for what I'd done to the THINK SAFETY sign all those years ago.

I looked at my watch. It was 12:15. "We have an hour and fifteen minutes before the briefing. Let's go to Tilly Heights and visit Fitzgerald's store."

"But that's the other side of the lake. We don't have time for that."

"It's not that far." Rod didn't say anything, so I added, "Think of all the people who must be there trying to buy supplies at the last minute. We can shoot video about the evacuation and ask questions about the drowning."

I could see he liked the idea, but was still wary. "I can't miss the briefing. You heard Callum. I'm supposed to ask questions. I'm the entire press corps tonight."

"I promise we'll leave in time. No matter what. We'll pick up and walk out in midsentence if we have to."

He didn't say anything.

"Please, Rod. I need your help."

His blue eyes shifted down and he looked at me.

"This is why I asked you to come up here. It wasn't because of the governor. I need you to help me get answers about this drowning."

I drove back south on the Lake Road in the live truck and Rod followed in his news van. We passed the turnoff for Search and Rescue headquarters down at the lake, and then the complex of local government buildings the sergeant had thrown me out of. The road hooked around and suddenly we were in Tilly Heights. A drive of a few minutes, and property values had tripled.

The original Fitzgerald's, or Fitz's as everyone called it, had opened over thirty years ago in Elizabeth. The store wasn't fancy, but served the needs of its customers. Five years ago it had closed and reopened in Tilly Heights. The new Fitz's stocked gourmet groceries, electronics, home goods, and even hunting and fishing supplies. It had become a locally owned, upscale Target.

I pulled into the large parking lot. It was paved and well lit, unlike the lots common on the western shore. The bright electric FITZGERALD'S sign was shining from the top of the storefront. Rod and I each found spaces. The constant flow of cars in and out had created ridges of ash, one of which Rod stepped in getting out.

He tried to dust off his shoes with a Kleenex, but it was a losing battle. "Is it just me, or is the ash worse here?"

"The smoke is worse too." I took my camera, sticks, and gear bag and locked the truck. Rod knew better than to try to help me with my gear. "This side of the lake is closer to the fire. I hate to break it to you, but your clothes are probably starting to smell."

He nodded in a bearing-his-burden-stoically kind of way that reminded me of Brad Egan.

Near the store entrance, we passed an overweight man on a ladder nailing plywood to the large store windows. He wore a handkerchief over his nose and mouth as protection from the smoke. Half of the windows to the left of the automatic door were covered, but he was working by himself and looked as if he had a long night ahead of him.

The man looked at my camera, but then turned back to his work as though he hadn't noticed us. That was an unusual reaction, but I put it down to his urgent need to finish his task.

The automatic doors opened. Perfumed air blasted us as we stepped inside. The lighting was soft and tasteful. The employees all wore green dress shirts and khaki pants. Wreaths of dried flowers hung at every checkout. Everything in the store felt elegant and relaxed. Everything except the people.

"That was mine," a woman at the checkout said. "I saw you take it right off the belt." She lunged and tried to rip a bottle of water out of a man's hands. The checker jumped in between them.

Behind the registers, the aisles were bumper-to-bumper with carts and shoppers. The noise from so many voices almost drowned out the tasteful classical music playing overhead.

Rod pulled me back against the windows as a man rushed past. He was pushing a cart with his elbows and texting with his hands.

I gestured to the row of checkout stands. Only half of them were open, despite long lines. "We should ask for the owner."

Rod didn't move. "Before we do that, let's make a game plan for how we're going to handle the interview."

"Okay. What would you like me to do?"

"Don't accuse anyone of murder."

I gave him a dirty look. "I'm not an idiot."

"This is outrageous," a woman screamed at a nearby clerk. "You knew there was a fire. Why didn't you stock more decaf vanilla roast?"

Rod looked back at me. "I'm going to ease into the interview and only come around to the drowning at the end. He'll be less likely to throw us out that way."

"I promise not to accuse anyone of murder, but you should know going in, I don't particularly care if this ends with us getting thrown out. All I want is to find out what really happened to Jessica. If we run out of time, I'm going to get aggressive."

He sighed. "What do you want me to do while you're getting aggressive?"

"Watch for lying. You're much better at reading people than I am."

He agreed, so we approached a salesclerk and asked for the owner. The manager came to speak with us instead. I shot while Rod asked questions about the high demand for essentials such as bottled water and canned goods. There'd also been a run on garden hoses and batteries.

After the brief interview I shot B-roll of the store. Rod stood nearby with the manager. I heard him casually ask, "How much longer will you be open?"

"I'm not sure. About half our employees have already called out, so we may have to close after tonight."

"Are the owners around? Maybe we can speak to them directly."

"You can try, but Mr. Fitzgerald's not a big talker." The manager pointed to the man outside nailing plywood to the windows. "And he's trying to get the windows covered in case there's looting tomorrow."

We went outside. Fitzgerald wore the same outfit as his employees, but his green dress shirt had sweat stains under the armpits.

"Hi. We're from KJAY," Rod said. "I understand you're Mr. Fitzgerald. Can I ask you a few questions about your plans for the store?"

Our interruption didn't distract him from hammering the next nail. "Mr. Fitzgerald was my dad."

I set down my sticks. "Fitz, then?"

He glanced over his shoulder and looked at us for the first

time. I couldn't see his mouth under the handkerchief, but his eyes crinkled as if he was smiling. "That was my dad too. My name's Lee." He placed another nail on the plywood and hammered it in.

Rod waited for him to finish, then said, "Can we ask you some questions, Lee?"

Fitzgerald tested the piece of wood with the palm of his hand, then got down from the ladder. He was probably about forty pounds overweight. "You should come back later and talk to my wife. She's good with public speaking and stuff like that."

Rod wasn't deterred. "I'm sure you'll do a great job."

"Sorry, but I have to get more plywood." He began walking down the front of the store past the still uncovered windows.

Rod glanced at his watch. "We don't mind waiting."

Fitzgerald stopped. His back was to us, but after a pause he turned. "I don't want to talk about the drowning."

NINE

L ight poured out the store windows and covered Fitzgerald, but the handkerchief hid most of his facial expressions. "It's a sad thing. We were all in school together. My wife is very upset. Neither of us wants a bunch of publicity."

I spoke first. "Did the police warn you we were asking questions?"

"An officer called my wife and said you'd been trying to get our name." He actually sounded a little embarrassed. "I think he was giving us the VIP treatment. It's probably not ethical, but we're a small town."

I hadn't expected a blunt admission and was momentarily thrown.

In contrast, Rod knew exactly what to say. "You must see how suspicious that kind of deference looks, even if you didn't ask for it. And refusing to answer a few of our simple questions only makes it look worse."

Fitzgerald shook his head. "I told you, I don't want to go on camera about Jessica."

"We won't record you." Rod glanced back at me and I reluctantly nodded. "And it won't take long. There's a one-thirty briefing with the governor. We need to leave soon if we're going to make it." Rod walked to Fitzgerald, passed him, and continued down the front of the store. "Come on. We can help you with the plywood while we talk."

Fitzgerald hesitated, but then joined him. "I guess it wouldn't hurt, just to talk."

I grabbed my gear, but stayed a step or two behind. I wasn't happy about Fitzgerald not being on camera, but at least he'd agreed to answer questions.

"It's bad luck I guess." Fitzgerald had a slow, almost shuffly way of walking that made him look short even though he was fairly tall. "You know, bad luck that it happened at all, and at a time like this."

In contrast, Rod looked lean and fit. "Why was Jessica Egan staying with you? It does seem like an odd time for a visit."

"She came to check on her father, but by the time she arrived, he'd already evacuated."

"Has she stayed with you before?"

We passed the last of the windows and the light abruptly fell off.

Fitzgerald continued in front of the dark garden center. "No. Jessica left home after high school and we didn't see her again until last fall. She came into the store one day out of the blue. She and Byrdie got to talking—that's my wife. It was sort of like old times."

He stopped before a padlocked iron gate and pulled a set of keys off his belt. "I've seen her in the store four or five more times since then, but we haven't talked much."

I tried to sound easygoing, like Rod, but wasn't very successful. "Her brother said she'd only visited once this past year."

Fitzgerald glanced back at me. Between the darkness and the handkerchief, I had no idea how to read him. "I guess she didn't tell her family she was here." He unlocked the gate and we all entered.

This part of the store was enclosed by mesh and open to the air and smoke. The space was dark except for light coming through the open doorway of a room in the back. Fitzgerald led us past long displays of plants and flowers covered in plastic tarps. Everything had ash and soot on it. I could feel the fine sandy substance in the slide of my boots as they hit the ground.

We reached the room at the back. "Sorry for the walk." Fitzgerald pulled the handkerchief down so it hung around his neck.

He had a pleasant face, but a roll of neck fat was threatening to swallow his chin. "My office is separate from the others. I prefer it back here."

A desk was in the corner, but a long table in the center was clearly the heart of the room. The only lights hung above it. Someone had been potting seedlings, but had abandoned the job.

"I'd prefer it here too," Rod said as he looked around. "This is much nicer than a cramped office with fluorescent lights."

The air smelled like soil and reminded me of my early childhood on the farm. A muted flat-screen TV hung on the wall playing a cable news channel. It looked out of place in what was basically a really big garden shed.

Fitzgerald knelt at a large stack of plywood sheets. "The Garden Center has always been my baby." He gestured back to a framed photo on his desk. "My wife, Byrdie, is the one with business sense. I just like playing in the dirt."

I thought I recognized the smiling woman kneeling in front of a flower bed. Jessica hadn't had any friends the summer I knew her, so it was unlikely I'd met her then. The same woman was in several more pictures with two young boys.

Fitzgerald passed a waist-high stack of plywood sheets, then unlocked a set of double doors onto a rear alley. "My truck's out here. If you don't mind helping me load the wood, I can drive it around front."

"Of course." Rod took off his suit jacket and laid it on Fitzgerald's desk. His vest, like everything else, was tailored perfectly to his body.

As Fitzgerald opened the doors, a shower of built-up ash fell. He coughed and waved his hand in front of his face. He turned toward the alley and began to raise the handkerchief again.

"Hold on." I set down my gear. "We're happy to help, but before you go out there, I'd like to hear an account of what happened yesterday."

He shrugged. "Jessica called Byrdie and asked if we could put her up for the night. Her dad's place was locked up and there weren't any motel rooms to be had. Byrdie ran home to let Jessica in, but only stayed a few minutes before she had to get back to work."

He reached for the handkerchief again. "I figure Jessica got bored there by herself and decided to visit Road's End. You add alcohol to the equation and you get a sad ending." He pulled the fabric up over his face and stepped into the alley.

Rod knelt by the stack of wood and made several attempts to pick up the plywood in a way that wouldn't damage his clothes. "Where were your children?"

Fitzgerald lowered the back on a flatbed truck. "We sent them to stay with relatives in Merced last week."

Rod carefully picked up several pieces of plywood.

Fitzgerald pointed. "That's heavy. Maybe you shouldn't . . ." He trailed off as Rod easily carried the load.

I'd made the same mistake when we first met. Just because Rod was dapper and not especially big didn't mean the man wasn't packing muscle under his hand-sewn Italian shirtsleeves.

Rod offered the sheets. "Was it your boat that Jessica Egan took out last night?"

Fitzgerald took the plywood, but had to quickly drop the weight in the truck. "Our house is on the lake and we've got a tiny dock. Nothing fancy, but I like taking our boys out fishing like my dad took me."

I followed Rod with another sheet and handed it to Fitzgerald. "Why would Jessica go to Road's End?"

"The summer before she left town, Jessica got in with a wild crowd that liked to party out there."

Truthfully, I was the one who liked to party out there, not Jessica, but for obvious reasons I didn't say so. Instead, I waited for him to turn back around and face me. "How did a woman with a bad shoulder start an old two-stroke motor?"

He stared at me for a moment. The fabric covering his open mouth moved in and out with his breath. "You're right. I do remember something being wrong with her shoulder, but it's been so long. She must have had therapy or surgery or something."

I stepped back so Rod could bring more wood. After the hand-off, Rod stopped and waited for Fitzgerald's attention. What he said next surprised me.

"I don't mean to be offensive, Mr. Fitzgerald, but I sense that perhaps there's something you're holding back?" Leave it to Rod to call someone a liar while still sounding polite and respectful. "Maybe there's something on your mind that you're not sharing?"

Fitzgerald looked Rod straight in the eye and pulled down the handkerchief. "I didn't like Jessica. That's probably what you're picking up on. It seems wrong to speak badly of her now, but I feel like a hypocrite."

Rod nodded. "That's very understandable."

"When we were kids, we were all friends because our parents were all friends. It was easy. We loved this place. The lake and mountain were our playground. Then in middle school, Byrdie and I fell in love and Jessica went steady with my best friend, so the four of us were always double-dating."

"What happened to change things?"

"After her mom died, Jessica got into radical environmental stuff and lost her way. She picked up bad habits. Stuff Byrdie and I didn't want any part of. By our senior year of high school, we'd completely cut ties with her."

"What kind of bad habits?" Rod asked.

"I suspected drugs. It's very possible she was doing more than drinking last night." He tilted his head down. His chin disappeared completely into the roll of fat. "And monogamy definitely wasn't her thing. She always had a different guy around."

I felt my anger start to simmer.

"I don't mean to be indelicate," Rod said, "but could she have been meeting a man last night? Maybe out at this island?"

"Byrdie might know better than me, but, yes, it's possible." Fitzgerald hesitated. "And earlier, when you mentioned her visiting without telling her family, I didn't like to say . . ."

"It's okay," Rod said. "I know you don't want to speak ill of the dead, but you can tell us the truth."

"Back in high school, Jessica didn't join up with those protesters because she believed in their cause. She did it because they had easy access to drugs and they liked to party. Poor Jessica was a lost soul." Fitzgerald shrugged. "If she's been visiting this past year without her family knowing, she was probably doing more of the same."

"That's it." My hands shot to my hips. "I'm not going to stand here while you slander a dead woman."

Fitzgerald stared back at me. "I'm not slandering anyone. How would you know what Jessica was like?"

"Because I knew her."

Rod's mouth opened in surprise.

Fitzgerald just looked confused. "Is this some kind of bad joke?"

"I used to live here and I knew Jessica before she moved to L.A." I walked toward him. "She was smart and principled. She fought for the environment and animal rights because she believed in it. She was not some drug-addict party girl."

I stopped directly in front of him. "So why are you lying? What really happened last night, Lee? Did you come on to her? Or maybe you two were having an affair?"

Rod tried to intervene. "Hold on, Lilly."

"I would never cheat on Byrdie." Fitzgerald didn't sound especially upset or emotional. "And definitely not with Jessica."

"Prove it," I said. "Where were you last night when Jessica died?"

He didn't hesitate. "Right here. There are plenty of people who can vouch for me." He looked at Rod. "And my wife has plenty of people who can vouch for her. She was only home long enough to let Jessica in before she had to go back to work."

"Of course." Rod stepped between us. "I'm very sorry for my colleague's offensive tone. She's been working for seventeen hours straight."

Lee walked to his desk where a box of Chips Ahoy! sat next to his computer. "It's okay. I don't mind answering questions about our alibis. I'm relieved, actually." He took a cookie from the box. "I was worried you were doing a story about Byrdie pressuring the police and Forest Service to look for Jessica's body."

He reached for the TV remote with his free hand. "If you really think there's something suspicious about Jessica's death, you should try talking to her current friends." He gestured to the monitor. "I saw her in the store with this group a couple different times this past year." He raised the volume. "I think they all live together in a house on the other side of the mountain."

The clip of the mad scientist I'd seen Slim feeding back to L.A. was on. He gestured wildly as he spoke in his Bond-villain accent. "They are not lizards. They're salamanders and evacuating would be morally reprehensible." A group of college students stood behind him like minions. Among them was the young man with the glasses and ponytail and the blond girl in the tank top whose sound bite was going viral.

Fitzgerald pointed at the mad scientist. "This guy is notorious in the store. Hits on all the female employees. He actually pinched a salesclerk's behind."

"Who is he?" I said.

Fitzgerald muted the TV again. "I don't know, but the young man with the ponytail and glasses—I think he said his name was Farris—he was in the store earlier tonight asking about Jessica. She was supposed to meet him today, but never showed." Fitzgerald's voice dropped. "I had to explain why." He reached for another cookie.

Rod looked at me. "I think it's time we left."

"Hold on." I turned to Fitzgerald. "I want to talk to your wife."

Fitzgerald laughed. "Be my guest. She's over at the school in Elizabeth."

"What? You mean Incident Command Headquarters?"

He nodded. "You'll see her at the briefing. She'll be the one standing next to the governor." He gestured to one of the photos on his desk. "Byrdie is our mayor."

I took a closer look at the woman in the photos. I pictured her with a lot more makeup and high-heel shoes. I'd met her in the briefing tent.

"You promised not to accuse anyone of murder."

I glanced around the parking lot to make sure no one could hear us. "I didn't accuse him of murder. I accused him of adultery. I only implied that he killed her."

Rod pulled me into the relative privacy of the live truck. "Have you lost your mind? You're on assignment. You represent the station."

I began putting away equipment. "I'm sorry, but this is more important than the station's reputation."

He paused. When he next spoke, his voice was softer. "Why didn't you tell me you knew her? We're a team. That's a huge piece of information to hide."

There was no chance I was going to tell him the truth. Saying that I was ashamed of the girl I used to be would be like introducing him to the girl I used to be. "I knew you'd think it was unethical for me to work on the story, and I can't stop. I owe Jessica."

"It is unethical." He tried to get me to look at him, but I knelt and secured the Velcro straps over my sticks. "But I don't think that's why you kept it from me."

I didn't say anything.

I heard him take a deep breath. "I'm sorry about your friend."

I suddenly felt like a woman who'd been working for seventeen hours. I sat down on the floor of the truck and leaned my back against the wall. "She wasn't my friend."

Rod sat down too. He didn't even try to protect his clothes from the accumulation of dirt and grime on the floor. "Even if it's been a long time since you knew her, that doesn't mean she wasn't your friend."

"You don't understand." I didn't want to open this can of worms, but there was no way out now. "I was her alibi."

He did a double take. "You're going to have to elaborate on that."

"When I was almost nineteen, I came up here at the start of the summer to live in Bud's mobile home by the lake. Jessica was a year younger than me and had just finished high school. She'd been working with a group of environmentalists called Green Seed to stop development, but her dad didn't approve. I agreed to say she was with me so he wouldn't find out she was still helping them." I left out the part where Jessica was paying me to lie, but I was hoping to get out of this conversation with Rod's respect still intact.

"But why do you think you owe her? If anything, it should be the other way around."

I rubbed my head. I must have looked really upset because Rod put his arm around me. He was warm and strong in a way that felt, well, dependable. I know that's not a sexy word, but maybe it should be.

"Jessica had my back once." I leaned my head against his chest. "I did something bad and she could have gotten herself out of trouble by turning me in, but she kept her mouth shut."

"What did you do?"

"It's not important. It was just a stupid prank that . . . it was stupid."

Rod pulled me closer, but didn't say anything.

"But someone saw me doing it," I continued. "And since Jessica and I were supposed to be together at the time, we both got hauled in by the police. Jessica was a minor and her dad gave them permission to interview her for as long as they wanted."

I flashed again to waiting at the old Elizabeth police station while they questioned Jessica in the back. Even from across the lobby, I could smell the Old Spice on Jessica's father as he waited too. I remember thinking he'd probably doused himself in the stuff to cover up some other smell, such as beer or cigarettes.

I pulled back and looked at Rod. "Jessica could have told the truth. I even confessed to her about the prank after the fact." Bragged was more like it. "But when the police questioned her,

Jessica refused to say anything at all. Finally they had to let us both go."

I took a breath. I was in danger of losing control. "And to make matters worse, now it looks like her family and the police always assumed she was guilty because she wouldn't talk."

"I understand why you feel like you owe her." Rod kept his voice level and calm. "But you're having an emotional reaction. You practically took Fitzgerald's head off in there."

"You're right, I'm angry, and Fitzgerald isn't the only one who makes me feel that way."

Rod patiently waited for me to continue.

"I'm not an environmentalist, but I admire Jessica. She stood up to her family, her friends—basically, this entire community—all because she believed in something. That takes guts."

I pulled away and turned so I was facing him. "Jessica may have been a little weird and awkward, but she was strong, and now that she's dead and can't defend herself, all these jerks are remaking her as weak and pathetic. It's like, it's not enough that she's dead, they have to take away the best thing about her, the thing she probably cared most about."

The alarm on my cell phone began ringing. "It's one fifteen. We have to go if we're going to make the briefing."

"Are you going to be okay?"

I nodded. "Thanks for letting me get that off my chest." I shut off the phone and then stood. "When we get back to headquarters, I'm going to find the L.A. shooter and ask him about the mad scientist and his minions. The protests thirteen years ago were about a lizard so maybe his research is connected to the nonprofit Jessica works for."

Rod followed me up and dusted off his pants. "I think the mad scientist was pretty clear that it's a salamander, not a lizard."

"You know what I mean."

He smiled. "I understand you want to find out what happened to Jessica, but promise me that if we see the mayor at headquarters, you won't treat her like you treated her husband."

"If you promise me that you'll ask her questions about the drowning."

"Of course."

"Then I promise too."

He gave me a good-bye kiss—the kind that makes dependable seem sexy—and then we left in our own vehicles.

When we parted, I fully intended to meet Rod at headquarters. But as I drove, I kept thinking about Jessica's death. I couldn't see any motive for the Fitzgeralds to murder their childhood friend. They even had alibis—still unconfirmed, but why offer them if they weren't going to hold up?

Slim could tell me where to find the mad scientist and his minions, but since he'd needed a ride-along to interview them in the first place, there was little chance of my being able to interview them. Arnaldo Bedolla hadn't returned my calls, and I couldn't reasonably leave any more messages on his cell. I could always track down his diving partner, Pukey the Kid, but since his family also lived on the other side of Mt. Terrill and were busy trying to evacuate their ranch, I'd need an escort to see him too.

Tracking down the McClellan family was probably just a matter of speaking with enough locals. If any members of the family still lived here and were angry about the protests thirteen years ago, it would have to be common knowledge. Lastly, someone was going to need to go down to Venice and ask questions about Jessica's life there, if only to discover the truth about her shoulder.

That's when I passed the turnoff for Search and Rescue. Seeing the dirt road leading down to the lake reminded me that the police had never searched Road's End.

By the time I reached the turnoff for Elizabeth, I didn't even consider stopping. Using the speakerphone and the speed dial, I tried Rod's cell several times during the drive. Between my bad reception and his bad reception, the best I could do was leave a message.

"Hi, it's Lilly. I'm making a stop. I'll catch up with you at headquarters. Don't worry. It's not a big deal and I don't have anything to do during the briefing anyway. . . . Okay, so, see you soon."

I hung up. See you soon? Had that sounded as lame as I thought? Should I have said I love you? It was against the no-public-displays-of-affection-on-the-job rule, but I felt guilty.

I slowed several miles before the Forest Service airstrip where the governor had landed. I found the dirt road and passed two mobile-home parks and a few private residences. At the end of the road I stopped at the final property.

I got out and jumped up the few steps to the mobile home's covered patio. I banged on the door and rang the bell at the same time. Finally I heard footsteps.

"I'm not leaving," the old man yelled from inside. "I've got a shotgun and this is my property and you can't make me evacuate."

"Mr. King? It's Lilly Hawkins. I was here earlier today with Leanore Drucker."

The door opened. Mr. King wore boxer shorts and a soiled undershirt. He hadn't been lying about the gun. "From the TV?"

"That's right."

"I saw myself on the news at five." His face lit up. "That was something. Folks were calling me all night saying how they saw me on TV." He paused. "Is that why you're back? You want to ask me some more questions?"

"No. This time I need a favor."

"Sure. You name it."

I pointed toward the lake. "I need to use your boat."

TEN

You know why they called it Road's End?"

I carefully stepped into the motorboat. I was momentarily thrown by the odd sensation of the floor moving, but I managed to keep my footing. "No."

Mr. King was already at the rear of the small utility boat. He had the cover up on the engine and was putting the key in. "Back before they flooded this valley in the fifties, there were houses and trees and things where the lake is now. Cars had a habit of driving off the side of a steep hill there. Folks started calling it Road's End, meaning, your road was coming to an end if you drove up there."

He checked something, then closed the cover. "After they flooded the valley, the top of that hill became an island in the middle of the lake. Folks started rowing out there for picnics and things. Everyone forgot how it got its name."

"That's a great story." I felt a sudden desire to double-check the clasps on my life jacket. "Maybe Leanore can use it in one of her pieces."

"I didn't tell you that so I could be on TV again." He paused, then smiled. "But I sure wouldn't mind being on TV again."

I cautiously sat on the shelf at the front of the boat. "I've been doing this job for almost six years, and everyone wants to be on television. It's human nature."

"I like sharing our history too. It makes me feel good to get the stories out there."

I had an idea. "Do you remember the protests thirteen years ago?"

"Sure. Went on for over a year."

"Was anyone ever violent?"

"I wouldn't say violent, but Loys McClellan was sure angry. Finally they came up with some kind of compromise where he'd sell for a nature preserve. He agreed, but wanted to keep the land where he'd built his own house. It was in a beautiful spot called Bonny Hazel, after the hazelnut trees."

I remembered the support officer saying something similar when I'd talked to her at the police station.

He laughed. "It's hard for an old fart to leave the house he loves—I'm living proof—but the environmental folks said all or nothing and McClellan finally agreed."

Mr. King paused to take a ragged breath. "There's a bunch of students living there now, studying the nature preserve. They've probably trashed the place."

My head jerked up. "Wait, are they the ones who've been on TV all night? The scientist and the blond girl who said the firefighters had to save her no matter what?"

"I don't know if it's the same ones, but I hate that girl on TV." He had to pause to take another labored breath. "I got an e-mail from a friend so I got on the Facebook and liked a page saying how I didn't like her."

"Does Green Seed still own the house?" He looked confused so I said, "Green Seed is the group that was protesting. They own the nature preserve now."

"I guess. In the end they got all of McClellan's land."

If Green Seed was sponsoring the mad scientist's research, then naturally Jessica would be visiting him and his minions—it was probably even part of her job.

"Whatever happened to the McClellans?" I said. "Do any of them still live here?"

"I heard Loys McClellan moved to Santa Barbara or some place like that. I don't know what happened to his kids. They'd probably be middle-aged by now."

I was absorbed in my thoughts and didn't notice right away when Mr. King took out an inhaler and breathed in a blast of medicine.

"I'm sorry." I stood and took the few steps to the rear. "You should get out of the smoke."

"I'm okay." While he took a moment to normalize his breathing, I stood in front of the engine. It had a backup starter cord in case the battery died. I reached down with my left arm and pulled. I barely got the cord halfway.

"You don't have to do that. This engine is one of the new ones with a battery." He pumped the primer, then hit the ignition switch. The small engine roared to life.

I raised my voice so I could be heard. "I just wanted to see how hard it would be for a right-handed person to start an old pull-cord engine with their left arm."

"Just about impossible, but you might get lucky if you tried enough times." Mr. King climbed onto the dock. He looked up the dirt path to his mobile home. "If the smoke weren't riling up my asthma so bad, I'd come with you."

"Don't worry, I've made this trip before." I looked out onto the lake. The lights from Tilly Heights on the opposite shore looked gauzy and muted. Above the mountain, the belly of the smoke was lit with an orange glow from the fire on the other side. The lake itself was a black hole, without any signs of life.

I sat down so I could hold the throttle with my right hand. "I'm not scared," I lied. "I've got a life jacket on and I'll be very careful."

He knelt down and unhooked the boat from where it was tied to the dock. He tossed the rope in the boat and I turned the throttle.

A mounted light lit the area directly in front of the boat. I also used the light from the shorelines to judge my location and navigate my way. I went slowly.

After what felt like an eternity, but was probably ten minutes, something appeared ahead of me. I stopped the engine and allowed momentum to take the boat forward. The silence that replaced the roaring motor made me uneasy, so I glanced at the lights on the shore to remind myself I wasn't entirely alone. As I got closer, the rocky outline of Road's End appeared.

I neared the island and grabbed a protruding rock in an attempt to slow the boat. After several tries I succeeded, then tied off the line to one of the many informal rings hammered into the island. I retrieved a flashlight from the emergency kit and turned off the boat's light. If I ran down the power, I'd never make it back to shore in the dark.

A low, flat rock protruded near the tie-off and I was able to climb safely onto it. How difficult would it have been if I'd been drinking? Was it really so hard to believe Jessica had slipped and fallen in the water? Maybe Byrdie Fitzgerald had started the boat for her before she left and was afraid to admit it.

But even drunk, the Jessica I'd known would never have come without a life jacket. The bulky weight of the one I wore was a hindrance, but it also guaranteed I wouldn't end up in a mesh body bag.

I scrambled over a few more rocks, then lowered myself onto a large stretch of relatively flat ground. Road's End is only about thirty yards long. It's a mixture of dirt and rocks. People use it for fishing and sunbathing, but its real attraction is as a make-out spot. Some of the larger rocks give cover for couples wanting privacy. I appeared to be in one of the recesses because I couldn't see either shoreline. Everything was black outside the weak beam of the flashlight. I raised my free hand toward my face, but couldn't see it. The only sound came from my own quick breaths, interrupted by the occasional gentle thud as the current pushed the nearby boat into the island.

This kind of situation makes a person afraid. I don't mean rational fear, such as being afraid a wild animal might be hiding in the dark. I mean irrational fear, such as being afraid the monster from *Alien* is hiding in the dark.

I shone the flashlight in every direction, trying to reassure myself. Nothing appeared but rocks and warning signs advising water safety. Then something caught the light in the distance to my left. It was all the way on the other end of the island. I guessed a wet rock was simply reflecting back the light, but decided to check it out anyway. I walked carefully and kept the flashlight shining on the ground as I navigated the uneven surface. I'd gone two-thirds of the way before I glanced ahead and got a good look at what I was walking toward.

I forgot about being careful and ran the rest of the way.

A grocery bag sat on the ground. Something heavy inside kept the flimsy plastic from blowing away. I pulled apart the opening at the top. A six-pack of beer and two bottles of wine were inside. Was it possible? Had Jessica really come out here drinking and fallen in the water?

I reached into the plastic bag to make sure I'd seen everything. My hand touched the bottle of wine and I froze. It was cold.

It had been over twenty-four hours since Jessica's death. The wine should have been as warm as the air going in and out of my lungs.

I jerked the flashlight back toward the darkness of the island. Nothing but rocks and dirt. I swung in the other direction, toward the lake and the lights of the shore.

I didn't have time to scream. The man was steps from me. So close, the light only revealed his legs and the end of the boat oar as he raised it. I dove. The wood missed me. I heard it splinter on a nearby rock.

I jumped up to run, but the flashlight had broken and I couldn't see. I heard a noise on my right and stepped back. A pair of powerful hands seized me. I shoved and tore—anything to break free— but he was too strong. He threw me back on the ground. I clawed the darkness and made contact. I dug in my nails. He cried out and then a fist smashed into my ribs. I couldn't breathe. When I'd finished gasping for air, his hands were already ripping at my shirt.

I screamed, but it had no effect on him. I would have given anything for the Mace I kept in my gear bag. All at once he stood up. His strong hands dragged me back toward the lake. That's when I realized he hadn't been trying to remove my clothes, just the life vest.

He stopped, pulled back, then thrust me forward. I fell headfirst into nothing. The ground simply wasn't there. I can't describe the terror. I waited to hit rocks, dirt, anything except what I knew was coming at the end of the fall—water.

I broke the surface. The shock and cold stung like needles. I kicked. I tore. A thick blanket of water trapped me. I opened my eyes, but saw only black. What direction was up? My lungs ached. How much longer could I hold my breath?

A light came on. I saw the surface above me and recognized the underside of a boat. How could I have sunk so far? I turned upright and swam toward the surface. The current held me. I tried harder and got nowhere.

Above me, the boat's engine started. It shot away. The light left with it, but not before I saw how close I was to the submerged part of the island. Instead of continuing to struggle upward, I reached over to the rocks. I pulled my legs into a squat and launched myself.

I broke the surface coughing. I started to sink again, but reached out for the island and found a rock. Some part of me was vaguely aware of the boat and its light speeding away in the distance, but it hardly registered. All I wanted to do for the rest of my life was breathe.

After wasting time finding my boat again in the dark, I returned to Mr. King's. Judging from the expression on his face, I was not a pretty sight.

He leaned out the open doorway and gaped at me in horror. "What happened?"

I ran my hand over my face. It felt like fine sandpaper from the ash and grit that had dried there. "Someone tried to drown me." Before he could respond I continued, "Can I use your phone? Mine is at the bottom of the lake."

He stepped back from the doorway to allow me to enter. "It's right there, by my chair. Are you calling the police?"

I crossed to his recliner and picked up the phone. "Yes, but there's someone else I need to call first."

Bud didn't pick up his cell, so I hung up and dialed again. This time he picked up immediately.

"Bud, it's Lilly."

"What are you doin' callin' from somebody named Henry King's phone?"

"I borrowed his boat. It's a long story, but basically, someone just tried to kill me."

"Little Sister!" I heard metal crash in the background—probably a baker's tray. "Are you all right?"

I looked down at myself. My hair had dried on the boat ride back, but my clothes were still damp, and my cargo pants were torn. "Pretty much."

"Where are you?"

"I'm at Henry King's house." I managed not to say the *duh*, but I'm sure it was in my tone. "Listen, I'm sorry to bother you, but I may need your help with bail or talking myself out of police custody or something."

"Hold on, I thought someone tried to kill you?"

"Yes, and now I have to go tell the police what happened, but they already threatened to arrest me once tonight, and they're going to be really pissed when they find out I was out at the crime scene, so I need you to be ready in case I need bail. It's just a precaution."

"Hold on, Little Sister. What crime scene?"

"Road's End. I took a boat to look around because the police aren't investigating the drowning I told you about earlier."

His tone changed. "And you went out there and somebody tried to kill you?"

"Yes, but it was too dark to get a good look at him."

"You got any witnesses?"

"No."

"You got any proof at all?"

I thought for a moment, then reluctantly admitted, "No."

"And you were breakin' the law bein' there in the first place?"

I hesitated. "It's a gray area."

"If you didn't do nothin' wrong, then why are you worried they're gonna lock you up?"

"I'm only calling you as a precaution. I was out at Road's End in an official capacity, as a journalist. It's my job to investigate."

"Then why are you callin' me and not the outfit you work for?"

I glanced at Mr. King. You can always tell if you did something wrong when it comes time for other people to hear about it.

"Lilly?" Bud said.

I turned my back on Mr. King and lowered my voice. "I may have, sort of, given my word to Callum that I'd stop looking into the drowning."

He sighed. "And why aren't you callin' Rod?"

"I may have, sort of, told him I'd meet him at headquarters, but came here instead."

"Little Sister, you fixin' to lose your job, your man, and get ill of the cops all in one night?"

My voice rose. "Don't be melodramatic. I only called you to arrange bail because someone tried to kill me."

"Can you hear yourself?"

"I thought after all the jams you've been in, you wouldn't be judgmental."

"Did you ever think I want better for you than takin' after me?"

That shut me up. I've never been good with touching moments, and seeing as I was sleep-deprived, hungry, damp, dirty, and had swallowed an unhealthy amount of lake water, I was incapable of responding.

Fortunately, Bud changed gears. "Now listen. Don't go to the cops right off. We need to get together and make a plan. Maybe there's some other cops to talk to that you haven't got all bowed up."

"Lucero!" Mr. King jumped, so I lowered my voice. "I can call the detective in charge from the Sheriff's Department. I know him and he'll probably listen."

"Good." Bud paused and then came back on the line. "I got some doughnuts to deliver right now, but I'll be free in an hour or so. Why don't you go find Rod and tell him what you done and make nice?"

"Rod's at headquarters."

"Perfect. I'm supposed to be deliverin' there. I'll make it my last stop and the three of us will have a war council."

I was surprised at how relieved I felt. The idea of facing the sergeant again and telling him where I'd gone and what had happened, without any proof, was not appealing. There was also the issue of bailing on Rod when I'd promised to meet him at headquarters. If I got tied up all night with the police, I wouldn't be available to shoot his material on the fire.

"That's a good idea. I should explain to Rod in person." I looked at my watch. "He's probably already worried about me."

I parked the live truck in the same place behind the grandstands. Rod's van was there as well as the L.A. satellite truck. It looked as if the briefing was over. There was no sign of Rod, but Slim was back sitting out the open side door of his truck. He leaned over a different graphic novel while eating a sandwich. Where was he getting all this food?

Instead of asking that, I said, "Have you seen my reporter? His name is Rod Strong?"

He looked up and frowned. "What happened to you?"

I tried to rub some of the grit off my damp clothes. "I almost drowned. Have you seen my reporter?"

"Seriously?" Apparently he thought the situation important enough to lower the sandwich. "How'd you manage that?"

"I was working on a story."

"Man. That's why I hate these kinds of assignments. Everything is so friggin' dangerous. Nobody ever drowned at a pastry competition." He raised the sandwich again. "I'm just sayin'."

"Have you seen my reporter?"

"Sure." He gestured to the graphic novel. "What a great guy. He knows all this cool stuff about Joss Whedon's *Wonder Woman* movie that never happened."

I tried to interrupt him. "Where is he?"

Slim didn't hear me. "You would never guess he was a geek from how he looks. If anything, he reminds me of the guys who used to pick on me in high school." Slim gestured to me with the sandwich. "And what about you going to Jareth's Ball? When he told me that, I almost choked."

I started to ask where Rod was, but stopped. "How do you know Jareth?"

For a moment Slim looked confused, but then all at once he laughed and pointed. "You have no idea what the ball is, do you?"

I shook my head.

He finished laughing. "You know that Jim Henson movie *Labyrinth* with David Bowie?"

"Stop." I raised my hand. "Stop talking. This day can't possibly get any worse."

"You'll have to coordinate costumes, of course." He took a bite and spoke while chewing. "But it's better if Rod explains. He's got other stuff to tell you too. I guess he knows our assistant news director, Helen Henry." Slim smiled. "But I'll let Rod tell it. He said I should wait for him."

"Where is he?"

Slim gestured toward the hill at the end of campus. "Up in the gymnasium with the IO. He tried calling your cell a bunch of times. He's got an interview lined up. He was worried he'd lose it if you didn't show up soon."

Rod was the best at getting people to go on camera, but I hadn't expected the IO to give anyone a sound bite so quickly.

I got my gear out of the truck. Before heading for the gymnasium, I stopped and spoke to Slim one more time. "I'm going to shoot Rod's interview, but when I'm done, I need to talk to you about that sound bite of yours that's been running all night."

He rolled his eyes. "You mean the bimbo who won't evacuate?"

"I need to find her and the people with her. Especially a guy named Farris who had a ponytail."

"They were at a house on the other side of the mountain with a weird name. I don't remember, but the turnoff's easy to spot because it's right by some fruit stands."

"Was the house called Bonny Hazel?"

"Yeah, that's it. It's actually inside a nature preserve." I started to walk away, but he called after me, "Don't you want to change clothes before the interview and clean up a little?"

"I don't have any other clothes and I don't have time for a shower." I glanced back. "Don't go anywhere, okay? I need to talk to you about Bonny Hazel."

I crossed a dirt field and climbed a small slope to the high school gymnasium. This was where the incident commander had set up his war room. Press had never been allowed inside before, so despite my plunge into the lake, I was excited to shoot an exclusive look at the operation.

My anticipation was heightened by the two men in black suits standing guard at the door. They checked my ID, patted me down, and searched my gear bag before allowing me in. The patdown was especially awkward given the state of my clothing.

After all that buildup, the war room was a letdown. The basketball court inside had been filled with rows of tables and more computer and communications equipment. Cables carrying electricity to all those devices ran along the floor. Officials were everywhere—some in ties and slacks, some in uniform, but nothing I hadn't seen before. At the end of the court a large movie screen hung in front of the basketball hoop. It showed a computer-generated map of the fire.

I scanned the crowd for Rod. Maybe the mood in the room was what gave me the feeling of disappointment. Judging from the dour expressions on people's faces, we were losing the war. I finally saw Rod with the IO and two other men in the corner. The men looked like generic officials, drinking coffee in their rolled-up shirtsleeves.

I walked straight up to Rod. "I heard you've got an exclusive. Sorry, I lost my phone."

"It's okay. Are you ready to shoot?" Rod took a good look at me and stopped smiling. "Wait a minute. What happened?"

I set down my sticks, then locked down each leg. "I almost drowned, but I'm fine." I attached the camera to the tripod head. "And I'm always ready to shoot."

One of the men with Rod laughed. "And I thought my job was hard."

I took a good look at the man. I recognized him immediately.

He offered his hand. "Pleased to meet you, Miss Hawkins."

And that's how I met the governor of the great state of California for the fourth time; damp, smelly, and from about two feet away.

ELEVEN

I shook the governor's hand. His grip was perfect. Not too tight. Not too loose.

He smiled. "Rod's been telling us all about your adventure last winter."

"You mean when I was wanted for murder?"

The IO flinched, but the governor laughed.

Two of the governor's aides laughed too. The third, aka schedule Nazi, glared.

"What do you mean, you almost drowned?" Rod turned me toward him and touched a tender spot on my forehead. "You've got a huge cut here. Do you need a doctor?"

"I'm okay. It's nothing."

He started to pull me toward the exit. "We'll go to the Red Cross."

Schedule Nazi came as close as he probably ever got to looking happy. "Sir, we really need to go. You should have left ten minutes ago."

"I said I'm okay." I refused to be pulled by Rod's gentle grip. "And if you think I'm giving up an exclusive with the governor, then you don't know me at all."

The governor looked at his aides. "I'd like to make time." His voice was friendly, but it also conveyed finality.

The schedule Nazi frowned. "In that case, there are a few things that need your attention." He gestured to the other aides, and one got out an iPad. "I can go over the interview format while you're doing that."

The two aides joined the governor while schedule Nazi walked over to us.

Rod looked at me. "Are you sure you're okay?"

"I'm fine."

The schedule Nazi pulled us farther away so no one could hear us. "I don't care if you're fine or not. I want you to back out of the interview."

Rod did a double take. "Why?"

The schedule Nazi spread his arms. "Because it's going to kill my schedule. Why else?"

"Then you'd better grab Eva Braun," I said. "And a couple cyanide pills, and head for the Nazi bunker, because your schedule is going down."

Rod and I started to walk away.

"You owe me from that *thing*, before."

I stopped. My hands shot to my hips. "You only kept your mouth shut about that *thing* because it was in your own best interest."

"Hold on." Rod quickly looked around, then dropped his voice. "How does he know about the thing before?"

Schedule Nazi didn't give me a chance to answer. "When a person looks the other way on a *thing*, then you owe them. That's an understanding people everywhere have. It's part of the social contract."

I stepped back to him. "I'm sorry. I never got that memo when I joined the people-everywhere club."

Rod looked from one of us to the other. "I'm sorry, but as long as Lilly is physically able, we're doing the interview."

"Have it your way." The schedule Nazi passed us and approached the governor. Rod and I followed.

"Sir, I have concerns about this reporter. He has issues and I don't think it's wise to grant him an exclusive." The schedule Nazi glanced back at Rod, then leaned closer to the governor. He cupped his hand into a C-shape and raised it back and forth to his mouth.

The governor cast a concerned glance at Rod, then entered into a whispered discussion with all of his aides.

"I owe you an apology," I said. "It is the international symbol for alcohol."

Rod didn't take his eyes off the governor. "Are you sure you're not hurt?"

"Why? Are you going to kill me?"

"Something like that."

From the look on the schedule Nazi's face, and his mannerisms as he spoke, I guessed he was embellishing Rod's behavior beyond even what he'd mistaken.

Finally the governor raised his hands. "Enough." The aides were all silenced. "We're making time for this."

The schedule Nazi opened his mouth, but the governor cut him off. "I said, I'm making time for this."

The aides got out their BlackBerrys and began making phone calls and e-mails.

Rod, the governor, and I walked over to a nearby table so I could hook up the wireless mic. The governor had to pull his shirt out and run the cord up underneath so it would be hidden. A man and a woman from the Bureau of Land Management, who'd been working on computers nearby, got up to go get coffee and give the governor some privacy.

Rod took the opportunity to try to do some damage control. "If it's all right, sir, I'd like to try and explain something. Your aide may have gotten the mistaken impression that I was indulging—"

The governor cut him off. "Is it okay to speak in front of Miss Hawkins? It's obvious from the way you were talking about her earlier that your relationship is more than professional."

Rod and I glanced at each other.

"Yes, sir," Rod said. "But Lilly is actually the one who can explain—"

The governor placed a hand on Rod's shoulder. "Part of the reason I agreed to this interview was so we'd have this chance to talk. You're a remarkably intelligent and talented young man. Those questions you asked during the briefing were sharp, but addiction is something you have no control over."

Rod's eyes widened. "Sir, no . . ."

The governor covered the mic clipped to his shirt. "I'm going to be frank with you, Rod."

Rod held up his hands. "No, sir, please don't be frank."

"Even though you're a journalist, I know you'll keep it private because of your own difficulties."

"He doesn't have difficulties," I rushed to say.

Rod shook his head. "Sir, please don't share your—"

"I had a problem myself when I was a young man."

All the color drained from Rod's face.

"It started with social drinking, then I was drinking on the job." The governor took his hand off Rod's shoulder. "You have a bright future ahead of you, but alcohol can't be a part of it. Don't let yourself fall as far as I did before getting help."

The governor tucked his shirt back in and walked over to the incident commander.

Rod watched him go. "That did not just happen."

"It's sort of flattering. How many people can say the governor cares about their sobriety?"

Rod looked at me. "In all seriousness, we can't ever tell anyone about this. He told us in confidence, and if his past difficulties got out, it could ruin his political career."

I nodded. "You're right, but knowing he struggled and overcame his problems makes me more inclined to vote for him."

We spent the next ten minutes doing a walk and talk around the gymnasium. The IO, the aides, and the governor's security guard hung back and stayed off camera. Sometimes Rod and the governor would stop and face each other for a series of questions, and other times they'd stop and look at something on a computer or talk with a third person. Rod kept things loose and easily switched gears to accommodate the changing situation. His questions were smart and direct, but mostly he listened to the answers and asked great follow-ups.

I went handheld, something I almost never do, and followed

Rod's lead. For me, the greatest challenge was not tripping over all the cords and cables running along the floor.

We finished by speaking with the incident commander. He wore a Montecito Fire Department uniform and said he was halfway into a six-year rotation as the head of Team 18. He talked in a relaxed and comfortable way, despite the severity of the subject matter. It spoke well of his performance under pressure.

He walked our entire group to one of the tables and sat down at a large computer monitor. "Most of this was in the briefing, but it may come across better if I show you on the map."

He gestured above us to the projection at the front of the room. It showed Lake Elizabeth, Mt. Terrill, and Terrill Valley next door. The whole thing was sliced down the middle by Highway 55, running from the lake, up through Tilly Heights, and then over into the valley. The burnt area was indicated by a huge ocean of red shading.

"We believe the point of origin for the fire was here." He used the mouse and a flashing dot appeared in Terrill Valley. "It began on uninhabited lands north of Highway 55 and then spread into the Sequoia National Forest.

"On Monday the winds shifted to the west." He clicked the mouse a few times and moving arrows appeared going in the direction of Mt. Terrill and the lake on the other side. "It took everyone by surprise. I mean everyone. The fire jumped the containment lines. The two men we lost were falling back when their truck went off the road." His voice wavered. "It's a hell of a thing. I've never lost a man before."

The governor struck the perfect tone to convey both grief and strength. "Our entire state is mourning them."

The commander nodded, but said, "I don't intend to mourn anyone else. The fire is in the valley right now, but if it reaches the foothills by tomorrow afternoon, the conditions will be perfect for a blowup."

He used the mouse and drew lines on the map. "If that happens, it's going to race straight up these sections of Mt. Terrill like chimneys." He looked up. "It's imperative that all of our personnel and local residents are evacuated by then."

"Assuming the worst," Rod said, "and it does burn all the way to the communication towers on the ridge of the mountain, how likely is it that the fire would then come down this side to Tilly Heights?"

The commander shook his head. "Fires burn much more slowly down a mountain than up, but there are no guarantees in a situation like this. That's why we've got dozers and hand crews constructing indirect fire lines in the steep terrain on both sides of the mountain ridge."

"But if it did reach Tilly Heights, the property damage would be in the hundreds of millions of dollars, right?"

The governor jumped in and answered, without answering. "The really tragic thing about disasters like this is that most are preventable."

Rod accepted the change in subject, but turned it for his own end. "Is there any word yet on what started the Terrill Wildfire?"

The commander shook his head. "We've eliminated lightning, but we don't have access to the point of origin yet. It's still too dangerous."

One of the aides walked over with his BlackBerry out. He showed the governor something on the screen, then the two of them stepped away.

The commander got up as though done, but Rod continued asking questions. "You said the land at the point of origin was uninhabited, but someone must own it. Have they been questioned?"

"It's part of a nature preserve that runs all the way from the top of the mountain and then down through the valley. Almost all the land north of Highway 55 is part of it."

I started to ask about Green Seed and the preserve, but managed to stop myself before I ruined Rod's interview.

"What about campers or hikers who were trespassing?" Rod said.

"Careless campfires are a common cause of wildland fires, but we have no evidence to support that at this point." The commander looked at Rod. "And there are no signs of human intrusion on the aerial photographs taken by the marijuana patrols."

We'd done several stories about Mexican drug cartels using uninhabited land to grow pot. If they'd started the fire, it would be a huge story. Rod kept his voice neutral. "Have they found any evidence of other marijuana farms in the area?"

"No," the commander said. "There's nothing but normal vegetation and trees on the photos. No sign that anyone was using the land at all."

The governor returned. He removed the mic himself and offered his polite good-byes. He made a point of telling Rod he'd be e-mailing the phone number of someone Rod could speak to about his *issue.*

After the governor and his entourage departed, I walked up to where the information officer and incident commander were standing. "Is it all right if I shoot some B-roll of the room? Just some generic shots of people working?"

The incident commander nodded. "As long as you don't get in anyone's way."

I set up my sticks. Rod came and stood next to me and went over his notes. I was rolling on a wide shot when I heard Byrdie Fitzgerald. Her high-heel shoes made a loud crack with each determined step she took across the basketball court.

The incident commander saw her coming too. Was that a frown I saw on his face? If so, he recovered immediately. He actually stepped forward to meet her. Instinct made me turn the camera and tighten my shot on them.

Despite the rough conditions at headquarters and the late hour, Byrdie Fitzgerald looked impeccable. Her dark purple suit may have collected some stray bits of ash, but her hair and makeup were perfect. She stopped immediately before the commander and information officer. "I have one question for you gentlemen." She was smiling and her voice sounded sweet. "I want to know why you looked me straight in the eye and lied."

Before either of them could say anything she continued, "You promised me you'd protect Tilly Heights, and now I discover you're devoting resources to protecting empty land where nobody lives." Her voice stayed pleasant, despite the harshness of the words.

That may be why the incident commander didn't get angry. "Of course the preservation of human life is everyone's top priority."

"Is it?" She tilted her head slightly. "Then why are you protecting a lizard instead of people?"

Rod cleared his throat. "I think that's a question we're going to want answered too."

The IO turned. We were only ten feet away with a camera pointed at them. Let's just say, he didn't look happy. "Are you recording?"

I nodded.

"Please, stop."

I reached over and pressed stop. "Okay." The school campus was private property and I couldn't record without permission.

Byrdie Fitzgerald leaned toward us while squinting her eyes. All at once she pulled back, smiling. "Are you Rod Strong?"

"Yes." Rod walked up to her. "Why do you think the incident commander lied to you?"

The commander bristled. "I did not lie."

"Of course not." The IO took charge. "Lilly and Rod, let's go outside with Mayor Fitzgerald. We're in the way here."

"Hold on," the commander said. "Am I going to be called a liar on the news?"

The IO looked at the commander. "Absolutely not. I promise that will not happen."

We all walked outside and stopped near the bike racks. Looking down the hill we had an amazing view of the campus. I'd only seen individual pieces of the operation at close range, but this was like seeing a living map. There was movement everywhere as people and vehicles came, went, or just traveled from one task to another. Color popped in unexpected places, such as the blue of the Porta Potties and the giant green bladders that held water for the laundry and shower trailers.

"Rod Strong," Byrdie said. "I can't believe this. I'm such a big fan."

Rod flushed. "Thank you. Why don't you explain what this is all about?"

The IO jumped in. "The mayor has been pressing her concerns that we don't waste manpower thinning and back-burning on the mostly unpopulated lands on the other side of the mountain." The IO, usually the picture of diplomacy, was having a hard time hiding his dislike of Byrdie Fitzgerald. "And we agree with her. Our priorities are Tilly Heights on this side of the mountain, and the antennas on the mountain ridge."

"I wish that were true." Byrdie continued to smile. "But I've discovered you've got at least three crews on the western end of the nature preserve. . . ." She leaned toward the IO. "Which is on the other side of the mountain. You're protecting a lizard."

"They're protecting human beings." The IO turned to Rod. "You probably saw a clip of a girl refusing to evacuate. It's been all over television and the Internet tonight." The IO took a breath and tried to regain his professional calm. "I assure you, everything humanly possible is being done to protect the residents of this community and not the endangered lizard."

"It was never endangered." Byrdie's sweet facade finally cracked. "We can't get rid of them. You can't have a picnic around here without the blanket landing on one."

"And it's a salamander," Rod said. "Not a lizard."

The IO looked ready to pull his hair out. "The point is, we're not diverting resources to protect the nature preserve."

"Prove it," I said.

"What's that supposed to mean?"

"I want my ride-along."

The IO stared at me. No one spoke or moved. Below us a

tanker truck made the turn onto the back side of campus. Farther away, a group of firefighters tossed a Frisbee to one another while waiting to use the showers.

Finally, the IO laughed.

"You owe it to me." I set down my gear. "And this is a great opportunity to show us exactly what you're doing on the other side of the mountain. We can see with our own eyes that no one misled Mayor Fitzgerald."

His laughter receded. "You know what, if that's all it takes to make this go away, then I will arrange for Firefighter Bell to take you on a ride-along. I'll tell her to give you full access to anywhere and anyone you want." The IO turned to Byrdie Fitzgerald. "And you're welcome to come look at the work that's being done to protect Tilly Heights."

"Thank you." Byrdie Fitzgerald's perky smile returned. "I'd love that."

Rod took an excited step forward. "We'd also like permission to go live from the top of the mountain."

"But there's no Internet up there," I said. "We can't do any kind of live shot."

"Trust me," Rod said.

The IO considered for a moment, then nodded. "As long as you broadcast from a specific place that we all agree on, and you evacuate when you're told."

"Agreed," Rod and I said in unison.

I took the IO aside, mostly so Byrdie Fitzgerald wouldn't hear, and told him I had specific people I wanted to interview on my ride-along. He quickly agreed to my visiting Bonny Hazel, but was uncertain about Jessica's brother, Brad Egan. He might be difficult to locate or it might not be safe.

The IO left to coordinate with Bell, and I rejoined Rod and Byrdie.

"I can't believe Rod Strong has come out of retirement. What an honor for our community." Byrdie had a moment of inspiration. "Would you like to interview me? I can talk about how everyone is pulling together."

I answered before Rod. "I'd like you to talk about Jessica Egan."

Rod turned and tried to discreetly say, "You promised to be nice."

"No, I didn't. I promised not to be rude. There's a difference."

Rod looked back at Byrdie. "I don't know if you've spoken with your husband, but we saw him earlier tonight and I'm deeply sorry for anything inappropriate that might have been said."

"I did speak with him, and it's okay." She looked at me. "Lee said you used to know Jessica. I'm glad someone else cares about her death. I was beginning to feel like the only one. You know they were going to leave her body in the water indefinitely?"

"I understand using your influence to have her body found." Thanks to those heels she wore, I actually had to look up to make eye contact. "But why didn't you force an investigation? You must have known about her bad shoulder."

She shrugged. "I assumed it had been repaired."

"Do you know for sure?"

She spread her arms. "I really don't know anything about Jessica anymore, for sure. Outside of a few conversations in the store this past year, we haven't seen her in almost thirteen years."

Rod's cell phone rang. He looked at the screen. "It's Callum. I should take this." He looked at me. The unspoken question hung in the air.

"Don't worry. I promise to be nice." But as soon as he'd stepped away, I said, "I'm no good at sugarcoating things, so—"

"You want my alibi?" She giggled sweetly. "My husband told me you were asking. If it gives you peace of mind, then I'm happy to oblige."

She got out a pen and piece of paper and began writing something down. "I was at city hall all day and all night, except for a brief dinner break from six to seven. I drove home, let Jessica into the house, and then drove back in time for a seven-o'clock meeting with city council." Despite the subject matter, she still sounded chipper.

She handed me the paper. It had her address on it. "We live on the far north end of Tilly Heights so it takes about twenty-five minutes. Feel free to check the distance online."

Byrdie could have murdered Jessica in the ten minutes she was home, but towing the body and boat out to Road's End would have taken at least half an hour. More if she'd had to change her clothes and clean up afterward.

I looked down at the paper and then back up to her. "I'm sorry if I've been rude. I'm only pushing so hard because I feel like I owe it to Jessica."

"You don't have to explain. Her death has been difficult for me too."

"Do you mind telling me what she was like during those ten minutes you saw her? Did she talk about meeting anyone?"

Byrdie shook her head. "Mostly she was upset about the fire."

I thought for a moment. "Did the police search her belongings, check her messages—that sort of thing?"

"The police are confident that this was an accident."

I took that to mean they hadn't done anything. Hopefully the police would go back and rectify that once I told them about the man at Road's End. "At least tell me Jessica's things are secure."

She nodded. "Lee moved her car into our garage to get it off the street, and I think he said there's a suitcase and purse inside. Her father is supposed to come get everything once the fire passes."

Rod waved at me to indicate he was wrapping up his call with Callum.

I nodded and looked back at Byrdie. "Thanks for talking with me. I really am sorry if I was rude."

She stopped me as I reached down for my gear. "If you want to, there is something you could do for me."

I felt an instinctive apprehension. "What's that?"

She looked behind me and I followed her gaze to Rod. "It

would be a big political boost if someone with a high profile interviewed me." Byrdie smiled, but it looked much shyer than the plastic one she usually wore. "Maybe you could put in a good word for me with Rod?"

"The mayor of a small town like Elizabeth shouldn't need a political boost." Then again, she wasn't dressed or acting like the mayor of a small town. "Do you have larger aspirations?"

"I'm running for county board of supervisors next year."

TWELVE

Friday, 3:10 a.m.

We were interrupted by an official from Cal Fire who came out of the gym.

"Mayor, I'm glad I caught you." He rushed up to Byrdie. "Before you go home, I need you to sign off on the city staffing plan."

He drew her back into the gym, just as Rod returned.

"Callum loves us." Rod tried to pick up my sticks, but I got to them first. "When I told him we had access to the other side of the mountain, he flipped out. He wants us to hurry, though." Rod had a sudden thought. "Unless you need to see a doctor about your head. He said not to take any chances."

"I'm pretty sure he didn't say that, but thank you for lying about it." I picked up the camera and gear bag. "Don't worry, though. I'm fine."

He stepped close to me. "Are you sure?"

I nodded. "Yes, but we need to talk."

"Let's talk on our way back to the truck." Rod started down the path. "Callum wants us live at four instead of four thirty."

I followed. "I'm sorry, but I can't go anywhere until Bud gets here."

"Bud, as in your uncle Bud?" After I nodded, Rod continued, "What on earth is he doing in Elizabeth, let alone Command Headquarters?"

"I have a confession to make."

Rod reached the bottom of the hill and paused. "Is this about how you almost drowned?"

I quickly told him the whole story while we walked down a small road toward the baseball field. When I got to the part about the man at Road's End, he abruptly stopped. It took me several steps to realize.

I turned around and went back. "I think the man was going to leave the alcohol so when the police finally did check the island, it would look like Jessica came out there to drink."

He took hold of my arms. It wasn't easy because I was carrying all my gear. "Lilly, I want you to drop this."

I stepped back. "What?"

"You could have been killed."

"But if someone was planting evidence, then that proves Jessica was murdered. I can't drop it now." I waited for a forklift to pass us on the road and then started walking again.

Rod followed. "Did you see his face?"

"No. He was strong, and trim, I guess." I shook my head. "But it definitely wasn't Fitzgerald. He's got a gut." I paused. "Why aren't you madder at me?"

"I'm grateful you're safe."

"I ran off without you and did something impulsive and almost got killed. You should be mad."

He smiled. "It's not exactly a shock to me that you're impulsive."

"Okay, but why aren't you madder at me?"

"Because I have something to tell you."

We had to stop so a tanker truck could navigate the turn onto the track field. While we waited, I remembered what Rod had said to the IO. As soon as the noise from the truck receded, I said, "Why did you say we could go live from the top of the mountain?"

He put his hand up. "Don't overreact."

"Did Callum make a deal with KBLA?"

"It's the right move. They don't have a reporter and we don't have a satellite truck."

I put down my camera and sticks. "But now we've got two shooters, and I don't want to work with Slim. He's lazy and won't do anything."

"Who's Slim?"

I gestured toward the baseball field. "That shooter from L.A. He's a slug and his name is Tim or Jim or something." Several passersby were looking, so I tried to lower my voice. "I call him Slim."

"His name is Dennis."

"Who cares? The point is, he's a slug and I don't want to partner up with him."

"But isn't this what you've wanted for the last two weeks: the chance to broadcast live pictures from where the fire is actually happening?"

He was right. It was the kind of opportunity a breaking-news junkie lives for. I wanted to cover the fire just as much as Rod, probably more. But was it right to run off chasing a big story while Jessica's killer quietly got away with murder? And someone had tried to kill me too. Was I supposed to ignore that?

I shook my head. "I have to go see the Elizabeth police. Hopefully when I tell them about the man at Road's End, they'll start a real investigation." I suddenly remembered something. "Crud. I was supposed to call Detective Lucero, but my station phone is at the bottom of the lake."

"Lucero from the Sheriff's Department?"

I nodded. "He's technically in charge of the case and hasn't threatened to arrest me."

"You mean he hasn't threatened to arrest you *today*." Rod handed me his work phone. It was from the same set as the one I'd lost.

"Very funny." I scrolled through his contacts looking for the Sheriff's Department's nonemergency number. "Let me make this call, and then I'll catch up with you."

"Go ahead and keep the phone when you're done." He picked up the tripod and started to walk away. "I can use my personal cell for the rest of the night."

"I see what you just did, and for the record, I'm only letting you carry my sticks because I almost drowned."

He turned around and smiled. "Let me have my tiny chivalrous victories."

The dispatcher that answered said Detective Lucero didn't work the overnight shift and transferred me to his voice mail.

"Hey, it's Lilly Hawkins. So, okay, I'm just going to put it all out there." I paused to take a breath. "Jessica Egan, the drowner from today, I mean yesterday. Anyway, the body you took back to Bakersfield, she was murdered. She had a bad shoulder and couldn't have started the boat herself. So, I went out to Road's End and I surprised a guy planting evidence and he tried to kill me, but I didn't get a good look at him . . . so call me back, okay?" I started to hang up, but then rushed the phone back to my ear. "Oh, and the local police don't like me and didn't want to investigate when I told them about her shoulder. . . . But that was before the guy tried to kill me. I mean, I still knew she was murdered. That's why I went out to Road's End. But I think the local police are going to be mad about that too, not just me yelling at them . . . which I shouldn't have done and regret now. I mean, not that I regret pushing them to investigate, but I shouldn't have—"

Beep.

The voice mail cut me off.

When I reached the live truck, Slim—I mean Slennis—and Rod were in the middle of an amiable disagreement.

"But Ultimate Universe Nick Fury is just better." Rod took a bite from a doughnut.

Slennis spoke while chewing his own glazed old-fashioned. "He may be better but he's not canon."

"Where's Bud?" I said.

"Right here, Little Sister." Bud walked around from the other side of the truck, carrying a bucket of water and a towel. "I tell you, there's so many folks wanderin' around this place, you could stir 'em with a stick." He set the bucket down in front of me. "This here's clean water if you want to wash up."

"Thanks. How'd you know I needed it?"

He gestured to Slennis. "Your friend here said you didn't have time for a proper shower."

Slennis reached back into the truck and then tossed a pair of jeans and a T-shirt at me. "I grabbed these for you too. From the commissary."

That was it. No way I could keep calling him by a derogatory nickname. "Thanks, Dennis."

He answered while still chewing a doughnut. "No problem. I figure we're a team now."

Bud leaned against the side of the truck. "Little Sister, since we're all poppin' for the same patch, why don't you fill us all in on the details of your latest escapade."

I gave everyone a quick recap. Rod added a few details I'd forgotten. When I finished, I asked Dennis about the interviews he'd done earlier in the evening at Bonny Hazel.

"The mad scientist and his minions were weird, but they certainly didn't seem like murderers." Dennis looked troubled, but still took a bite of a doughnut. "And they definitely weren't there to party. They've got all kinds of expensive lab equipment. I think they said it was all run through the University of California."

"I don't mean to interrupt." Rod looked at his watch. "But Callum's expecting us to go live in half an hour."

I shook my head. "I have to go see the police."

Dennis grabbed a rag from inside his truck and wiped the doughnut glaze from his hands. "For what it's worth, I wouldn't do that tonight. This is the absolute worst time to get in trouble with them."

"Why's that?"

"The governor declared a state of emergency. It's not martial law or anything, but due process is going to be hard to come by. It sounds like they already threatened to arrest you for harassing witnesses. What if they decide to hold you and sort out the business at Road's End tomorrow?"

I found my opinion of him rising. "Thanks for pointing that out, Dennis."

Rod shook his head. "And you have no proof that the man who attacked you had anything to do with Jessica Egan's death. You could have walked in on a drug deal, or he could have been a crazy homeless man who stole a boat. Anything's possible."

I managed not to say the denial on the tip of my tongue. Rod was right. As obvious as it seemed to me that the two events were connected, there was no real proof to force the Elizabeth police into action.

"What about that other cop?" Bud said. "The one you were goin' to call at the Sheriff's Department. The one you ain't poked in the eye with a stick."

Rod laughed. "If you're speaking metaphorically, then she has poked him in the eye with a stick, just not today."

"That's probably the most we can hope for with my little niece."

The three of them laughed.

"Ha-ha," I said. "If everyone is done judging me, maybe we can get back to the issue at hand." I waited for their laughter to die down. "I left a message for Lucero, but I doubt he'll get it until tomorrow morning."

"Then I suggest you hold off goin' to the cops until then," Bud said. "It's almost mornin', anyways. You're only talkin' about a few hours."

I nodded. "But if we're not going to the police, then at least let me stop at Byrdie and Lee Fitzgerald's house on the way to the live shot. All of Jessica's things are still there, and no one has even bothered to look through them. For all we know there's a threatening letter or a diary explaining exactly who wanted her dead."

Rod opened his mouth to say no, but I cut him off.

"It's not very far out of the way, and you have all that footage of the governor to edit. While I drive, you can work in the back of the live truck." I looked at Dennis. "And then we'll meet you as soon as we can at the top of the mountain."

Rod looked uncertain, but didn't say anything.

I used the GPS on Rod's phone to find the address Byrdie had given me. Rod edited in the back of the truck while I drove.

Byrdie hadn't lied about the drive to her house. I timed us beginning at the local government buildings near search and rescue. It actually took us longer than the twenty-five minutes she'd said. Being a speed demon behind the wheel didn't fit with Byrdie Fitzgerald's sugary demeanor, but from the way she'd attacked the incident commander, she obviously wasn't really all that sweet.

Byrdie was some kind of unholy combination of Ladybird Johnson and Lyndon Johnson—a hybrid that could give gardening tips while breaking a political opponent's nose.

I parked in front of the Fitzgeralds' house. Their McMansion had its own gate across the driveway and a high masonry fence that hid the house.

I joined Rod in the back. "How's the governor's material."

He finished an edit, then looked up from the small screen. "We've got great stuff here. And the camerawork is phenomenal."

"I'm sorry to drag you away from it, but I doubt Byrdie will let me into the house unless famous journalist Rod Strong is along to interview her."

Rod cringed, but said, "You owe me big-time for this."

"Are you sure? I found out what Jareth's Ball is."

He laughed, then gave me a peck on the cheek. "You'll be the most beautiful faerie there."

I opened the side door and stepped out of the van. I looked down at the jeans Dennis had bought me and the dirty KJAY polo shirt I still wore. I was about as far from a beautiful faerie as was possible.

Rod followed me out of the truck and put on his suit jacket. "The smoke sure is worse."

I picked up my gear and locked the truck. "This side of the lake is closer to the fire. Everything's worse."

The front gate was locked, so Rod pushed the button on an intercom. Through the bars, I could see lights on inside the house.

After a moment the doors opened and Byrdie Fitzgerald came out. "My goodness. What are you two doing here?"

"Sorry," Rod said through the bars. "I know it's late, but we have a brief window in our schedule and Lilly thought you might be available for an interview."

Byrdie's high-heel shoes clicked as she hurried down the walkway. She wore the same skirt and blouse as before, but had removed the jacket. "I only have a few hours to get some sleep before I have to be back at headquarters. Can we do it tomorrow?"

Rod shook his head. "I doubt we'll have time." He began to step away. "But I understand that it's the middle of the night and you need your rest."

"No, wait." She unlocked the gate and opened it. "Maybe we can do something quickly out here."

"The smoke is too thick," I said. "Rod needs to protect his voice."

She glanced back at the house. "Of course." She hesitated, then held the gate open for us. "I have to apologize for the state of the house. Our cleaning lady didn't come this week and I haven't been able to do much myself."

I carried my gear and we walked through the gate. The house was constructed in the California mission style. White plaster arches and dark brown trim made the perfect backdrop for bright red bougainvillea vines climbing the walls. Much less ash was on the tile walkway than the grass, which meant someone had taken the time to sweep it earlier in the day.

"Is your husband home now?" Rod asked.

"No. He's still at work. People are desperate for supplies and he doesn't feel like he can close."

I turned around and glanced up. I couldn't see the red glow in the sky above the mountain. Either we were too close or the thicker smoke was blocking the light.

Byrdie opened one of the double doors that made up their elaborate front entrance. "Please come in."

Rod and I passed into a foyer. If the immediate area was any indication, Byrdie Fitzgerald's idea of sloppy housekeeping did not match mine. I would have had no problem eating off the gleaming marble floors.

She closed the door behind us. "Would you like some coffee or tea? I don't have any made, but I can brew something."

The living room was filled with expensive furniture in pristine condition. Large windows looked out on what I guessed was the dark lake. There were lots of photos similar to the ones on Lee Fitzgerald's desk, but nothing to indicate that children actually used the room.

"I'd love some coffee." Rod looked around. "Maybe we can talk and do a sort of pre-interview while you're making it?"

I set down my gear. "I'll need some time to set up anyway."

Rod followed Byrdie into the kitchen. The door swung closed behind them, but I could still hear their conversation.

"Why did you call the incident commander a liar?" Rod said. "You don't really believe that, do you?"

"No." I heard cupboards opening and closing, then Byrdie's clear voice. "But I have to keep the pressure on them. It's my job."

I unzipped the gear bag and found my Mini Maglite and a pair of rubber gloves I'd taken from the truck.

"But according to the IO, your wishes are being honored," Rod said. "They're focusing on saving Tilly Heights and hardly giving a second thought to the nature preserve."

I crossed the room and headed for a hallway.

"You don't know how irrational the decision-making process can become when environmental concerns are raised. I can't risk the citizens of Tilly Heights losing their homes because someone decided to try and save a lizard."

The last thing I heard was Rod saying, "It's a salamander, not a lizard."

I found the laundry room—it was immaculate—and then the garage. Inside was a giant red SUV. Parked next to it, like a tiny bunny cowering next to a rhinoceros, was a hybrid Honda Civic. I had little doubt which belonged to Byrdie and which belonged to Jessica. As I put on the rubber gloves, I couldn't help but wonder what had drawn two such different women into a friendship. Even as children their basic personalities must have been present. Even if they'd later grown apart, what had those two little girls seen in each other?

The Civic's doors were all unlocked, and the keys were in the ignition. A black carry-on suitcase sat in the backseat.

I quickly searched the case, but didn't find anything more than clothes and toiletries for a quick trip.

Just as I opened the door to the front seat, Rod's cell phone rang in my pocket. It was Bud. "What were you able to find out?" I said.

"Fitzgerald's been at his store all night nailin' plywood up. Just left twenty minutes ago. No way he was the fella sent you for a swim."

I opened the glove compartment and looked through the registration and insurance. "What about the night before?"

"Also got what you'd call a cast-iron-type alibi. He was out on a register all night."

A black backpack sat on the floor of the passenger seat. I reached for it and opened the clasp. An iPhone, a metal water bottle, and a wallet fit neatly into what was more purse than backpack.

"Where did you get your information?" I said.

"Several of the lady clerks were kind enough to help me with my shoppin' needs."

I removed the wallet. "Are you sure Annette would approve of that?" Annette was Bud's girlfriend in Bakersfield. He'd met and begun dating her seven months earlier when I'd been wanted by the police.

"No harm in shoppin', Little Sister."

The driver's license in the wallet belonged to Jessica Egan of Venice, California. Some credit cards and a gym membership were also in the wallet. "Did you find out anything else while you were shopping?"

"Word around the store is that Mrs. Fitzgerald's got all sorts of political ambitions, but they're havin' trouble raisin' the cash on account of they bought some fancy house."

I thanked him and said good-bye. A small case in the back-pack's side compartment held Jessica's business cards. There was also a vegan cheat sheet of easily available products in most grocery stores. I hit a button on the iPhone. It powered up, but a screen appeared asking for a security code. I returned everything to the purse, then got out. I glanced over my shoulder at the door, then slipped Jessica's iPhone into my back pocket.

This was probably inappropriate, but hadn't the police aban-doned it for Jessica's father to collect? If I got past the security screen and discovered an important piece of information, then I'd be doing them a favor.

I noticed a trash can pushed up against the wall nearby. It was too full and the lid wasn't closed all the way. I saw something in-side and quickly opened the lid.

Someone had been doing a lot of shredding. I ran my hand through the confetti, but couldn't make sense of the tiny squares. Then a larger piece caught my eye. It was about the size of a half-dollar. It felt thick and I realized it was the corner of a picture. Something about it was familiar, but I couldn't place it.

I pocketed it and then looked at my watch. I'd only been gone four minutes. How long did it take to brew coffee? Was there time to take a quick look out at the dock?

I decided to push my luck. I wasn't really all that afraid of get-ting caught. I would have asked permission when we arrived, but didn't want to risk Byrdie saying no. Easier to gain forgiveness.

Outside, I found stairs at the rear of the backyard. I carefully held the railing so I wouldn't slip on the steps. At the bottom I used my flashlight to examine the dock. No one had bothered to sweep out here. A thick layer of ash and soot rested on the simple green planks.

No boats were tied up, so I shone the flashlight into the water. The ash and muck on the surface reminded me of my recent plunge. The combined smell of the fire and the rotting vegetation normally along the lakeshore made me wish I'd brought a hand-kerchief.

A light came on. "What are you doing out here?" Lee Fitzgerald stood at the top of the steps.

THIRTEEN

Friday, 4:20 a.m.

Lee grabbed the railing and carefully walked down.

"I was just looking around," I said. "I thought maybe the police missed something."

"Does Byrdie know you're out here?"

"I doubt it."

He stopped at the bottom step. "Why didn't you just ask to see the dock? You could have fallen stumbling around in the dark."

"Sorry. I only wanted a quick look."

"Well, there's nothing to see." He gestured to the side. "Except the empty space where our boat used to be."

"Lilly?" Rod appeared at the top of the steps.

"She's down here," Lee called.

Rod started down, but his cell phone rang and he paused to answer it.

I looked at Lee. "Did the police talk to your neighbors about the night Jessica died? Did they see anyone coming or going from the house?"

"None of our neighbors were here. Either they already evacuated or this is their second home." Lee covered his nose. "Do you mind if we go back inside? We shouldn't be out here without handkerchiefs." He turned and started back up the steps.

I followed and we joined Rod at the top.

"That was Dennis." Rod put away the cell phone. "He's waiting for us at the top of the mountain. We need to go." He turned to Lee. "I'm sorry. We'll have to postpone the interview."

"That's probably best." Lee headed back toward the house and we followed. "I appreciate you giving Byrdie this kind of exposure, but it's the middle of the night and she's exhausted."

We followed him through a sliding glass door and then back through the house. Lee continued into the kitchen to speak with Byrdie, but Rod and I stayed with my gear in the living room.

As soon as we were alone, Rod whispered, "Sorry I couldn't stall her any longer. Fitzgerald came home unexpectedly."

I returned the gloves to my gear bag. "It's okay. I had enough time." I handed Rod the piece of the photo I'd found in the trash. "Someone shredded a bunch of stuff. It looks familiar, but I can't place it."

He turned it over in his hands. "The photo is in black and white, but the paper's not old. There aren't very many kinds of modern photos that are printed in black and white."

That's when I recognized it. "I've seen this background before. It's in the Elizabeth yearbooks. The Fitzgeralds shredded their old school photos." I looked up at Rod. "They must be hiding something. We need to confront them."

"Shredding photos is definitely odd, but it hardly qualifies as a smoking gun." Rod shook his head. "And we need to go do our live shot."

I turned and entered the kitchen. Byrdie and Lee stopped talking when I entered.

The black granite counters and stainless-steel appliances looked modern and sharp. They clashed with the kitschy knickknacks and lace doilies decorating the room.

Byrdie looked up from pouring the contents of a stainless-steel carafe into a china coffeepot. Cups and saucers with the same flowery pattern sat on the counter. Lee hovered nearby at a plate of cookies.

"Why didn't you just ask to see the dock?" Byrdie said.

I held up the scrap I'd found in the garage. "Why are you shredding your old photos?"

She flushed. "You had no right to go through my trash." Byrdie returned the carafe to the coffeemaker on the counter, then looked at Lee. "I'm sorry, sweetie. I shredded the old pictures we still had of Jessica. I was too upset to . . ." Her voice choked.

He put his arms around her. "It'll be okay, honey."

I held up the fragment of the photo. "Why didn't you want anyone to see these pictures?"

"I don't care if people see them or not." Byrdie blinked back tears. "I shredded the pictures so I wouldn't have to see them. They make me feel guilty, and I don't like feeling guilty."

Rod stepped forward from the doorway. "What do you have to feel guilty about?"

"Nothing." Lee pulled a tissue from a pink box and handed it to her. "You have nothing to feel guilty about."

"That's not true." Byrdie dabbed the tissue at her eyes. "I only saw Jessica for a few minutes last night, but she was heartbroken about the fire. She wanted me to stay. She said she needed to talk to someone, but I left her alone because I had a meeting."

Rod gave Lee a moment to comfort her, then said, "Given that the meeting was with the city council concerning a deadly wildfire, you really don't have anything to feel guilty about."

"He's right," I said. "So there must be something else bothering you."

Lee pointed toward the door. "I think it's time for you to go."

"It's okay." Byrdie pulled away from his grasp and took a moment to compose herself. "She's right. There is something else."

She threw away the tissue in a bin under the sink, then poured coffee into a china cup.

Lee opened the refrigerator. "You need something stronger than that. Don't we have a bottle of chardonnay in here?"

"No." Byrdie frowned at him. "I told you it was gone. I think Jessica drank it last night."

"Oh, sorry." Lee bent over and began looking through the shelves. "Isn't there anything left?"

Byrdie turned back to us. While she spoke, she added cream and sugar to her coffee cup. "Jessica's mother had cancer. It dragged on for years before she died. When it finally happened, Jessica was a different person. She broke up with her boyfriend and stopped caring about the things that normal teenage girls are supposed to care about."

"So you dumped her?" My voice had sounded much angrier than I'd intended. "That's why you feel guilty?"

"Hey," Lee said. "It wasn't like that."

"I thought she'd snap out of it or something." Byrdie added a packet of Equal to her coffee, in addition to the sugar, then stirred. "But then Green Seed arrived and Jessica joined right up. This was before all the development in Tilly Heights, and this area was pretty old-fashioned. A bunch of, well, hippies start telling people what they can and can't do on their own land . . . everyone hated them."

"So you dumped her," I repeated.

Byrdie tossed the spoon down. It made a loud clank as it hit the granite. "Yes, all right. I dumped her."

Lee flinched.

"But that was the least of her problems," Byrdie continued. "She got arrested for doing some outrageous thing with the protesters, I can't even remember what, but her father flipped out. It got really ugly between them."

"She chained herself to a tree," I said. "How ugly did it get between them?"

Byrdie took a drink of coffee, then lowered her voice. "He threatened to beat her if she saw anyone from that group again. I think he may have hit her once to show he meant it."

"He hit her?" Jessica had never said anything about her father being violent, but it would explain why she'd gone to such lengths to fool him. "Did you tell someone? A teacher or your parents?"

"How do you think I found out about it? I overheard my parents talking." Byrdie turned to Lee, who was watching her tell the story. "Sweetie, you're letting all the cold air out."

He glanced down at the open refrigerator. "Oh, right. Sorry." He shut the door, then took a cookie from a plate on the counter.

Rod stepped farther into the room. He looked upset. "If your parents thought Jessica's father might be abusive, why didn't they intervene?"

"Nobody thought he was abusive. I told you, everybody hated Green Seed and thought he was right to keep Jessica from seeing them. And they felt sorry for the man. His life unraveled after his wife died. He lost his job, and then his daughter starts chaining herself to trees."

"What about her brother?" Rod said. "Why didn't he do something?"

"Brad Egan had his own problems." Byrdie topped off her coffee cup and added two more sugar cubes. I guess she needed it because her tone was no longer sweet. "He was a big deal around here, but out in the real world he didn't do so well. His big claim to fame was almost making it onto the Olympic team for archery." She paused for emphasis. "Almost making it. He was washed-up at twenty-one."

"Still," Rod said. "You'd think he would care that his father was beating his little sister."

"He was already grown and living somewhere else. And it wasn't like Jessica had bruises all the time. I think it was just this one time when her dad really put his foot down about the protesters."

"And by put his foot down," I said, "you mean literally, on her face?"

"Don't be melodramatic." Byrdie took her coffee cup and started toward the living room. "Jessica wasn't a saint. She was always putting things like lizards above human beings."

"Salamanders," Rod said as we followed her.

Byrdie didn't appear to hear him as she crossed into the living room. "Like the nature preserve. She didn't want to protect the land for future generations, or whatever. She wanted to put it under a glass dome and it would be this perfectly preserved place, and nobody would ever be allowed to use it or enjoy it. She wanted it all for herself."

Byrdie passed my camera and tripod and took a seat on the pristine sofa.

Rod glanced at his watch and then looked at me. I nodded and began collecting my gear.

Rod turned back to Byrdie. "If the nature preserve has always been so important to Jessica, then why did she only begin visiting this year?"

"I told you before." Lee had followed us out. "She was involved with those people, the ones she kept coming into the store with." He hesitated near the sofa, presumably afraid to bring the plate of cookies any closer to the furniture.

"I thought she was more than involved with someone." Byrdie's sharp eyes focused on Rod, then on me. "Maybe I'm wrong, and I don't know who it was, but when I saw Jessica in the store, she looked like a schoolgirl in love. It reminded me of the old Jessica, before her mother died. Bright, open, excited."

"Then maybe her boyfriend wasn't new." I zipped up my gear bag and lifted the strap over my head. "Maybe she reconnected with someone she dated back when you were young?"

Byrdie shook her head. "No. She only ever dated Arnie—the four of us were practically best friends—but he's happily married now and hasn't seen Jessica in over a decade."

"But he's still living here?" Rod said.

"Oh, sure." Lee finished a cookie and wiped powdered sugar from his shirt. "Arnie's born and bred. He'll never leave. We used to run a landscaping business together out of the store, but then he quit to sell real estate."

I paused in the middle of picking up my sticks. "Is Arnie, Arnaldo Bedolla?"

Byrdie and Lee glanced at each other and then nodded.

I turned to Rod. "He's with Search and Rescue. He's the one who pulled Jessica's body from the lake."

We'd only driven a few yards from the house before I called the IO and put him on speaker.

"I know you wanted to interview Brad Egan on your ridealong," he said, "but I haven't been able to pin down his location yet. How about in the meantime Firefighter Bell takes you to that house in the nature preserve? The scientist and his students are still refusing to evacuate."

"Things have changed." Speaking with Jessica's brother again didn't seem so important anymore. "I need to interview a man named Arnaldo Bedolla with the local Search and Rescue. I think he's doing first aid or something down near the fire line."

Rod made a noise, but whatever he'd started to say, he thought better of it.

"Okay, but consider us even after this. I appreciate your not using the tape of the mayor calling us liars, but I can't keep doing you favors."

I agreed, then he promised to call back when he'd found Bedolla.

Next, Rod called Callum. I wanted to avoid Callum for as long as possible, so I asked him not to put it on speaker. I listened as Rod apologized for missing our 4:00 a.m. live shot, but promised we'd be in place soon. He didn't mention the drowning.

When the call was over, Rod returned the phone to his inside coat pocket. "I'm going to finish editing. With some luck I'll be done by the time we get there."

I kept my eyes on the road. "Was Callum mad we missed our slot?"

"Yes, but he didn't waste time dwelling on it."

"Does he know we've been working on the drowning?"

"No, but you'll have to tell him eventually." Rod started to get up.

"Hold on." I reached into my back pocket. "See if you can do anything with Jessica's cell. It needs a security code and I don't know anything about iPhones."

He took it from me. "Where did you get this?"

"It was in her car."

His voice rose. "Lilly. It could be evidence."

"Which is why I thought it was a bad idea to leave it sitting in an unlocked car like the Elizabeth PD did."

He shook his head, but took the phone with him into the rear.

I got off the Lake Road where it intersected with Highway 55. This was the main highway over Mt. Terrill. It began at the lake, climbed through Tilly Heights, continued over the ridge, and then down into Terrill Valley. At first we had to fight against cars evacuating, but the farther up into Tilly Heights we drove, the less traffic came down.

We stopped briefly where the road was closed. Only emergency personnel or property owners were being allowed through. Fortunately, the IO had called ahead. We were waved through and continued our climb. As we neared the top of the mountain, the sky began to warm. It looked like a sunrise trying to peak through the smoke. Sadly, it was at least an hour too early for that. I knew what was really making the sky glow with soft reds and oranges, but didn't want to think about it.

"We're almost to the top," I called back to Rod. "I figure we'll do some live hits for Callum and KBLA, and then when the IO finds Bedolla, he can send Bell to take us on the ride-along."

"I'd rather he didn't." I couldn't see him, but Rod's voice sounded tired and apprehensive.

"What do you mean? He was the dead woman's boyfriend and never said a word about it the whole time he was pulling her body from the lake. Who knows how he could have sabotaged the autopsy? We need to get him on camera and let him have it. Maybe we can even get him to implicate himself."

"We're talking about a potentially dangerous man and you almost drowned once already."

"So what are you saying? You won't go? You want to do live shots for KBLA for the rest of the day?"

Rod paused. After a few moments he said, "Don't worry. If the IO finds Egan and Bedolla, I'll go with you. But you're right. I'd rather do the live shots."

We managed to avoid the topic for the rest of the drive. It wasn't hard, since Rod was editing and I was busy navigating through equipment and firefighters amassing to protect Tilly

Heights. After we passed the final developed lots with their expensive homes, a dense forest of ponderosa pines began. At this transition point, a firebreak was being constructed. When it was done, a twenty-foot-wide line of cleared ground would run straight across the mountain so that if the fire approached, it would run out of fuel and die.

We passed a convoy of flatbed trucks loaded with enormous bulldozers. Teams of Hotshots like Brad Egan were gathering here too. They'd cut down trees and remove brush in the steep terrain bulldozers couldn't reach. My headlights caught the reflective strips on their yellow helmets as the groups of mostly young men checked their supplies and equipment. They'd need to carry food, chain saws, tents, axes—everything they required to work and survive—on their backs.

Just before reaching the top of the mountain, I turned left at a dirt road cutting through the trees. We were meeting Dennis at an abandoned Forest Service lookout on the ridge. In my headlights, I saw his wide tire tracks running through a thick layer of ash on the ground. Ash also covered the trees. The dirt road eventually ended in a large, flat clearing with trees on all sides. My headlights illuminated a three-story lookout tower surrounded by a chain-link fence.

Rod shut down the editor. "I could have used another five minutes, but that's going to have to be good enough."

He opened the side door, but immediately pulled his head back in. "The smoke is worse. It may be time for handkerchiefs or masks or something."

I'd seen the thickening haze in the headlights, so I wasn't surprised. I went to my gear bag and removed two handkerchiefs I'd brought from Command Headquarters. We each tied one around our face so it covered our nose and mouth. We looked a little like old-time cowboy bandits.

We got out. The ash was much, much thicker here. Our boots left prints as we walked to the other side of the building where

Dennis had parked his satellite truck. I assumed he was inside, hiding from the smoke. The dirt road continued on the back side of the building and disappeared down the other side of the mountain into the trees.

Dennis had set up his sticks and camera at the top of the road. It wasn't a terrible place for a live shot. Despite trees blocking the view down into the valley, the striking red horizon would make a nice backdrop. But I wasn't in the habit of settling for nice, and never on a story this big.

I carefully walked a few feet into the thicket of trees. As my boots touched down, dead vegetation crackled under the ash.

I got my flashlight out and continued. After roughly ten yards I stopped.

Ahead the terrain took a sudden dip. Through a break in the trees I saw the mountain spread downward and flow out into the valley. The uninhabited land looked almost black, like an ocean at night. It suddenly ended in a horizontal line of fire.

The explosions of yellow and orange reached into the night sky and turned the horizon bloodred. In some places, what looked like miles of pine trees were lit from within by a burning forest floor. In others, giant columns of flames strained upward into the polluted air. It looked to me as if this mass of fire, scorched ground, and smoke could swallow a person like the waters of an ocean.

This was the land Jessica had fought to save thirteen years ago. Byrdie had even accused her of valuing it more than human life. Is that why she finally came home after all these years? Because the land was in so much danger?

I pictured Jessica Egan walking out of her father's old house with a box.

"Why didn't you tell them I painted the THINK SAFETY sign?"

"I didn't like the way they asked." She opened the trunk on the old Civic hatchback in the driveway. It was already packed to the roof. "My dad and the police thought they could bully me. I enjoyed showing them they were wrong."

"Thanks, I guess."

"You're welcome." She moved something in the trunk and slid in the box.

I nervously shifted my weight to the other leg. "You're really going to L.A.?"

She nodded. "I'm eighteen today. Dad is going to be mad I took the car, but he can deal with it. It was my mom's anyway." She moved a large, flat rectangle that looked like a wrapped painting. "I only wish it didn't have leather seats."

"You really believe in all that stuff? Animal rights and all that?"

She turned and gave me a dirty look. "What do you think I've been doing all this time?"

I shrugged. "Trying to make your dad mad."

She went back to packing the car. "Is that what you've been doing the last few months?"

I didn't answer. I watched her shift a few more things to make space. When she finished, I held an envelope out to her. "I brought you this."

She opened it and frowned. "Where did this come from?"

"It's the money you paid me this summer, for lying to your dad. It's not a lot. Just a hundred and fifty."

"I paid you fifteen dollars a week for nine weeks. That's a hundred and thirty-five, not a hundred and fifty." She tried to shut the trunk with her hand holding the envelope. The door slipped. Her right hand instinctively reached for it, but then she grimaced in pain.

I jumped in and helped her.

"Thanks." She rubbed her bad shoulder. "Besides, I thought you spent that money."

"I did."

She looked at the envelope again, then her eyes shifted up to me without moving her head. "Why is this money in an envelope from Otto's Pawn?"

"I sold a couple things." I laughed. "But it's okay. I'll get a real job now that the summer's over and buy it all back."

She held the envelope out to me. "You don't have to pay me just because I didn't tell them you painted the sign."

"It's not for that."

"Then what's it for?"

I hesitated. "Bad things happen down in L.A. You might get into trouble or something."

She laughed.

I looked away, embarrassed by my own sincerity. "You might need a way home. This can be your emergency bus money or something."

She looked back at the house. "This hasn't been home since my mom died, and I don't have anything in common with my friends anymore. I'm not coming back."

"Then don't spend the money." I started backing up. "You can hold on to it in case things go wrong and you have to make a porno or something." I was half serious, but we both laughed.

"I have a job waiting for me." She held out the envelope. "You need this more than me."

"I'm already home. Even if I'm a screwup, at least I'm home." She opened her mouth to protest again, but I cut her off. "If your mom were alive, she'd be giving you this money. Everyone needs a way home, even if they never use it."

FOURTEEN

Friday, 5:05 a.m.

illy?" Rod's voice brought me back from the memory.

"I'm over here," I called. "Watch your step."

I heard the crunch of his approach. The sound abruptly stopped right behind me, followed immediately by a sudden gasp.

"My camera won't do it justice," I said.

"No wonder Jessica Egan was heartbroken." Rod took the final step and stood next to me. He gazed out at the red horizon rising from the flames. "I've never been here before, and this breaks my heart."

Behind us I heard someone approaching. "Rod, where'd you go?"

"We're out here," he said.

Dennis joined us. He whistled. "Some view."

We moved Dennis's camera out to the edge of the trees and ran more cable. Once we had a signal back to the station, Rod fed his edited video followed by the raw stuff. My biggest problem was getting a light set up for Rod. I didn't have enough extension cord to reach, but found several more coils in Dennis's satellite truck.

I let Rod work out the content of the live shot with Callum and the L.A. assignment manager, while I focused on getting the technical details perfect. We were on the air by five thirty. Rod stepped out of the camera's view almost immediately so we could show a live picture of the fire while he spoke. He gave updates on the evacuations and then tossed to the package he'd edited in the van. While tape was playing, he put the handkerchief back over his face.

My phone vibrated at one point during the half hour we were live, but I had to ignore the call. As soon as we were clear, I checked the caller ID. It had been the IO. I sent Rod back to the satellite truck to escape the smoke and rest his voice. When he was gone, I called the IO back.

"We're still trying to locate Arnaldo Bedolla," he said. "But Firefighter Bell is on her way to your location. Once she arrives, you can start the ride-along, or if you have more national live shots scheduled, she can wait."

"What do you mean, *national*?"

"I just saw Rod on CNN." The IO's voice was casual, as though this were no big deal. "I assumed you were doing the camerawork. Nice, by the way. I think you'll get some job offers out of this. Rod too, obviously."

"Obviously," I managed to say.

"If you want to wait, just let Bell know. You'll have to change positions in a couple hours anyway. They're coming through there to thin the trees."

We said good-bye, then I immediately dialed the station.

I was breathing hard through my handkerchief when Callum answered. "KJAY, we're on your side," he started, but then abruptly changed tone. "Listen here, you puke-face pervert, I've told you a thousand times to stop calling. We're not—"

"It's Lilly."

"Lilly? What's with the heavy breathing?"

"I'm mad and I'm wearing a handkerchief."

"Why are you wearing a handkerchief?"

"I'm outside and the smoke is bad." My voice rose. "Don't you want to know why I'm mad?"

"Not particularly. If the smoke is bad, why are you calling from outside?"

"Never mind that. How dare you put us on national TV without so much as a heads-up?"

I heard his chair creak and knew he was leaning back. "CNN wanted to dip in. It was the right call not to tell Rod. He would have been a nervous wreck."

I hadn't realized Callum knew about Rod's stage fright. It had been a surprise to me when I'd first discovered the truth, but then I'm usually the last to know.

"And don't get snippy with me," Callum continued. "You're in no position to play the outrage card. How about that promise you made me earlier tonight?"

I lowered my voice. "What do you mean?"

"Don't even try to lie." I heard the sound of his chair snapping forward. "I know you've been chasing the drowning and ignoring the biggest story of your career."

"Callum, I—"

"And you're dragging Rod right along with you, sabotaging his best chance to make it to a big market."

"I'd never sabotage Rod."

"People do stupid, dishonest things when they're scared of losing the person they love."

"Don't you get it, Callum? I've always known he was going to leave. It was over before it started." I paused to get control of myself. "But I don't want him to fail. I would never go behind his back to sabotage him."

Callum sighed. "You might not mean to, Lilly, but that's exactly what you've already done."

Fear quickly replaced anger. "What do you mean?"

"That four a.m. live shot you missed."

"What about it?"

"The *Today* show wanted Rod. They're three hours ahead, on East Coast time. Rod could have been doing live shots with Matt Lauer, but instead he was running around with you, following your freaky, contrary self off a cliff."

I didn't say anything.

Callum's tone softened. "For once, listen to me. I know you and I know Rod. For some reason, you've decided the drowning is your story. You're just the kind of crazy newshound who bites somebody's butt and doesn't let go. Even if the world is about to end up there, even if you could make your career by sticking with the fire, even if you lose your job, you will chase your story because that's who you are." He paused. "And because I know Rod, I know he's going to back your play."

"What's your point?"

"Whatever shenanigans you've got planned, don't mess up his chances. Don't ruin this opportunity for him. Don't make his being in love with you turn out to be a bad thing."

"I won't."

"Good."

For a moment neither of us said anything. Then Callum broke the silence. "You have another hit in twenty minutes. KBLA is taking it live, and probably CNN."

I ended the call and double-checked all the camera settings and connections. I walked back to the clearing. I passed the satellite truck and got my gear from my own live truck. I left the keys in the ignition. By the time I was done, a red SUV with the Santa Theresa Fire Department logo had pulled up. It had the same windshield-wiper eyes as my live truck. Bell got out. She wore a yellow firefighter's jacket over her black uniform.

"Thanks for coming." I quickly loaded my gear and then got in the passenger seat. "Let's go."

"What about Rod?"

"He has to stay and do a live shot."

Instead of doubling back the way she'd come, Bell drove down the other side of the mountain, toward the fire. The trees blocked most of our view, which was fine by me.

I dialed Rod's cell phone.

It took several rings, but he answered. "Sorry. Dennis and I fell asleep." I heard him yawn. "Do we have another hit?"

"You do. In five minutes. I'm on my way to interview Jessica's brother and then hopefully Arnaldo Bedolla."

"What?"

"I knew you wouldn't let me go alone, so I left without you."

Bell glanced at me in surprise, but quickly put her eyes back on the road.

"Lilly." The grogginess vanished from Rod's voice. "Come back. I mean it."

"I'll only be gone for an hour or so. Dennis can handle things."

"This is not okay, Lilly."

"I know you're mad," I said into the phone. "But I also know I'm right. You're the only reporter in a sixty-mile radius and you have a functioning live signal. We have a responsibility to broadcast the fire. KJAY is counting on us." I paused. "And more than that, it's good for your career. We both know you're going to get job offers after this."

"I don't want offers if it means we'll end up living in different cities."

I took a deep breath and said it. "You don't need to use me as an excuse anymore. You haven't been nervous going live once tonight. The stage fright is gone."

He didn't answer so I said, "We'll talk about it when I get back." I hung up.

There was an uneasy moment between Bell and myself. In the background two portable scanners played from where they were attached to the dashboard. The only light came from the SUV's headlights on the dirt road ahead. Several times Bell looked as if she was about to say something, but then stopped herself.

Finally I crossed my arms. "I'm sorry for spewing my personal life all over you."

"It's okay."

"It's not very professional. I usually do a better job of keeping my personal and work life separate."

She didn't take her eyes off the road. "You know how hard it is for a man to become a firefighter?"

I was taken aback by the abrupt change in subject, but managed to say, "Hard."

"You know how hard it is for a woman?"

"I'm guessing harder."

She smiled and nodded. "I was an intelligence officer in the navy. I didn't believe anything could be more difficult than my military training. I was wrong. I flunked out halfway through my first time at the fire academy."

"But you made it eventually."

"On my third try." Her smile softened into pride. "My point is, I know what it's like to hide the mushy personal stuff because you're afraid male coworkers will think less of you. But sometimes worrying too much about that stuff only makes it a bigger deal."

"It's not just the mushy stuff that I'm afraid people will see."

"Then what?"

I tried to turn away and look out the window, but it was too dark to see anything. "If people know I'm happy now, then if it ends, all they'll see is a sad girl with a broken heart, and not their boss who's going to kick their butt if they're late again."

"Maybe it won't end."

I didn't answer.

A few moments later, a tall chain-link fence appeared in our headlights. We turned and joined another dirt road running parallel with the fence below and the ridge of the mountain above. A bulldozer had already come through tearing out anything flammable in a line along the side of the road. Hopefully the firebreak would hold and protect the antennas on the ridge.

I pointed to the fence on Bell's side of the car. "Is that the nature preserve?"

"Yes. It's their western property line."

Since the IO hadn't located Arnaldo Bedolla, I had to choose between visiting Bonny Hazel inside the nature preserve or Jessica's brother where his hand crew was working in the valley. I easily chose Bonny Hazel.

The closer I got to seeing Brad Egan again, the less I wanted to do it. I didn't like the way he'd talked about Jessica on camera, and I was angry that he hadn't done more to help her after their mother died. But mostly my reluctance stemmed from guilt that he'd been blaming Jessica for vandalizing the sign. When I saw Brad again, I'd have to tell him the truth.

As if sensing my reluctance, Bell said, "Why do you even need to talk to Brad Egan again? There are lots of other Hotshots you could interview."

"I think his sister was murdered. I need to tell him and get his help with the police."

Bell's head whipped from the road to me and then back again. "Really?"

"Really. I'll shoot what I can of the fire, but that's not my primary reason for taking this ride-along. I'm working the drowning." I looked at her. "Is that going to be a problem?"

She shrugged. "The IO said to help you however I could. It's between you and your boss what story you shoot."

"Thank you." I guess it was also between me and my boss if I defied him and ended up getting fired. "How long do we have? When is the blowup happening?"

She chuckled. "We're not scheduling it."

"But it's going to happen, right?"

"No one knows, but late this afternoon will be the most dangerous time. The National Weather Service is predicting freakishly strong winds then, which is also when humidity will be almost nonexistent and the temperature will be at its highest. You add all that to the fire reaching the foothills and you get a potential blowup."

I took out a map and, in the light coming off the dashboard, tried to see where the valley and mountain met. "Why the foothills? Why can't it blow up anywhere?"

"The upward slope of the mountain and the shape of the terrain could create a chimney. The speed of a blowup is completely unpredictable. It could be sixty miles an hour or only five. Or it could never blow up. There's no way to predict." She smiled. "So I prefer to be optimistic and think it won't happen at all."

"When my life is at stake, I prefer pessimism." I also prefer pessimism when nothing's at stake, but I kept that part to myself.

As we neared Highway 55, Bell slowed the car. This was the same highway Rod and I had used to climb through Tilly Heights.

Bell and I were just catching it on the other side of the mountain. From here it continued straight down and into Terrill Valley. It actually went all the way out to Mojave when there wasn't a massive wildfire blocking the road.

Bell waited to make sure there was no cross traffic, then turned down the highway. The red horizon filled the windshield. I couldn't help but think there was something very wrong with anyone who chooses to drive toward a view like that.

We hadn't gone far before Bell slowed. On our right was a clearing with several shuttered fruit stands advertising local citrus and honey.

Bell pointed to a dirt road across the highway where there was a break in the nature preserve's fence. "This is the only way in to Bonny Hazel. Since the house is actually on the nature preserve, it's been that much harder to get equipment in and out."

She made the turn. It was a relief to be back inside the forest and not looking straight down into the burning valley. About a quarter mile in, the road forked. Our headlights illuminated a padlocked gate on the right. On the left, a pretty wood sign with an arrow said BONNY HAZEL.

Bell followed the sign, and a quarter mile later we emerged at a huge swath of cleared ground. It was as though a giant circle had been stamped out in the middle of the forest. Harsh work lights illuminated row after row of tree stumps. I guessed many of them had once been the house's namesake hazelnut trees.

The ground between the stumps was black from a controlled burn. This was another way to remove flammable material—actually set a fire on purpose so there was nothing left to burn when the wildfire arrived. Several Hotshots walked back and forth checking for flare-ups. The still-smoldering areas glowed against the dark landscape, and thick smoke hung in the air.

At the center of the blighted land sat a large, two-story house with all its lights on.

We parked in front of the long front porch with several other cars. We pulled our handkerchiefs up over our noses and mouths and got out. I gagged, but then began adjusting to the smell of freshly cut timber and burnt grasses.

I noticed for the first time that the driveway continued past the house and looped around to another structure some fifty yards away.

Bell handed me a yellow firefighter's jacket like the one she wore. "Put this on."

It was still early in the day and the temperature hadn't risen, but the jacket looked bulky and hot. "I'd rather not."

As if on cue, a warm gust of air blew ash into our faces.

"On second thought . . ." I put on the stiff fabric. It was a little big for me—the sleeves hung down to the tips of my fingers—but to my surprise the fabric was fairly light.

Bell gestured to three fire engines in the distance. Work lights running off portable generators lit crews loading cut trees and other debris onto a huge truck. "I need to check in with the superintendent before I do anything else. I know you said the fire's not your primary focus, but do you want to interview any of the crew?"

I told her I doubted it, but wanted to keep my options open.

After she left, I glanced up at the house. The white wood planks covering the house's exterior were coated with ash and soot. I recognized a screened-in porch at one end of the house. Above it on the second floor was a glassed-in porch, which probably had spectacular views of the valley. The house itself was even bigger than the Fitzgeralds' McMansion, but felt more personal. Above the front door was another wood sign, reading WELCOME TO BONNY HAZEL.

I noticed an open trunk on a nearby Prius. I decided to take a quick look. It was full of plastic containers roughly the size of shoe boxes. Air holes were punched in the lids and each contained a lizard—I mean salamander. I felt a twinge of regret that Rod wasn't with me.

Only a tiny amount of ash had accumulated inside the trunk, so it probably hadn't been left open for long.

I heard a noise and then a woman walked around the side of the house.

She crossed into the light coming from the front windows. She had long, wavy gray hair and carried more of the plastic boxes.

I thought there was something familiar about the woman, so I stepped forward to intercept her. "Can I ask you a few questions?"

"No." She had a bohemian air, but still managed to look elegant in a long skirt and peasant blouse. "I don't live here and I'm about to leave." She continued past me to the Prius with the open trunk.

"Season." The cry came from a girl running out the front door and was directed at the woman. The girl had pronounced the name like the word *season*, but I remembered a more exotic spelling from the Green Seed website.

The nonprofit's former executive director had spelled her name Ceasonne. Even with the handkerchief covering most of her face, I now recognized her from one of the pictures I'd looked at online. She'd been wearing an orange sarong at a black-tie fund-raiser. Her husband, in a tuxedo, had been the one with his arm around Jessica.

"I just checked my e-mail, and it's horrible." The girl who'd run out of the house had blond hair and wore shorts and a tank top.

Ceasonne loaded the boxes into the trunk. "Cathy, I told you not to get on the Internet. You upset a lot of people and it's going to take time to die down."

The girl came into the light. Cathy didn't wear a handkerchief and I easily recognized her from Dennis's video. Her sound bite had gone national, then viral. This was the girl who'd been cavalier about putting firefighters' lives in danger.

"But it's so awful," she said. "There's even a Facebook page about how terrible I am, and it's got over three hundred thousand fans." She started crying. "And I clicked to look and my grandma is one of them."

Ceasonne made a few final adjustments to the boxes in the trunk. "That's why I told you not to get on the Internet. Did you think I was making it up?"

Two more young women had followed Cathy out of the house. One of them hurried to Cathy's side. "I'm sorry about your grandma, but I'm sure it was an accident."

"That's what my mom says." Cathy wiped her eyes with the back of her hand. "I guess Ma-Ma thought she was liking me, but instead she liked the page that hated me."

"I'm sorry to interrupt." I took a few steps so I stood between Ceasonne and the girls. "But I really need to speak with you. It's about a woman named Jessica Egan."

Ceasonne froze, about to shut the trunk. For a moment everyone was silent, then she slammed it closed. "This isn't the best time. Can I give you my business card?"

"No. I'd really like to talk now."

"It's terrible." Cathy sounded emotional, but I wasn't sure if that was sadness for Jessica or residue from Ma-Ma's Facebook accident. "Farris told us what happened. I can't believe it. I was just down at the lake taking samples on Tuesday."

I straightened. "Do the people who live here have access to a boat?"

Cathy glanced at the others before answering. "Dr. Polignac keeps one. We use it to study the Terrill salamander." She gestured away from the house. "The creek here used to be its only known habitat, but now it's migrated to the lake."

I looked at the young women. All three were tall, thin, and blond. "And you all live here with Dr. Polignac?"

They nodded. "We're undergrads at UCLA," one said. "But we're doing internships this summer in molecular biology."

I looked at Ceasonne. "And you?"

"I live in Los Angeles, where I'm going now." She pointed to the girls. "Are your cars packed and ready?" All three said they were. "Then we need to get on the road."

"Wait, please," I said to her. "I need to talk to you about Jessica."

Ceasonne reached into her car and pulled out a purse. She found a business card and walked back around to the rear to give it to me. "Call me, but if you're looking for Jessica's next of kin, I believe her father lives in Elizabeth. He's probably the one you should talk to."

The business card said CEASONNE POLIGNAC, EXECUTIVE DIRECTOR, ART FOR LIFE. There was an L.A. address and phone number.

I started to tell her I wasn't with the police, but stopped myself. "Do you know if Jessica had a shoulder injury?"

She walked back around to the driver's side. "A bad one. Rotator cuff I think."

"Do you know if she still had the injury when she died?"

"I assume so." She pointed to the front door. The mad scientist rushed out with an armload of clear plastic boxes. "Ask my husband. He's seen her much more recently." Her tone implied he wouldn't be her husband for much longer.

FIFTEEN

The mad scientist hurried down the porch steps. "Ceasonne, wait." He wore a lab coat, but his legs were bare. For a moment I feared he wasn't wearing anything underneath. Then the white fabric fluttered and I saw a pair of khaki shorts.

Ceasonne pointed to the three girls. "We're leaving." She got in her car and slammed the door shut. Cathy hurried to a loaded Jeep while the other two girls got inside an SUV.

"Wait." The mad scientist ran around to Ceasonne's window. Just like in Dennis's video, his graying hair stood up in places. "Darling, I know you're angry, but I can't leave. I have to protect my research."

I had a hard time believing that the mad scientist, with his ridiculous accent and hysterical tone, was the same debonair man in a tuxedo who'd been in the photo with Ceasonne and Jessica.

Ceasonne rolled down her window. "I'm not angry, dear. Do whatever you think is best." She started to roll her window back up, but he tried to stop her.

"Wait. I need you to take more samples with you."

"All full, dear." She finished raising the window and backed up.

The mad scientist ran to the SUV. He was able to pass the boxes to the two girls. All three cars backed up in preparation to leave.

I approached him. "Can I talk to you?"

He looked at my yellow jacket. "I have rights. You can't force a free man from his lawful property." He stormed back into the house.

I started to go after him, but stopped when I heard a voice.

"Wait." A young man ran around the side of the house chasing the departing cars. "Please, stop."

The final car's red brake lights came on. The young man ran to catch up. Although he wore a handkerchief over his face, I recognized his ponytail and glasses.

Cathy opened the driver's-side door.

"Can you take these for me?" He passed her two laptops. "Just leave them at the lab and I'll pick them up later."

"Of course, but I don't feel right leaving you here. Promise you won't wait for Dr. Polignac."

"I promise." He gestured to the Hotshots working nearby. "I honestly never thought he'd hold out this long. It's crazy."

Cathy glanced ahead. The other two cars were already gone. "I'm sorry. I have to go."

They said good-bye and she drove away.

The young man was walking back when I intercepted him. "Are you Farris?"

He stopped. "Yes?"

"Are you also an intern here?"

"No. I'm a doctoral candidate at UCLA." He looked offended. "I have a paid fellowship with Dr. Polignac."

"Is Green Seed sponsoring your research?"

He gestured to the house. "Only in that they're letting us use this property. We get logistical support from the University of California and are funded by private donors." He looked at my yellow jacket. "Are you with the Forest Service or the local fire department?"

"Neither." I didn't pause to elaborate. "Did you go to Fitzgerald's in Tilly Heights yesterday evening and ask about Jessica Egan?"

He continued to look confused for a few moments longer, but then nodded. "Is that why you're here? I still can't believe she's dead. It's so sudden." He glanced toward the house. "Do you mind if we talk while I pack. I still have a lot to do before I can leave."

I looked for Bell in the distance, but didn't see her.

Farris didn't wait for my answer. He jumped up the steps to the porch and entered the house. I followed. By the time I'd shut the door behind us, he was halfway up the stairs to the second floor.

I glanced into the dining room as I followed. A dirty plate and utensils from a hastily abandoned breakfast sat at the head of a long table. Next to it was a rifle.

I continued up the stairs. "Why is there a gun on the dining room table?"

"That's just Dr. Polignac being melodramatic." Farris went down a hallway and into a room on the right. "He wants to prove he can defend the house if the authorities try to force us to leave. Don't worry. It's not loaded."

I followed him into the bedroom. The room had nice pine floors, but the generic furniture looked as if it had come from a dorm. Farris had lowered the handkerchief and was in the middle of redoing his ponytail.

"Are you the only grad student here?"

"The other two evacuated yesterday, and you just saw the interns make their escape." He finished the ponytail and crossed to a wood dresser. He opened the top drawer and carried an armload of clothing to a large, open suitcase on the bed.

"Who here has access to the boat down at the lake?"

He paused on his way back to the dresser, glanced at me, then continued. "I guess we all do. The key is in a drawer downstairs. Why on earth do you want to know that?"

"Did anyone use it a couple hours ago? Maybe between one thirty and two thirty in the morning?"

"We were all asleep."

"Could someone have snuck out?"

"I suppose so. But why on earth would they?" He looked genuinely baffled, but I kept thinking about the predatory glance he'd given Cathy in the viral video. There was clearly more to him than the nice-guy image he projected.

"When did you last talk to Jessica?" I said.

He returned to the dresser and emptied another drawer. "I called her Wednesday morning because Dr. Polignac was refusing to evacuate."

"Why didn't you call his wife in L.A.?"

"I did, but Ceasonne said telling him to leave would only make him dig in further. She wanted us to pretend like we didn't care." The suitcase was full, so he zipped it up. "She refused to drive up so I called Jessica instead."

I remembered the way Polignac had his hand on Jessica's back in the photo. "Were they particularly close?"

"Dr. Polignac's heavily involved with Green Seed and Jessica worked there." Farris added a laptop bag to the pile of things by the door.

I noticed a sketchpad sitting on the desk. The light coming from a desk lamp highlighted it. The pad was open to a pencil drawing of the famed Terrill salamander. For the first time I didn't think it looked creepy.

"Did you do this?"

"Uh-huh." He continued to pack. "I got my undergraduate degree in biology with a minor in scientific illustration. I try to keep it up."

I leaned in. The salamander's eyes appeared thoughtful and wise. Its body, which I usually thought of as slithery, looked regal as it rested on four short legs. "Wow, you're really good."

Suddenly he was standing behind me. "I do my best. It's important not to let your own ego get in the way. You have to bring out the soul of the animal. It's really important to try and connect on a spiritual level with nature."

He reached around me so he could gesture to the sketchpad. His body came into contact with mine—separated by lots of clothing, but nonetheless, ick. "I can see you must have a deep connection yourself."

"Are you hitting on me?" It seemed impossible given how rough I must have looked after my dive in the lake, but that had definitely been the vibe.

He jumped back. His face flushed as he straightened his glasses. "No. Why would you say that?"

"Because it seemed like you were hitting on me." I set the sketchpad back down. "Did you ever sleep with Jessica Egan?"

"What?" His mouth gaped. "I mean, no. Of course not."

"What about Dr. Polignac? Did they have a relationship?"

"Why would you even ask that?"

"It's a simple question. If you have to think about it, then the answer is probably yes."

"The answer is no." He opened the closet. "Dr. Polignac is a shameless flirt, but he loves Ceasonne."

"Then why has Jessica visited Bonny Hazel so much this past year?"

He shook his head. "She didn't. I've had the fellowship for ten months and Jessica only visited once." He added a guitar case to the pile. "And she was abrasive and unpleasant on that visit. She threatened to kick us out if we damaged the house or trespassed outside of this small area designated for research. . . . Why are you looking at me like that?"

"Because Jessica was seen shopping with members of your group."

He shook his head. "I don't think that's possible."

"Could she have been visiting and you didn't know? Maybe she was spending time with a member of your group and keeping it secret."

"Dr. Polignac and I are the only two men here." He hesitated. "Although he sleeps out in his motor home, so I suppose I don't know what he's doing at night." Farris disappeared into the closet. "The only thing I really know absolutely is that I wasn't sleeping with Jessica." I couldn't see him, but his voice sounded snide. "Jessica wasn't my type."

"Why not?"

He emerged with an armload of camping equipment. "I volunteered at the Green Seed offices in Venice. I thought it might give me an edge for getting the fellowship."

He slung a collapsed tent over his shoulder by a carrying strap. "I saw Jessica a couple times a week around the building. She was obsessed with her job. No time for fun." He grinned. "Not my type." He picked up the suitcase and sleeping bag, then exited.

I grabbed the guitar case and followed. "Are Cathy and the other interns more your type?"

"What's that supposed to mean?" He paused on the steps and looked back.

"They're all young, pretty, blond, and stupid. Whoever is selecting the interns isn't being very subtle about their preferences."

"It's Dr. Polignac, but regardless of how it looked in that TV clip, Cathy's not stupid. She scored a perfect 2400 on her SATs and she's at UCLA on a full scholarship." He turned and continued down the steps.

I followed him outside and raised the handkerchief back over my face. It was still mostly dark, but the coming sunrise had begun to lighten the sky.

Farris was opening the trunk of his own Prius when Bell approached.

"Lilly, the superintendent is cleared to go on camera, if you would like to interview him." She recognized Farris. "Good to see you again. I'm glad you've changed your mind and decided to evacuate." She continued past. "I'm going to talk with your professor and see if I can convince him to evacuate as well."

After she'd gone around the side of the building, Farris looked at me. "Wait a minute. She was the one escorting the photographer yesterday."

I set down the guitar case. "There's been a misunderstanding." I lifted my official press pass from where it hung around my neck. I angled it so light from the house would hit it. "I'm a photographer from KJAY in Bakersfield."

He stepped back. "So that's why you asked about Jessica's sex life. You're doing some sort of sleazy tabloid story."

"Not at all. If I were doing a sleazy piece I'd have sandbagged you on camera." I laughed. "Surprising someone while they're on camera is the only way to be sleazy. Warning them in advance ruins it."

"Well, whatever you have planned, leave us out of it." He started back into the house.

I raised the handkerchief back up over my face, then followed Bell around the side of the building.

Even before I cleared the corner, I heard the mad scientist shouting, "You have destroyed this beautiful place. You have committed this crime against nature, and now you suggest I abandon my research like garbage."

Bell stood on a large brick patio lit by a single bulb above the back door. "I suggest you not die in a fire."

Dr. Sebastian Polignac, aka the mad scientist, saw me and pointed. "I don't care how many storm troopers you bring, I won't be forced out."

I've been called a lot of things, but never a storm trooper. "I'm with KJAY in Bakersfield. I'd like to ask you some questions."

"What?" His accent got even thicker. "You vultures. You evil scavengers of pain and humiliation, descending like carrion crows to feed on the dead flesh of humanity."

"I think there's been a mistake. I'm a shooter, not a reporter." I made Bell laugh, but Polignac didn't get my inside joke. "Sorry. I'm here about Jessica Egan."

His accent became unintelligible. I think he said something like "Is there no blank you won't blank for your own blank? The poor blank's blank is blank blank and you pick over it like blank blank."

This was a complete waste of time. The man could confess and I probably wouldn't know. I had nothing to lose, so why not follow his wife's advice to Farris.

"You're absolutely right. Don't talk to the media. Don't answer questions. It's the worst thing you could do."

He looked as if he was about to yell something, but then paused. "Why?"

"You'll say things that you'll regret later. Do not talk to anyone from the media."

He stepped toward me. "I'm perfectly capable of deciding what I'll say and to whom I'll say it."

"I'm sure you are, but the bottom line is, even though I don't have a camera, and only want to talk to you off the record, you still shouldn't agree."

His spine straightened. He adjusted the lab coat. "As it happens, I have much to say about how our rights are being trampled." He gestured to the structure in the distance. "I have work to do, but you're welcome to come with me. I would be very happy to tell you all about the obscene injustices committed here." He turned to Bell. "You're not invited."

Instead of taking the driveway from the front of the house, he walked straight through the field of charred earth and tree stumps toward the other structure.

Bell joined me. "What just happened?"

"Whatever you tell him to do, he'll want to do the opposite."

"Who says?"

"His wife."

"Oh." She nodded and drew out the syllable. "Good luck, then. I'll be in the car, out of the smoke."

I took the driveway so Polignac got there quite a bit before me. The structure was a modular classroom like the ones schools use when they outgrow their facilities. A large directional antenna rose from the roof. The creek was nearby, and someone had strung netting from one bank to the other. There were also buckets and other containers on the shore.

A motor home was parked to the side of the building. I glanced back toward the house. Before the trees were cleared, it would have been impossible to see the house from here, and vice versa.

Several Hotshots walked back and forth, looking for flare-ups in the controlled burn, but I didn't see Polignac.

I walked up the wooden wheelchair ramp to the modular classroom. The door was ajar, so I entered.

Bright fluorescent lights lit several lab tables and metal stools. White cabinets and a black counter lined two of the walls.

"Hello?" I called.

Polignac's voice came from a room in the back. "In here, please."

I crossed the lab and entered a small room with two computers and a printer. The computer monitors were big, old-fashioned cathode monsters. The dated technology went well with the fake-wood paneling and metal folding chairs in this room. I kept going and reached the back.

The mad scientist was working at a table near several refrigerators with glass doors. Inside were rows of rectangular flasks lying flat on stainless-steel racks.

"Excuse me if I continue working." His legs and the lower half of the lab coat were both black from walking through the charred field. "These tissue cultures are extremely important."

I glanced around the rest of the room. The walls were covered with bulletin boards. A large machine with a white body sat on a second table. It looked like an advanced microscope and was hooked up to a new computer.

"What exactly is your field of study?" I said.

"Comparative regenerative biology." His head turned. The smile on his face indicated I had hit on one of his favorite topics. "I'm studying tissue and organ regeneration in the Terrill salamander and its potential use in humans."

"Wait, what?"

He opened one of the refrigerators and carefully transferred one of the flasks to a Styrofoam cooler on the table. "Salamanders possess the ability to regenerate limbs after injury. The Terrill salamander does it twice as fast as other species."

"Are you actually trying to transfer that ability to human beings?"

"I'm isolating the genes responsible for the proteins, and the triggers." He continued transferring the flasks. "My partner at UCLA is growing transformed human cell lines containing the salamander regeneration genes. One day we may be able to cure any number of diseases."

For a moment I was just awed by the possibilities. Then I realized what the natural by-product of his research would be. "Wait a minute. Are you killing salamanders?"

"It is an inevitable side effect of the process, yes." The small cooler was full, so he closed the Styrofoam lid. "We're also amputating limbs and watching the speed at which they regenerate. We must determine if the salamanders down at Lake Elizabeth are regenerating at the same pace. There might be an environmental factor."

He picked up the cooler and carefully carried it out of the room.

I followed. "But Jessica Egan never would have approved of that. She was a vegan and in PETA."

He stopped and turned around. At some point he'd flattened his hair. That combined with the ebbing of his accent and reasoned tone had transformed the mad scientist into the dapper man in the tuxedo. "You knew Jessica?"

I nodded. "She grew up here. We knew each other before she moved to Los Angeles."

"Oh, my dear. You should have said something." His voice sounded gentle and sympathetic. "It is a terrible thing to lose a friend. I'm so sorry."

His accent was actually pleasing when almost dormant. I decided attention from a brilliant older man might turn a lot of young women's heads. It would certainly be more pleasant than Farris's creepy come-on.

"You have my condolences." He turned, still holding the cooler, then continued toward the front of the building.

"We weren't exactly friends." I followed him. "But I know Jessica never would have approved of killing animals."

We passed back into the lab. He stopped at the outside door and turned around. "You knew Jessica when she was still young and idealistic. If only we could all stay that way."

"Are you saying Jessica compromised her beliefs, because I'm not buying it."

"She remained very vocally opposed to Green Seed's support of my research until the day she attained the ability to actually stop it." He backed up and used his weight to push the lever down and open the door.

"That doesn't make any sense." I held the door open for him, then shut it behind us. I raised my handkerchief and followed him down the ramp.

He waited for me at the bottom. "My wife, Ceasonne, used to be executive director of Green Seed. It is because I alerted her to the potential destruction of this species, and its potential scientific value, that they moved to block the plans for development here thirteen years ago."

He began walking and I joined him.

He stepped carefully and kept the cooler level. "After we raised the funds to purchase the land, Jessica learned the unfortunate side effects of my research. She lobbied Ceasonne and the board to deny me access to the property."

"Wait a minute. Green Seed raised the funds to buy the land from the McClellans because of your research, and then Jessica turns around and asks your own wife to deny you access? You must have been irate."

"No." He smiled fondly. "She never had a chance of succeeding, so it was very easy to look kindly on, what was for her, a moral stand. And knowing Jessica, you had to admire how strong she was in her beliefs." We reached the side of the building and continued toward the RV.

"But she took over when your wife left," I said. "Couldn't she have stopped you then?"

"When Jessica became executive director, she dropped her objections."

I was losing patience. "But why?"

"Because it's easy to stand outside and complain and criticize, but once Jessica had the power, she also had the responsibility. She didn't approve of exploiting animals, but at the same time, she wanted to cure disease."

We stopped at the RV. I reached up and opened the side door for him. He climbed the steps and disappeared inside. I followed and shut the door behind me.

The small interior looked like a hoarder's secret cave. All sorts of equipment and materials from the lab were haphazardly piled inside.

Polignac set the cooler down on the kitchen counter and opened the refrigerator. He checked the temperature on a digital thermometer, then began transferring the flasks from the cooler. "Part of getting older is understanding that a certain amount of compromise is necessary in life. Sadly, Jessica had to grow up."

I'd never thought of growing up as a sad thing. The years I'd spent being reckless and irresponsible embarrassed me now. Growing up seemed like a moral obligation. "Are you equating Jessica's commitment to animal rights with some kind of youthful folly?"

He finished the transfer and shut the door. "No. I'm equating her commitment to animal rights at the expense of everything else with youthful folly. But as silly as it was, there was something wonderful in her passion, and it made me a little sad to see it diminish."

He glanced over his shoulder. A stack of boxes blocked the aisle behind him. "Excuse me." He climbed over the boxes, then disappeared into the bedroom.

"Farris told me that you usually sleep out here," I yelled. "Why, when there's so much room inside the house?"

"There are also students inside the house." He climbed back over carrying a second cooler. He knocked a roll of toilet paper off the kitchen counter while trying to pass. "I prefer it out here where I'm not disturbed by their music, or television, or impulsive desire to bake cookies at one in the morning."

We exited the RV. Just as Polignac was shutting the door, we both heard the sound of a helicopter approaching. We looked up into the gray sky and saw the Chinook pass carrying a basket of water.

He came down the steps and joined me.

"Why was Jessica visiting here so much?"

He shook his head. "She didn't visit. I saw her at the Green Seed offices in Venice on occasion. During the school year I still teach a class once a week at UCLA so I must split my time."

"Does your wife split her time?"

"Sadly no." He glanced at the helicopter as it passed from view. "Her work keeps her in Los Angeles."

The door to the lab opened and Farris walked out. "There you are. I've got the rest of the—" He saw me and froze. "Don't talk to her. She's a reporter doing a sleazy story. She thinks you and Jessica were sleeping together."

The mad scientist reasserted himself. "I'll talk to whomever I choose."

He then turned to me and spoke in a flirty voice. "I appreciate the compliment, but, alas, I was not sleeping with Jessica."

Farris abandoned any attempt to control Polignac and switched to me. "If you don't leave, I'll call Green Seed. This is private property and they can have the police force you out."

"Don't worry. I'm going." I started toward the driveway.

"But I don't want you to go." Dr. Polignac took several steps after me. "I haven't even told you how our rights have been trampled."

"Don't worry. I promise to take your word for it."

Farris insisted on escorting me back to Bell's car. I paused before getting in. "A word of advice: I'd do what his wife says. The more you tell him to evacuate, the less likely he'll be to actually do it."

SIXTEEN

W e drove back out the dirt road and exited the nature preserve across from the fruit stands. The IO still hadn't been able to locate Arnaldo Bedolla, so I'd asked Bell to take me to see Jessica's brother at the fire line. We turned and continued down Highway 55. The burning valley still appeared in Bell's dirty windshield, but the sun had risen and we'd returned to the twilight that passed as daylight.

A plane flew into the view. It was probably the first of the morning. Red fire retardant streaked in a trail behind it. The mixture of water, dye, and chemicals scattered downward, where it was swallowed by a flaming section of trees.

I looked at Bell. "We are safe, right?"

"We're fine, but if I say it's time to go, you don't ask questions. You run for the car." She managed to glance away from the view ahead. "Understood?"

"Understood." I glanced down as we crossed an overpass. Even in the reduced light I could see the creek below was barely flowing. It had looked fine at Bonny Hazel. Had Dr. Polignac and his minions done something to disrupt the flow while researching salamanders?

The wind increased the closer we got to the valley. Sudden gusts blew ash and burning embers like a light rain. My apprehension also increased—and not just because we were getting closer to the fire. How would Egan react when I told him the truth?

I turned to Bell. "Bedolla had a diving partner—a young college-age kid. His family owns a farm or ranch over here. They were trying to evacuate, but they had a lot of horses and cattle and stuff."

She gestured to the side of the highway that didn't belong to the nature preserve. "There's a ranch not far ahead. Other than the group at Bonny Hazel, they're the last residents on this side of the mountain."

If Bedolla had compromised the autopsy, Pukey the Kid might have seen something. Pukey even being there—a young, inexperienced diver instead of a trained member of Search and Rescue—could have been something Bedolla orchestrated. "Let's stop. If it's not the same family, I'll interview them about the fire."

The pine forest began to thin near the foothills and then ended. We approached a turnoff with a large, old iron gate. It was open so we went ahead and turned onto the dirt road.

I tensed. Black smoke blew from over the next hill.

Bell saw it too. "Don't worry. That's probably just a controlled burn to remove the dry fuel around the property. They did the same thing up at Bonny Hazel."

"Does that work? I mean, if the fire comes through here, it won't really skip over the house just because the land around it has been cleared, will it?"

"Sometimes. I've seen perfectly intact structures surrounded by miles of scorched earth."

We followed the road as it rose over the hill. A farmhouse, barn, and several outbuildings appeared before the red horizon.

As we neared, I saw an engine crew pumping water from a nearby pond and giving cover to a team of Hotshots managing the controlled burn. We parked and got out. The blistering wind slapped my face. I inhaled an ember and had to bend over coughing. When I'd gotten my breath back, I yanked the handkerchief up over my nose and mouth.

Bell left to speak with the superintendent. I heard noise on the other side of the barn. I took my camera from the vehicle and walked around the building.

Two men held the reins of a nervous horse. They both wore handkerchiefs, but I recognized one as Pukey the Kid. The other man was older and I guessed he was Pukey's father. They were leading the horse to one of two open trailers. The horse wore a mask to protect its eyes, but neighed and pulled back each time the wind gusted.

I threw the camera on my shoulder. I cranked up the iris to adjust for the reduced light, then hit record.

Just as the horse took its first step onto the ramp, a shower of sparks pelted us all. The horse reared. The father lost his rein and fell flat on his back. Hooves crashed into the dirt.

"Get her, get her." An old man came running from the barn.

The kid dug his bootheels into the dirt. His arms strained against the power of a blind, panicked animal six times his weight.

The horse screamed as it reared again. The father rolled away. The horse's hooves smashed the ground where his head had been moments earlier.

"Hold on." The old man grabbed the other rein.

The father tried to stand. He was shaky and winded from the fall, but rushed to take the reins from the old man. "I got her, Dad."

The three of them forced the horse into the trailer and slammed it shut.

I turned off the camera and walked toward them. As I neared, the grandfather took a rag from his back pocket and dabbed at his eyes. "That's all we need today. You getting yourself killed." He said it as a rebuke, but the old man was wiping away more than sweat from his eyes.

The father put a hand on his own son's shoulder. "Good work, Pete. You probably saved my life."

"Your rope was bad, Dad. That's all." The young man showed none of the boasting or jockeying for attention that was present at our first meeting. Probably because building up his own accomplishment would diminish his father.

I felt regret for how snidely I'd judged him at the lake. As awesome a nickname as Pukey the Kid was, I was going to have to retire it. "Hello," I said loudly.

It took a moment, but Pete recognized me. "Hey. You're the reporter lady."

"Sort of. I'm a shooter." I gestured to the closed trailer. "I recorded you with the horse. Is it okay if I interview you too?"

His smile under the handkerchief faded. He glanced at his father, who'd already gone back to work spreading wood shavings on the floor of the second trailer. "I don't know. We're leaving as soon as my mom gets back."

"Running away is more like it." Grandpa took off toward the house. "Eighty-five years I've been here and more fires than I can count. Never left. Never left once . . ." His rant petered out as he got farther from us.

"Dad, wait." Pete's father started after the old man, but stopped when he saw a woman approaching on horseback. He pointed at his son. "Here she is. If there's anything else you want in the house, get it now. We may not be able to make another trip." Pete's father turned and ran to the house.

Pete hurried to meet the horse and rider.

I followed. "Do I have permission to videotape you?"

He reached out for the horse's reins. "I guess so." He held the horse steady while the woman dismounted. "How'd it go?" he said to her.

I put the camera back on my shoulder and started recording.

"As well as it could, under the circumstances." She wore a handkerchief and goggles. "I got them down to the lower pasture, at least."

She saw me so I said, "I'm from KJAY in Bakersfield. What are your plans for your animals?"

She lowered her goggles and handkerchief. "I'm getting this one into the barn."

I followed as she led the horse inside.

I immediately adjusted my camera settings for the different light while she and Pete removed the saddle. The smell of hay and animals inside the old wooden structure almost overpowered the fire.

"Can you talk a little bit about your plans?" I turned the camera on the woman. "And where your animals are going?"

She began walking the horse up and down the length of the barn. "We've got three horses at the shelter in Elizabeth already and we'll drop off these last two now." She pointed at Pete. "Go make sure the trailer's ready."

Pete ran out.

"What about the cattle?" I said.

She turned the horse at the end of the barn and began walking back toward us. "We got about a dozen out, but there's no more time. We have to go."

"What's going to happen to the ones left behind?"

"I don't know, but leaving them is one of the hardest things I've ever had to do."

"You're talking like they're dead already." Pete had returned and overheard her. "But they'll be okay in the lower pasture. There's marshland down there." He turned to me and I instinctively swung the camera to him. "Animals survive all the time if they can make it to water. One of the firefighters told me."

"I hope you're right," Pete's mom said, bringing the horse forward. "Except with the drought this year, there's less water coming down the creek feeding the marshes."

They loaded the horse into the second trailer. Once the door was secured, Pete's mom pointed at him. "Check the trucks again. Make sure everything is secure. I'm going to check the barn one last time."

I followed her back inside. "Do you know what happened to the McClellans who used to own all the land on the other side of the highway?"

She stopped and looked at me. "The kids were grown and moved away long before old Mr. McClellan sold everything. I think he moved to San Diego." She went back to checking the stalls. "Probably better that way. He didn't have to stay and see the weirdo living at Bonny Hazel now with his own personal harem."

She joined me at the doors and shut off the overhead lights. "We may be a little gossipy around here, but there are too many stories about those people's shenanigans for it all to be untrue."

Her husband appeared in the doorway. "I got Grandpa in the truck. Let's go."

We all went back outside.

The mother stopped. "The vet papers. I left them by the door." She started toward the house.

"No." Pete started running. "Let me get it. Grandpa needs your help."

I ran after the young man. I was slowed by the camera. By the time I caught up, he'd already gone inside. He picked up some papers by the door and then hesitated. He glanced around the living room. The lights were off, but you could recognize the obvious missing pieces—a dark square on the wall where a picture once hung, the end table sitting by itself without a chair.

"I need to ask you a couple questions about the lake yesterday," I said. "Does Arnaldo have access to a boat?"

Pete looked surprised by the question, but answered, "Sure. He's practically in charge of Search and Rescue."

"Could he have used the Search and Rescue boat to go to Road's End?"

"Anyone with a key to the gate can take the boat out." Pete frowned at me. "What's this about?"

I didn't answer. "When you and Arnaldo went to do the dive yesterday, did he tell you the dead woman was his ex-girlfriend?"

It was obvious from Pete's expression that Arnaldo hadn't. "I don't know anything about that, but if you think Arnaldo did something wrong, you're way off base. He's a great guy. He's working, like, three jobs so his wife can stay home with their daughters. He's the guy who takes care of everybody."

"Did you come up to the surface after the two of you found the body?" I watched as Pete's annoyance with me turned into dislike. "How long was Arnaldo alone with the body? Could he have sabotaged the autopsy?"

"Arnaldo would never do that." Pete walked forward and forced me out the door. "If you have questions, go talk to him instead of asking me behind his back."

"I don't know where he is."

Pete shut the door. "He's doing first aid."

The trucks pulling the horses stopped in front of the house. Their headlights backlit the smoke in the air.

I followed Pete around to the passenger door. "Where is Arnaldo doing first aid?"

"I don't know." He opened the door. "He was here last night helping us with the cattle. Then he left to go help the Red Cross." Pete got in the truck and reached for the door.

I shoved my shoulder into the gap before he could get it closed.

"Hey, what's going on here?" the father said.

"I need to know where Arnaldo Bedolla is."

He reached across Pete and grabbed the door. "He's at the spike camp."

I stepped back. Both pickups drove away towing the horse trailers.

Bell's SUV pulled up. I walked around to the passenger side and got in.

Bell turned on her windshield wipers and sprayed cleaner on the glass. The dirty area outside the wiper's path was almost black. "Sorry. This crew's too busy for interviews."

"That's okay. I got what I needed."

She gave it some gas and we started back out to the highway.

"Can you take me to the spike camp?" I said. "That's where Bedolla is."

"Which one?"

I turned to look at her. "There's more than one?"

"This fire is over seventy thousand acres. Yes, there's more than one spike camp."

Spike camps were remote and usually near the fire line. Hand crews such as the one Brad Egan was on needed a place closer in where they could replenish supplies and get access to first aid.

"I guess start at the closest one."

She nodded. "All right. Brad Egan's down that way too.

At the highway we turned right. We passed two trucks going

the opposite direction and had to shield our eyes from their powerful headlights.

"They're starting to clear out," she said. "We've probably only got another hour or two before we have to leave too."

A little farther ahead, we slowed and then turned at a sign advertising a public campground. Bell switched on her windshield wipers and left them on. The stream of ash and embers was constant now. We followed the twisty dirt road through pine trees until we reached the campground.

It was still fairly dark, but I was able to make out several fire trucks and other official vehicles parked there. Among them was a large SUV with the Elizabeth Search and Rescue logo.

Bell looked out the windshield. "Hopefully my car is here."

"Your car?"

"I gave it to Brad Egan last night so he could drive back to his crew. I need to get it back in case the fire blows up." She smiled. "That is, if you don't mind driving this one."

"I can't take it all the way to headquarters. Rod's expecting me."

"We'll work something out."

Bell parked the SUV next to a large truck two men were loading with supplies. We raised our handkerchiefs and got out. A burning leaf floated between us and landed in the ash. Bell put it out with her boot.

"How far are we from the fire line?" I asked.

Her eyes crinkled up and I knew she was smiling. "Don't worry. We're not close and the winds are still fairly low."

I looked around. Several Hotshots sat at a picnic table devouring sandwiches under their handkerchiefs. It was so dark that they had a Coleman lantern on the table with them.

Bell pointed to a large tent next to the campground's public restrooms. A light inside made the white fabric glow in the half-light. "That's first aid. If Bedolla is helping the Red Cross, he'll be inside."

I collected my gear and started walking. The closer we got, the more hopeful I felt—as in, I was hoping a murderer was inside. Not the everything-will-work-out, spiritual-grace kind of hope.

We entered. The tent's fabric made a thumping noise as the wind jostled it. A work light on a stand illuminated a folding table, cot, and several camp chairs. In the corner, clear plastic bins filled with medical supplies were stacked in rows. More supplies were laid out on the table. Arnaldo Bedolla was using them to replace the dressing on a shirtless Hotshot's arm. The young man's pants and boots were caked in dirt and grime. His torso wasn't much cleaner.

Bedolla wore the same dark green pants and orange Search and Rescue shirt as he had at the body retrieval. I tried to recognize the man who'd almost drowned me, but couldn't. All I'd seen were a pair of men's legs in dark pants. It could have been Bedolla or Farris or Professor Polignac or just about any other man in the area.

He glanced up at us. "Hello." He looked older than the day before. Exhaustion does that to people.

The firefighter turned to see who'd entered. When the relatively young man saw my camera, he grinned. I doubted I could muster that kind of enthusiasm while smelling as bad as he did. Then I remembered that I probably did smell as bad as he did.

I lowered the handkerchief and spoke to Bedolla. "I'm Lilly Hawkins from KJAY. We met yesterday at Lake Elizabeth."

"I remember." He didn't sound alarmed or worried. "What can I do for you?"

"I'm Firefighter Tracy Bell with the information officer's staff." She gestured to me. "I'm escorting Lilly on a ride-along. She'd like an interview, when you're free."

Bedolla finished applying a piece of tape to a gauze pad on the firefighter's arm. "I'm free now, but I'm no good at that sort of thing. You should talk to one of the boys."

He'd declined to be interviewed at the lakeshore too, which in retrospect should have made me suspicious. Everyone wants to be on TV.

A truth the young Hotshot was about to illustrate. "I'll give you an interview." He pulled a clean navy-blue T-shirt over his head and covered his perfect abs. "My mom'll go crazy if I'm on TV."

Bell started to say something, but I cut her off. "Sorry. I'm looking for civilians."

The Hotshot was disappointed, but he recovered and turned to Bedolla while touching the new bandage. "Thanks, you're the best."

"You need to be more careful out there." Bedolla spoke like a caring but reserved father. "It's not a bad cut, but you need to do a better job of keeping it clean."

"I promise I will." The Hotshot's tone abruptly changed. "Grandpa."

Bedolla grinned at him. "Get out of here." The Hotshot left and Bedolla spoke to Bell. "You should wait until the Red Cross nurse gets back. She ran down to the fire line to assist with an injury, but she'll be back soon."

Bell frowned. "Nothing serious, I hope."

"Broken ankle." Bedolla picked up the bloodied gauze pads and threw them away. "She's getting the kid stabilized until the medevac chopper arrives."

It took all my willpower not to run for the car. Video of a fire-fighter being airlifted to the hospital would get played over and over on every major news outlet.

"I didn't hear anything." Bell's head dropped. She immediately began adjusting knobs and buttons on the radio strapped to her chest.

"Why don't you call them from outside while I shoot this?" I planted my sticks in front of Bedolla.

If this worked, it would remove my biggest obstacle. Bell had been ordered to help me and knew my primary focus was the drowning and not the fire, but she had no idea I suspected Bedolla of wrongdoing. There was no way she'd stand by once I began hammering him with accusations.

Bell glanced at Bedolla. He nodded his head and then sat down in the folding chair next to the table. Bell looked relieved. "Okay. I'll only be a minute or two."

I attached the camera to the tripod, then hit record. "Say and spell your name for me."

Bedolla complied while removing his rubber gloves.

I took a seat next to the camera. "Tell me about Jessica Egan."

Bedolla froze. "Jessica? Why do you want to know about her?"

"You pulled her body from the lake yesterday, right?"

He nodded. "You know I did. You were there."

"And you found her boat out at Road's End?"

"Not just me. There were three of us." He thought for a moment. "You didn't really come all this way to ask about Jessica? Don't you want to know about the fire?"

I ignored his question. "Why didn't you tell anyone you knew her? Isn't it against protocol to pull your ex-girlfriend's body out of the water?"

He frowned. "No, actually it's not, and I did tell people."

"Who?"

"I said right away, as soon as I heard it was Jessica." He looked at me. "And not because it was a conflict of interest, like you're implying. I was upset. I didn't want to see her like that."

I thought back to his behavior at the lakeshore. Bedolla had stood by, silently loading equipment, while the local officer talked about the trashy bimbo who'd gotten herself killed. "So your official statement is that the officer on the scene knew about your prior relationship?"

He shook his head. "I don't remember specifically if he knew or not, but I told plenty of people. I had to be talked into making that dive. It's bad enough pulling a body from the water. It's horrific when it's someone you care about."

"Were you still in love with her?"

"Of course not. I haven't seen Jessica in almost fourteen years." He stood up. "I don't want to talk anymore. Turn that thing off."

This is where Rod would have stepped in and said something nice. That was pretty much beyond me, so I turned off the camera and stood too. "I think Jessica was murdered."

"What?"

"Pete freaked out and returned to the surface when you found the body, didn't he? You had ample opportunity to sabotage the autopsy."

"Why would I do that?" He stared at me for a moment, then understanding flashed across his face. Unfortunately he started laughing. "You think I killed Jessica? Are you serious?"

"She broke your heart. You've probably hated her all these years."

He laughed again and sat back down. "Jessica and I were friends when we were kids. Our going out just sort of happened when we hit puberty, but I wouldn't say my feelings were particularly deep. More like, neither of us knew there were any other options."

"That's the only reason you dated her?"

He raised one of his legs and set the ankle across his knee. "Jessica's older brother, Brad, was a big deal around here. We went to all his football and basketball games. Jessica used to worship him. We all did." He lowered the leg he'd just raised. "I'm not proud of this, but dating Brad Egan's sister was like dating royalty."

"But she dumped you. That's humiliating."

He shook his head. "I didn't mind when she broke it off. After her mother died, she turned into a freaky hippie, and not even at a time when everyone was doing it, like in the sixties. This was the nineties. People were watching *Seinfeld* and figuring out the Internet."

This was not going well. Bedolla was giving reasonable answers to all of my questions. He wasn't nervous or panicking.

"Let's cut to the chase here. I couldn't have hurt Jessica." He began putting medical supplies away. "I was here from noon Wednesday to noon Thursday. I only left because they needed me to dive."

"Oh," I said.

He smiled. "Apology accepted."

SEVENTEEN

The adrenaline I'd been running on started to fade. I sat down and rubbed my head.

"Sorry to disappoint you," Bedolla said.

"It's not personal. It's just that I'm back to square one. I have no idea what happened to Jessica."

He looked up from the supplies. "You really think she was murdered?"

"She had a bad shoulder. She never could have started the boat by herself."

He thought for a moment. When he did finally speak, he sounded troubled. "That's right. I remember. She busted up her shoulder really bad trying to impress her brother."

"Trying to impress him, how?"

"Brad was hot on archery and Jessica kept bugging him to teach her. He finally got annoyed and dared her to even try to draw his bow. It was a recurve, probably as tall as she was." Bedolla shook his head. "It did not end well."

After a pause, he looked at me. "But Jessica must have gotten the shoulder fixed after she moved to L.A., or else there's some other explanation. Why would anyone hurt her?"

"You tell me. You're her first love."

He turned away. He resumed putting away supplies, but I had the feeling it was just an excuse not to look at me. "That may be true, but I don't know anything about her life now. None of us saw her after she left town. Honestly, I hadn't thought of her in years."

"But you, Lee, and Byrdie have all stayed close? You and Lee even worked together."

"You mean the landscaping business?" When I nodded, he continued, "That was a side thing we ran out of the Garden Center. Lee and I both have green thumbs so it was easy."

The flap opened. I moved so a Hotshot could enter.

"I pick up a lot of side jobs like that," Bedolla continued. "Before all the development in Tilly Heights, that's how everyone was around here. Even Lee's dad—he ran the store, but he also worked as a handyman. That way of life is disappearing fast now."

The new Hotshot finished closing the flap behind him. He was in his early thirties and had a captain's insignia on his uniform. "Sorry to interrupt."

Before he could continue, I jumped in. "Was Arnaldo working here two days ago? I'm interested in Wednesday afternoon through midnight."

"Sure he was." The captain looked from me to Bedolla and back again. "Why on earth do you want to know that?"

"She's checking my alibi." Bedolla's tone was amused, not angry.

"Are you sure he was here," I pressed. "On Wednesday evening and night?"

"Of course." He looked at Bedolla. "What's going on?"

"Don't worry. She's just doing her job." Bedolla shifted gears. "How about that kid with the broken ankle? Any word yet?"

"That's why I came to see you." A gust of wind battered the tent and the captain had to wait for the noise to fade. "The injury's not as bad as we thought."

Bedolla brightened. "That's great news."

"And it means the Red Cross nurse will be back soon and you can finally get out of here."

"Thanks. I'd stay as long as you needed me, but I have to admit I'd like to get some rest."

The captain started to go, but stopped and looked at me. "Are you being escorted by someone? Because you should think about getting out of here too."

"Don't worry, I'm with Firefighter Bell."

He was frowning as he pulled his handkerchief back up over his face and walked out.

I gathered my equipment. "I don't suppose you know if any of the McClellan family is still in the area?"

He shook his head.

As I started to leave he said, "I hope you're wrong about how Jessica died."

I stopped. "Would you prefer that she died because she was stupid? It's pointless."

"Would you prefer that she died because someone hated her? That's pointless and sad."

I found Bell by our car. I hadn't put my handkerchief up and couldn't now with my arms full. "I'm getting in," I said while trying to breathe. I quickly loaded my gear in the back.

Bell got in the front seat moments after me. "It's only a sprain, and it looks like they managed to carry the kid out to a vehicle. They're not using the chopper."

"That's good news." I should have been glad for the firefighter. But mostly I was glad I didn't have to feel guilty about blowing off a great story. "I'm done here. Let's go find Brad Egan."

"I know exactly where he is. The sprained ankle came from his crew." She paused. "But we should make it fast."

"Why?"

"The fire's gained more ground. They're evacuating all nonessential personnel from this side of the mountain and pulling back the hand crews another five miles."

We started back toward the highway, but before we got there, Bell turned down another dirt road. Even with the headlights and windshield wipers on it was still difficult to see through the smoke and blowing ash. We drove for two or three miles like that.

Eventually flashing lights appeared on the road ahead. I couldn't tell how many vehicles there were, but Bell pulled in behind a truck from the Fish and Game Department. "I'll go ask for Egan. You can wait inside if you'd like. We can even do the interview in the car."

I pulled the handkerchief up. "I didn't come all this way to sit in the car."

We both got out. The darkness could have passed for night. It was probably a good ten degrees hotter than it had been at Bonny Hazel. A hand crew worked nearby, desperately trying to strengthen the natural firebreak the road provided. A nearby tree, lit by an engine's headlights, violently swayed in the wind. I cringed in anticipation of its snapping, but it continued to whip back and forth.

Bell went to find the crew's superintendent. I got my camera out and tried to shoot video. Two Fish and Game officers passed carrying rifles. I stopped one and asked for an interview.

"Sorry." The man had to shout to be heard over the wind. "We're pulling back to the spike camp."

I turned on the camera light and hit record anyway. "Just a couple questions." I gestured to the rifles. "Are you part of the team hunting the cougars?"

He nodded. "We got one overnight, but there are reports of two more. They've been displaced by the fire and are probably disoriented and hungry."

"If you leave, does that mean the firefighters here are vulnerable? What if they get attacked?"

"Worst case, each of the trucks has a weapon on it, but it'll never come to that." He gestured to the fire. "The cougars are smart enough to run the opposite direction. You and I should follow their lead." He turned and jogged to the waiting SUV. Moments later I saw a pair of retreating taillights.

I set up my sticks and attached the camera. The body of the wildfire was still far away, but the flames from a small spot fire burned in a nearby field. An enormous length of hose ran from two Kern County fire engines out to where the firefighters were working to put it out.

In my camera, the men appeared as black silhouettes against the red horizon. The burning backdrop made the water from their hoses look like a spray of red sparks.

I stopped recording when Bell approached. "Egan's here, but his captain pulled him off the line. They're sending him back to headquarters."

"Why?"

"Said he was distracted. There's no room for that out here." She glanced over her shoulder. "Nobody wanted to say so, but I think Egan not being at a hundred percent might have contributed to their man getting injured." She pointed to one of the trucks. "He's waiting over there, out of the wind."

I packed up and we walked around the truck.

Egan sat on the ground with his back against one of the massive tires. A pair of headlights down the road lit his profile. He wore a handkerchief, but I didn't have to see his face to know he was miserable. Whatever I thought about him personally, something was sad about this big man's being crumpled and low.

He heard us approach and looked up. For a moment he stared, but then he saw the camera and turned away. "Oh, please, not now."

I set down my camera and sticks. "I need to speak with you about your sister."

"No." He shook his head. "I never should have talked to you in the first place."

Bell touched my arm. "This isn't a good time. If he doesn't want to talk, you have to respect that."

I came around and stood in front of him. "Why did you say all those bad things about Jessica?"

"Everyone's going to see it, aren't they?"

"No. I told my assignment manager to only use the part at the end."

"The end?" He looked up. "What did I say?"

"That when you were both kids she followed you around trying to get you to teach her stuff. You said she loved the lake and you hoped she was at peace."

He pulled down his handkerchief and swiped his face with it. "Thank you for not using the other stuff."

202 | Nora McFarland

"I need to ask you about Jessica's shoulder."

"That's what I keep thinking about." He winced. "Her drowning may be because she could no longer swim, and Mom always saying her shoulder was my fault because . . ."

He started crying.

I waited a moment or two, hoping he'd pull himself together. "Okay," I said. "Okay. I know you're upset, but we need to talk." I waited. The wind gusted around the truck. Ash and embers blew though the space under the vehicle and hit my legs. Egan put a hand up to momentarily shield his face, but still didn't compose himself.

I pulled down my handkerchief. "You need to stop crying. We have to talk about how Jessica died." The contrast with our first meeting could not have been greater.

"Lilly, that's not an appropriate tone." Bell gave me the kind of look my mother used to give Bud. She knelt and placed a hand on Egan's shoulder. "It's okay. Your sister is in a better place now."

"Actually, she's in the Bakersfield morgue."

Their heads both jerked to me.

"And she's there because someone murdered her." I knelt down. "I know I'm being a jerk, but you need to pull yourself together and help me find out who did it."

"Murdered?" he said. "The police didn't say anything like that."

"Jessica couldn't have started the boat with her bad shoulder."

"But they've got engines now that—"

"It was an old engine with a pull-cord starter. I saw it myself." I gave him a second to digest this, then continued, "You need to go see the Elizabeth police and demand that they launch a full investigation."

"Me? Why?" He straightened and pulled back. "They're the police. They know what needs to be done."

"They're ignoring Jessica because of the wildfire, and by the time they get around to investigating, there isn't going to be any evidence left."

He thought for a moment. From the look of alarm on his face, he was probably struggling to come up with an excuse not to get involved. "Maybe she got her shoulder fixed," he finally said. "How do I know what she was doing all those years down in L.A.?"

"Stop thinking about yourself. You owe Jessica this."

"Owe her?" Egan stood up. He towered over me without even trying. "She left us and never looked back."

My voice rose. "I've been talking to people who used to know your family, and after your mom died, things were really bad for Jessica. Your father unraveled. He was drinking and from what I've heard, even abusive."

I expected Egan to deny it or yell at me, but instead he glanced at Bell. That glance spoke volumes about what Egan knew, or at least suspected, about his father's parental fitness.

"You had a responsibility to help your little sister," I continued. "But you were too busy worrying about yourself to come back home. At least speak up for her now that she's dead. You're the only family she has."

His eyes closed and he leaned against the truck. The light from the other truck's headlights shone behind him, so I couldn't see his face.

"Wouldn't you want her to do the same for you?"

"Fine." His head turned. The harsh light emphasized the bags under his eyes and deep wrinkles, making him look much older. "It's not going to change anything, but I'll go talk to the police."

"Thank you."

The raised voices of the unseen Hotshots had been getting steadily louder and more frequent. The wind gusts were also strengthening.

Bell stepped back. Her voice was polite, but firm. "If that's settled, I think we should give Senior Firefighter Egan his privacy."

"I just have two questions."

Bell dropped polite all together and concentrated on firm. "Senior Firefighter Egan doesn't want to go on camera."

"It's not on camera and it'll just take a minute, I promise." Before either of them could say no, I turned to Egan. "You said Jessica was having an affair with a married man. Why do you think that, and who's the man?"

He cast an ugly glance up the mountain. "There's some creep living up there studying the lizards. Jessica was sleeping with him."

"How do you know?"

"I went out with some old friends last time I visited Dad. After a couple beers, they all started making cracks about Jessica being back in town."

My voice rose. "But that doesn't mean she was having an affair. Her nonprofit owns the nature preserve. She was probably here on business."

He shook his head. "No. I made them tell me. It was humiliating, but I wanted to hear it." He grimaced, as though reliving the moment his frenemies had told him. "She was spending the night there on weekends. Sometimes sneaking in on Highway 55 from Mojave so she didn't have to drive through Elizabeth or Tilly Heights."

Why would everyone at Bonny Hazel lie about Jessica's visits? Were they all lying to cover up something, or was Jessica meeting one of them secretly? I would have sworn Farris and the mad scientist had been telling the truth. Then again, I wasn't the best judge.

I looked at Egan. "How did your friends know about it?"

"There's a spot where people sell fruit and stuff by the highway. Jessica stopped and bought something, told somebody who she was. They all knew her car after that. Word got around." He shook his head. "I guess the creep practically has a harem with young girls coming and going all the time."

A voice cried out on the other side of the truck. Several more voices quickly followed. I couldn't understand the words, but I knew what panic sounded like. Egan and Bell ran around the front of the truck. I picked up my gear and followed. Without the truck as a shield, a windstorm of burning shrapnel pelted us. I stumbled and covered my eyes. "Pull back," someone screamed.

I managed to open my eyes. The flames spread like a bucket of water thrown into a wind machine.

Egan raised his goggles and ran to help pull in the hoses.

"Get out," a man shouted at Bell. "We got a spot fire jumping the line. Air support is on its way. Everyone needs to clear out."

We leapt back as an SUV raced past. I hit record and raised my camera.

Bell grabbed my arm. "Not now." Two more vehicles tore past. "Come on."

We both ran for her car. I kept the still-recording camera on my shoulder.

As soon as Bell started the engine, I rolled down my window. Flames were now burning on both sides of the road.

Bell floored the gas pedal. "What are you doing?"

I rested the camera on the open window. "I'm shooting."

Bell slammed on the brakes. Crew members sprinted across the road. Behind them a tree exploded. I turned the camera and felt heat on my hand and face. A horn blasted and seconds later I saw one of the fire engines fly past in the viewfinder. Bell floored the gas again.

We left the flames behind. After a few moments I pulled back and raised the window. I wasn't moving, but my heart raced. I turned and looked out the back window. "Don't take this the wrong way, Firefighter Bell, but why is everybody else driving the opposite direction, and should I be worried about that?"

She laughed. "A, call me Tracy. B, they're all driving the direction their vehicles were facing. C"—Bell pointed ahead to a pair of taillights barely visible through the windshield wipers—"not everybody is going the other way, and D, this road loops back around to the spike camp." She laughed. "And we still need to pick up my car."

"You're worried about your car? What about the wind? Is this the blowup? Shouldn't we be hauling butt back up the mountain?"

"That was just a tiny spot fire that jumped its containment. A blowup would be a hundred times worse."

I couldn't imagine an experience that intense, but more than that, I couldn't imagine surviving it.

Bell must have sensed my fear. "Don't worry. If something really catastrophic had happened, and there were no other options, we could've deployed a personal fire shelter." She hooked her thumb back. "I've got two in the rear. Anyone working on or near the fire line is required to carry one. It's sort of like a sleeping bag, but the fabric is silica and fiberglass."

"You mean I'd actually be able to crawl into this thing and not get burnt?"

"Not you." She smiled. "You'd have to share mine so I could deploy it properly. All fire personnel train on how to use them so when the time comes, we know how to trap breathable air. In a real firestorm, you wouldn't survive without knowing how to use it."

I heard the whipping blades of a helicopter. Bell paused as it passed overhead flying low. The sound filled the car. The metal frame shook and I felt the vibrations rattle through me.

When the noise faded, Bell continued, "They used to call the shelters shake-and-bakes, but that's discouraged now for obvious reasons."

The road did eventually loop back around to the spike camp. We entered from the opposite direction, but even in the reduced light I recognized the same bathrooms and picnic tables. The crews that had pulled back were congregating here to regroup. Several vehicles from Egan's crew that had fled in the opposite direction were already parked here.

The infrastructure of the spike camp was almost completely dismantled. Even the first-aid tent Bedolla had been working in was gone.

Bell pulled in next to an Orange County FD vehicle. She got out and checked in with whoever was in charge. I got a couple sound bites from some of the men from Egan's crew. I asked where he was, but no one knew for sure. He'd officially been pulled off duty so he'd probably gotten a ride back to headquarters.

I still hadn't confessed to Egan that it was me, and not Jessica, who'd vandalized the THINK SAFETY sign all those years ago. I wanted to believe it was our abrupt departure that had denied me the opportunity, but hadn't there been several chances to tell the truth before the spot fire erupted? Was I now going to let the matter quietly fade away, appeasing my conscience by saying there was no right time?

I was running back to the car to try to get out of the wind and smoke when my phone rang. I didn't know the caller, but recognized the area code as L.A.

I shut the door and answered, "This is Lilly."

"I'm sorry," a woman said. "I was calling for Rod Strong."

I remembered that Rod had given me his station phone after I lost mine in the lake. "This is his shooter. I'm using this phone today."

"Can you put Rod on real fast? He knows me. Tell him it's Helen Henry from KBLA."

"I'm not with him. I'm down at the fire line shooting video."

"Are you the one who shot that interview with the governor?"

"Yes."

"Fantastic work." She paused. "Look, we should talk later. You and Rod make a great team and we're always looking for talent."

"You can reach Rod on his personal cell phone. I'll give you the number."

"I've already got it. We go way back." I heard her clicking a mouse. "Here it is. Okay, good talking to you." She hung up.

Bell returned. "What's wrong?"

"Nothing. Let's get going. I want to get back to the satellite truck and start feeding this video."

Bell gave me the keys to her car and told me to follow.

"Don't you want to drive your own car?"

She shook her head. "The Santa Theresa rig belongs to the IO. I wouldn't feel right letting someone else drive it without his permission—especially a journalist."

I agreed to follow her over the summit and down to Tilly

Heights, where someone else would take it the rest of the way. Bell promised to then take me back to Rod and the satellite truck. At the highway we turned left and started toward the mountain. I felt an almost instant release of tension. The mass of red, gray, and black filled my rearview mirror instead of my windshield.

The smoke lessened. Halfway up the mountain I switched off the windshield wipers. I kept the headlights on, but not because I couldn't see the road without them.

We neared the overpass and I slowed to glance down at the barely flowing creek. I thought about the cattle Pete's mom had taken down in the marshes. How could they survive a firestorm a hundred times worse than the one I'd just witnessed?

The sound of tires shrieking against asphalt brought my attention back to the road. Bell's taillights jerked and then jumped into the air. I slammed on my brakes. Her SUV flipped. Glass shattered and metal smashed into the pavement. I jerked hard to the left as the massive vehicle rolled past me and into the nature preserve's fence.

EIGHTEEN

My SUV tilted and for a moment I thought I was going to roll too, but then it righted and came to a stop. With my engine still running I jumped out and raced to Bell. I heard a sharp pop in the distance and then behind me the sound of breaking glass, but I was too focused on getting to Bell to care.

The SUV had gone straight through the fence and landed right-side up in the trees. It faced out toward the road, but I couldn't see Bell through the web of shattered and cracked glass that was now the windshield.

Without slowing I continued my sprint around the SUV to the driver's-side door. The window had fallen out and I reached in, trying to deflate the air bag. "Tracy? Tracy, can you hear me?" With my other hand I pulled the phone out of my pocket and checked for bars. I had none.

"Get . . . ," I heard her say.

I hit the air bag and what looked like talcum powder flew out of it. "Tracy, it's Lilly."

"Get down."

I gave the bag another punch. "Don't worry. I'm calling 911. I just need to get a signal."

"No," she said. "Get down."

"We'll get you down from the mountain. I promise."

"Not me," she managed to say. "You get down." Bell turned her head. Pieces of glass fell from her hair. Blood trickled from cuts on her forehead and nose. She took a gasp of air and said, "Sniper."

Another pop sounded in the distance. A bullet pierced the metal frame of the windshield inches from my head. I dropped to the ground. The SUV gave me cover, but Bell was exposed. I yanked on her door, but it was too damaged to open. "Tracy, you need to get down on the seat. Can you do that?"

"I think so." I heard the seat belt unbuckle, then she cried out.

I jumped up. "Tracy?"

She was lying on her side. "I think my ribs are broken."

Another pop. A bullet cracked the windshield and continued through the driver's headrest.

I fell to the ground again. "I don't have any bars and we're pinned. Is your radio working?"

"No. The air bag hit it." She paused to take several difficult breaths. "I think that's what broke my ribs."

"Do you know where the sniper is? Did you see anything?"

"There was a muzzle flash from the fruit stands when he shot my tire out." Her voice was fading and the pauses were getting longer. "He was waiting."

If she was right, then the trees would probably hide the rear of the SUV. Should I try to get a signal back there? Was it safe enough to stand?

I rolled over onto my belly and looked out the underside of the vehicle. Directly across the road, my SUV sat with the engine still running and the door ajar.

I sat back up and leaned against the driver's door. "Tracy," I said. "Can you hold on until someone drives by? They'll have to stop when they see the accident."

No answer. "Tracy," I repeated. Still no answer.

I grabbed the door handle and pulled. "Tracy, can you hear me?"

The door wouldn't budge. I jerked it with all my strength. The SUV rocked back and forth.

Another crack. As I dropped backward into the dirt, a terrible pop exploded from the remaining front tire. Pain and a high-pitched ringing filled my left ear. I watched as the entire SUV slowly tilted down toward the deflating tire.

I crawled to the rear. I didn't cautiously inch my way up or throw something in the air first to make sure it was safe. I leapt to my feet. My hand held the phone in the air and pointed it in every direction. No signal. I thought about running into the trees, but that would leave Bell defenseless.

I tore off the yellow jacket. It easily covered my forearm. I pulled back, then smashed it into the fragile rear window. The cracked glass fell like a curtain. I put my arm through and pulled out the first thing I touched. First-aid supplies. I reached farther in and threw aside two fire blankets. Underneath, a jack, a tire iron, gallon jugs of water, a fire extinguisher. Nothing I could use.

A black plastic case sat out of my reach up against the rear of the backseat. I put my torso in through the window and reached for it.

My ear still rang, but I thought I heard Bell moan.

"Tracy?" I said.

My chest stung where it rested against the glass at the bottom of the window, but I pushed myself even farther and grabbed at the plastic briefcase. I made contact and pulled it toward me.

I opened it, paused for a moment, then crawled with it back to the driver's-side door. The sniper must have seen movement because a bullet hit the dirt near my foot. "I've had just about enough of this," I mumbled.

I took both flare guns from the case and loaded them. I raised one and shot straight into the air. Without pausing I dropped it and grabbed the other. I leapt up and fired straight across the hood of the SUV. The sparking red missile tore through the twilight and exploded into the fruit stands.

Nonessential personnel were kept out. Bell, still unconscious, was stabilized first by firefighters who quickly drove up from the bottom of the mountain, and then by two Red Cross nurses who were allowed in from Tilly Heights. At some point a hand crew arrived. They went to work cutting down trees lining a designated section of highway so the medevac chopper could land. This all felt like hours, but in reality was probably only twenty minutes.

I tried to explain what had happened, and why I thought I was the target, but knew I sounded overwrought.

"Whoever the gunman was," I said, "he must have fled back into the trees behind the fruit stands." I pointed. "There's a driveway there too. You need to warn whoever lives up there. They might be in danger."

"They've all evacuated." The deputy took out a map and pointed to where we were. "And that area back in there is full of unmapped dirt roads. If this fellow had a car in the trees, then he's already gone."

"Then at least go check Bonny Hazel. The gunman could have run across the road into the nature preserve when I wasn't looking."

The deputy didn't say anything.

"You should hurry. If it was someone at Bonny Hazel, they could be destroying evidence."

"The thing is, miss, are you sure it was deliberate?" His voice had the slow quality people use when speaking to small children. "Isn't it possible someone was shooting at an animal and your vehicle got hit? Everyone knows we've got cougars in the area. Some idiot might have decided to drive up here and bag one."

Before I could finish yelling at him, he got pulled away by a call on his radio.

That's when Byrdie Fitzgerald arrived in her SUV. She wore a pink-and-black suit and black heels.

I went to meet her. "You got here fast."

She tied a black handkerchief over her face and shut her car door. The burnt oil smell from the chain saws and the sharp odor of freshly cut timber were actually worse than the smoke. "I was getting a tour of the firebreak above Tilly Heights when the call came over the radio."

"I thought only essential personnel were being let in."

"I told them I was essential." She was back to sounding sweet and upbeat, but I didn't doubt her ability to force her way through a roadblock. "Would you mind bringing me up-to-date on what happened?"

I gave her the quickie version and finished by saying, "It's time someone called in the BII." The California Bureau of Investigation & Intelligence was sort of like the FBI for California, but their assistance had to be requested.

"My police chief won't like bringing in outsiders, but you're right, we need help. I'll push him." She looked at me and frowned. "Maybe you should think about getting some serious medical attention."

"Do I look that bad?"

She smiled. "Let's just say, you've seen better days."

We both heard a sound and looked up. Seconds later I was running for my camera. I stayed tight on the helicopter and then did a smooth pullout to a wide shot as it landed. I was above it on the road, so the red sky appeared behind the gradually sinking chopper.

I was speaking with the pilots when the KBLA satellite truck arrived.

Rod jumped out and ran to me. "What happened? Are you all right?"

I started to tell him that I'd never been in any real danger, but stopped. Why even try? Rod could smell a lie on me from a mile away. "I think I almost died, again."

He put his arms around me. For once I let him.

I brought him up-to-date on what I'd learned and included how everyone at Bonny Hazel had lied about Jessica's visits. When I finished, I handed him my tape. "Here's everything I shot."

He took it. "Why are you giving it to me?"

"I'm also going to need you to take my gear for a little while."

"I love you too," he said.

"I'm serious."

"So am I. I've never seen you trust anyone with your gear before. It's like a normal person declaring their undying love."

"Very funny." I gestured to the medevac. It was backlit by the red-and-black view down the mountain. The pilots looked almost ready to go. "They're taking Bell to Bakersfield and I'm hitching a ride. I need to get a definite answer about whether or not Jessica had her shoulder repaired when she lived in L.A."

I waited, but Rod didn't say anything. "I thought you'd be happy I'm leaving. This gets me out of the line of fire. Whoever keeps trying to kill me won't get a third chance."

He reluctantly nodded. "You're right. I'll drive down to Bakersfield after you and we'll make a plan from there."

"No. It'll take you hours to get through traffic and down the canyon. Besides, you're needed here." I gestured down the mountain to the sea of flames and smoke. "The fire is too important a story and you have a lot riding on this . . . career-wise."

"I could care less about my career."

I shook my head. "You should care. You're bored out of your mind producing the eleven. I didn't want to see it, but tonight you've been like a kid in a candy store."

Dennis approached. He handed Rod a handkerchief. "We should be ready to go live in a couple minutes.

Rod thanked him and tied the handkerchief over his nose and mouth.

Dennis looked at me before starting to walk away. "Glad you're okay, Lilly. We were pretty scared when we heard the radio call."

He returned to his truck and Rod pulled me toward the tree line.

After we'd taken a few steps into the forest he lowered his handkerchief. "Maybe I have been bored, but that doesn't mean I want to go back on camera." He took a breath. "And that's not me using you as an excuse to stay here because I'm afraid to try. You're insulting us both if you really believe that."

"Then why are you still here?"

His forehead creased. "What's that supposed to mean?"

I lowered my handkerchief too. My voice was remarkably calm considering how I felt. "You're handsome and rich. You've got a doctorate from one of the best schools in the country. You're practically a celebrity. Why would you choose to live in the meth capital of California with a contrary, breaking-news junkie who has a high school diploma and a trashy past she can't talk about?" I paused. "It makes no sense."

His face melted and he put his arms around me. "Sweetheart, I wish I had your past. While you were having fun, I was pretending to be someone I'm not, and hiding all the things I really love because they weren't cool. There's nothing you ever did that could be more pathetic than that."

Maybe it was the lack of sleep, or maybe I felt guilty about not confessing to Brad Egan, but I didn't hesitate to try to prove Rod wrong. "Oh, yeah? You know what the prank was, that Jessica got blamed for? I went out to the THINK SAFETY sign with a couple guys I'd known five seconds. We took two six-packs of beer and some spray paint and I got up there and changed the wording. I changed 54 LIVES LOST SINCE 1955 to 54,000 LIZARDS LOST SINCE 1955. Then I drew a green thing on the bottom with a red stripe."

"Sweetheart, that's terrible." He pulled back to look at me, but didn't let go. "It's a salamander not a lizard."

His face was deadly serious. Then the corners of his mouth began to twitch.

"You're making jokes?" My voice rose. "It's not funny."

"It's a little funny."

"No, it's not. Don't you get it?" I pulled away. "The sign didn't mean anything to me, but it means something to the people who live here. Those numbers are human beings. There were parents of kids that drowned who had to see what I did to that sign."

Rod's voice was getting hoarse. "I'm not saying it wasn't bad, but it doesn't define who you are right now."

"Rod, there is no magic do-over button. We don't get second chances to erase mistakes and try again."

An engine started, followed by the whine of the propeller blades beginning to spin. I ran back out to my gear bag and Rod followed.

"Hey," one of the pilots shouted. "We're ready to go."

I picked up my gear bag and then turned to Rod. "Please, please take good care of my camera."

"I love you too," he yelled as I ran for the chopper.

I climbed inside and with some help got strapped into a chair. "Hey, you want some coffee?" One of the pilots turned from the front seat. I recognized him from the airstrip. "I've got a fantastic fair-trade Sumatra. It's not a great morning coffee, but I like the juicy acidity."

Lilly Hawkins drinking coffee is one of the biblical signs of the apocalypse. In a mark of just how messed up I felt, I said yes and drank it all.

Twenty minutes later we landed on the roof of Bakersfield Medical Center. I ducked into an elevator while everyone was focused on Bell. I walked out the main entrance. A KJAY news van was double-parked outside. I opened the sliding side door and climbed in. "Do you know what the ticket is for parking in an ambulance zone?"

Freddy turned from the driver's seat. "You're welcome, dude. It's a total pleasure to chauffeur you around on our day off."

"I'm sorry." I fastened my seat belt. "Thank you for coming to get me. I'm only giving you a hard time because I don't want Trent to fire you."

"I totally told him not to park here." Teddy reached back from the front passenger seat and offered a white Smith's Bakeries bag. "But he was freaking that you shouldn't be walking out to the parking lot, you know, 'cause you're, like, messed up."

I took the bag and then turned to Freddy. "Really?"

He shrugged. "I can't let anything happen to you, dude. It would take months to break in a new chief."

I pulled one of my favorite sun-shaped, smiley-face cookies from Teddy's bag. "Thanks."

"So where to?" Freddy said. "Back home to Casa Hawkins in Oildale?"

"How do you feel about a road trip?"

I slept most of the way. I awoke at one point to the sound of the Wonder Twins' angry voices.

"Dude, get your head out of your butt," Freddy said. "If John

Mellencamp went on a murder spree, and Bruce Springsteen took him down, Springsteen is totally the get."

"I totally think it's Mellencamp," Teddy said. "He's the one who acted all crazy and out of character. You expect Springsteen to stop him because he's a badass. He's just doing what he always does, being awesome. Mellencamp is the get because he did the weird thing."

"I'm sleeping," I said.

Teddy turned to the backseat. "Sorry, chief. We'll dial it down."

"And for the record"—I raised up on my elbow— "Mellencamp's final victim, the one Springsteen saved, is the get."

"Dude," Freddy yelled, "why didn't I think of that?"

"That's why she's the chief." Teddy reached back and high-fived me.

This time I fell into a much deeper sleep. I awoke to see Teddy's tentative face above mine. "Dude, we're here. Are you sure you're okay?"

I sat up. I shook my head to clear the drugged feeling. "What time is it?"

Freddy handed me a bottle of Mountain Dew. "A little after twelve."

I opened the bottle and chugged it. The carbonation burned my throat and forced me to wake up.

I lowered the bottle and looked out the car window. We were double-parked in front of a two-story brick building. GREEN SEED was etched into the glass door. The block was full of similar storefronts and offices. They all looked expensive.

I took another quick drink. "Why don't you go ahead and park?"

"Good luck with that." Freddy cackled. "We'd bag our own reality show before a free parking space opened up in this town."

I took the phone from my gear bag, then reached for the door. "I guess, try and wait for me here then. I'm using Rod's station phone, if you need to call me."

Freddy nodded. "Cool."

I slid open the door and smelled something new. I've never done a lot of traveling. Bakersfield is my home and I've always been happy to stay there. The odor I smelled now reminded me of a farm, but at the same time was something completely different.

I looked down the block and saw the Pacific Ocean. Only a sliver of its true scope was visible, but the smell, the moisture in the air, the intangible weight of knowing it was there, all combined to make it feel massive. It reminded me of the fire, but without the terror.

I stepped down from the van. A man in an expensive suit walked by carrying a briefcase. His Bluetooth headset gave him the appearance of talking to himself. "You and all those soft-rock apologists can figure it out. . . . Am I talking to the Japanese? Am I in Tokyo right now?"

A second man passed, but his soiled clothing and matted hair made it unlikely he was also on a call. "It's all about Lorne Michaels. He's the key. I saw him put it in the reservoir. And these are good eyes. The Canadians want these eyes."

"You disrespect her like this and somebody is getting bloody." The first man hit a button on his key chain. A Porsche beeped in a nearby driveway.

The sound made the second man jump, but he recovered and continued his monologue. "He said it was just fluoride, but I know the truth. My eyes can think for themselves. They aren't sheep."

"So this is Venice," I said.

"Isn't it awesome?" Teddy leaned out his window. "We'd totally move down here, but it's way too expensive."

"Totally," I said.

I slid the door shut.

"Hold up, dude." Freddy walked around the front of the van holding out a comb. "You look like Medusa on her bummerest day."

"Thanks." I took my hair down and tried to comb it out. My long, dark curls were some new kind of frizzy that until that moment hadn't been seen on our planet. They also had a sandy texture that I guessed was ash and soot. I shoved them back up into a ponytail. "Better?"

"Totally." Freddy grinned. "Now you look like Medusa on an awesome day."

I opened the glass door and entered. The exposed-brick walls contrasted with a futuristic-looking, black metal staircase leading to the second floor. On the wall above a reception desk hung a large green pod with a giant earth sprouting from its center.

A young woman in a headset was sitting there. "Green Seed, how can I help you help the earth?" She paused, then said, "She's not in right now. Would you like her voice mail?"

As she performed the transfer, her face scrunched up and she sniffed. She looked up, trying to find the source of the odor, and saw me. "Can I help you?"

"Sorry. I just came from the Terrill Wildfire. That's why I smell like this."

She nodded, but I saw her pull back a little from the desk.

"Is this where Jessica Egan works?"

"This is difficult to say, but I'm afraid Jessica may have passed away." She eyed the logo on my polo shirt. "Is that why you're here? Are you doing a story about her?"

"Something like that."

She asked me to wait, then walked into a glass-walled office on the other side of the metal staircase. She spoke to a man wearing dark slacks and a dress shirt. He stared at her, then me. He picked up a phone and dialed.

I looked around. On the other side of the stairs, another glass-walled office sat beyond a row of empty desks. I approached. There was no name on the door because there was no door. The lights abruptly came on when I entered. A motion sensor eyed me from the wall where you'd expect to see a light switch.

A large oil painting was the only decoration. The landscape, painted in thick, lush strokes, looked like the view from the top of Mt. Terrill. Of course no horrific natural disaster was marring this scene. I looked for a signature and was surprised to see *C. Egan.*

Several cacti sat on a long filing cabinet under the painting. But in contrast to the thriving plants in the picture, these looked withered and brown.

A quick glance inside the stacks of folders on the desk showed budgets, lists, and complicated spreadsheets I couldn't understand. The only other thing on the desk, besides a phone and Macintosh computer, was an open metal water bottle. It gave the eerie impression that Jessica had just stepped out and would be right back. I quickly opened the desk drawers. A set of house keys sat in a pencil tray. I pocketed them, then searched the rest of the desk, but didn't see anything personal or revealing.

More stacks of papers and folders covered a table in the corner. I was looking though them when a man said, "That's private material."

I turned around. It was the man the receptionist had gone to speak with. "This is Jessica Egan's office, right?"

His studious-looking wire-frame glasses contrasted with his militaristic hairstyle. "Yes, and you don't have permission to be here. Just because you're a reporter doesn't mean you can trespass."

"My name's Lilly Hawkins. I'm a shooter with KJAY in Bakersfield, but I'm not doing a story."

"Then why are you here?"

"I knew her." I took the metal water bottle and poured the contents into the cacti. "It was a long time ago, but I knew her."

He pushed his glasses back up from where they'd slipped down his nose. "I don't understand. Did you come all this way to tell us in person?"

"Not exactly. I don't think her death was an accident." I paused. "Did Jessica have a bad shoulder?"

He nodded. "The worst. Could barely raise her arm."

NINETEEN

I felt intense relief and immediately wondered why. Was Bedolla right? Did I want Jessica's death to be murder? Was I secretly afraid Jessica had stopped being strong and smart and become just as weak and stupid as I used to be?

"I believe she went to a doctor about the shoulder," he continued. "But it had been too long since the injury for surgery."

"You need you to contact the Elizabeth police and tell them that."

He glanced over his shoulder. "I'm going to have to insist that we continue this discussion in my office. I don't care if you knew Jessica or not, you have no business being in her office and looking through her work papers."

I went with him partly because he was right, and partly because I'd already looked through the desk and found what I hoped were the keys to Jessica's house.

As we passed, the receptionist gave me a dirty look. I didn't blame her. I smelled bad, looked bad, and had gone into a dead woman's office and began searching it without permission. I would probably have been glaring too.

We entered his office, and he sat down behind a desk. It was just as covered with paperwork as Jessica's, but a Captain Underpants figurine gave it some personality. "I'm Tyler, by the way."

I took a seat. Judging by the wall of pictures behind him, Tyler had done a lot of traveling—and not the Paris-in-spring kind of travel. His smiling face looked out at me from deserts, jungles, and even glaciers. In some of the pictures he wore military fatigues.

"Were you in the army?"

He glanced back at the photos. "I did ROTC and then got called up to active duty."

"Iraq?"

"One tour. The rest of the time I was in Germany."

I didn't say anything.

"You look surprised," he said.

"The stereotype for leftist environmental groups doesn't include military service."

"Taking care of the earth isn't a left or right issue. And neither is military service."

"Did Jessica see it that way?"

"Jessica doesn't care if you're straight, gay, right, left, religious, atheist, you name it. You can be anything you want as long as you work hard, respect the environment, and support animal rights."

He eyed me suspiciously. "But if you were really her friend, you'd probably know that."

"We weren't exactly friends and it was a long time ago. The summer before she moved here. I actually gave her cover so her dad wouldn't know she was working with Green Seed."

"Wait a minute." He pulled back and then pointed. "Did you spray-paint some sign up by the lake?"

I felt my cheeks burn. "She told you that story?"

"She saw you on the news last winter." His entire demeanor softened and he looked much less guarded. "She said you'd caught a murderer and taken on a gang or a smuggling ring or something."

"Or something."

"She was really excited. She wanted to try and get you to do a story about pesticide overuse in the Central Valley."

"That's ironic. She didn't have a very high opinion of me back when we knew each other."

"You wouldn't know it from the way she was going on. She said something weird . . . what was it?" He thought for a minute. "She said, 'Everybody needs a way home, even if they never use it.' " He shook his head. "None of us could figure out what she meant."

"It's the last thing I ever said to her, thirteen years ago." After an awkward pause, I changed the subject. "I have some unanswered questions about Jessica. I'd be very grateful if you'd help me settle them."

"I can't comment for a story." He gestured to the phone. "I called our PR person and they don't want me to say anything."

"I swear I'm not doing a story. My interest is personal. If I end up doing a story later, I'll get your permission before using anything you've said."

He adjusted his weight in the chair. "Why don't you start by telling me why you think Jessica was murdered?"

I gave him a quick recap of the official version of Jessica's death.

"There's so many things wrong with that. I don't know where to start." He shook his head. "I mean, even without the shoulder, I've never seen Jessica overindulge in alcohol. Even at fund-raisers with open bars, she always kept it to one glass of wine."

"I think her father may have become an alcoholic after Jessica's mother died."

"That explains a lot." He leaned back in his chair. "Jessica insisted on mandatory drug tests every six months. It's good policy, but she always seemed a little bit too worried about substance abuse."

He glanced back at the pictures on the wall. "It's funny, we worked here together for two years and I hardly know anything about her. She was always nice, but there was something closed off in her manner."

"Is there anyone around who knew her better?"

He thought for a moment. "Ceasonne Polignac. She and Jessica go way back and she happens to be upstairs right now. She used to be executive director here."

I couldn't help but turn around and look at the stairs. "I know who Ceasonne is—I met her at Bonny Hazel—but what's she doing here?"

"She's unloading salamanders." He made a goofy face of mock aversion. "It's a temporary measure until Dr. Polignac evacuates and can take them to UCLA."

"Was Jessica close to both the Polignacs or just Ceasonne?"

"I wouldn't say she was close to either. Just that she'd known them for a long time."

"Did Jessica ever visit Bonny Hazel on behalf of Green Seed?"

He shook his head. "Not really. I think once this past year. She wanted to make sure the students weren't abusing the property."

That's what Farris and Polignac had both said. Then why did the Fitzgeralds see her in the store with people from Bonny Hazel, and why was she seen driving into Bonny Hazel on weekends?

Tyler continued, "And of course she went up on Wednesday to make sure everyone evacuated."

"What was her reaction to the wildfire?"

"She was very disturbed." He hesitated. "The truth is, she had a meltdown about it on Monday. It was completely out of character. I've seen her angry, sad, frustrated, but never crying."

"Did something in particular set her off?"

"When the fire jumped its containment lines and those men were killed." He spread his arms. "It was terrible news, of course, but Jessica's reaction seemed completely out of proportion. Later I heard her brother is a firefighter, and it made more sense."

If that was true, then Jessica cared far more for Brad than he did for her. "Was she better on Tuesday?"

"She didn't come in at all, which is almost unheard of. Then Wednesday she called and said she was going up to Elizabeth and wouldn't be in for the rest of the week." He leaned forward for emphasis. "You don't understand how out of character that was. I mean, Jessica practically lived here."

"Is that true for weekends too?"

He considered. "Before this past year it was."

"Why the change?"

He shrugged. The movement was small and casual, but it felt artificial.

"Did you ask her?"

"No," he said too quickly.

"But you must have had some idea."

He stood. "Like I said, Jessica and I weren't close." He walked around the desk. "I'll take you up to Ceasonne now. She worked with Jessica for much longer and is a better person to talk with."

He walked out and waited for me just outside the glass wall. I couldn't remember a time when I'd been so effectively stonewalled and wondered if it was his military background.

I followed him, but said, "So what exactly are you hiding?"

He'd already started up the black metal staircase, but his head whipped around to glance at me. "Nothing."

It had to be connected to why Jessica stopped working weekends. We reached the second floor, and I was about to say that exact thing, when I saw we weren't alone.

Cathy, the intern from Bonny Hazel whose sound bite had gone viral, stood at one of several tables. She wore the same shorts and tank top as the last time I'd seen her. On the tables were clear plastic boxes with salamanders inside.

Cathy looked up from feeding a cricket to one. "Hey, it's you."

I turned to Tyler. "We met this morning at Bonny Hazel."

He nodded and then looked at Cathy. "Have you seen Ceasonne?"

"She went out for coffee. Should be back any second."

"I'll go look for her." He quickly left.

I suspected his real reason for leaving was to avoid my asking more questions about why Jessica had stopped working weekends. I would probably have followed him and done just that, except I wanted to talk to Cathy alone.

"What are you doing here?" I said after Tyler had disappeared down the steps. "I thought you'd be unpacking or sleeping or something."

Her mood shifted dramatically. "I can't go home. People won't stop calling my parents about that TV interview. Some people even recognized me when we stopped for gas. They called me horrible names." She looked at me with big, open eyes. "It was fifteen seconds. I opened my mouth and talked for fifteen seconds and now that's who I am forever."

I didn't know how to help her, so I repeated what Rod had said to me. "It may have been bad, but it won't define who you are in the future."

"I really didn't mean it the way it sounded. It was such a bone-headed mistake." She gently moved the box with the salamander to where the others were stacked. "I was so excited to be on TV. I wanted everyone to think I was brave for not evacuating. Which is total BS because I was the loudest one telling Dr. Polignac we had to get out."

"How old are you?"

"Eighteen."

Of course she was young, hardly a surprise, and inexperienced and unaware—all the things you'd expect an eighteen-year-old to be. But what surprised me was how unguarded she was, as though she invested every part of herself in what she thought and felt. If I saw her again in twenty years, would she still look that way? Hadn't she already learned from the disastrous interview to hold pieces of herself back?

The impulsiveness, the ignorance that even small acts might have permanent consequences, even her childish desire to sound brave—everything that had led Cathy to those disastrous fifteen seconds—morphed into something precious and fleeting. I felt an overwhelming desire to protect it.

The words came out before I even knew what was happening. "Stay away from Farris. He likes you for the wrong reasons and he'll treat you badly."

She laughed.

I immediately backpedaled. "I'm sorry. I don't know why I did that. It's none of my business."

She laughed again. "It's okay. I was onto Farris's whole routine before I even got up to Bonny Hazel." She lowered her voice. " 'My art keeps me in touch with nature. Maybe we can go camping and I can sketch you.' " She giggled some more and then spoke in her natural voice. "One of the other interns warned me about him. He's used that move on every girl who came through."

"Did he try it on Jessica?"

Cathy took a bag of crickets and placed them on the table. "She's a woman and he met her, so probably."

"What about Dr. Polignac? Does he hit on all the interns too?"

She shook her head. "He flirts like a horndog with anything blond, but I think he's secretly faithful to Ceasonne. He's just terrified of getting older."

I heard footsteps and we both turned to the stairs. Ceasonne walked up. Cathy's cheeks turned scarlet.

"I've got your latte." It seemed impossible that Ceasonne hadn't heard at least part of our conversation. Yet from watching her as she crossed the room, you'd never guess it. "I'm sorry it took so long."

"No problem." Cathy took the latte without making eye contact. She almost spilled it trying to take a drink.

Ceasonne's own hand was rock solid as she took a sip of her own. "I just spoke with Tyler downstairs. He says you're an old friend of Jessica's. I'm sorry. I didn't realize when I saw you at Bonny Hazel. I thought you were an official or something."

"It's okay. You were focused on evacuating."

She turned to Cathy. "I don't mean to be rude, but would you mind giving us some privacy."

"Not at all." Cathy looked relieved. "I should go home anyway. You can only delay the inevitable for so long." She picked up her purse and took her coffee. "I gave them all crickets and only the ones on the far tables need water."

On her way out she looked at me. "If I don't see you again, thanks for the advice."

"It really will be okay. You won't feel this bad forever."

Cathy left and Ceasonne pulled a phone from a pocket on her long skirt. She checked the screen, then returned it to the pocket.

"When did you hear about Jessica?" I said.

"My husband called last night. I was shocked. Jessica is almost thirty years younger than me. How can she be gone and I'm still here?"

Those were hardly the words of a grieving friend. "Were you close?"

"No. But we worked together for ten years. She was a big part of my life then."

"Did Tyler tell you I think Jessica was murdered?"

Ceasonne walked across the room and retrieved a plastic spray bottle. "Yes, but I can't believe it. Jessica wasn't a friendly person, but nobody could want to kill her." She checked the bottle, then walked to the far table.

I followed her. A bank of frosted windows filled that end of the room with soft lighting. Ceasonne looked beautiful while still seeming completely natural.

"Do you know anyone she was close to?" I said. "Maybe someone she might have confided in?"

She removed the top from a box and misted the contents with water. "No. This job was her life. She dated a couple times over the years, but never seriously, and she never mentioned friends." She looked up suddenly. "Except, maybe you should talk to her neighbor. I remember he was her emergency contact."

"Do you remember his name?"

"No, but Jessica said he took care of her yard."

"Is that code for something?"

Ceasonne laughed. "No. Jessica has notoriously bad luck with plants. She's killed so many of them in the office that some of the less charitable volunteers started saying, 'Jessica may love the environment, but the environment doesn't love her.'"

I must have frowned because Ceasonne said, "I know it sounds mean, but in the early days if someone wanted to make a joke at your expense, they'd lace your coffee with LSD."

I followed her as she moved down the table to the next boxes.

"The early days sound pretty extreme. How many years were you with Green Seed?"

"I joined in the seventies when we were nothing more than a loose coalition of activists. Everyone had their own agenda. We were completely disorganized, but we made up for it by being loud and annoying." She was describing discord and chaos, but her tone was almost nostalgic. "But those days are long gone. Green Seed has been squarely in the mainstream for more than twenty years."

"Why did the organization change so much?"

"We all got older. The movement got older. By the time Jessica became involved, we were already an organized nonprofit with a board of directors and a five-year plan."

"Could Jessica have been killed because of her work for Green Seed?"

Her forehead creased. "It's not a controversial organization."

"What about the McClellans?" Ceasonne looked confused so I continued, "The family that owned the property in the Terrill Valley. Could they still be angry that you protested and stopped their plans?"

"Why would they be? In the end, we paid them a fair price to buy the land, and they didn't have to invest time and money in developing it. Everyone was happy." She checked the phone again, then replaced it before moving to the next table.

I followed her. "Jessica's friends and family seem to think your group alternated between drug orgies and chaining yourself to trees."

Ceasonne rolled her eyes. "Jessica was the only one who was ever crazy enough to trespass on private property and chain herself to something—and it was a bulldozer, not a tree." She shook her head. "We told her not to do it. Everything was about PR and paperwork at that point. We were working through official channels."

"I have a hard time believing there were absolutely no shenanigans or recreational drug use in your group. I was living up by Elizabeth at the time and I remember the stories."

She tried to suppress a small grin. "There were a few hangers-on who were into that sort of thing. Those types were always around. Leftovers from the early days."

"Did you know Jessica was a minor and her father didn't approve of her involvement?"

She shook her head. "Not until the chaining incident. Her father showed up making a lot of threats. We told him we didn't like it any better than he did, but he wouldn't listen."

"But you still let her help once a week, didn't you? Every Saturday."

She froze in the middle of removing a lid. "How did you know that? Nobody knows that."

"Jessica told me."

"You really must have been close." She finished removing the lid, then misted what was inside the box. "I should have sent her away, but Jessica typed a hundred words per minute. It was too much of a temptation. As soon as she turned eighteen, I offered her a real job here in our main offices. And when I told her she'd need a college degree to move up in the organization, she went to school at night."

"No wonder she didn't have a personal life."

"Everything for Jessica was about Green Seed and doing the good work. She may have died young, but her life mattered. She made the world a better place. Some people live to a hundred and can't say that."

Ceasonne set down the bottle and rubbed her eyes. I couldn't tell if she was crying or just tired. I wondered if she cared more for Jessica than she'd admitted, but then decided she probably wasn't even sure herself.

She looked at the cell phone. The skin around her eyes sagged. "I should go talk to her neighbor. Someone needs to tell him."

"Why don't we go together? We can finish talking in the car."

She replaced the final lid. "I'd like to go straight home afterwards. You won't have a way back here."

"I have someone waiting in a car downstairs. They can follow us."

She let out a deep breath. It wasn't as obvious as a sigh, but the implication was the same. "Okay, but I'll be a minute." She picked up the phone and stared at it, as if willing it to ring. "When you left Bonny Hazel, was my husband still refusing to evacuate?"

"He was." I smiled. "But I told Farris to follow your advice and act like he didn't care."

Her head jerked to look at me. "Really?"

I nodded. "I think Professor Polignac will go. He's got the RV loaded and is moving the remaining salamanders into the basement."

"I don't know why he's being so stubborn. The equipment and property are all insured, and when the University of California takes over next year, they'll invest even more money in the facility."

I straightened. "I thought UC was just providing logistical support. Are they taking over the property?"

She looked away. "I believe so."

I thought about the empty desks downstairs. "Is Green Seed selling them Bonny Hazel? Does Green Seed need money?"

Ceasonne returned the mister to where she'd gotten it. "I'm no longer privy to their private financial business."

"But you've heard things?"

"I'll be ready to go in a few minutes." She flipped open the phone. "If you don't mind, I'd like a few moments of privacy while I call my husband."

I went downstairs. Tyler wasn't in his office so I approached the receptionist. "Where's Tyler?"

"He's out back in the alley." She hesitated. "We have a situation out there."

"What kind of situation?"

"It's just something that comes up every once in a while." She took a quick look around. "We call him the poo fairy."

"Who?"

"Tyler thinks he must be a homeless man, but we don't really know who it is. He leaves his . . . presents for us."

"You've got to be joking."

She shook her head. "I wish I were."

"I can't believe I'm saying this, but how do I get to the back alley?"

She pointed behind me. "Straight back, behind the staircase."

"If Ceasonne comes down, tell her I'm out there with Tyler."

I found him hosing down the asphalt between Ceasonne's Prius and an Insight. He heard me coming and shut off the hose. "This must look odd, but you see we have—"

I raised my hand. "I got the basics and I don't want the details."

He looked embarrassed. "It's worth putting up with some inconvenience for this location, and it's rent-controlled."

"Is Green Seed in financial trouble? Is that what you were trying to hide earlier?"

He stepped back. "I'm not going to talk about private financial matters with a reporter."

"I'm a shooter, not a reporter, and I'm not doing a story."

He turned the hose back on and resumed spraying the ground.

I started to yell at him, but at the last moment stopped myself. I tried to muster enough self-control to sound polite. "You can trust me. I'm not here to cause trouble. I'm here for Jessica, because I owe her and because nobody else cares enough to speak up for her."

He stopped the hose.

"I'm not trying to harm Green Seed," I continued. "Or publicize whatever financial trouble you're in. And by not telling me, you're making it seem much worse than it probably is."

He looked at me. "Do I have your word this won't end up in a story?"

I nodded. "You have my word."

He glanced up and down the alley. "Perception is important for fund-raising, and what I'm about to say is not for public consumption." He stepped close to me and lowered his voice. "The recession has been very hard on all nonprofits. Charitable giving is way down."

"Was Jessica going to lose her job?"

"No, nothing like that, but we've been cutting costs and looking for ways to increase revenue." He took one last look around. "A little over a year ago I floated a plan to liquidate our land holdings near Elizabeth."

"You don't mean . . ."

"I tried to sell the nature preserve."

TWENTY

Tyler looked around again. "The land used to be environmentally significant because of the Terrill salamander, but now it's thriving down at the local lake. There's no reason to hold on to that property. And we've been paying to maintain it all these years."

"I'm guessing Jessica didn't see it that way."

"She threatened to quit, and the board gave her a one-year reprieve to raise the money. But they made it clear that if revenue didn't dramatically increase, they'd begin selling lots next year."

"You're subdividing the land instead of selling it in one piece?"

He nodded. "Except Bonny Hazel. We're donating that to the University of California so they can maintain a research post there."

My voice rose. "But selling the land in pieces, for subdivisions and strip malls, is exactly what you prevented the McClellans from doing thirteen years ago."

He raised a hand at me. "I'm the first to admit it's unfair, but that doesn't change the reality of the situation. Green Seed acted in good faith when we bought the property, but now we need to liquidate assets."

"But Jessica was goofy about that land. She'd never sit by and allow this to happen."

"She acted like the money was going to come in somehow, but it was bluster. She had to have known it was a lost cause." Tyler began coiling the hose. "When you asked me earlier why she stopped coming in on weekends, I couldn't tell you all this for obvious reasons, but I think she was angry. She gave her entire adult life to this organization and she felt betrayed."

I suspected it had more to do with the weekend trips to Bonny Hazel her brother had mentioned, but before I could say so, the door opened and Ceasonne walked out. She looked down at the puddle. "This is still going on?"

Tyler finished coiling the hose and stood up. "I'm calling the police this time."

"What are they going to do?"

He shrugged. "It's something at least."

Ceasonne hit a button on her key chain and the Prius beeped. "Have fun with that."

I thanked Tyler and gave him my business card in case he needed to get in touch. I was about to get in the car, but stopped. "E-mail me that story Jessica wanted to do."

"Pesticide overuse?"

"If you send me something, I'll see what I can do with it."

From the car I used Rod's cell to call Teddy and Freddy and let them know the plan. They were illegally parked in a driveway down the block and had no trouble following the Prius.

Ceasonne turned and drove toward the ocean. Even from several blocks away I could see the sun sparkling on the blue water. "It's beautiful here, even if there is a poo fairy and nowhere to park."

"What?" she said.

"The ocean, it's beautiful. I guess people would put up with a lot to be able to live near something like that."

"You'd be surprised what compromise can do to you." She turned onto Venice Boulevard. Trendy restaurants and boutiques competed with medical-marijuana shops and tattoo parlors. Every car was either an SUV or a hybrid.

"What do you mean?"

"The longer you compromise, the less the bad things bother you, but eventually, you stop enjoying the good things too." She glanced at the ocean as we drove through an intersection. "Eventually you don't remember which was which."

"That's one of the saddest things I've ever heard."

"Sorry." She glanced at me, then returned her eyes to the road. "I'm upset because I couldn't reach anyone at Bonny Hazel. Let's talk about something else."

"Do you mind if I ask why you left Green Seed?"

"I was upset about cuts to art programs in the public school system. When I heard Art for Life needed a new director, I jumped at the chance." The answer was simple and made sense, but it rolled off her tongue as if it were something she'd memorized.

We passed yet another marijuana store. This one had valet parking. "How many medical-marijuana stores do you have down here?"

"A lot."

"Is that why Jessica started drug testing?"

"You know about that?" I nodded. "She pushed that through six years ago while I was still in charge—and not just for employees. She made volunteers test too. But despite that, she actually approved of medical marijuana."

"Why the exception?"

"Her mother died of breast cancer. Jessica told me about it when she was campaigning for the ballot initiative. It was one of the few times she really opened up about herself."

"What did she say?"

"It sounded pretty horrible. Her mother suffered through chemo, radiation, a double mastectomy, and then more chemo. It went on for years before she died."

"Is that why she allowed the salamander experiments to continue at Bonny Hazel. Was she hoping it could lead to a cure?"

"Jessica never said." Ceasonne slowed the car. "This is her apartment." She pulled into a driveway and cut the engine. Jessica's apartment was one of three units in a simple, one-story building. Bars covered all the doors and windows and a FOR RENT sign hung on the first apartment.

I turned back from looking out the window. "Did she talk about her father or brother?"

"Jessica has a brother?" I nodded. "I had no idea. She did mention her father a couple times, and I picked up a little bit here and there over the years. It sounded like Jessica got stuck doing most of the caretaking when her mother was dying. I think her father couldn't handle losing his wife and lost himself. Jessica had no choice but to grow up fast."

"Or maybe her father was always weak and Jessica was always strong. Maybe instead of being changed by what happened, what happened brought out what they'd always been."

"Maybe. Jessica was definitely strong. She had a way of exhausting you. By the end of my time at Green Seed, I could barely keep up with her."

"Is that why you left?"

"You want the truth?"

I smiled. "That's the general idea."

"What I told you earlier wasn't a lie, but it's not why I left." Ceasonne paused. "Jessica wore me out. She was constantly pushing. She wasn't ambitious for herself, but she thought Green Seed could always do more. She's a big part of why we got into animal rights. And she was right. We could do more, but after ten years I was exhausted."

She looked past me at the apartments. "The problem is, I'm still exhausted. Now more than ever. Maybe it's like you said about her father. Maybe I was always weak and Jessica just brought out what I'd always been."

"I wasn't talking about you."

"I know." She pressed the engine button. "I'm not coming in. Apologize to the neighbor, if he even still lives there."

I thanked her for talking with me and got out. She drove away, and Teddy and Freddy pulled up.

I opened the side door and took out my gear bag. "Do you want to go look for a place to park and I'll call when I'm done?"

"Dude." Freddy laughed. "Seriously, no point in even trying."

They pulled into the driveway and waited for me. A small, striped awning covered the door to 201. According to the address I'd seen on Jessica's driver's license, this was her residence.

I took the keys I'd found in her desk and tried the locks.

No hungry cat greeted me inside the apartment. No secret boyfriend walked out of the bedroom in a towel. The apartment was empty except for the objects and things that Jessica had left behind. In another month it would all be in a landfill.

I shut the door and locked it. The layout was simple. One open room that served as living room, dining room, and kitchen, then a bedroom and a bath were down a short hallway. A breakfast bar separated the kitchen area from a dining room table. A sliding glass door on the other side of the table offered a view of the yard.

More folders and spreadsheets covered the table, and I would have had a hard time telling it apart from her desk at work. The apartment had almost no knickknacks or photos. The furniture was generic and looked as if it had hastily been ordered from an IKEA catalog. There was no personality. Nothing that was uniquely Jessica.

My eye kept coming back to the yard. Most of the lawn had been taken out and replaced with raised beds. Flowering jasmine covered all three sides of the fence. The view out the square windows reminded me of the painting in Jessica's office. Maybe that's why there was nothing on the walls of the apartment. Jessica preferred to let the yard be her decoration.

I turned on the TV and put a cable news channel on. The story wasn't about the fire, but it was just a matter of time before it came up in the rotation. Jessica's cupboards were empty except for organic fair-trade coffee. The refrigerator contained six prepackaged vegan meals, soy milk, and an open container of baking soda.

I turned on a laptop sitting on the dining room table. It had never completely been shut down and quickly came back to life. I glanced through her work files, but didn't see anything noteworthy. I closed all the folders and documents. Jessica's virtual desktop was much neater than her physical one. The only document saved there was labeled #'s.

I opened it. Halfway down the list I stopped reading and called

Rod. I got his voice mail and left a message. When I looked over at the TV, his tired face filled the screen. I turned the volume up.

"As more ground is lost, it becomes a virtual certainty that the powerful evening winds will drive the fire up Mt. Terrill." Behind him was a red sky mixed with black smoke. "The real question now is if it can be stopped before reaching the communication hub on the mountain's ridge."

I returned to the laptop to print Jessica's list of important numbers and passwords, but then couldn't find the printer.

"An army of over a thousand fire-suppression personnel are amassing here to protect those structures," Rod continued. His voice sounded hoarse. "But after the two tragic deaths earlier in the week, authorities have vowed to take no chances . . ."

I walked down the hallway to the bedroom. I found the printer and also a little bit more of Jessica's personality. The comforter was rose-colored with elaborate beading. It reminded me of the grown-up version of a little girl's princess bed. Another oil painting like the one in her office hung on the wall. It had a similar look and was also signed *C. Egan.* On the opposite wall were framed photos.

Some were black-and-white of people long dead. Others showed Jessica as a little girl with her brother and both parents. One showed a smiling woman with a pregnant belly lounging by the lake. I guessed it was her mother. There were also childhood photos of Jessica and Byrdie running for student council together, and several of Byrdie and Lee's sons. Arnaldo Bedolla, a woman I guessed was his wife, and their two daughters were there too. One of the largest photos was of Jessica with the Polignacs. It looked like a party for Ceasonne when she'd left Green Seed, which was probably an important day for Jessica since it marked her ascension.

I turned on the printer. The document printed immediately. While I was looking through Jessica's closet, which contained a shocking number of gray pants suits made of hemp or bamboo, my phone rang.

"Where are you?" Rod asked.

"Jessica Egan's apartment."

"In L.A.?"

"Uh-huh. You sound surprised."

"You hate big cities in general and L.A. in particular."

"The ocean is pretty."

He laughed, but his voice cracked.

"You should rest your voice until your next hit."

"It won't help. It's the smoke, and my next hit is in five minutes. I feel like a hamster on a wheel."

"I just saw you on CNN. You look good. Tired, but good."

"Tired about sums it up." He paused. "You know how you said I was like a kid in a candy store last night?"

"Yes."

"It turns out this is a lot less fun without you."

"That's sweet of you to say."

"And by a lot less, I mean no fun at all."

"I miss you too."

"Three minutes," I heard Dennis call in the background.

Rod made a noise that sounded like "Ugh."

"Do you still have Jessica Egan's phone?" I said.

"Yes, but I haven't had any luck getting past her security features."

"I may have her password." I picked up the printed list and read him the code. He promised to try it and call me back as soon as he had a free moment.

I finished going through the bedroom. On the floor of the closet I found a fire safe. I checked the printed list and found the combination.

Inside was an insurance policy, a college diploma still in its cardboard mailer, a passport, a birth certificate, and a last will and testament. It had been drawn up by a local lawyer the previous year. Brad Egan was the beneficiary of a 401(k) containing over $100,000. Jessica also left him the oil paintings in her office and bedroom. They'd been done by their mother, Celia.

Of her nonretirement assets, $50,000 was to be converted into cash and divided equally among Byrdie and Lee's sons, Arnaldo's two daughters, and an adult man named Micah Reynolds. His address was listed as the apartment next door. The rest of her money and assets were to be donated to Green Seed. It actually looked as if she had several hundred thousand dollars saved. I guess if you're a workaholic and don't care about where you live or how you decorate it, you can save a lot of money.

I folded the document and slipped it back into the sleeve. That's when I saw the envelope on the bottom of the safe. The Otto's Pawn logo peeked out from under some other papers. At first my mind refused to believe it. I counted the money inside twice. One hundred and fifty dollars—Jessica's emergency coming-home money.

I don't know how long I wasted crying. It was a silly and sentimental thing to do. The time would have been much better spent trying to solve Jessica's murder. But all at once I felt real heartache that she was dead, and there was nothing else to do but cry.

After slipping the envelope in my back pocket, I finished searching the apartment. I didn't find anything else. I turned off the TV and computer, then locked up.

I walked the rest of the way down the driveway. A homemade sign was taped to the last door.

NO VISITORS!!!
UNLESS YOU ARE MEALS ON WHEELS, OR A NURSE,
OR AN UNDERTAKER, DO NOT KNOCK ON MY DOOR.

I rang the bell. I could hear *The Price Is Right* playing inside. After a few moments I rang again. Still nothing. This time I leaned on the button and didn't let go.

The front door opened. Behind the bars of the still-locked security door, an old man glared at me. "What?"

Despite his age, the man was tall and I had to look up at him. "Are you Micah Reynolds?"

"No visitors." He started to close the door.

"I'm here about Jessica Egan."

"Can't you read? This is 202. She lives in 201." He started to slam the door shut.

"Hold on. I need to talk to you about Jessica." Normally I'd have thrown my ample foot into the door opening, but the bars prevented it.

The door stopped two inches from the door frame. "What about Jessica? I don't know when she's coming back, if that's what you're after. I don't keep tabs on her or anything."

I started to tell him she was dead, but hesitated. "Maybe you should sit down."

The door opened. "Where exactly am I going to do that? I'm standing in the hallway."

"I'm sorry. It's just . . . I have some bad news to tell you."

He snorted. "What, is she dead?"

I didn't know what to say. "Maybe you should sit down."

He looked down at me. His eyes were black dots peeking out from a face full of rough and cracked skin. A few strands of thin, oily hair ran back over his patchy scalp. "She's dead?" he said in a quieter voice.

"I'm sorry. I tried to break it to you gently."

"Don't be an idiot." He unlocked the security door, then turned back into the apartment. "There's no gentle way to break that kind of news."

I entered. The smell was intense. A strange combination of bacon grease, air freshener, and old-man stink. I reluctantly closed the door behind me.

"Come in here," he called from the living room.

The apartment layout was a mirror of Jessica's, but the decor was very different. The space next to the sliding glass door, where Jessica had a dining room table, had been turned into a garden shed. A heavy-duty plastic tarp covered the floor, and a potting bench leaned against the wall. Bags of soil and fertilizer were in the corner, and tools hung neatly along the front of the breakfast bar.

The living room looked more normal. A fifty-inch flat-screen television hung on the wall. Opposite it, Mr. Reynolds sat in a recliner and wiped his eyes on the back of his arm. I wondered if I should sit down, but then I realized the only other piece of furniture was a large end table with a lamp.

He pointed to the closet. "There's a chair in there, if you want to sit."

I opened the closet. It was packed from floor to ceiling in a precarious puzzle of shapes and colors. I recognized boxes of Cheerios, Andes mints, a tackle box, shoes and sweaters stored in clear plastic containers, soap, motor oil, envelopes, a giant bag of red and green rubber bands. Leaning up against the front was a folded beach chair. I pulled it out and set it up across from him.

"I keep it for Jessica. For when she comes over."

I had no idea how to act. He looked sad, so I thought I should be gentle, but he'd rebuffed my sympathy at the door. "Do you have any family I can call for you?"

He shook his head. "Had a wife and kids once, but it wasn't for me."

I forgot to be gentle. "You mean you ran out on them?"

He forgot to be sad. "I only got married because I was going to Korea and I wanted to get in her pants. Then stupid me went and lived."

"Bad luck," I said before I could stop myself.

He looked up and smiled. "You're right. I'm a creep, but I tried. I couldn't stand family life. I wanted to kill myself so bad. I used to take out my dad's old gun just to show myself I had a way out."

What was I doing here? I felt an overwhelming urge to run out, but instead I managed to say, "Sorry."

"Don't be. I finally figured leaving would be better than blowing my brains out."

"What about your kids?"

"I loved them, but I still left." When I didn't say anything, he added, "I don't expect you to understand. Not many people would."

I adjusted the lawn chair and sat down. "Did Jessica understand? Is that why you two were friends?"

"We weren't friends. She paid me to work her garden, that's all. Twenty-five dollars a week." He gestured to my chair. "Don't get ideas because I kept that for her. It didn't matter to me if she came or not. Most times I don't even have that stupid soy milk she puts in her coffee."

I smiled. "I take it you're not a vegan?"

He rolled his eyes. "None of my business what she wants to eat, but you couldn't pay me to live like that." He paused. His momentary show of strength faded. "How'd it happen?"

"She drowned in the local lake where she grew up."

"That doesn't sound like her. She was a real careful girl."

"She was murdered."

His head shot up. "What? Who would do something like that?"

"I think I know, but I'm not sure why."

"What about the police?"

"They're too busy with the fire to do much." I inched my chair closer. "That's why I drove down here. I used to know Jessica a long time ago. I'm trying to find out what happened to her."

"Nobody would want that girl dead. All she cared about was saving animals and global warming and all that junk. And I thought she was goofy for doing it, but who'd want to hurt her for that?" I waited while he took a breath and wiped his eyes. "I told her, the planet isn't going to save you, but she said it was her calling. I told her nobody would thank her for it, but she didn't care."

"All the same, I'm pretty sure someone did kill her." He didn't say anything. "Was there anything unusual going on this past year?"

He shook his head.

"Did she start going away on weekends?"

"Sometimes, I guess. She used to work all the time anyway, so who could tell?"

"Could she have been dating someone and keeping it a secret? Maybe a married guy?"

His head shot up. "Do I look like some girlfriend she'd tell that stuff to?"

"Then try and think." My voice matched his for crankiness. "There must have been something wrong." He shook his head. "She was closer to you than anyone else. You must have noticed something."

His head stopped shaking. He took an almost involuntary glance toward the yard.

"What?"

"It's nothing."

"See, I'm not really believing you right now."

His face turned angry. "Jessica's business is Jessica's business and my business is my business. That's the way we both like it." He got up. "I think it's time for you to go. I'm an old man. I can't be agitated like this."

I stood up and he followed me down the hall. At the door I stopped. "I saw Jessica's will. She left you ten thousand dollars."

He looked away. "Why'd she go and do a stupid thing like that?"

"If I had to guess, I'd say it was because she liked you."

"Jessica didn't like people. She never was comfortable around 'em. That's why she was so goofy about animals and plants and stuff." He glanced back toward the yard again. "I don't know. None of my business, anyway."

"Are you trying to protect Jessica or yourself?"

He took a deep breath. "I'm sure it's nothing. I never asked her about it." I waited, then after a moment he gestured for me to come back inside. "Come on. I'll show you."

He shut the door again and I followed him through the apartment and into the backyard. He opened the gate and we stepped into Jessica's yard. He led me to one of the flower beds. He pointed to a medium-size plant sandwiched between two larger ones.

"I don't understand."

"It's probably nothing." He looked around the yard—everywhere but at the plant.

I looked straight down on it. The plant appeared to my untrained eyes like a generic green shrub. It blended almost seamlessly into the two larger ones around it. "I don't get it. It's just a plant."

He reached down and tore a leaf from the underside. Without saying anything he handed it to me.

I looked at the leaf and then him. "Is this what I think it is?"

He started backing away. "I don't know anything and I never asked." He turned and went back to his own yard.

TWENTY-ONE

I decided to call in a team of experts to confirm my suspicion.

"Dude, it's totally pot," Freddy said.

Teddy looked up from where he was examining the plant on all fours. "But it's like some kind of awesome hybrid or something."

I knelt down. "If you smoked it, would you get high?"

Freddy grinned and reached for a leaf. "Only one way to find out."

I stopped him. "It's evidence in a murder investigation."

He straightened. "Bummer."

"It's not budding yet anyway." Teddy stuck his head in underneath the leaves to get a better look. He might have been a mechanic looking under a car. "I think the point wasn't, like, to make weed that didn't mess you up. 'Cause who'd want that?"

"Totally," Freddy said. "That's like a crime against humanity."

Teddy continued, "I think they bred it so it wouldn't look like itself, when the stuff was being grown."

"You mean, they were trying to hide the grow?"

He nodded.

I looked at Freddy and pointed outside. "Go get your gear. We need to shoot some video."

I left the plant where it was, but made sure we had plenty of tape documenting it. The cell I'd gotten from Rod had died, so as soon as we got on the road, I called Callum on Teddy's phone. I explained where we were and what had happened. He said Lucero had been looking for me and I suggested we all meet at the station. I slept most of the two-hour drive back to Bakersfield.

I awoke about twenty minutes from town. The land on each

side of the freeway ran in flat planes. Neat rows of lettuce and grapes stretched into the distance. The horizon was open without any skyscrapers or hills boxing us in. Occasionally an oil derrick would appear between farms, pumping at its own slow pace.

Freddy got off the 99 near downtown. We passed the turn for Buck Owens' Crystal Palace. Buck's gone now, but his restaurant/nightclub is still going strong. As if cued to my thoughts, Freddy turned on a CD of Buck singing "Streets of Bakersfield."

The Wonder Twins both sang along as we drove. The wide, flat streets and excess space between the buildings, cars, people, trees—everything—felt luxurious after being in cramped and over-built L.A.

Freddy drove the van into the KJAY lot and parked next to Granny Pants, our backup live truck. It's really just an old Chevy Suburban with a collapsed microwave mast on its roof.

Freddy kept the engine running. "Mind if we drop you here, chief?"

"Don't worry." I slid toward the door. "I'm going to talk to Trent about getting you two paid for today. Since we came back with tape, it's a justifiable expense."

"It's not that," Freddy said. "We just don't want to get con-scripted."

"Totally, dude, we got class tonight."

I froze reaching for the door handle. "What class?"

Always upbeat Teddy smiled. "We're signed up at BC."

"You're going to Bakersfield College?" I looked from one to the other. "When did that happen?"

"It's just one class, dude." Freddy kept facing forward in the driver's seat. "Not a big deal."

Teddy turned and looked back toward me. "It's sort of a big deal."

"It's not a big deal," Freddy said again.

Teddy twisted and stretched even farther toward me, as though about to confide a secret. "We're getting too old to be, like, every-body's favorite jackasses. I'm going to be twenty-four next month."

"I never said we're too old to be jackasses." Freddy still didn't turn around. "And we're not jackasses."

"The new sports guy is actually younger than us. That's never happened before."

"I totally said we needed to be proactive about our futures, dude." Freddy finally turned to look at me. "I never said anything about getting older. I never said that."

"It's okay. I understand." I smiled at Teddy. "Let me know if you need to shift your schedules. I won't tell Callum or Trent why."

I took my gear bag and got out. The triple-digit heat was a shock to my system. I rushed to get inside where there was air-conditioning.

I entered the newsroom from the back. KJAY was in live breaking-news coverage of the fire. The rows of desks were all full. Everyone was working. In addition to the conversations, phone calls, and screaming matches, a blur of different audio came from the many TV monitors placed around the room.

The new sports reporter Teddy had just mentioned saw me and got up from a desk. He'd recently graduated college and was annoying everyone with his great attitude and sunny disposition. "Hey, Lilly," he called. "Can I have Freddy on Saturday?"

I passed the bin where I'd normally put my video and walked straight up to the assignment desk. This raised platform in the rear corner of the newsroom was where Callum kept his eagle eye on the rest of the room.

Callum's unibrow dipped in the middle when he saw me. "Lucero's not here yet."

The new guy came up behind me. "Can I have Freddy on Saturday? I've got a competitive-swim thing to cover and need a second shooter."

"I have to look at the schedule to confirm," I said. "But we should have coverage."

"All right." He raised his hand for a high five. " 'And it's a Breaking Blast.' "

He'd gone through several attempts at creating a signature tagline for his sports highlights. I could only assume this was the latest.

I looked at him and shook my head. "No."

His hand dropped. "You really don't like it?"

"Besides its inherent lameness," Callum began, "it's perfect."

The door to the studio opened and the floor director's head popped in. He covered his headset's mic as he yelled toward the assignment desk, "We still need relief at prompter. Kylie has to pee."

"I'm working on it," Callum shouted.

The new sports guy cleared his throat. "How about, 'and it's a Bouncing Blast.' "

"No," Callum and I said in unison.

"You're right. That's no good." He shook his head and started to walk away. "It sounded okay in my head . . . Miracle Blast . . . Blowout Blast." He trailed off as he got farther from us.

I raised my hand with the tape and offered it to Callum. "You want to see my exclusive video? This is a story with both murder and drugs."

He smiled. "I bet you say that to all the boys."

"Just you." I handed him the tape. "And sometimes Rod."

Callum took the tape and swiveled around to the wall of decks and monitors behind him. He killed the audio on a live shot Rod was doing and played my tape. After watching it, and listening to my commentary, he rubbed his hands together. "Try and get Lucero to comment on tape. He won't, but try." He paused and thought for a moment. "At the very least we can say we're assisting in their investigation."

He wanted copies made before Lucero got there. I hooked my phone up to a charger and started to leave.

"Hey, Lilly?" Callum said. "You'll never hear me say this again, but thank you for lying to me and completely going against a direct order. This story is going to be huge for us."

"You're welcome."

I took the tape to one of the edit bays lining the newsroom. I'd made several copies when I heard a knock.

Leanore slid open the sliding glass door. "Last time I saw you, you were throwing my purse at me."

"I'm sorry." I hit eject on the deck. "I know this is small consolation, but I wouldn't have stopped to throw that purse at just anyone."

She laughed. "So leaving me stranded in a hundred-and-five-degree weather is proof of how much you like me?"

I labeled the tape and added it to the pile. "When you put it like that, I sound pretty messed up."

Leanore frowned. "Hey, you know I'm teasing, right?"

"I'm sorry. It's not you."

She walked in, then slid the door closed behind her. "The word around the newsroom is that you knew the lady who drowned up in Elizabeth."

"I hadn't seen her in thirteen years."

"You're obviously troubled." Leanore sat down in the other chair. There was barely room for both of us in the small space and our knees touched. "Do you want to talk?"

I paused. "The dead woman was a really strong person." I glanced at Leanore, who nodded as though she understood. "There was no gray with her. Most people who believe in animal rights become vegetarians, but then they eat fish and dairy and, you know, just do their best with it. Jessica became a vegan. She refused to exploit animals in any way. Her principles were absolute and I really liked that about her."

"How did she die?"

"That's what so depressing. She started compromising. I think it got harder for her as she got older and the stakes got higher." I felt an odd reluctance to tell Leanore any more, as though I should protect Jessica's reputation. "Then this past year Jessica did something really bad, something she knew was wrong and illegal. She must have thought it benefited a greater good, but it led to her death."

Leanore's concern enhanced the crow's-feet around her eyes. "Are you sure your own fear of making bad choices isn't influencing the way you see this woman's life?" She gestured to the muted television where Rod was doing a live shot. "It's obvious that all this attention is going to bring Rod job offers."

I turned away from the monitor. "He says he doesn't want to leave, but that seems crazy to me. He could have his dream job and go home to L.A., where his family and friends all live."

"Can't you go with him? With your talent, you'd have no trouble getting a job there." She paused. "I know you haven't been out of Kern County very much, but maybe if you—"

"It's not that," I said louder than I meant to. "I'm not some hick."

"I don't think you're a hick."

I sighed. "Okay, it's a little that. It's scary. It's a lot of change all at once." She nodded. "I also plain don't like L.A. The ocean is pretty, but the rest of it is either loud and angry, or loud and snobby. And you have to pay to park in front of your own house. And the freeways." I looked up. "But I'd put up with that for Rod."

"Then why don't you? Isn't that the simplest way to solve your problem?"

I didn't say anything.

"What is it, Lilly?"

"I've had this job for almost six years. When I started here . . ." I trailed off. Leanore waited. "My life was crazy and out of control."

She laughed. "A lot of people would say it's crazy and out of control right now, the way this job keeps you running around."

I looked up and our eyes met. "But that's the thing, it's controlled chaos. There's structure to it. I make sense here and I like myself doing this job. I feel good about myself."

"I think I'm going to puke." I looked up and saw Callum standing on the other side of the glass. His voice was muted, but I could still hear him, as he'd undoubtedly heard us. "Stop feeling sorry for yourself."

I cupped my ear and leaned toward the door. "I'm sorry, what did you say?" I looked at Leanore. "Did you hear him?"

Leanore cupped her ear. "Try again, Callum, and this time e-nun-ci-ate."

He looked at Leanore. "Stop encouraging her."

"Still no good," she said. "Try saying it louder."

He ripped open the door. "Stop whining around like some pimply-faced teenager in an after-school special."

"Callum." A panicked desk assistant ran up. "I lost the bird. I swear we had it booked for another ten minutes, but it's gone."

"Give what you have to an editor, and then get on the phone and find out what happened."

"I swear I booked it," she continued. "But it just went to black in the middle."

"I already said get on the phone." Callum's wide middle was jiggling, but he didn't look jolly. "Find out what happened."

She left and then Callum turned to me. The crankiness vanished from his face. He took a breath and prepared to speak.

"I got it." The new sports reporter ran up with such force that he actually pushed Callum out of the doorway. " 'It's a Blowup Blast,' " he shouted.

"No," I said.

Callum righted himself. "You got some kind of fixation with explosives?"

Even Leanore shook her head and muttered, "No, no." She thought for a moment. "How about 'It's a Bakersfield Blast.' "

Callum and I both froze.

The new guy smiled. " 'It's a Bakersfield Blast.' "

"That works," I said.

Even Callum nodded. "That's it."

The new guy turned around and shouted into the newsroom, "Ladies and gentleman, it's a Bakersfield Blast."

Applause erupted from half the room, then he jogged a victory lap around the desks high-fiving people as he went.

Callum watched him for a moment, then turned back to me. "I've got multiple ex-wives and I've made a mess of every friendship I ever had, so maybe you'd rather listen to Leanore's flowery love-will-find-a-way talk."

An uncomfortable feeling settled over the edit bay. Callum looked vulnerable in a way I'd never seen and I wasn't sure I liked. Leanore must have seen it too because she didn't snap back after the obvious dig.

Callum took a breath. "But if you were my kid, I'd tell you life isn't about making the right choice. There is no right choice, just a bunch of lousy compromises. Life is about being strong enough to live with the consequences. And you are strong, so stop whining around and wringing your hands."

He handed me several papers and abruptly changed his tone. "Here's what I got on the McClellans, and Lucero is waiting for you in the conference room."

He slid the door shut again and left.

I got up. "I can't keep Lucero waiting." I shut off the monitor and deck. "Thanks for listening to all my weird personal stuff."

Leanore grabbed my arm as I turned to go. "Lilly, it may sound flowery and trite, but sometimes love does find a way."

"Sometimes?"

She smiled. "Pretend I said *always.*"

I looked over the papers on my way to see Lucero.

The McClellan patriarch had taken his money from the sale and moved to Santa Barbara, where he'd died two years ago. His childless son lived in Seattle, but he owned a patent on some kind of handwriting software and was a rich man in his own right.

When I entered the conference room, an intern was asking Lucero if he wanted coffee.

He saw me and stood. "This better be good. We're about an hour from losing all emergency and police communication for a third of the valley. You better not be wasting my time here."

"I'm fine, thanks for asking. How are you?"

"Cut the smart talk. If you pull this kind of emergency lever, and I take the bait, then you better have some major 911-type info to share. So start sharing."

"Jessica Egan needed money to keep her nonprofit from selling their land in the Terrill Valley, so she farmed marijuana."

He sat back down and looked at the intern. "Black with two Equals."

I told him about Green Seed's plan to sell the nature preserve, Jessica's secret weekend visits, and finished by showing him the video I'd shot of the plant.

"Most of that's guesswork," he said. "But even if you're right, how'd she end up a drowner? If the cartels got wind of what she was doing, they'd have killed her, but not like that."

"This wasn't a professional murder, just like Jessica wasn't a professional drug dealer. These were amateurs, improvising."

"Plural?"

"Jessica never could have managed a marijuana grow on her own, even if she drove up from L.A. on weekends. She needed local help."

"But if the partner wanted to kill her, they would have waited until after the fall harvest. No sense in killing off your labor pool before the hard work is over."

"Jessica wasn't killed for her share of the profits." I sat down. "I know how you must feel about people who farm pot, but Jessica really was a good person. She genuinely wanted to make the world a better place. I think she came up to Elizabeth on Wednesday to turn herself in."

"Why now?"

"The wildfire turned deadly on Monday. I think Jessica blamed herself."

Lucero pulled back.

"I don't have to tell you how many wildfires are accidentally started by people tending marijuana farms." I pointed at the monitor. "And these plants are hybrids. They don't look like marijuana from the air. That's why they don't show up on aerial photos taken in the days before the fire."

He thought for a moment. "You got any ideas about who the partner is?"

I told him my theory and why.

"I have to talk to the detective sergeant," he finally said. "Then we'll get some warrants and take a forensics team up there." Lucero took his two tapes and started to leave.

"Wait." I stopped him. "There's something you're not going to like."

"What's that?"

"Rod's got Jessica's cell phone. I took it out of her unlocked car last night."

He read me the riot act, but in the end admitted I wouldn't be in any trouble.

He left and I checked in with Callum. The evacuation was being declared a success, and the canyon road had been reopened to eastbound traffic. Unfortunately, the humidity had continued to drop and the winds were due to rise in about an hour. Rod and Dennis were doing one final live shot before evacuating back to Command Headquarters.

I checked my phone and found a message from Rod. He'd gotten into Jessica's iPhone and found two voice-mail messages from Farris asking Jessica when she was coming to Bonny Hazel. There were no other messages. Rod's voice sounded even worse than when I'd spoken with him from Jessica's apartment. He said he missed me and couldn't wait to come home.

I took a news van without asking since I doubted Callum would have approved of a third station vehicle being taken up to Elizabeth. I went through the drive-through at John's Burgers and got three orders of chili fries—Rod's favorite junk food. I headed out of town toward the mountains. Traffic was still evacuating down the canyon, but it was sporadic and moving quickly. As I climbed back into the mountains, the skies darkened and I had to flip on the headlights.

At Command Headquarters, I parked in the same spot behind the grandstands. It was weird to be back on campus, even though it had only been half a day since I'd left. The news van Rod had driven up the night before was still parked where we left it. The KBLA satellite truck was also parked there.

Dennis jumped out of his truck and met me halfway.

"Where's Rod?" I handed him one of the styrofoam containers. "He sounded tired on the phone. I thought I'd come up and help."

"He's in your station's live truck."

"Where's the live truck?"

He glanced toward the mountains. "He said it would just take a minute. I told him it was a bad idea, but—"

I cut him off. "What was just going to take a minute?"

"He drove down the mountain. He wanted to check out a spot in the woods by that house with the funny name."

"But didn't they tell you to evacuate?"

Dennis shook his head. "I told him it was a bad idea, but he said it would only take a minute, but now it's been an hour and I'm really starting to worry."

"Why would he go to Bonny Hazel now?"

Dennis got a map out of his truck. "After he called you about the phone messages, he found a GPS program on the dead lady's phone." He opened the map to Mt. Terrill. "There were a bunch of saved locations down in L.A., but only two here."

Dennis pointed to where Rod had drawn a small red circle in the valley and scribbled a set of coordinates directly on the map. "He got all excited because this is where the wildfire started two weeks ago. The dead lady had the exact spot saved in her GPS." Dennis's finger ran up the mountain and stopped at a similar circle to the northeast of Bonny Hazel. "He said he needed to go check the other location before the fire came through and destroyed whatever was there."

I tried to take a deep breath, but my heart was beating too fast. "Have you tried calling him?"

"There's no answer, but that doesn't mean anything. The worse the smoke gets at the top of the mountain, the worse cell reception gets."

"How long has it been since you split up?"

"An hour. Maybe a little more."

"Okay." I looked one direction and then the other. "We need the police right now."

"There's nobody here. Looting broke out in Tilly Heights. They got groups of kids mixed in with real criminal types. They're all running around busting windows, grabbing stuff. They got houses getting broken into. It's a mess over there."

I pulled out my phone and dialed the station. Callum picked up on the first ring. "Lilly, good. You took a news van without asking, which normally I'd be mad about, but since we need you and Rod over in Tilly Heights, I forgive you. Get over there right away. We're hearing all kinds of scanner traffic about—"

"Stop talking and listen. I think they were growing the pot in two locations. Rod got the coordinates of the second grow off Jessica's phone. He went to go check it out and now he's missing."

"Did you try calling his cell?"

"He's not answering." I barely paused before continuing. "If they were trying to salvage plants before the fire, then Rod would have walked right in on them."

"Okay. I'm getting numbers and making calls." I heard him pounding on a keyboard, then he screamed into the newsroom, "Everybody, over here. I mean everybody."

"You need to get help," I said. "I'm counting on you. Everyone here is gone fighting the fire or the looters."

"I'm putting you on hold for a second."

"No. I'm hanging up and then texting you the coordinates."

His voice rose. "Why are you hanging up? Don't do anything stupid."

I hit the end button, then texted the coordinates.

Dennis looked pale and shaken. "You don't really think something could have happened to him?"

I dug into my gear bag and found Lucero's business card. "You need to raise the alarm here. Tell anybody you can find." I handed him the card. "Call this detective too. He knows all about the murder." I got back in the news van. "Give them the coordinates and tell them we need help."

"Wait." Dennis tried to stop my shutting the door, but failed. "You'll never get through. They've got the highway blocked off at Tilly Heights."

I started the engine. "I know a back way."

Dennis pounded on my window. "You don't have time. The fire could blow up any minute."

"Then you better get help fast."

TWENTY-TWO

Friday, 4:55 p.m.

I drove like a madwoman. I should have been stopped and arrested for reckless driving, but all the police were in Tilly Heights.

I pulled in behind the building and cut the engine. "Bud," I screamed, before I was even out of the van. I ran to the back door and threw it open.

Inside the kitchen, Bud froze with a baker's tray in his hands.

I tried to catch my breath. "Rod's trapped on the other side of the mountain at a marijuana grow and the fire is coming and if we don't go save him, he's going to die."

Bud dropped the tray and started for the door.

Outside, he stopped me on the way to the news van. "My ride this time." I barely had time to retrieve my gear bag before he'd jumped in the Double Down Donuts van and started the engine.

If I'd driven like a madwoman, Bud drove like a madman on speed. I tried to give him directions to the back road over the mountain—the one the officer thought the sniper used—but he knew that route better than me. "I've been usin' it to make deliveries," he said. "You just make sure your seat belt works."

He made incredible time, and soon we'd driven up the southern side of Tilly Heights, crossed over the ridge, and were on the other side of the mountain. Bud had a radio in his car and we listened for emergency traffic. Bell had said that the fire wouldn't blow up until it reached the foothills. Once that happened, the blowup might occur immediately, never, or any point in between.

Fortunately, the fire still hadn't reached the foothills when we emerged on Highway 55 from behind the fruit stands. Bud barely slowed before crossing the road and entering the nature preserve.

I told myself not to look down the mountain as we crossed. The view ahead was upsetting enough. If it weren't for the heat, we could have been in a snowstorm in the middle of the night. The windshield wipers couldn't remove the ash and debris fast enough. The wind gusted and roared against the sides of the van.

We reached the fork where the BONNY HAZEL sign pointed to the left. I gestured to the road on the right, where a gate blocked access. "According to Rod's map, the grow is about two miles in."

Bud backed up. "Hold on."

He floored it. Fortunately, the gate had been left unlocked. One of Bud's headlights cracked, but otherwise the damage was minimal.

I don't know how long we drove. My perception of time was alternately slowed down and sped up. We didn't have a GPS, so there was no way to know how close we were to Jessica's coordinates.

I saw the KJAY truck in the headlights. "Stop."

The truck was unlocked, but empty. I found the yellow firefighter's jacket inside with my camera and sticks. I put on the jacket and tied a handkerchief around my mouth. The digital camcorder we'd used at the airstrip was sitting on the counter with Rod's laptop. I dropped it into one of the coat pockets along with my Swiss army knife, Mace, and two flashlights. I got out.

Bud stood next to the entrance to an even smaller dirt road cutting straight down the mountain. He was shielding his face from the wind so I handed him a handkerchief. After putting it on, he pointed down the road. "It's down there, Little Sister."

"How do you know?"

He shone a flashlight on a pile of shrubs and tree branches. "They must have been usin' these to hide the entrance."

I started down the road.

"Hold on. We can't go straight down. They probably got guns." He pointed into the trees. "You circle 'round until you come to the creek. Come in slow. I'll come in from this side."

Bud switched off his light and disappeared into the trees. I turned off my flashlight too. My eyes adjusted and I found I could see fairly well. I walked for a few minutes until I found the creek. I followed it down the mountain, staying in the trees until they abruptly stopped. I turned on my flashlight. A field of marijuana plants began and ran on past the edge of the light. They reached up to my chest and reminded me of a cornfield halfway to maturity.

The field bordered the creek, but I could tell something was wrong with the water. I stepped to the edge and shone the flashlight down. A short distance from where the trees stopped, a large vinyl dam blocked the creek. Its edges were smooth, as though the long tube were filled with air. The creek water was being diverted into a nearby pool to irrigate the grow. The temporary dam wasn't stopping all the water, nor was it probably meant to, but it did drastically reduce the flow down the mountain.

I touched it and the vinyl easily gave. It was too solid and heavy to be filled with air, and I guessed it had water inside.

I heard an engine and quickly shut off my flashlight. I thought I saw a light from somewhere among the marijuana plants. I cautiously began walking toward it. The light got stronger. Finally I saw a truck parked in a clearing. The wind sent smoke swirling in its headlights.

Something moved and I stopped. A man walked quickly through the beams. It was Arnaldo Bedolla.

He wore a handkerchief, but I easily recognized him. "This is your own fault. Don't try and make me feel guilty."

I couldn't see whom he was speaking to, but from his anxious body language I guessed it wasn't a pleasant conversation. "If you and your girlfriend had minded your own business, you wouldn't be here now." He paused to listen, but what he heard upset him even more. "I'm fighting to survive. This is life or death for me. I can't go to jail like some—"

Noise came from a radio attached to his belt. He ripped it off, listened for a moment, then took off running into the darkness.

I hurried to the clearing. Rod sat on the ground leaning against stacks of gardening equipment and fertilizer. His hands were tied behind his back and he wore a handkerchief over his mouth.

"Lilly?" He looked up at me. A bead of sweat ran down his forehead, leaving a track in the accumulated ash. "You're in Bakersfield." His voice was weak and raspy.

"No, I'm here, but I'd rather be in Bakersfield, so come on." I tried to help him up, but he moaned and pulled away. He had a dark stain on his suit jacket. "Are you hurt? What happened?"

"You need to go. Bedolla's radio . . . the fire's at the foothills. You need to run."

I took the Swiss army knife from my pocket. "I'm not going anywhere without you." I glanced over my shoulder before cutting his hands free. "Is it just Bedolla or are the Fitzgeralds here too?"

"They're here too." He struggled to take a breath, then his glassy eyes focused on me. "How did you know?"

"All three of them claimed not to have seen Jessica since she moved away, but there are pictures in her apartment of their kids and she left them money in her will. They never lost touch with her."

"In retrospect it was probably a mistake to lie about that." Byrdie Fitzgerald stood at the edge of the clearing pointing a rifle at us. Even though she'd been acknowledging an error, her voice sounded bright and upbeat. "But since the four of us were partners in this extremely illegal farm, I thought it best to downplay our friendship."

The color of the shirt tucked into her jeans coordinated with the handkerchief covering her face and the gloves on her hands. She gestured with the rifle. "Please stand up and put your hands where I can see them."

I started to stand.

A man ran out of the darkness struggling to carry something. "Why aren't you in the truck? Arnie says we need to go. It's at the foothills." Lee Fitzgerald adjusted his hold on the marijuana plant. The root-ball had hastily been wrapped in a trash bag. He saw me and stopped.

Byrdie glanced at him. I took the opportunity to hit the record button on the camera in my pocket. Rod and I locked eyes. I was sure he'd seen me.

264 | Nora McFarland

Byrdie looked back. "I said, please put your hands where I can see them."

I put my hands in the air. "There's no point in hurting either of us. It's too late for that. I already told the Sheriff's Department everything."

"You're bluffing." There was no doubt or uncertainty in Byrdie's voice. "You don't know enough to tell them anything. And a few photos in Jessica's apartment aren't proof of murder."

"I found one of your marijuana plants there too."

Lee's handkerchief popped into his mouth as he took a quick gasp.

Byrdie glanced at him. "What did you do?"

"I didn't see any harm in letting Jessica take one. You know how she was with plants. I thought it would be dead in a week."

"You were wrong," I said. "The Sheriff's Department has it now, and they know you lied about your friendship with Jessica. They're getting warrants as we speak. They're going to go over your house, your boat, your dock, Lee's office."

She giggled. "They won't find anything. I was smarter than that and we all have alibis."

"You sure do," I said. "And Lee and Arnaldo's are even real. Too bad yours isn't."

Byrdie didn't say anything, but her knuckles turned white as she grasped the gun.

Rod managed to raise his head. "But Byrdie was only home for ten minutes. She didn't have time to commit the murder."

"She didn't have time if she drove home." I looked from Rod to Byrdie. "But Search and Rescue is just down the road from city hall. All she had to do was get the key to the gate from Arnaldo. Then Wednesday night she left her meeting at six, drove down to the lake, and then took the Search and Rescue boat for a quick ride home. It cut her commute time in half."

"Byrdie, they know," Lee said. "She told the police everything and they know."

"You let Jessica into the house," I continued. "Lured her down to the dock, knocked her out, towed your own boat out to Road's End, dumped her in the water, and then returned to Search and Rescue. Even if you changed clothes, you still would've had plenty of time. It was very clever."

Her eyes stayed fixed on me. "It was even more clever than you realize. Jessica very stupidly got into the Search and Rescue boat before I hit her over the head with a rock. Any evidence they find is useless because the same boat was used to retrieve the body."

Lee couldn't look at her. "How can you talk about it that way? Like you're proud of it?" He leaned his weight against the truck and took deep breaths.

"Why did you agree to this, Lee?" When he didn't answer, I continued, "Were you the one who started the fire? Did Byrdie tell you she had to kill Jessica to protect you?"

"The fire was an accident. Even Jessica understood that." Beads of sweat ran down from Lee's hairline. "I was spending the night out there. I wasn't even being careless, but sparks from my camp-fire ignited some brush."

Byrdie's voice rose. "Everything would have been fine if Jessica hadn't insisted on confessing. She was as good as killing the rest of us."

There was a noise behind the truck. Arnaldo Bedolla came running out of the darkness. He carried another plant. "Why are you still here? You're blocking me. I told you to take the truck and—"

Bedolla saw me and abruptly stopped. He hesitated for only a moment, then looked at Byrdie. "Shoot them. There's no time. We have to go."

I saw movement in the trees behind her.

"Just for the record, Arnaldo"—and considering that I was recording him, I meant it literally—"you were the man at Road's End who tried to drown me, right?"

He shook his head. "It wasn't personal. I thought you'd seen me."

"The sniper ambush felt very personal."

Byrdie smiled. "That's because I was the one shooting, and by then I didn't like you. When Arnie phoned with a description of your car, I was only too happy to try and stop you."

"We don't have time for this." Arnaldo looked at Byrdie. "The fire could blow up any minute. Shoot them or give me the gun and I'll do it."

Byrdie steeled herself and tightened her grip on the rifle. Lee reluctantly looked away.

Bud lunged out of the darkness. He grabbed the rifle right out of Byrdie's hands and pushed it straight into the air. Lee ran to help her, but I dove at him. He was twice my weight, but I made up for it by being crazy fierce.

That left Bedolla. I turned from my position on top of Lee to look. Rod was on his feet. He swung his good arm and connected with Bedolla's jaw. He leveled him in one punch, but immediately collapsed to the ground.

"Back up," I heard Bud say. I looked in the other direction and saw him holding the rifle.

"Rod?" I ran to him. He didn't answer. The stain on his jacket had doubled in size. I ripped the sleeve off. There was blood everywhere.

A shriek came from Bedolla's radio, then a voice. Even before my brain processed the words, I knew from the panicked sounds that we were in trouble. "I'm pulling my shots off the ridge. I got visual on a blowup with flames thirty, maybe fifty, feet high. I've never seen it this bad, over."

Arnaldo Bedolla was the first to move. He didn't say anything. He jumped up and ran into the darkness.

"Go," Byrdie yelled at Lee. They ran for the truck.

And Bud let them. He lowered the gun and hurried to us. "We gotta run. I'll carry Rod."

I tried to rip Rod's sleeve off. "They shot him earlier and I think the bullet is still in his arm. I'm not sure we can move him. He's lost too much blood."

Lee slammed shut the rear of the truck.

"Rod," Bud shouted. "Boy, can you hear me?"

Lee jumped into the driver's seat. I recognized a Fitz's logo as they flew past.

Bud, his face grim, looked up from Rod. "You try and stop the bleedin'. I'll be back with the van as fast as I can."

Another set of headlights followed the Fitzgeralds'. A Search and Rescue truck tore through the clearing without stopping.

Bud waited for Bedolla to pass, then ran up the road.

I applied pressure to Rod's arm.

Through the trees, the sky swelled with orange and gray light. It lit the outlines of the grow, and for the first time I could see how far it stretched. There must have been four or five hundred plants.

I heard a roaring engine in the distance and for a second wondered if another car might come barreling out of the darkness. I put my hand up to shield my eyes from the burning embers in the wind and tried to look. There was no car. That's when I realized the sound came from the fire, and it was getting louder.

The delivery van sped down the road and stopped.

I ran and opened the back. Bud threw a box of flares out the open door, followed by an aerosol can and a bottle of vegetable oil.

"What are you doing?" I yelled.

He jumped down and ran to Rod. "You get his feet."

We carried him into the van and set him down. "Get rid of anything like to explode in heat. Just throw it out the back."

He jumped into the driver's seat and started the engine. "And get off all your clothes that's not natural."

"What?" I grabbed the back door and barely got it shut before the van moved.

"Anythin' that's not cotton or wool or natural-type cloth. Take 'em off you and Rod both."

"Why?"

"There's no time, Lillian. Just do it."

He drove straight into the grow.

"Where are you going?" I yelled.

He didn't answer. Instead he increased our speed.

I struggled to keep Rod steady as we plowed through the marijuana plants. "We're going the wrong way."

"It's too late. The creek is our only chance."

"What do you mean it's too late? It can't be too late."

"Judgin' offa what I saw when I went for the van, we only got minutes. It's blowin' up real bad." He quickly glanced back. "I told you to get those clothes off. Anythin' polyester is gonna melt."

I must have wasted several seconds in blind terror. The thought of a heat so intense that your clothing melts will do that do a person. But all I remember is whipping off my KJAY polo shirt and being grateful my bra was cotton. Fortunately Rod's clothes are all so nice that most everything he wears is a natural fiber.

"Get his watch too," Bud yelled. "The metal will burn into him."

I removed the watch, then put it in my gear bag with the digital camera. The Mace and some other flammable things went out the window. I tried to keep pressure on Rod's wound, but it was hard with the van jostling around so much. Then all at once the van stopped. Bud peered out the windshield. He looked both ways, then appeared to decide something.

"Hold on," he shouted.

He hit the gas and then the road dipped. I held Rod down. He moaned as a box of doughnuts flew into the air and spread chocolate glazed with sprinkles everywhere. The van stopped and Bud shut off the engine.

I tried to see out the windshield. "Where are we?"

"The creek." Bud jumped out of his seat. He tossed a metallic bundle at me. "Open that up and lay it down on the floor." He began tearing through the contents of the van. "I'm not gonna lie to you, this is bad. I was countin' on the creek bein' a firebreak, but it's hardly flowin'. Best we can do is park down in the creek bed and pray there's enough water to keep the temperature down."

The bundle was a fire shelter, or a shake-and-bake as Bell had called it. I ripped the red cord and opened the plastic bag. The metallic fabric was folded like an accordion. The two handles were labeled RIGHT and LEFT.

"I saw a temporary dam." I grasped each handle and pulled while shaking the fabric out. "We could drive up there. There's tons of water on the other side."

"It's no good. The trees start up again. If we get hit by a fallin' branch, we'll be dead for sure, don't matter how much water there is."

I laid the small tent on the floor of the van and straightened it. "But is there going to be enough water here?"

Bud didn't answer.

"Bud?" I yelled.

"I don't know what to say, Little Sister. It's real bad." He gestured to the tent. "Best thing is you and Rod get in here."

Only two of us were going to fit. We got Rod safely inside and then I said, "Have you trained with one of these before?"

"Yes, and you gots to remember to try and keep your hands—"

A gust rocked the van. The roaring sound got louder and I cut him off. "Get inside with Rod. I won't do it right and we'll both die anyway." I pulled out my Swiss army knife and opened the blade. "That's the only way it's going to work."

I jumped out the back and slammed the door shut. My eyes and lungs burned, but I ran straight up the shallow creek bed. Through the smoke and wind I saw something dark. I ran straight at it. I stabbed the thick vinyl with all my strength. A small hole opened.

I heard a freight train coming behind me. I raised the knife and pounded it down over and over again in a frenzy. The world around me brightened in shades of orange and red. I felt the center start to give. I brought the blade down in one fluid motion, then ripped it toward me.

The dam broke. A wave knocked me flat on my back as everything exploded.

TWENTY-THREE

held my breath. I slid headfirst with the current and slipped under the van's submerged back bumper. I grabbed a tire to stop myself. I opened my eyes and tried to see through the flowing water. Blurry streaks of orange glowed all around the edges of the rocking van.

My lungs ached. I had to breathe. I tried to look up, but the van's underside was an indistinguishable dark mess. I reached up. My hand touched strange shapes, sharp edges, and then finally air. I rose up and found the air pocket running up into the engine. I pushed, trying to squeeze my head past the front axle. I opened my lips and sucked in the beautiful, foul air.

I held my breath and lowered back down. I opened my eyes again underwater. I could see a tire moving back and forth as the winds battered the van.

I held my breath as long as I could, and then scrambled up to take another breath. How long would I have to do this? How long could I do this?

I heard a terrible explosion followed by another and another. A gust like a tornado must have hit the van. The seven-thousand-pound vehicle jerked to the right. The two left tires lifted, but then fell back to the creek bed.

Finally the van's movements slowed and then went still. I was later told that the blowup lasted eight minutes. For me, it felt like eight hours. I waited as long as I could, and then allowed the current to take me below the front bumper. I lifted my head and took a breath. The hot air burned my throat and lungs. I coughed and took another breath. I tried to sit up, but the higher I got, the hotter the air became. I sank back down so just my head rose out of the water. I took short, shallow breaths. The water flowed around me making gentle trickling sounds like on a nature CD.

I stayed like that. My eyes stung, but I could see. The marijuana field was a scorched memory. Random hot spots still burned, but most of the crop had been reduced to ashes by the intense heat. Beyond that, a burning forest heaved black smoke into the sky. The core structure of each tree was still visible, but flames filled out the branches instead of pine needles. Occasionally a tree would collapse and there'd be a thunderous crash.

The other side of the creek was completely untouched. With the water flowing at its normal levels, the natural firebreak had held.

The temperature slowly dropped to the point where I could sit up. The light from the still-burning trees shimmered on the dark surface of the water, so at first I didn't recognize movement. When I did finally realize something was walking up the shallow edge of the creek bed, I had a goofy thought that it was probably a Terrill Mountain slender salamander. All the flames and light were behind it, so the animal appeared as a black silhouette. It stopped roughly five yards from me and stared.

The cougar didn't look angry or frightened. Maybe that's why I was so calm. Nothing in its manner suggested pride in the triumph of survival, and if events had played out differently, I doubted the animal would have wasted time feeling sorry for itself. It simply was alive, and one day it would be dead, just like the trees, and the salamanders, and Jessica, and me.

Something crashed in the van behind us. The cougar leapt up and ran off into the brush on the safe side of the creek.

The chopper found us fairly quickly. Dennis and Callum had given the authorities the coordinates of the grow, so they knew exactly where to look.

Bud was able to stop crying long enough to signal them. I had expected some emotion from the old codger, but not for Bud to completely break down when he saw I was alive.

As visibility increased, I saw another reason the fire hadn't spread across the creek: a line of fire retardant had been dropped onto the land there. The van had survived fairly well. Its body was charred on one side, but the water and humidity in the air had deflected the worst of the flame front. Bud's proper use of the fire shelter had protected him and Rod from the superheated air. None of us had burns.

For the second time in twelve hours I was airlifted to the Bakersfield Medical Center. Rod was taken straight into surgery to remove the bullet. Bud and I were examined and released. We went to the surgery waiting room and found Callum and Leanore already there.

Each jumped up. Leanore hugged me while crying. Callum awkwardly patted me on the back while trying to hide that his eyes were wet. He then admonished me for destroying the live truck. It had been left up on the dirt road and, without the benefit of the creek, was a burnt-out shell.

My cotton gear bag had survived in the doughnut truck. I gave Callum the digital camera. "I recorded everything, including their confessions, but there's no picture and the camera was exposed to insanely high temperatures."

"We'll get something." He looked at the camera instead of me. "Good job getting tape . . . and the whole not-dying thing."

We waited a little longer and then Lucero arrived.

"They found the Fitzgeralds and Bedolla." He took a seat next to Callum. "I guess Bedolla realized they weren't going to make it and they all detoured to a house nearby with a weird name."

"Bonny Hazel?" I said.

"That's it. Place was empty, but they broke in and rode out the fire in the basement with a bunch of lizards."

I laughed. "They're salamanders."

"Whatever they are, I'm sure they'd never turn on each other as fast as the three humans who were down there with them."

Bud grinned. "No honor among thieves, take my word for it."

Something in his tone got Lucero's attention—such as maybe Bud had a little too much experience with thieves—but Lucero let it go. "Bedolla is already trying to cut a deal. Says how he got into trouble flipping houses and needed cash, but the Fitzgeralds were really behind everything."

Callum took out a cell phone. "Is this on the record? Can I go with this?"

Lucero straightened. "No. It's not on the record."

"Okay. Calm down. I won't use it."

Lucero's eyes narrowed. "Then who are you calling?"

"Nobody. I have to check on a thing." Callum walked down the hall and out of earshot.

Lucero watched him. "He's going with it, isn't he?"

Leanore offered him some of her vending-machine pretzels. "You have to say 'off-the-record' before you start talking."

"Cheer up," I said. "I may have audio of the Fitzgeralds and Bedolla confessing."

He frowned at me while chewing. "Why don't I already have it?"

"You'll have to talk with Callum. He's in charge of it now."

Lucero jumped up and ran after Callum.

Leanore finished her pretzels, then went to get coffee for everyone from the cafeteria. I scooted down to the seat next to Bud and took the envelope out of my rear pocket. "Here. It got wet when I was in the creek, but it should still be good."

"What's this?" He looked at the runny ink on the outside of the envelope. "Does this say Otto's Pawn? They been closed for five years now." He pulled the soggy bills out. "Well, I was never one to turn down money, but what did I do to deserve this?"

"It's yours. It's the money I got for selling your TV and stuff thirteen years ago."

He stared at me for a second, then erupted into whoops of laughter. "Little Sister, you are growin' up if you're payin' off your debts." He leaned in and lowered his voice. "That's why I make a habit of owin' money all over town."

He placed the envelope on my leg. "But all the same, this is yours."

"No, I want to pay you back."

A man in scrubs came through a pair of double doors and walked toward the waiting area. I had to pick up the envelope so I could stand.

"You did, Little Sister, and I thank you for it." Bud stood too. "This here's a gift, from me to you."

The doctor said Rod was out of surgery and improving. I went to see him, but he was still unconscious. He was so pale. His chest hardly rose and fell with each breath. I started crying and decided it was time to leave.

I stopped and checked on Bell. She was awake and feeling better. When I told her the Elizabeth mayor had been the one shooting at us, she laughed. It hurt her broken ribs, but she couldn't help it.

I laughed too, harder than I can remember laughing in a long time. Maybe it was because I'd just been crying over Rod, and this was the pendulum swinging the other direction, but the entire mess seemed hysterical to me.

"If you think that's funny," I said, "wait until I tell you why Mayor Fitzgerald didn't want manpower wasted defending the nature preserve."

"Why?"

"She didn't want the firefighters to accidentally discover her pot farm."

We both laughed again. I actually had tears in my eyes.

Bell did too, but they were from pain. "Oh, this is cruel of you."

I wiped my eyes. "You're right. I should let you rest." I got up to go.

She gestured to the muted TV mounted on the wall. Images from the fire were playing on a cable news channel. "You and Rod are going to be big news. You could parlay this into a fantastic new job somewhere."

"I have a fantastic job right here."

The laughter faded a little from her eyes. "For how long? Most stations your size already have reporters shooting their own material. How long before one-man bands come to Bakersfield?"

"Probably not long." I tried to smile. "Sometimes I wonder if I might be able to transition over to the assignment desk, but I'd die in a desk job."

"I used to think that too." She raised her knee a few inches under the blanket. "You may have noticed I have a limp."

I shrugged, not wanting to make her feel self-conscious.

"Before I busted my knee, I worked on an engine crew. I was like you. I couldn't imagine leaving the field, but then life happens and we adjust."

"I'm not good at adjusting."

She smiled. "You might surprise yourself."

I went home to shower and change clothes. Even if I hadn't been in a hurry to return to the hospital and check on Rod, I wouldn't have slept. I was too nervous and keyed up. I showered, put on clean clothes, brushed my teeth, and started to feel like a human being again.

I passed the bed where my things had haphazardly been tossed on the quilt. The envelope stuck out from the pocket of my jeans. I stood for a few moments looking down, then called the IO. He called back ten minutes later with the address.

The house was in Oleander, an older neighborhood near downtown. It was almost midnight and most of the houses on the tree-lined street were dark. I parked Rod's Prius and walked up the front steps. The lights were on so I didn't hesitate to knock.

A woman pulled back the curtain from a window near the door.

I tried to speak loudly so she could hear me through the glass. "I'm here to see Brad. He should be expecting me."

The curtain fell back into place and the door opened. Jessica's brother stood in the doorway. He wore sweatpants and a T-shirt.

"I'm sorry for the late hour," I said.

Brad Egan looked even more tired than this morning. "It's okay. The IO said you were very insistent, so I figure it's important."

"There's something you're going to find out about Jessica and I wanted to be the one to tell you."

He gestured for me to come in.

I hesitated. I didn't want to run into Jessica's father. I may have matured to the point where I could hide some of my feelings, but holding my tongue around a man who hits his daughter was not going to happen. On the other hand, it seemed unlikely that Brad would conduct a sensitive conversation on his aunt's porch at midnight.

I stepped inside the cottage-style house from the 1930s. It smelled normal. Not gross, and not overly sweet with air freshener as if they were hiding something.

Brad introduced me to his aunt, then shut the door behind me. "I already got a couple calls from friends still in Elizabeth saying there are all kind of rumors about the Fitzgeralds and Jessica."

His aunt tightened a terry-cloth robe. "Would you like some coffee?"

I said yes because I didn't know what else to say. We all went to the kitchen. It had been remodeled in the 1980s. The oak cabinets and tile counters clashed with the older style of the rest of the house.

Brad and I sat at the kind of small two-person table you can buy at Wal-Mart, or Target, or any other number of stores. The aunt poured two mugs of coffee and set them down in front of us. She wasn't very old, probably early fifties, and it reminded me how much older Brad looked than his real age.

"I'm sure the police will be here tomorrow to talk to you about Jessica." I looked from the aunt to Brad. "They're going to tell you she was farming marijuana with the Fitzgeralds and Arnaldo Bedolla, and that Byrdie murdered her."

I watched his face expand as the shock of the news hit him.

The aunt made some noises and started for the door. "I should wake your father up."

Brad shook his head. "He won't care."

She stopped in the doorway and turned around. "She was his daughter." She left before Brad could say anything else.

"I know this all sounds bad," I continued. "And you probably think it confirms every bad thought you've ever had about Jessica, but you're wrong. Your sister wasn't the person you think she was."

His lips collapsed into thin, angry lines. "How would you know?"

"Because I knew her. Thirteen years ago I lived in Elizabeth and I knew Jessica."

"Why didn't you say so before?"

"I didn't know it was her at first, and the second time I saw you there wasn't time."

He thought for a moment. "Exactly how did you know her?" His look hovered somewhere between distaste and anger. "Were you one of those protesters she took up with?"

"No, but you have the wrong idea about that too. Jessica had a genuine belief in animal rights and protecting the environment. She fought for that. She never partied or ran around with any of those people. The only reason she got that reputation was because I did those things. People thought she was spending time with me and my reputation became hers."

He didn't believe me, so I explained our arrangement and why Jessica didn't want their father to know. When I was done, I took a deep breath. "You should also know that I was the one who vandalized the THINK SAFETY sign."

He shook his head. "You expect me to believe Jessica had nothing to do with that?"

"It was all my doing. Jessica covered for me, but that was it."

He didn't say anything. After a few moments he picked up his coffee mug and moved it several inches to the right without taking a drink. "I don't know what you want from me, telling me all this."

"Nothing. Just maybe think about it and don't judge Jessica so harshly about the marijuana. She meant it for the best."

The aunt returned. We both looked at her. "He's not coming." She held the robe closed at her chest. "He said we could tell him about it in the morning."

Egan didn't say anything.

She looked nervously at each of us. "You know how he is, ever since your mom died. He just doesn't care very much, about anything."

I stood up. "I need to go, anyway. I have to get back to the hospital."

The envelope was in my back pocket. I wanted to take it out and place it on the table in front of Egan. Hadn't I told Jessica to think of the money as coming from her mother? Who better to give it to now than her brother? And wouldn't it be symbolic of settling my debt to Jessica? It made sense, and in a bizarrely sentimental way I wanted desperately to do it.

In the end it was the sentimentality of it that stopped me. I was embarrassed by my foolish, sappy desire for emotional closure. It really was a corny thing to do, and Egan would probably laugh in my face.

"Thank you for listening," I said. "I'm sorry to disturb you so late."

Egan followed me to the door.

We said polite good-byes and I started to go.

"What you said this morning." Egan stepped out onto the porch. "About how bad it was for Jessica after my mom died."

I nodded.

"I don't want you to think I didn't care about Jessica." He looked down the dark street. "It was hard to come home. Things didn't happen for me the way I thought they would. I got injured and lost my football scholarship. It sort of went downhill from there." He looked back to me. "It was hard to come home knowing everyone thought I was a failure."

I thought again about giving him the envelope. If there was ever a moment, this was it. Brad was being vulnerable and honest. I should have felt safe enough to be vulnerable and honest too.

But I didn't.

"You shouldn't feel that way," I said. "I interviewed a lot people up in Elizabeth. Everyone who mentioned you said how proud they were of the work you're doing for the Forest Service. No one even mentioned when you were younger."

He easily believed the lie. Not because I was particularly adept at telling it, but because he wanted to.

I returned to the hospital. Rod had been moved from the ICU to a private room.

I pushed through the door.

On the other side of a curtain I heard Freddy. "So, dude, I figure you're the get."

Teddy shook his head. "No way, it's totally Lilly."

I pushed the curtain aside and went to the side of the bed. I set down my gear bag. Rod looked pale, and he was definitely on some kind of narcotic, but I could tell he was much better.

He smiled as I leaned down to kiss him.

"Eww," Freddy said at the exact same time as Teddy said, "Ahh."

I sat on the edge of the bed. "You guys can stay, but there's going to be mushy stuff."

Teddy smiled and pulled Freddy's arm toward the door. "We're going."

"I totally would stay for the mushy stuff." Freddy raised his fingers like pistols and shot them off in unison. "If Rod were a chick."

Rod smiled. "I'm not sure if that's a compliment or not."

"We're glad you're okay, Rod." Teddy pulled Freddy out the door.

I leaned down and kissed him again. "I called your parents. They're on their way."

Rod took a deep breath. "How long do we have?"

"An hour, maybe less."

"How freaked-out are they?"

"On a scale of one to ten, I'd say ten thousand million." I picked up my gear bag. The fabric was scorched and smelled like it too. "You know, I don't have a purse. I should get a purse." I took the DVDs out of the bag and then Rod's laptop I'd brought from home. "I brought you some stuff to watch." I held up *Labyrinth*. David Bowie gazed out from behind a magic orb. "I figured I should study up for the ball."

He laughed. "Don't worry. I won't hold you to that promise."

"No, I want to go. It'll be . . . different." I set the DVD down on the laptop. "You want to watch now?"

"Maybe in a minute." His arm with the IV reached out. He took my hand in his. "Why'd you leave me today?"

"In case you hadn't noticed, from the fact that you're alive, I did not leave you. I saved you."

"I think you know that's not what I mean. Why'd you leave me with Dennis this morning? Why'd you go off by yourself? We're supposed to be a team."

"I didn't think of it like I was leaving you." I sat down on the bed. "It's great to be a team, but I need to know I can take care of myself if you're not around."

He shook his head. "I'm not going anywhere, even if you were right about me being bored at work. We'll figure something out, and I won't have to go all the way to L.A. to do it."

"But it's your home. Don't you want to go back there? Don't you feel about it the way I feel about Bakersfield?"

He paused. Rod looked so calm. Maybe it was the narcotics or the near-death experience, but he radiated relaxed confidence. "You asked me earlier, before you flew out on the medevac, why I'm here. Obviously, the answer is that I'm crazy in love with you, but it's more than that too."

He squeezed my hand. "Home is where you can be yourself. It's where a person's comfortable in their own skin. That's how I feel when I'm with you."

"Oh, Rod" was all I could manage to say.

"Every other relationship I've ever been in, I had to pretend to be someone I'm not. But when I'm with you, I'm exactly myself. So wherever you are, that's my home."

I lay down on the edge of the bed next to him. "I'm crazy in love with you too, and when I thought you might die, I just about lost my mind." I took the envelope from my back pocket and set it on his chest.

His good arm reached for it. "What's this for?"

"So you'll always be able to come home."

ACKNOWLEDGMENTS

As always I must begin by thanking the Friedrich Agency. Molly Friedrich, Lucy Carson, and Paul Cirone are the best of the best. Their guidance, support, feedback, and promotion have made my entire writing career possible. This book simply would not exist without them.

I've also been blessed with the greatest editor. Sulay Hernandez was instrumental in shaping the first Lilly Hawkins mystery, and now her continued support and guidance have made this book possible.

Also at Touchstone I'd like to thank Shida Carr, Marcia Burch, Stacy Creamer, Trish Todd, Ashley Hewlett, and Justin Mitchell. I especially want to thank the incredible production, marketing, and sales departments!

The design of my first book was absolutely perfect. I owe a huge debt to Cherlynne Li for designing a beautiful, eye-catching cover and Renata Di Biase for designing the interior pages. Even the Reading Group Guide was created with amazing care and intelligence.

Thanks to my heroic copy editors, Steve Boldt and Jessica Chin. I don't know what I would do without them. For example, in my original draft of this page I managed to misspell the word acknowledgments and my publisher's first name. Thank you for saving me over and over again!

Special thanks to Linda Brown, Rachel Brown, Becky Ferreira, Jo Imhoff, Tracy Imley, Ceasonne Reiter, Molly Schullman, Peter Schuurmans, and Kim Zachman for reading and giving invaluable feedback.

Thanks to Roscoe Cross, Jon Doll, Alec Gerry, and Yvonne Stockwell for helping me with all the technical details.

Thanks to Marcia Muller and Lisa Scottoline for giving their support and endorsement to my first book. They each took time from their busy schedules to read my unpublished manuscript. As a longtime fan of each of those amazing writers, it was deeply meaningful to me.

Finally, I thank my dear husband, Jeff, who always believes in me.

Hot, Shot, and Bothered

INTRODUCTION

In *Hot, Shot, and Bothered*, the second Lilly Hawkins mystery, Lilly uses her top-notch "shooter" skills to cover a deadly wildfire burning in the California mountains. But the natural disaster isn't all she ends up covering after a dead body is found near the scene of the fire. When the dead woman turns out to be Jessica Egan, someone from Lilly's own past, Lilly decides to look into Jessica's death herself. What she discovers isn't pretty.

FOR DISCUSSION

1. The novel opens with Lilly Hawkins chasing after a coroner's van in pursuit of a big story. How does this affect your initial impression of her? Does this seem consistent with Lilly's character in *A Bad Day's Work*? In what ways has she changed since that novel? Compare and contrast the portrayal of her character in both books.

2. Lilly takes great pride in her ability to take care of herself and do a job most women wouldn't or couldn't do. Does this trait help or hinder her career? Discuss the effect it has on her relationships.

3. Lilly is one of the best camera operators, or shooters, in the news business. How is this job different from what a reporter does? Why do you think Lilly chose to be a shooter rather than a reporter? Use examples from the novel to support your opinion.

4. What we do for a living often affects how we view our surroundings, our experiences, and even the people we meet. How does Lilly's profession influence her view of the world?

5. The local police believe Jessica Egan's death was an accidental drowning. What causes Lilly to doubt this? How much of that doubt is based on her knowledge of Jessica's character and how much on hard fact?

6. Lilly insists on carrying her own equipment, won't make reference to her relationship with Rod in public, and generally doesn't like to show vulnerability. Why do you think she acts this way? Is there anyone she's willing to let her guard down around? If so, who and why?

7. Lilly initially keeps her relationship with Jessica a secret from everyone, including Rod. Why do you think she does this? How does Rod react once he finally learns the truth? Is his reaction what Lilly expected? Is it what you expected? In what way do you think his reaction influences how she feels about him?

8. Social media, such as Twitter and Facebook, are mentioned several times throughout the novel. What role does social media play in the story? How does social media affect Lilly's ability to solve Jessica's murder? Discuss the role social media plays in spreading news and solving crimes. Identify ways in which these outlets can be positive and negative, both in the novel and in the real world.

9. Because Lilly works for a smaller news operation, she finds herself in a position where she has to partner with the "big guys" to get the story. How does her opinion of the L.A. shooter change as she gets to know him better? Is this consistent with Lilly's relationships in *A Bad Day's Work*?

10. We all have fears that affect how we behave and even who we become. Rod has stage fright and Lilly is afraid of intimacy. Eventually they both overcome their fears and are able to grow in new ways. What fears do you have and in what ways have you taken steps to overcome them? How were you changed by this?

11. Though Lilly was covering for Jessica and taking money for doing so, she eventually returns the money, saying: "Everyone needs a way home, even if they never use it." What do you think Lilly meant by this? She later gives the same money to Rod, saying something very similar. Compare and contrast the exchange of money in both cases and discuss what Lilly meant by "going home" in each situation.

12. Callum, Lilly and Rod's boss, essentially tells Lilly to drop the drowning story or risk ruining Rod's career. How does Lilly choose? Why does she make this choice and how does it affect her relationship with Rod?

13. Jessica made a compromise between her beliefs in animal rights and her desire to find a cure for the disease that killed her mother. How does this discovery influence your opinion of Jessica? Have you ever come to a point in your life where you had to make a similar compromise? Identify other characters in the novel who are forced to weigh what they want with the realities of what it will take to get it. Do you agree or disagree with their choices? Explain your opinion.

A Conversation with Nora McFarland

Hot, Shot, and Bothered **is the second novel in a trilogy starring Lilly Hawkins. Did you have an idea how the entire trilogy would play out before you started writing the series? If so, did** *Hot, Shot, and Bothered* **turn out as you planned? If not, how did it differ from your original expectations?**

I know exactly where I want Lilly to be at the end of the trilogy in terms of her growth and the changes she's made in her life. The rest isn't mapped out, and even if it were, I'm sure it would change as I wrote. For example, I originally planned for the third book to be about a wildfire, not the second. I switched them after having a hard time mapping out Bud's history, which is essential to the story I'd had in mind. Now I'm going to explore Bud's background in the third book.

How did the process and experience of writing your second book compare to writing the first?

I had to do it much faster and the stakes felt much higher. When I wrote *A Bad Day's Work*, I didn't even have an agent, let alone a book contract. There was a big part of me that never thought anyone would read it. When I wrote *Hot, Shot, and Bothered*, I had contractual deadlines and all the pressures that came along with them.

You've created a very strong and independent character in Lilly, yet you've also given her weaknesses and vulnerabilities. What guided you in developing Lilly into such a well-rounded character that readers can relate to?

I've never been a fan of stories where the main character is a generic nice guy or gal. I believe some of the obstacles that the main character faces, and the dangers they encounter, should be of their own making. I don't have any interest in writing stories about characters who are passive or perfect. We all make mistakes and we all change over time. I want my characters to reflect that.

Readers saw several of the characters from *A Bad Day's Work* reappear in *Hot, Shot, and Bothered*. Was it always your plan to bring them back for the second novel? What is it about these characters that made you want to keep them around?

I love the fictional newsroom at KJAY and everyone who works there. I hope that at least some of those characters will appear in every Lilly Hawkins Mystery. And of course Uncle Bud is a hoot to write.

I also keep coming back to these characters because it's a terrific way to highlight how Lilly has changed. She began *A Bad Day's Work* with shallow or mistaken views of her friends and co-workers. By continuing those relationships, it's easier to see the way Lilly is growing and changing. It's also fun to allow those characters to experience their own growth. Teddy and Freddy, for instance, are getting to the age where it's no longer as much fun to be out partying every night. They're looking at their lives and trying to figure out what the next step looks like.

This novel is centered on the murder of an environmental and animal rights activist. Why did you choose to make Jessica a vegan and member of PETA? Are you also interested in environmental conservation and animal rights?

I do support those causes, but not to the degree that Jessica Egan's character did. Mostly I wanted to show someone who saw things in black and white, but who as she got older couldn't sustain that kind of absolute belief. To a certain extent learning to compromise is a healthy part of being a mature adult, but too much of it can ruin you. Lilly is terrified of the latter.

In this series, you take on murder and other serious topics with a touch of humor. What role does humor play in your writing and in your life? How do you think injecting humor into serious stories affects your readers' experience of the work?

The humor comes from my personality. There was a point when I was outlining *Hot, Shot, and Bothered* that I tried to sit down and plan the humor. I couldn't come up with a single joke. But once I began writing, it just happened. It's my natural voice. The few times I've tried to write something serious, it came out as pretentious and dreary.

You were a shooter yourself for a time. Did you encounter any life-threatening situations similar to the ones Lilly often finds herself in? Did you have any particularly memorable experiences behind the camera?

Nothing as dangerous as Lilly's adventures. There was an incident where someone threatened me and the reporter I was with. There had been a gang related drive-by shooting and we went out to do live shots from the block where it happened. Several young men appeared and threatened to hurt us if we didn't leave. My reporter and I were both very shaken, but unharmed. That was unusual and the only time something like that ever happened.

The more memorable experiences all involve crime scenes. Most of the dead bodies I saw were under tarps. The worst was if the body under the tarp was small because you knew it had to be a child. That was more upsetting than seeing an uncovered adult body.

Lilly isn't the only female character in a male-dominated field in this book. Was this a conscious decision on your part? What appeals to you about strong female characters like Lilly and Fire-fighter Bell?

I decided that Lilly needed a friend—someone who she didn't supervise and someone closer to her own age than Leanore. When I was doing research into wildfires I came across an article about how difficult it was for women to become firefighters. It's a grueling process with physical requirements that many of the strongest men fail. The women who do make it often have to take the test several times. I had a flash that a woman with that kind of determination and discipline was the perfect friend for Lilly. I hope Bell will be a recurring character.

Throughout the novel, Lilly struggles to keep part of her past a secret from Rod. When he finally finds out the truth, he doesn't respond the way Lilly expected. Was this what you planned all along, or did his reaction surprise you as well? What were you saying to readers with this choice?

I always planned that Rod wouldn't be bothered by Lilly's past. His character is very accepting of other people because he craves that in return. What I didn't expect was that he would make the joke about the salamanders and lizards. That came to me as I was writing the scene. I was also surprised by Lilly's reaction. I think she's a little annoyed with his almost unconditional acceptance because she genuinely believes that actions have consequences. Later, when she runs into Cathy who's become a pariah after making offensive comments on TV, Lilly feels compassion for her and better understands Rod's viewpoint. She even repeats to Cathy what Rod had said to her.

How do you think Lilly has evolved as a character since your first novel? Was this evolution deliberate or do you feel like your characters take on lives of their own?

Lilly is more in control of how she appears. She's a little better at holding back what she's thinking and feeling, which is part of gaining maturity and discipline. Her worldview has also become more nuanced and she has much better relationships with other people.

All that was planned. What was a surprise is that Lilly is a little sad about those changes. Lilly looks at the young intern Cathy who, although impetuous and unwise, has a purity and truth to her. Then she looks at Ceasonne Polignac who has the wisdom and self-control of age, but is tired and full of regret. Lilly worries that by finally growing up she's sacrificing something in herself that's honest and strong. She also sees what happened to Jessica Egan, and how she began to compromise, and this frightens her as well.

Social media like Facebook and Twitter also play a role in *Hot, Shot, and Bothered.* Are you active in social media? How do you feel about social media in general? What do you think about its influence on our world today, particularly where the news is concerned?

It's funny, but when I originally wrote *A Bad Day's Work* I made Lilly twenty-four years old. My editor felt that Lilly wasn't credible as a person in her early twenties because she didn't use enough social media. In particular she didn't send text messages or Tweets from her cell phone. My editor was right and I changed her age to thirty-one before publication.

But in a very short time the world has changed. Tweeting, YouTube, Facebook, and other social media aren't just for young people anymore. Everyone has a cell phone with them at all times. My ninety-one year old grandmother has a Facebook account. Whether it's GPS, e-mails, or status updates, everyone is logged in somewhere.

This has sped up our access to everything. Word of mouth can spread in minutes. Videos go viral and rack up enormous hits overnight. We all have access to first-hand accounts of disasters and revolutions as they're happening. The danger is that there's no filter. No one is fact checking. No one is corroborating stories.

What can we expect from the next book in the Lilly Hawkins trilogy?

Lilly's Uncle Bud has always been a bit of a shady character. In the third book, something from his past comes violently back to haunt him. As Lilly tries to uncover the truth and protect Bud, she becomes the target of a killer who wants to keep his own secrets buried.

ENHANCE YOUR BOOK CLUB

1. Jessica was a staunch animal rights activist and she lived her life as best she could in support of her beliefs, even to the point of changing her diet. For your next book club meeting, plan a potluck and have everyone make and bring a vegan dish (and the recipe) to share. Discuss in your group reasons why animal rights activists and devotees may choose to live a vegan lifestyle.

2. Lilly sees the world through the lens of her camera and the filter of what is newsworthy. Try looking at the world through Lilly's eyes. Take out your video camera or cell phone and see what (real or imagined) stories you can stumble on. How did looking through the lens of a video camera change how you saw your neighborhood? What did you find yourself looking for or gravitating to when you were behind the camera? Did you find that your perspective change? In what ways? At your next book club meeting, share and discuss what you discovered with the group.

3. To learn more about Nora McFarland, visit her website at www.noramcfarland.com. If you haven't read *A Bad Day's Work*, consider selecting it for your next book club pick. Discuss with your group the ways in which you think the author's history and background influence the stories she tells. How is the first novel in the Lilly Hawkins series similar to and different from the second? Did the author's style remain consistent? What themes and topics does the author seem to touch on in both books?

STAY TUNED FOR

NORA McFARLAND'S

NEXT LILLY HAWKINS MYSTERY!

Coming summer
2012